I0780810

POISONED SPLINTER

POISONED SPLINTER

AJ PARK

StarTree Press

ISCHAR

CHAPTER 1

B EING SMALL SOMETIMES CAME with advantages. No one saw Sam reach up to grasp the door handle and tiptoe out of the library, his lessons undone. Only a few moments later, he slipped through the door and down the steps to the dungeon, his small feet barely making a sound. Despite the oppressive stone walls and the gloom, he came here often. Grandfather hadn't locked anyone down here in decades, and it was the one space Sam could play undisturbed, his secret place.

Sooner than he expected, he heard the sound of footsteps on the stairs, and Sam darted to hide behind a stack of storage crates, fitting neatly into the narrow space. When he peeked out, he recognized a member of the royal court, Halderan, an older man with a long thin face and gray hair, dressed in formal robes. It was best to keep out of his way. Sam had never seen any of the important people in the dungeon before. Halderan wouldn't be looking for a small boy sneaking away from his lessons. There must be another reason he'd come.

Still hidden, Sam waited silently as a second person descended the stairs. At the sight of the tall form and familiar features of his uncle Adengo, Sam almost rushed out to greet him. But Halderan was still there, wearing an unpleasant look on his narrow face that informed Sam he shouldn't be bothered.

"Well?" Halderan asked. "Why did you ask me to come down here, Your Highness?" He looked around, his face pinched in disapproval. "The dungeon, of all places."

Instead of his usual easy smile, Adengo wore a serious expression. At his belt hung a dagger with a beautiful purple gem set into the hilt. Sam had seen him use it, only in practice, but Adengo knew how to fight. Sam wanted to be just like him when he grew up.

Adengo faced the older man. "I just received word that another two-dozen people in Kulin have fallen ill."

Halderan stared back at him, his heavy brows drawn together. "That is indeed unfortunate. We are all gravely concerned in these trying times."

Straightening his shoulders, Adengo faced Halderan, his eyebrows lowering in anger. "Unfortunate? How can you say that? You are well aware of the origin of this mysterious disease."

Halderan took a step toward Adengo, anger etched into the heavy lines of his face. "What are you implying?"

Adengo refused to back down. "It's you. They're sick because you're draining their hallan to increase your own power."

At the words, Halderan trembled with rage. "How dare you?" His eyes never left Adengo. "After all I have done for you? I came to Kulin specifically to instruct *you*, and now you claim that I practice dark sorcery?"

Hidden behind the crate, Sam shivered at the sharp malice in his tone, pulling himself even farther out of sight.

Adengo shook his head. "I didn't want to believe it. I hoped it wasn't true. But the more I learn, the more signs point directly to *you*. I haven't told the king yet. If you leave Kulin today, I won't say anything to anyone."

Halderan's complexion darkened in fury. "I placed my hopes in you. We could have accomplished great things together. It's been decades since I came across a student as talented as you are, and now you would betray me?"

"They're innocent people," Adengo exclaimed. "And you're killing them to fuel your magic!"

Sam's stomach clenched. He shouldn't be listening to this. Was Halderan really killing people? Sam should tell his father what he'd overheard. He would know what to do.

"You have *real* power," Halderan hissed. "Why should you care if a few of your unfortunate subjects fall ill? If you take a portion of their life energy, it's all for the greater good. Think what you could accomplish with the extra hallan!"

"But it's wrong. I'll never do that!" Adengo protested.

They stared at each other for a long moment. "Very well, Your Highness," Halderan said, lowering his eyes and his voice and stepping away from the other man. "There is no way we will reach an agreement over this. I will do as you suggest and leave at once."

Without further protest, Halderan turned and went up the stairs, leaving Adengo standing alone in the middle of the room, a frown of deep thought on his face.

Sam squirmed in his corner, accidentally bumping against the crate.

His uncle's gaze sharpened, focusing on his hiding place. "All right, Sam. Come out here."

Sam crept out into the open.

Adengo met his gaze. "What are you doing down here? You shouldn't have heard any of that."

Sam ran to Adengo, throwing his arms around his uncle's waist. "I'm sorry. I only wanted to play, and I didn't mean to hear. He scares me!"

Adengo hugged him, and then bent to one knee to meet Sam's eyes. "I'm going to make sure he doesn't hurt anyone else. Come on." Together, they climbed the stairs back to the palace. "Go to your mother," Adengo directed. "I'm going to see the king."

Sam ran through the marble halls of the palace, passing by the room where he was supposed to be working on his lessons, to the suite of rooms he shared with his parents. Ignoring the two guards watching over the door, he threw it open and ran inside. "Maman?" he charged into the sitting room. Finding it empty, he crossed the room to his parent's bedroom.

His mother lay crumpled on the floor in a pool of blood. Sam screamed, realizing a second later that his father lay just beyond her. Icy cold swept down his back, and for a moment, his entire body froze. He ran to his mother, dropping to his knees over her. "Maman!" he shook her shoulder, but she didn't turn to look at him. Her eyes stared up at nothing.

Two guards ran into the room, their eyes wide in horror as they took in the scene. One of them ran to Sam's father, searching for any sign of life. The other knelt beside Sam. He took in the still form of the princess, her staring eyes, and he placed his fingers under her chin, searching for any sign of a heartbeat.

More guards arrived a moment later. Sam heard his grandfather's voice in the hall. A moment later, he burst into the room, Adengo at his side. Both their faces were deathly white, and their eyes wide in shock. There was a moment of silence.

His grandfather, Hashoreth Algorian, King of Ischar, walked forward, kneeling beside the still form of his son. He took a crumpled scrap of parchment from his lifeless hand. His eyes widened as they scanned the few words written on it. "You will never rule Ischar." His gaze flew to Adengo. "It's your handwriting."

Shock froze Adengo's features. He struggled to speak, but no words came out. He took a deep breath and tried again. "I didn't write that."

Grandfather's eyes fixed on Adengo. "But your brother—it was in his hand. Is this about the *throne*? I never thought you were jealous of him."

Adengo's jaw clenched. "I'm not! I swear. No throne is worth losing my brother."

King Hashoreth bowed his head.

"Adengo didn't do it!" Sam cried. His strong, brave uncle would never harm his family for his own gain. In that moment, he felt sure.

Still bent over the body of his son, Hashoreth picked up something from the floor. He held up a knife with a purple gem on the hilt, the blade sticky with blood. Sam recognized the weapon immediately. Adengo's dagger.

Hashoreth held it up and turned toward his second son.

Adengo's eyes widened, all color draining from his face. "I didn't do this. Father, you have to believe me! I would never kill my brother!"

The king's eyes went to the empty sheath at Adengo's belt. "You had this knife with you?"

Adengo looked down at his belt. "I thought I did."

Sam stared at the empty sheath. Adengo had been wearing the dagger just a few moments ago in the dungeon, and now, here it was, covered with blood. Was it true? The king believed Adengo had killed Sam's parents.

"Seize him," King Hashoreth nodded to the guards, and they grabbed Adengo. The king nodded toward the door, and they dragged Adengo out.

"No! I didn't do it! Father, please! I didn't—"

In a moment, he was gone.

The king knelt beside Sam and put a hand on his shoulder. "Samanath."

Sam shook violently all over. He couldn't stop crying, and he clung to his mother, though her limbs were heavy and cold, and she didn't respond to him.

His grandfather gathered Sam into his arms and held him as he sobbed. "I'm sorry, Sam. So sorry." Sam clung to him.

The king stood up and walked toward the large windows. Outside in the courtyard, shouts and cries rang out. People looked upward, pointing at the sky. A shadow passed over the palace. From his place in his grandfather's arms, Sam caught a glimpse of an enormous dark bird. Wide wings carried it swiftly away. Only a moment later, it was gone.

CHAPTER 2

19 Years Later

T HE CARRIAGE JOSTLED DIA as it rolled over a stone in the road, startling her out of sleep. She straightened up abruptly.

Her younger sister, Lisenth, jabbed her sharply with an elbow. "How can you sleep? We'll be in Kulin in another hour, the home of the prince. In a few more weeks, we get to *meet* him. And you're sleeping." She shook her head in disgust.

Her sister's grumbling was so commonplace that Dia had learned to ignore it. Sometimes. Often, it was easier not to say anything at all than to argue with her. Dia tried to be patient. Before their father died, he'd begged her to take care of Lisenth, and Dia had promised she would do her best. She had no wish to bicker now. Instead, she straightened to sit taller in her seat and glanced out the window. Outside, thick, unbroken forest lined the road, as it had for hours. The afternoon faded into evening, and the light grew dim beneath the thick trees.

From the corner of her eye, Dia glanced at her sister. Lisenth looked elegant, even after a long day of travel. She appeared ready to meet her prince at any moment. Not a golden hair was out of place, and the ice blue silk of her veil draped gracefully from the crown of her head down around her shoulders. Sparkling gems hung across her brow.

Dia made a quick effort to smooth her own hair. But why should she worry? It's not like they'd meet anyone tonight.

Though dressed similarly, the resemblance between the sisters was distant. Dia was three years older, but shorter, plainer, more thoughtful, and much less ambitious than her sister. All facts that Lisenth took every opportunity to remind her of. Dia simply shrugged and glanced back out of the window. Her own goals were different.

Dia loved seeing new places. The unfamiliar scenery spoke to the place inside her that constantly searched for... something. She wasn't sure what it was, but she preferred to remain in the background while she looked. In contrast, Lisenth thrived on attention. Let her charm the prince if she wanted to. Dia had no intention of interfering.

As the sun dipped toward the distant purple horizon; the endless jostling paused and the carriage stopped. Roland, the footman who had been with their family for decades, opened the door and bowed. He was a plain-looking, sturdy man, his brown hair beginning to gray. "Ladies, would you care to stretch your legs for a moment? The view of Kulin is stunning."

Gratefully, Dia accepted his hand, allowing him to help her from the carriage. She straightened her spine and extended her arms, attempting to stretch the stiffness from her muscles. Lisenth alighted behind her. "You look ridiculous with your arms out like that."

Reluctantly, Dia lowered her arms to assume a more ladylike posture.

"Look at this!" Lisenth walked a few paces from the carriage to an opening between the trees. The last rays of sunset lit the green of the forest as it blended into open fields, a patchwork of crops. Central to the view was the city of Kulin, blazing with light. From this higher vantage point, they saw within the walls, all the way from small cottages at the outskirts to graceful towers in the center that could only belong to the king's palace. Kulin stood on the very brink of the cliffs that fell away around the edges of Ischar. Nothing could be seen of the precipice from up here.

"It's beautiful." Dia gazed at the city.

Lisenth sighed and placed a hand over her heart, looking at the distant towers. "When the prince falls madly in love with me, that will be my home."

If the prince behaved like any other man who met Lisenth, that would probably be his exact reaction. She was stunning, and by now, everyone expected that sort of thing to happen. Maybe it was inevitable.

"We're almost there," Lisenth said. "Let's go."

Dia wished for a moment of privacy to stretch again. "The view is lovely. I need just a moment more."

"But we're almost there!"

Her jaw tightened, but Dia drew in a breath, forcing the muscles to relax. "Only a moment."

Lisenth let out a breath of irritation and stalked back toward the carriage.

Enjoying the moment of solitude and the quiet, Dia took a deeper breath. The tight muscles in her neck loosened a little as she stood alone. Sunset lit heavy clouds with a touch of bright rose. Her eye caught a black shape moving along the horizon, silhouetted against the colorful sky. It circled the city before turning in their direction. A bird? The outline grew clearer as it approached. It had the shape of an eagle, except its wingspan was enormous. Even far away, it appeared big enough to carry off a horse if it wished. Perhaps because of the bright light behind, its feathers appeared black as night.

Dia's stomach clenched. If she truly saw what she thought she did, it had a name. Shadaroc. An omen of evil.

Before tonight, she'd never believed the stories she'd heard as a child of sorcerers who practiced magic and could change their form. When the Shadaroc resumed its human form, it could walk undetected among the people. If she truly saw one of them in Kulin, trouble would follow.

The dark shape of the mythical bird wheeled over the forest, drawing nearer every moment. Her hands tightened into fists. What could she do if it came to the clearing where she stood? She felt a sudden urge to flee and hide.

A moment later, it soared directly overhead, and Dia crouched instinctively as it passed. A sharp prickle raced over her skin, from the crown of her head to the soles of her feet. She couldn't breathe. The enormous dark shape turned and passed over her again. Frozen in place, she stared upward.

The great bird wheeled, flying lower to land nearby, out of sight among the dark trees.

It wasn't far from her. Dia needed to get away.

The sudden rattle of harnesses and carriage wheels brought her sharply back to the present. Drawing in a quick breath, she turned back to the road in time to see the carriage disappearing down the road.

"Lisenth!" Dia shouted in frustration. This wasn't the first prank she had been the victim of. The carriage quickly disappeared between the trees and silence fell.

She stood alone, staring down the road after them. They would come back for her. It was only a joke. Any moment now.

Roland and the driver had worked faithfully for the Ifereth family for many years, and they would never intentionally leave Dia alone in the forest. Her sister must have assured them she was already inside, ready to go. It wasn't their fault. When they discovered their mistake, they would certainly come back for her.

Thick silence covered the woods. A damp chill settled over Dia. The pale-yellow silk of her gown wasn't warm and her soft slippers had never been intended for walking in rough terrain. A few spatters of rain struck her. Lowering clouds quickly moved across the fading sunset, hiding any sign of the strange bird. It couldn't be too far away. Fear slid along her spine.

Darkness fell around Dia, and she shivered. Her sister had to be coming back soon. Letting out a breath of frustration, she stared down the empty road as rain began to fall. Clutching her arms around her body in an attempt to warm herself, Dia considered her options. She was alone. She had no light, no warm clothes, no transportation, and it was quickly becoming too cold to remain standing here. But they would be back any moment. Wouldn't they?

Lacking any other option, Dia started walking down the road in the direction of the city of Kulin. Maybe another traveler would come along and she could ask for help. As the rain fell harder, puddles formed, surrounded by patches of thick mud. She tiptoed around them in her yellow silk slippers.

The movement warmed her a little, but it was past time for the carriage to return. The darkness deepened around her, and the rain continued. Above the soft patter of raindrops on the leaves, she heard the howl of a wolf. Her body froze between steps, turning her heart to ice in her chest. A pack of hungry wolves would be happy to make their supper on a lost girl, defenseless in the woods. A second howl followed the first. After what she'd seen only a few moments before in the sky, she couldn't help but remember that, in the stories, wolves were loyal servants of the Shadaroc.

At the sound of another howl, Dia shook off her temporary paralysis and ran, leaving the road behind and plunging into the forest. Brush snagged at her long skirt. The fabric ripped as she jerked it free. Stumbling across a narrower path, she followed it. The howls grew closer.

Desperately, she searched the trees for one she might climb up into. When none of them had branches within her reach, she hurried on. She would have to take her chances on the ground. Wrenching the fabric of her gown free of the entangling branches, she pushed forward, emerging from the brush to find herself at the brink of a precipitous slope of bare earth and rock.

The world spun around her as she looked down from the height, and all her muscles clenched, but she couldn't pause. Branches rustled as the wolves pushed swiftly through the thicket behind her, leaving her no choice but to attempt the descent. Dia started down, her soft shoes slipping against the earth. On the wet soil, her footing grew worse every moment.

She shrieked as her feet slid out from under her, and she fell, tumbling and sliding down the long slope, finally coming to rest in the mud at the bottom. Pain raced through her arm and various other bruised parts of her body. Tears welled in her eyes, and for a moment, she didn't move at all, grateful to be still.

A howl reminded her that the wolves weren't far away. With a groan, she lifted her head and saw the black outline of one of the creatures at the top of the steep embankment. Hopefully, the animals had better sense than to follow her down the incline. Would they find a way around? Dia needed to move.

Dragging her aching body up, she got to her feet. Forest surrounded her in all directions. Which way should she go? Off through the trees, she glimpsed what might be an open area, and headed that way. Thick vegetation and brush attempted to block her way. She had several deep scratches on her arms before she stumbled out onto a road. If she followed it, perhaps it would join with the road to Kulin.

The distant whinny of a horse made the decision, and she followed the path in the direction of the city. She hadn't gone far when the square shape of a carriage loomed in the dark, its straight lines contrasting with the wild shapes of the trees. There was something wrong. Dia stared into the dim light for several moments, trying to piece together what her eyes showed her.

As she approached, she saw more clearly. The carriage lay awkwardly on its side. One of the horses must have broken its harness and bolted, leaving the remaining animal entangled, snorting nervously in its tethers.

Dia had no experience with horses. Was there a way to calm the frightened animal or even release it from the twisted harness? Putting that idea off for the moment, she turned toward the carriage. It must have carried someone.

Dia bent beside a shattered window at the back. Inside lay the crumpled body of a girl, her pale skin standing out against the darker interior, her skirts a tangled mass. A stain, black in the dim light, covered her neck and shoulder. Dia touched her hand. "Can you hear me?"

A faint groan was her only answer.

A howl from somewhere off in the forest reminded her that she didn't have time to linger. She shook the girl's hand. "Can you wake up? We need to get away from here before the wolves come."

"What happened?" the girl moaned.

"I don't know," Dia said. "But it's not safe to stay here. The wolves are getting closer."

That information appeared to motivate the injured girl. Dia used a branch to clear away the sharp pieces of glass remaining, and she helped the girl slide out. "How badly are you hurt? Can you walk?"

More howls came from the trees, closer this time. It was time to go. The horse might have helped them escape, but Dia didn't know how to ride, and she had no way to free it from the jumbled leather straps. There wasn't time to debate. She helped the girl to her feet, supporting her as they staggered away from the carriage.

"What's your name?" Dia asked.

"Carrina." The girl's features were tight with pain, her face white, and she held one arm cradled against her chest.

"I'm Dia, and we're going to try to find some help before the wolves reach us."

"Where's my father?" Carrina looked around at the dark trees.

"I don't know," Dia replied, "but we can't stay here."

Carrina started walking. They weren't fast, but at least they were moving. A little farther along, a dark shape lay in the road. With a cry, Carrina stumbled toward it, kneeling beside the still form of a man.

"Papa!" Reaching out with her uninjured arm, she shook him, but he didn't stir at all.

Dia bent down beside a middle-aged man in a fine tunic, now lying on his back in the muddy road. His skin appeared chalky pale in the faint light; his empty eyes stared upward. Dia shivered. She touched his forehead and found his skin damp with rain and icy cold. When she held her hand above his mouth, she felt no breath. He didn't move at all as Carrina cried and tried to rouse him.

What had happened to this family as they'd traveled? Had they been on their way to Kulin just as Dia and her sister had? Her questions would have to wait. She didn't want to tell the girl that her father was dead, but what choice did she have now?

She gripped Carrina's arm. "There's nothing more we can do now," she said, as gently as she could. "We'll find help and then come back."

Carrina nodded, accepting Dia's support as she got to her feet.

The chill rain still fell, soaking them both to the skin, and they shivered as they walked. Keeping the best pace they could, Dia realized it wouldn't be nearly fast enough. Where could they go? The trees on either side closed in thickly, but they were small, thin thickets here, nothing they could climb up to escape the wolves.

Would it have been safer to stay in the carriage? No. The wolves could have entered it just as easily as she had pulled Carrina out. Damaged as it was, it offered no real protection. Maybe if they could reach the main road again, they might find help.

They hurried on, exhaustion dragging at Dia's aching body as she tried to support Carrina. This evening had turned into a nightmare with no end in sight.

From the howls growing nearer, the wolves were quickly catching up. Dia looked desperately from side to side, looking for any means of defense. She picked up a sturdy stick, murmuring the words of a prayer to the Soul Mother under her breath.

Dia backed up until she felt the small trees against her back. Carrina huddled beside her, sobbing in fear. Several animals circled them, their eyes shining in the gloom. Her heart thudded in her chest. A growl ripped through the dark, and Dia clenched her jaw as she raised the stick.

This wasn't going to end well.

CHAPTER 3

A S THE WOLF RUSHED, snarling at her, Dia swung the branch with all her strength. It collided with the side of the animal's head, knocking it away from the girls. The blow slowed it, but it wasn't badly hurt. It turned and began to advance again. Before it could attack, a blaze of light and the pounding of hooves came through the trees.

Was it her carriage returning at last? Instead, the light revealed two mounted men, one carrying a lantern, the other a spear. Leveling it at the nearest wolf, he charged. With a snarl, the animal retreated. Its pack mates backed away from Dia and Carrina, and, in a flash of silver fur, they vanished into the woods.

Dia stood shaking, gripping her tree branch, Carrina still clinging to her, sobbing. All her muscles clenched in terror, and she searched wildly around for further danger. The man dismounted, staring at her in the lantern light, his eyes wide in surprise.

She looked back at him. Whether the wolves had been servants of a dark sorcerer or ordinary animals, the shock of the attack had frozen all her muscles.

He set down the spear and took a few steps nearer. "How badly are you hurt?" He looked her up and down, taking in the soaked, muddy ruins of her dress and the blood on her arms. His gazed moved to Carrina at her side. His companion had ridden up beside him and now dismounted, holding the lantern.

Still unsure of her voice, Dia tried to gather her breath.

He looked around the woods, searching for an explanation for the presence of two young women in the forest at night. "What are you doing here?"

"I..." How to explain the wolves, and the carriage, and their flight? Obviously, they weren't supposed to be out here. The rain still drizzled down.

He was prepared for the weather, dressed in heavy boots and a cloak to shed the rain. His eyes moved from her mud-soaked slippers to her dress, to the veil now straggling from her hair to the stick gripped in her white knuckled hand. His eyes softened. "Maybe now is not the time for so many questions. May we offer our assistance?"

Driving the wolves away had already been a huge help. The second man set his lantern down and came forward to help Carrina, wrapping his cloak around her.

A sharp gust of cold wind blew down on them. A huge shadow passed low over the treetops. It blended in with the dark and the rain, but the shape of the wide wings was unmistakable. It passed swiftly, only visible for a moment. Dia didn't move, her eyes fixed on the sky. Beside her, the man drew in a sharp breath.

Only gray clouds remained above them. Was it gone?

"You saw it too, didn't you?" he asked.

Tearing her eyes from the sky, she met his gaze. He came nearer. Even though he was a stranger to Dia, he had already protected her, and in that moment, she was grateful for any offer of help. If he hadn't come, she might be dead.

Gripping the tree branch, he gently pried it loose from her stiff fingers and dropped it. Unfastening his heavy cloak, he wrapped it around her. "I'm Sam." He nodded toward his companion. "That's Andar."

"D–Dia." Why did her teeth chatter as she tried to speak?

His voice was steady and comforting. "Can you tell me what happened?" He took a clean handkerchief from his pocket and held it against the worst cut on her arm.

"I was trying to get away from the wolves," she said. "I found a carriage back there," she pointed the way they had come. "Carrina was inside, hurt, but the wolves were coming and we tried to escape. We weren't fast enough."

He offered Dia his arm. "Can you show me where?"

She took it. "Yes. T-Thank you for helping us."

He felt strong and solid, and she leaned on him, still having trouble getting her feet to move. They made it to his horse, which stood patiently. Up close, the animal looked huge.

"Do you know how to ride?"

She shook her head.

He looked at her appraisingly. "You fought off a wolf. I'm sure you can do it."

From his tone, he believed she could. Dia gathered her determination. It would be a new experience, but she was willing to try.

"Put your foot here." He offered the stirrup. It was as high as her shoulder, and she was forced to assume an ungraceful position as she lifted her foot.

"Hold on here." He pointed to the saddle horn. "As I push you up, swing your leg over the saddle."

She had seen this done many times, but never attempted it herself, especially not in a rain-drenched gown. Reaching up to grab the pommel, she nodded to him. His strong hands took her waist and easily lifted her. Her skirts bunched uncomfortably around her, leaving too much of the pale, mud-streaked skin of her legs showing, but what else could be done? Of course, that was one of the reasons ladies in long dresses traveled in carriages. She was up. Once balanced in the saddle, her feet no longer reached the stirrups.

Sam bent to pick up the spear he had set aside. Gripping it in one hand, he put his boot where her slipper had been and swung easily onto the horse behind her. "All right?" he asked, reaching around her to take the reins.

"Yes." He had been so kind, while she'd been so overwhelmed with the situation that she could barely speak to him. She took a deep breath, and her voice came out stronger. "Thank you, Sam."

His voice sounded very near as he sat close behind her. "I'm glad I could help."

"Was the bird a Shadaroc?" she asked him suddenly.

He was silent for a long moment. She turned in the saddle to look at his face and saw his features were tight as he nodded.

"I fear so."

She nodded. "It landed in the woods, just before the wolves came."

He put a hand on her shoulder, and it felt large, warm, and comforting. "They're gone. For now, at least."

Andar lifted Carrina up with him and moved off. Sam directed his horse to follow. Dia clutched at the pommel as the motion jolted her.

Sams arms tightened around her. "I won't let you fall."

After only a few moments, the wrecked carriage came into view, and the man's body was still lying in the road.

"You can stay here," Sam said, sliding off the horse. Dia remained in the saddle, feeling unsure atop the horse without him.

He bent to one knee, placing his fingers under the fallen man's chin, looking for a pulse. After a long moment, he shook his head and got back to his feet. He approached the trapped horse, speaking soothingly to it. Drawing his knife, he cut through the tangled straps and led the animal away from the fallen carriage.

Hooves pounding on the road announced the arrival of several more riders. They gathered around the fallen man. "We need to get him back to the city," Sam said.

Several of them got down and lifted the man's lifeless body and draped it across the back of the carriage horse. "Take him to the guards for now," Sam ordered. "We'll sort this all out in the morning."

"We've searched the entire area," one of the riders reported. "The wolves fled from us, and we saw the bird heading away. I can carry your spear."

Sam nodded, handing the man the weapon. "It's time to go back to the city."

The men returned to their horses, leading the animal with its unmoving burden.

Sam came back to the horse and mounted again behind Dia. "I should have taken more time to tend to your injuries before we came back here."

"I'm all right," Dia said, though every part of her body ached. He wouldn't be able to do anything for the bruises.

"Are you sure?"

She nodded, and he directed the horse toward the city.

Sam's voice was close behind her as they rode. "Will you tell me what you saw?"

The fear that had clenched in her belly when she saw it returned as she remembered. "First, the bird, like an eagle but much bigger."

"Black?"

"Yes."

He cursed under his breath. "One of my men saw it from the city, and we rode out tonight, pursuing it. A Shadaroc in Kulin is a sign of disease and death. If we see it again, we will attempt to kill it or drive it away. In the meantime, will you tell me what you were doing out in the woods alone at night?"

Dia took a deep breath. "It was simply a… misunderstanding. I am traveling to Kulin with my sister. We stopped at the overlook to stretch our legs."

"Is that when you first saw it?" His arms around her tightened slightly.

"Yes."

"And how did you become separated from your party?"

"It was… only a joke." Her explanation sounded ridiculous, even to her.

"A joke?" His voice sounded incredulous.

"They would have come back for me any moment."

His voice rose a little. "Are you telling me they left you there on purpose? In the dark and the rain? Alone in the forest?"

Dia shook her head. Maybe other people's siblings weren't so hard on them. "It wasn't raining when she left."

"Your sister? She left you in the woods after you saw the Shadaroc?"

Dia sighed, shaking her head. "She didn't see it. And it was only meant to be a prank. I'm sure she's looking for me right now."

Sam's hands clenched around the reins. "Didn't she consider the danger she put you in?"

What could Dia say? Of course, her impulsive sister hadn't fully considered the situation. There was no denying that Lisenth had intended to make her feel small. It was also possible that something else had happened to them. Her mind went back to the broken carriage on the road behind them.

Andar, who still held Carrina in his arms, slowed to ride beside them. "Did you get the whole story?"

"I still have several questions," Sam admitted. "But she saw the Shadaroc land in the forest not far from here. It might have had something to do with the accident. I need to let my grandfather know about this immediately. But, since we are heading back to the city ourselves, we can search for Dia's family along the way."

Andar nodded, and they rode on.

The rain continued to fall, and Dia huddled gratefully into the warm folds of his cloak.

"Do you live in the city, or are you visiting?" Sam asked.

"We're from Bartal. My father was the late Baron Ifereth," Dia said. "We came to stay as guests of Lord Karvan, the Earl of Kana."

"So, he is expecting you?"

Dia nodded. She looked down at her muddy gown and ruined shoes. "Perhaps not in this condition."

"Don't worry about the earl, he's a good man, and he will help you. His countess loves to take care of guests. She'll make sure you're comfortable. Maybe they can sort out your family misunderstanding better than I can."

Dia didn't look forward to explaining it to the countess or anyone else. But that couldn't be helped now.

"It will be better not to tell anyone else about what you saw," Sam suggested, "at least not for now. If the rumor got started in the city, people would be frightened. After all, maybe the Shadaroc only passed us on its way to... somewhere else."

Dia fervently hoped that was true. For a moment, she was lost in the dark memory of a huge bird passing directly over her head. "Is there someone we should report this to?"

"Yes," Sam replied. "I will go to the palace and make sure the right people are informed."

She put her hand over his where he held the reins. "You saved my life tonight, and I thank you with all my heart for your service."

"It's my honor to assist you," he said.

The warmth of his words sent a shiver through her body.

Thick clouds veiled the sky as they rode, hiding any sign of stars. Dia couldn't help anxiously scanning the sky for any sign of huge black wings.

A short while later, they arrived at the overlook where she had stopped to look at the sunset. Now the place was dark and silent. No one was there.

Sam dismounted to look at the ruts in the mud by lantern light. He pointed at the ground. "Carriage wheels. You said they were here before. Did they come so far off the road the first time? It looks like someone turned around."

"No, they were over there, before," Dia pointed. "Just off the main road."

"At least they do seem to be looking for you," Sam growled. "I'd like to have a few words with that sister of yours."

"Please don't," Dia protested. "She can be... difficult sometimes, and that would only make it worse."

Sam shook his head. "Why would she treat you like this?"

"We don't always get along very well, but she's not so bad," Dia protested. "This really was an accident. I know she never meant it to go so far."

"If you say so," he muttered.

"You rode all the way out here from the city looking for the Shadaroc?" she asked him.

"Yes. And though I found only a couple of wolves, I was able to assist a young lady in distress, and that is more important. I feel very fortunate to have been in the right place at the right time." His tone sounded earnest.

Dia couldn't help but laugh. "Do you do that often? Rescue silly girls who find themselves in trouble?"

"Every day," he claimed solemnly.

She laughed again, feeling more comfortable with him than she had with anyone in a long time. "It does seem that you have some experience. You were excellent at it."

He bent closer to her ear. "You're not silly," his voice was warm. "You were very brave, and you made the best of a difficult situation. I saw you hit that wolf."

Heat rushed to her cheeks, but his praise felt good. How long had it been since anyone paid her a sincere compliment? Most people barely noticed her at all. "Thank you, Sam."

All too soon, they rode up behind a familiar carriage moving slowly toward the city. She recognized Roland who held a lantern high and appeared to be searching the woods beside the road as they moved. Sam rode up beside them, holding the light so they could see Dia.

"My lady!" Roland cried as the driver pulled the horses to a stop. He put his hand over his chest to exhale a breath of relief. "Thank the Eternal Soul Mother!" He eyed her muddy dress and disheveled hair. "Are you hurt? What happened to you?"

"I'm all right," she confirmed. "And I'll be sure to let the earl know this wasn't your fault."

"Thank you." He let out a breath of relief. "And if I get the opportunity, I will have a word with him about this whole incident. Lady Lisenth has been weeping for an hour. When she confessed what she'd done, we turned around immediately, but one of our wheels broke, and it took time to repair it. We've been searching for you ever since."

At that moment, Lisenth threw open the carriage door. "Dia?" She ran to the horse and looked up at her sister. "Are you all right? I'm so sorry. The wheel broke..."

"I'm all right," Dia replied.

Lisenth let out a dramatic sigh of relief.

Sam lifted Dia to the ground. She started to remove his cloak.

"Keep it." He grinned at her. "You're still cold."

She returned his smile and wrapped the heavy fabric more tightly around herself.

She glanced toward Andar where he still held Carrina. "Would she be more comfortable in the carriage?" She looked back at Sam.

He nodded. "Yes."

Lisenth put her arm around Dia's shoulders as they moved toward the coach. Roland helped them in. Dia took the empty seat opposite her sister. Andar and Sam lifted Carrina in. Her eyes remained closed. Dia supported her head and shoulders as she slumped in the seat beside her. Avoiding the girl's injured arm, she held her in place.

Dia turned back toward Sam. "Thank you from the bottom of my heart."

"It was my pleasure," Sam replied.

In the dim light, Dia could barely see Sam's face. "Will I see you again?"

"You will," he promised. "Soon!" With a smile, he disappeared. She heard the horses riding behind the carriage as they all turned back toward the city.

Dia wrapped his cloak close around herself. She hadn't realized until he was gone that the garment still smelled faintly of him. A combination of leather and the fresh scent of forest air and something else she couldn't name.

Sam had promised that she'd see him again soon. He'd agreed to take news of the Shadaroc to the palace, and he appeared to know the earl well. Maybe he'd call on them while they stayed there. She wished she'd thought to ask him more about himself.

Where did he live? What did he do? He seemed to be in command of the company of riders, so perhaps he was a soldier. She would be content with whatever occupation he'd chosen, but now she realized she wanted to know everything about him.

They rode on. Lisenth stared at her as if she didn't know what to say, and Dia silently thought of Sam, her cheek resting against the collar of his cloak.

Finally, Dia met her sister's gaze. "Why did you do that?"

Lisenth lowered her eyes and looked away. "I thought we could come back to get you in a few minutes, but... the wheel."

"And you didn't stop to think it might be dangerous in the forest at night?" Dia looked down at Carrina. "A man died out there tonight, and she barely survived. Didn't you think that could have been us? Any of us might have been killed."

Lisenth swiped at her eyes. "I'm sorry Dia. I didn't know there would be wolves!" Her eyes flew to Carrina. "I didn't know anything dangerous was out there."

CHAPTER 4

S AM AND HIS COMPANIONS arrived at the doors of the palace and dismounted, grooms leading their horses toward the stables. Andar lifted the injured girl with him as he got down. She lay limp in his arms, apparently unconscious. She hadn't responded at all when he'd taken her from the coach at the Earl of Kana's estate. The earl would have taken her in gladly, but here at the palace, the king's counselor Marek could help her. He would know how to care for her.

Sam clasped his friend's shoulder. "Thank you for your help. The evening wasn't exactly what either of us expected."

Andar nodded. "True enough." He looked down at the girl in his arms. "I'll take her to the infirmary."

"Good."

"Even if we didn't find the creature tonight, I'm glad we were able to offer our aid. The two young ladies were in serious trouble," Andar said. "You aren't one to ignore someone who needs help."

"No, of course not," Sam agreed. And he couldn't afford to forget the information Dia had given him. "I need to take news to the king, immediately."

Andar nodded, heading away toward the doors, carrying the injured girl.

Sam hurried through the halls toward his grandfather's study. He paused to speak to the guards at the door. "Is the king inside?"

They nodded, stepping aside for him.

Sam knocked, and at the invitation from within, entered the room. King Hashoreth Algorian sat behind an ornate desk, his oldest friend and counselor, Marek, across from him. The king smiled at the sight of Sam, accentuating the heavy age lines and creases in his familiar face.

"Sam?" He appeared to realize at once that something was wrong, and he waved at a chair. "Please, sit."

Sam pulled the chair to face the desk and sat down. "How are you, Grandfather?"

The old man smiled, a hint of sadness in his expression. "Well enough, though news has reached me today of an illness in the city. A few dozen sick." He looked across the desk at Marek, a frail elderly man, even older than the king, though his dark eyes remained sharp. "We were just discussing it."

Sam's stomach tightened. "I fear the news I bring is related. Several of our guards saw an enormous black bird from the city walls. I rode out earlier this evening with a company of men pursuing it. And I just met someone who saw the Shadaroc in the forest tonight."

His grandfather's eyes widened. "Are you certain? Did you see it yourself?"

"Only for a moment. But I met a young woman, the daughter of Baron Ifereth, who got a better look at the creature. She possesses sound reasoning and good judgement, and I believe her."

"Did she describe the bird in detail?" Marek asked.

Sam nodded.

"Are you certain she isn't just vying for attention?" his grandfather asked.

Sam almost laughed. The suggestion was the exact opposite of Dia's character. "Very certain. I've never seen her before tonight, and she didn't recognize me. She doesn't know who I am, and I didn't tell her. She saw the bird flying above the forest until it landed nearby. We both saw the wolves soon after."

"It sounds like we must believe it, then." His grandfather bowed his head and rubbed his temple. "I hoped it would never come back. And now, this illness in Kulin..."

"We brought an injured girl back with us," Sam said. "We fear the Shadaroc attacked her."

Marek got to his feet. "I would like to see her, at once."

"Of course," Sam said. "We hoped you would offer her your aid. She'll be in the infirmary."

Marek nodded to him and made a stiff bow to the king. "We will speak again soon."

His grandfather nodded as his counselor shuffled out the door, his back bent.

Sam got up and walked around the desk to put a comforting hand on his grandfather's shoulder. "We all hoped it wouldn't return. After that terrible day... there has been no sign of the creature in nearly twenty years."

His grandfather put his hand over Sam's and gripped it. "Neither of us will ever forget. It was the worst day of both our lives. We lost everything. All the rest of our family, gone, leaving us with only each other." His usually strong voice trembled. "It broke my heart to condemn my son. But how could I do otherwise, when all the evidence pointed to him? I never thought he would be capable of killing his brother. Or your dear mother."

Though it had been many years, Sam felt his gut twist at the memory. It wasn't something anyone should see, let alone a small child. He'd been an orphan since that day, raised by his grandfather.

Blinking rapidly, the old man took in a deep breath. "We have to stay strong, Sam," he said, his voice steadier. "Our people look to us for protection and leadership. Marek has done all he can to help. His magic has provided protection to us for nearly twenty years. I have already assigned some of our best people to help him investigate this strange illness. It can't be a coincidence that a Shadaroc appeared now."

"No, I agree," Sam said. "Marek will be able to tell if the sickness is related. We need to discover the truth."

His grandfather nodded, rubbing a hand across his forehead. "There is something else." He raised his eyes to meet Sam's. "I've tried to devise a pleasant way to say this, but I couldn't think of one, so here it is. I'm old, and I don't know how much longer I'll be here with you."

Sam didn't want to hear it. He loved the old man. They had grown much closer after Sam's parents died. They had to. When there was no one else, they leaned on each other. "You might be old, but not as old as Marek, and you're in excellent health," Sam protested. "Is something wrong that I don't know about?"

The old man smiled. "No. Not at all. I am very well, and I'm grateful for it, but it can't last forever. For nearly forty years, I've ruled this kingdom, and it will soon be time for a change. You have grown into a caring and intelligent man, someone who will make an excellent ruler for Ischar. But you shouldn't be alone as you take on the responsibility. I never wanted to rush you, but I feel the time is at hand. You need to marry and provide Ischar with an heir. It falls to you to continue our bloodline."

Sam's eyes widened. They'd had several versions of this same conversation over the last two years, but his grandfather seemed more determined now. Suddenly, Sam's mind flickered back to

Dia, how she had stood bravely in the woods in a soaking wet gown facing down the wolves. His mouth went dry as he recalled the way the wet silk had clung to her slender form. It felt so right to protect her. After only a short while getting to know her, he didn't want to admit to himself how badly he wanted to see her again.

"Sam?"

His attention snapped back. "Sorry, what?"

"This is a very serious matter," his grandfather said, his eyebrows lowered in a stern expression. "As I said before, I don't want to put additional pressure on you, but you can't wait forever. For years, you've spent time with various young ladies, but nothing ever became serious. You need to make a decision very soon."

Choosing a spouse was a serious matter, and Sam had given the matter a lot of thought. Now the weight of the decision settled over him. "What do you have in mind?"

The old man took in a deep breath. "As I said, I have no wish to rush you, but I can't escape the feeling that time is short. If I should die... I can't stand the thought of you being alone. I think you can admit that it's high time."

Somehow, for the first time, today, Sam agreed with him. "It sounds like you've already planned something."

"Of course I have. In a few weeks we will hold your birthday celebration. Invitations to the party have already been sent far and wide."

CHAPTER 5

DIA SPENT THE DAY quietly, enjoying a long bath and nursing her bruises and scrapes. After dinner, the maid tapped on her door and stuck her head inside. "One of the palace guards is here with a message for you, my lady."

"A palace guard?" Her brows raised in surprise. "Did he say what the message was about?"

"No, my lady. He's waiting for you in the drawing room."

Dia got to her feet, smoothing the fabric of her gown. With a slow, proper tread, she descended the stairs, moving along the hall to enter the drawing room. A young man in a gray uniform stood waiting for her. She recognized Andar immediately. He had been with Sam last night. They must both be members of the palace guard.

Andar bowed politely. "Lady Alladia?"

"Andar, is there news? Is Carrina all right? Did they find anything else?"

He straightened up and smiled. "Carrina is being cared for. I brought you a message... from Sam."

All her attention was instantly riveted on him. "What is it? Is he all right?"

He nodded hastily. "Yes, of course, he's fine. A small company of guards will be riding back to the forest tomorrow. We'll be returning to the area of last night's..." he cleared his throat, "...events. Would you consider joining us? We hope to learn more about what happened, and your perspective would be very valuable."

Was this only to learn more about what had happened, or did Sam want her to ride with him? Could he want to see her again? Dia felt a strange warmth in her belly. He'd promised she would see him soon. No matter how hard she'd tried not to think about him, he'd been on her mind every moment since last night, and spending a day with him sounded wonderful. But riding?

She took in a deep breath and looked up at Andar. "Does he recall my lack of skill on horseback?"

He grinned. "Yes, but don't worry. He will make sure you are safe. Unless your injures require you to rest tomorrow?" His eyes went to the cut on her arm. "We could postpone this errand. He has no wish to cause you discomfort."

Dia had no intention of admitting how sore and bruised she still felt. She weighed her options. Of course, she could remain and rest, but the idea of spending time with Sam made the decision an easy one. "I would be happy to assist you with your investigation."

Andar smiled. "You're very kind, Lady Alladia. Perhaps Countess Lavinia might help you borrow a riding dress?"

They seemed to have thought of everything. But why hadn't Sam come to ask her? "Why didn't he bring this message himself?"

Andar flushed slightly. "I'm afraid that... Sam had another duty he couldn't escape from tonight. He asked me to beg your forgiveness."

It sounded plausible enough. She nodded. "Very well, I will be pleased to join you."

He smiled. "Thank you, my lady. We will call for you in the morning."

Excitement flowed through her as Dia returned to her room to get ready for bed. She slept little. Every time she rolled over, her mind presented her with a memory of her time with Sam, the way his dark eyes had met hers, his strong hands at her waist as he'd lifted her into the saddle. How safe she'd felt with his arms around her.

Finally, she got up and took Sam's cloak from the wardrobe and laid it over her pillow. With her face buried in its folds, she finally dozed.

The earl and countess hadn't questioned her explanation that a group of the palace guards had asked her to return to the forest as they gathered more information about the accident. Countess Lavinia was a petite, plump woman, an inch shorter even than Dia. She had a sweet face and a kindly disposition, and she'd rushed to find Dia a riding dress with a divided skirt.

At a knock on the front door, Roland opened it, nodding to her, and they went out to see six men in uniforms. Another footman held the reins of one of the horses they'd brought from Bartal for Roland to ride.

Roland glanced at Dia. "Are you *sure* you wouldn't rather take the carriage, my lady?" He knew she didn't know how to ride.

She shook her head.

One of the soldiers stepped forward and bowed to her. "Lady Alladia, would you do me the honor of accompanying me?"

A quiver of excitement spread through her. Sam. His smile and his brown eyes were warm as he offered his arm. She took it, following him to his horse. With her foot in the stirrup, he lifted her into the saddle.

He gazed up at her. "Do you need anything else before we go?"

She shook her head, gripping the pommel. He mounted behind her.

Had he been this close when they rode together before? Her cheeks warmed. His thighs pressed against hers, and unless she kept her back perfectly straight, she leaned against the solidness of his body directly behind her. He reached around her to take the reins and the animal began to move. The twinge of unease in her belly loosened as she felt him close behind her, calm and steady. He knew how to do this, and he wouldn't let anything happen to her.

The road looked entirely different by daylight. Brilliant morning sun shone on golden fields and green forests, and when they rode beneath the trees, light filtered through the leaves in beautiful patterns. The terror of two nights ago felt far away.

"It looks so different," she said.

"The sky is clear, and the sun is shining," he agreed.

The journey allowed plenty of time for them to talk and laugh together. It didn't seem to take long at all to reach the remains of the carriage. The horses drew up, and Sam dismounted and helped her down. They examined the wreckage carefully. The carriage lay on its side. There was damage along the top, on the side now facing upward.

Roland stared at the ruined coach with wide eyes. "We're fortunate we didn't suffer more serious injury."

Dia met his eyes. "You're right."

"It looks like something struck it, here." Andar pointed to the top of the coach. Sam nodded. He gazed off into the trees in the direction the Shadaroc might have been going.

He was silent for a long moment. Finally, he pointed. "I think I see something. Maybe a cliff face? Look Andar, do you see it?"

Andar looked where Sam pointed. "I think I can see an opening in the rocks, maybe a cave. Let's take a closer look."

There was no path in that direction. Sam turned to Dia. "The brush is too thick to ride through. We'll have to walk. If you don't want to go, we can stay here and let the others explore it."

Shoving down the dismay she felt as she surveyed the thick undergrowth, Dia squared her shoulders. "I'll go with you."

Roland raised his eyebrows at her decision, but he didn't comment. Sam smiled and offered Dia his hand.

They left a few men with the horses while the rest of the group plunged off the trail into the forest. Sam held branches back out of her way, and now that it was daylight, good weather, and nothing was chasing her, the way didn't seem too hard.

After a few moments, they emerged from the undergrowth into a clearing. An imposing rock face rose above them, with a narrow opening near the base. When they walked nearer to peer inside the crack in the rock, they saw only darkness.

The others looked to Sam. He gazed down at Dia. "We don't know what's in there."

A shiver ran down her spine. He didn't intend to go inside, did he?

Two of the others were already picking up branches that might serve as makeshift torches. "We'll take a look and let you know if it's safe."

They struck a spark and, in a moment, had a steady flame at the end of each branch. The men disappeared into the narrow opening. For a moment, the orange light of their torches followed them, until it too was gone.

Sam took her hand. "They'll be fine," he assured her.

Dia had never explored a cave before. It wasn't the kind of activity young ladies usually pursued. What would they find inside? She sneaked a glance up at Sam, only to find him looking down at her.

"Thank you for agreeing to come with us today," he said, his fingers tightened around hers.

She smiled. "I'm glad you asked me." She paused for a moment. Maybe she shouldn't tell him exactly how she felt. Taking a deep breath, she told the truth. "I wanted to see you again."

His brows drew down in thought. "My lady, that can't be the reason you joined us. You only came on this expedition because you're a concerned citizen, helping the palace guards gather more information to make the roads safer."

"That's right," she nodded at him, one corner of her mouth turning up. An answering smile lit his face.

A flash of firelight announced the return of their companions. "It's safe," one reported. His eyes met Sam's. "You should see this."

Sam turned to look at Dia. "Shall we?"

She nodded. His hand held hers firmly as she followed him into the dark passageway. For a short way, the walls were close on either side of them until they opened up into a large chamber. At first glance, it appeared to be a natural cavern. Upon closer inspection, Dia saw rough stairs leading up to a high ledge beside a wide opening looking out into the tops of the forest trees.

One of the guards climbed the stairs to the ledge. "Look!" He held up an enormous black feather. It looked just like any feather dropped from a bird's wing, except that it was over six feet long. He carried it back down to the others and offered it to Sam.

He took it, examining it closely. Dia reached out to touch it, feeling the stiff smooth column in the middle and the sleek vane spreading out from the center.

Sam met her eyes. "So, it was here." He turned to the guard who had found it. "The king and Marek should see this. Will you please carry it back with us?"

The guard nodded, and Sam returned the feather to him.

As the men explored the corners of the cavern, Dia stood in the center of the space. She heard something, or maybe felt something. A hum of energy. For several moments, she couldn't tell where it came from. Finally, her eyes dropped to her feet, to the dirt and pebbles forming the floor of the cavern. She bent down, brushing some of the loose rocks aside. Her fingers brushed something smooth, and she felt a tiny shock of energy. She picked up a small shard of crystal, part of a tapered, hexagonal blue column. As she lifted it, the clear light shone through it. She felt a slight hum as it rested on her palm.

"Did you find something?" Sam came up beside her, gazing curiously into her open hand. "What is it?"

Dia shrugged. "It's only a little shard of rock. It felt important, so I picked it up. It hums. Can you hear it?"

A moment of silence fell at her question. Sam leaned close and cocked his head, listening. "I don't hear anything."

He couldn't hear it. She wasn't sure she even heard it herself, but she felt it. Color rushed to her cheeks. "Maybe it's nothing." She closed her hand around the crystal and tucked it into her pocket.

Her gaze went back to the wide opening, high on the wall. "The Shadaroc must have flown in."

Sam's eyes went to the high ledge, and he nodded slowly. "If not for the black feather, we might still question whether it could be someone else. There have been many others to practice magic in Ischar who didn't follow the path of evil. Marek is a sorcerer who has served King Hashoreth for nearly twenty years. He is loyal to the kingdom and has served and helped our people. I've heard that he can change his shape just as the Shadaroc does."

Until she'd seen it for herself, Dia had never paid much attention to the stories of magic. "Then not all sorcerers harm people?"

"No. Magic is like any sort of power." His brown eyes met hers. "It all depends on how you use it. An evil sorcerer takes much of his power from other people. It gives him an advantage and makes him more powerful."

As they made their way back to the horses, Dia's mind spun with thoughts of sorcerers and giant birds. "If he returned to his human shape, the sorcerer could be in Kulin."

Sam paused, standing still for a moment. Slowly, he nodded. "We fear he is."

"What will you do?"

He drew in a breath, his expression hardening. "I will do everything I can to make sure our people are safe, but I don't know how to find him."

"If you do, how will you fight his magic?"

Someone of great power wouldn't give it up easily. And this sorcerer wouldn't care if he killed many people to increase his strength. Dia shivered. Maybe she should never have brought Lisenth here. They would have been safer back in Bartal.

But in Bartal, she would never have met Sam.

CHAPTER 6

After their outing to the forest, two more days passed with no word from Sam. Dia began to feel restless. She'd been in the manor house too long. It was time to go out.

Countess Lavinia appeared to sense her pent-up energy. "You ladies should go and visit the market," she suggested over the breakfast table.

Lisenth's eyes widened in excitement at the suggestion. "We've heard the merchants offer many beautiful things. Some of them are even brought from far outside Ischar."

Lavinia nodded her head. "True, my dear. I'm sure you will both enjoy it."

A short while later, accompanied by Roland and another of the footmen, they left the carriage behind, making their way into the center of the bustling market. Dia paused to look at a booth of beautiful books. She touched their covers, fascinated. "Come on," Lisenth urged. "We need to see everything. No one wants to look at *books*. You're so slow."

Dia drew in a calming breath. "I'll be along in a moment."

Lisenth tapped her foot impatiently, her arms folded across her chest. Refusing to yield to the pressure, Dia picked up another book.

Letting out a disgusted breath, her sister stomped away toward a display of fashionable shoes, the footman on her heels.

Dia raised her eyebrows. "We'll meet up with them again later, I suppose?"

Roland rubbed his forehead. "I suppose, my lady."

Dia took her time surveying jewelry, fabrics, books, trinkets, and a huge assortment of foods. People of all kinds surrounded her: men in the gray coats of the palace guard, or the dark green uniforms of the king's army, city tradespeople or members of the nobility.

As she stood at a booth near the edge of the market, movement in a narrow side street caught her eye. A man in a cloak with a hood drawn down to conceal his features carried a large crate. At first glance, she thought he must be doing something wrong. He obviously didn't want to be seen. Should she alert the guards?

The man set the crate outside the door of a small narrow house, knocked on the door, and then disappeared around a corner. A moment later, a small child opened the door, gaping in surprise at the box. He went back inside, and a woman appeared. Her face was lined with worry. When she peeked into the crate, her eyes widened in surprise. Gratitude showed plainly on her face, and she placed her hand over her heart. She looked, first one way, then the other, not spotting anyone. The child helped her move the crate inside.

Someone must want to help them without being discovered. Who had the man in the cloak been?

No longer seeing him, she turned back to look over a selection of sweets.

"The ones with strawberries are very good," a familiar voice said beside her.

She jumped, for a moment feeling as if an entire flock of birds had taken wing in her middle. She hadn't expected to find Sam here. She looked up at his handsome features and warm brown eyes. "You startled me."

He grinned. "But you are happy to see me?"

She was. She couldn't deny it. Her lips curved up into a smile. "Yes."

Despite the pleasant weather, he wore a cloak with a hood that partially shadowed his face. Beneath it, he wore the same gray uniform as the other guards.

She looked him up and down. "Who are you hiding from?" The man she'd just seen in the alley had worn a garment very like this one. If it hadn't been him a moment ago, then it was someone else wearing a very similar cloak.

His eyes sparkled with mischief. He glanced to one side and then the other. "I'm not supposed to be here. I couldn't stop thinking about you, and I was supposed to work this afternoon. I told them I wasn't feeling well and went to my room to lie down."

Her eyes widened. He'd been thinking about her? He'd sneaked away from his duties to see her? "Won't you get in trouble?"

Tugging the hood a little lower over his face, he smiled. "Only if I get caught."

Warmth spread through her body. He wanted to spend time with her, and he'd found a way for them to meet again. She gestured to the crowds of shoppers and merchants. "How did you find me in all this?"

He nodded toward the edge of the market, where more men in gray uniforms stood. "One of my friends saw you and told me you were here."

They made their way through the market, laughing and chatting, and if Sam subtly kept his face covered, no one seemed to notice too much. "Come on, I'll show you where they sell the best sweets." He took her hand and led her through the maze of merchants to a booth stacked with dozens of kinds of chocolates and pastries. "You need to taste them all, but for now, may I buy a few for you?"

The sensation of his big, callused hand holding hers made her forget about any sort of food. He picked out one and handed it to her on a napkin. "These are my favorite."

She picked up the sweet, its outside coated in chocolate, and bit into it. Her eyes closed in bliss. "What is it?"

"Chocolate and coconut," he replied, watching her reaction closely.

"What's coconut?"

"A large nut." He formed the shape with his hands. "They grow in the jungle."

Dia drew in a sharp breath. The only jungle was far below, at the base of the towering cliffs. "Someone brought them up from down there?"

He nodded. "It's difficult, but once in a while, we are able to buy or trade for them."

She nibbled a little more. "They taste amazing."

He grinned, taking a bite of his own treat. After a quick conversation, the merchant handed him a box of sweets. He gave it to her. "Will you think of me when you eat them later?"

Dia nodded. Of course she would. Chocolate or not, her thoughts had a habit of wandering back to him.

"Shall I carry it for you, my lady?" Roland asked.

She smiled, placing the box in his hand. "Thank you." She turned back to Sam.

"Will you walk with me for a while?" he asked.

"I would enjoy that."

He offered his arm, and she took it. They strolled from the street out into a park, crossing the graceful stone arch of a bridge. Below them, the river gurgled as it slid by.

"I have to ask about you and your sister," Sam said finally. "Tell me more."

A respectful distance behind them, but apparently still listening, Roland coughed suddenly.

Sam turned to face him. "I gather you've been with the family for some time?"

Roland nodded gravely. "All my life."

"And is what I saw that night in the forest usual for them?"

Clearing his throat, Roland put a finger beneath his collar to loosen it, looking at Dia.

"It's all right," Dia assured him. "I'm fairly sure that Sam witnessed more of our family that night than most people ever see. You may tell him frankly what you observe."

Roland rubbed his chin, considering his words. "Every family has their share of... little troubles."

Half a laugh escaped Sam. "Is that what you'd call it?" He shook his head. "Don't worry. I understand. My family has more than our share."

Roland drew in a deep breath. "Lady Lisenth is a good girl, somewhere on the inside. But I fear that she resents not being in charge, being the younger sister. Sometimes she can be... unkind."

It was a tactful explanation. It didn't cover everything. Lisenth was so beautiful. She stood out in a crowd, loving people and blooming under their attention. In contrast, Dia attempted to remain unnoticed as much as she could.

They strolled and talked. Sam took her hand, and she loved the connection to him. He was a good man. Back in the forest, he hadn't had to help her, and he certainly hadn't needed to be so kind as he did. She must have appeared pathetic in that moment, lost, wet, covered in mud. She'd been in desperate need of his aid.

No one had forced him to seek her out afterwards. He could have simply offered his help in her moment of need and never given her another thought. No one had made him find her today. In fact, he had gone to a great deal of trouble to clear his schedule and meet her. Why would he do that if he didn't genuinely want to spend time with her?

Long before she even thought to worry about the time, they came around a corner to find Andar waiting for them.

He smiled and bowed. "Lady Alladia, how nice to see you again."

"And you as well."

Andar cleared his throat. "I apologize, my lady, but I'm afraid I must interrupt." His eyes moved to Sam. "I told them you weren't *feeling* well, but your grandfather still requested your presence."

Sam's lips twitched. "Either he doesn't believe me, or it's truly something urgent." He turned to Dia. "You have honored me by spending time with me today." He brought her hand to his lips and kissed it.

A surge of warmth ran through her at the look in his eyes, and the whisper of his breath across her skin. "I have loved spending time with you, too," she said. Maybe it was better not to be so forthright, but she knew he could tell anyway.

He smiled at her, bowed, and slipped away into the crowd with Andar.

***

Dia and Lisenth had been invited to join the earl and countess and their guests for tea. Countess Lavinia greeted her friends warmly, ushering them into the drawing room. "Lord and Lady Marith, may I introduce Lady Lisenth and Lady Alladia, old family friends visiting from Bartal."

Dia and Lisenth curtsied.

The countess smiled. "And these are their sons, Eldon and Thomas." Two young men entered the room. They both had brown hair with just a hint of red, and they were both handsome and polished. They smiled, kissing Dia's hand and then Lisenth's. And if their eyes followed Lisenth avidly, maybe it wasn't too noticeable.

The countess ushered them all into seats pleasantly spaced for conversation. Eldon and Thomas were charming, and Lisenth led the conversation. She always had more to say than Dia, but they both spoke of their home, and a little of the journey to Kulin, smoothly glossing over the disaster their travel had become.

"The Royal Birthday Celebration is only two weeks away," Eldon said. "Are you both as excited as the rest of the city to attend?"

"Of course." Lisenth smiled.

"I'm not sure I'd want to be the prince right now," Thomas added. "The king has been trying to get him safely married off for years. By now, the pressure is mounting. I think the king invited every eligible girl in Ischar."

"It only makes sense that he should meet someone," Lisenth pointed out. "I'm sure one of the young ladies will catch his eye."

Dia refused to allow any change to show in her expression. Lisenth meant herself, of course.

Thomas laughed. "He's going to meet *everyone*."

It must be difficult to meet so many people all at once. How would the prince ever get to know anyone when he was thrust into a crowd of people? None of them would be more beautiful than Lisenth, so perhaps her plans would work out after all.

The servants entered with trays of food and tea. For a moment, everyone was occupied by cups and plates. Balancing a small plate of food, Dia barely looked at Lisenth as she handed her a steaming cup of tea. There was a lull in the conversation as everyone ate and drank. Setting the plate down on a side table, Dia took a sip of tea.

Something was off about the flavor. It was hot, much too hot, burning all the way down her throat. Her mouth burned painfully, and despite her best efforts to stop them, her eyes watered. She couldn't think about anything else. The burning only got worse, and her face heated. She had to find some relief. Setting the cup down, she fled from the room.

Desperate for a way to cool the burning, she ran to the kitchen, taking up a glass of water and gulping it down. "What's wrong?" the cook patted her back.

Dia pointed to her mouth, barely able to get out a single word. "Hot!"

The woman's eyes widened with understanding, and she quickly brought a glass of milk. "Sip this, my dear."

Dia obeyed, and the cool milk gradually cooled her mouth until she could think again.

"What happened?" the cook watched her with wide eyes.

"The tea!" she managed to say. "There was something in the tea."

The cook looked alarmed. "How can that be? I prepared it myself only a few moments ago. You look like you swallowed half the bottle of my special pepper sauce. Tea wouldn't do that."

"Pepper sauce?"

"I keep a bottle of it just to add spice to certain dishes. But I only use a drop at a time."

"And where is the bottle?" Dia asked.

The cook searched through her cupboards for several moments before she turned back to Dia, her face creased in worried lines. "It's gone, my lady. I don't see it anywhere."

Of course she didn't. Dia finished her milk and set the glass down. "I'm very sure this was not your fault," she assured the cook. Dia returned to her room and washed her face. The red was slowly fading from her cheeks, and her eyes no longer streamed. Though she would have preferred to hide in her room until their guests were gone, she had to go back and explain herself.

When she entered the drawing room, everyone stopped what they were saying to stare at her.

"I apologize for my rude departure," she used her most gracious voice. "I suddenly felt unwell for a moment, but I am recovered."

The countess stared at her in confusion. When Dia looked at her sister, she detected a hint of satisfaction on Lisenth's face before she turned back to her conversation with Eldon.

◆

After the guests had gone, Dia knocked on the door of her sister's room. Lisenth opened it.

"Where is it?" Dia demanded.

Lisenth's eyes went round in surprise. "What?"

Dia glared at her, holding out her hand.

Lisenth broke eye contact, looking away before she attempted to look innocent once more. Dia remained exactly where she was, waiting, her hand held out. At last, Lisenth dug in her pocket, pulled out a small bottle, and handed it to her.

"Why would you do that?" Dia demanded.

"Why?" Lisenth giggled. "You should have seen your face! You ran out of the room like there was a fire!"

"It wasn't funny!" Dia protested.

Lisenth laughed even harder. Dia took the hot sauce, shut the door in her face, and stalked back to her own room.

Three nights later, with a small pop, a tiny pebble struck the window of her room. Dia jumped. Around her, the house was quiet, everyone in their rooms for the night, the servants all in their beds.

Tap.

Another pebble. Dia wrapped her dressing gown around herself and went to the balcony doors. Outside, the night air surrounded her, cool and fresh. Who could possibly be throwing pebbles toward her window? Was this another of her sister's pranks? Her room was on the second floor, the ground a significant distance below.

"Dia?" a voice whispered.

"Who is it?" She shrank back toward the open door. Should she wake one of the footmen for help?

"Sam," the voice replied.

The tight ball of fear in her middle relaxed instantly. Instead, warmth spread throughout her body. She moved to the edge of the balcony, attempting to ignore the black space beneath her, and looked down. He stood alone on the lawn, a black shadow against the starlight on the grass.

"Sam?" When he pulled back his hood, she saw his familiar features clearly. How had he gotten into the grounds without raising an alarm? "What are you doing here?"

"I know it's late, but I wanted to see you," he confessed. "I sneaked in."

She gripped the railing, not liking to be this high up, but she smiled down at him. It was so late that everyone was asleep, yet here he was. "But you're down there and I'm up here."

"If you will permit me, my lady, I'll climb up."

"Climb?"

With a gasp, she drew back from the railing. He couldn't be serious. Her balcony was high. He might fall and be hurt. Clamping her jaw shut on her protests, she waited. For several moments, she heard nothing, then a black shape appeared, climbing over the railing. She almost shrieked in surprise. He released his grip on the climbing vines and turned to face her.

"How?" she gasped. He'd climbed up the ivy. She knew it. What she really meant to ask was how he could climb like that in the dark, with no apparent trace of fear.

He stepped nearer. "Are you well?" He put his arms around her. "You're trembling. What is it?"

"I'm afraid of heights," she admitted. "How did you do that safely? I was afraid you'd fall."

Humor filled his voice. "It wasn't that bad. I could climb down and up again."

Her eyes widened at the suggestion and she clutched at him. "No! Why would you...?"

He was teasing her. She felt him shake with suppressed laughter, and she smacked his arm.

His tone grew suddenly serious. "Were you really concerned about me?"

He had caught her. There was no way now to hide the fact that she'd been worried. The thought of him falling into the dark space, with the hard ground below... she couldn't stand it. "I was," she confessed.

In the dark, his hand found hers. "I'm glad you care about my safety. May I sit with you for a while and watch the stars? I know it's late. If you need to sleep, I'll go..." He lowered his arms and took a step away.

"I'm not sleepy," she said. "I'm glad you came. Just wait here for a moment."

She darted back inside, scooping up the blanket from the bed and a couple of pillows. Returning to the balcony, Sam spread out his cloak and arranged the pillows on it. They sat down, side by side, and Dia draped the blanket over them.

They spoke in hushed whispers and muffled their laughter. They rested against the pillows, staring up into the heavens. Sam slipped his arm around her, and she moved closer, nestling against him. He felt so warm and solid. He was closer now than he'd ever been.

For a long time, they stayed as they were, watching the stars turn slowly above them. Sam turned onto his side, facing her. He brushed his fingertips along her cheek and then down her arm to her wrist. Lifting it to his mouth, he kissed her hand.

Dia almost allowed a gasp to escape her lips at the feeling of his mouth against her skin, the rough prickle of his beard, the warmth of his breath. Did he want more? She was very sure *she* did. But even though they were alone, and no one was watching, Sam didn't try to take advantage.

It was very late before he wished her good night and slipped away, disappearing silently over the balcony railing.

⋇

Dia couldn't believe the day had arrived so quickly. Tonight was the prince's birthday celebration. She sat at the dressing table in her room, preparing for the event. After everything that had happened in the last few weeks, Dia didn't care a bit about meeting the prince, but the whole city would be there tonight. Sam knew she and her sister were attending, and if there was any possible way he could arrange it, she was certain he would meet her. Perhaps he would already be there, on duty with other members of the royal guard. Better yet, he had the night off, and they would have time to talk or even dance.

She shook herself out of a daydream where they twirled together, floating along as the music played and Sam smiled at her.

Dia turned back to her mirror to finish getting ready. One of Countess Lavinia's maids had arranged her hair. Dia wore a sleeveless gown of soft green, trimmed with silver. It was nothing flashy, but she preferred not to attract too much attention. A veil of silver silk flowed down her back with the length of her light brown hair, and a single green gem sparkled on her forehead. A silver cuff with the pattern of their family crest wound several times around her arm, from just above her elbow to nearly her shoulder.

The fading remains of cuts and bruises from her adventure in the forest still marked her skin, but they were healing well. Hopefully, they weren't too noticeable. Sam would see them, but he knew exactly what had happened. As surreal as the events of that night seemed, her injuries were a stark reminder that she'd been lucky. She could easily have been seriously hurt or even killed. Others had not been so fortunate. Was Carrina safe and recovering? She'd lost her father that night, and Dia knew what that felt like.

As terrifying as the whole experience had been, it had allowed her to meet Sam. A shiver ran through her as she remembered how it felt to be close to him, the warmth and strength of him, and the heat in his eyes as he looked at her.

Finished with her preparations, she left the room to see Lisenth standing at the top of the stairs. Dia stopped, observing the picture her sister made. Lisenth was tall and elegant, her figure lush. Her hair hung in bright gold waves, and her eyes were a striking blue. Comfortable being the center of attention, she'd chosen a gown in vivid red with a daring neckline. Her cuff and veil were gold. A line of sparking gems draped across her forehead. Her high cheekbones were pink and her full lips a tempting red. Dia didn't know the prince, but any man would have a difficult time saying no to her. She was stunning.

It was no accident that King Hashoreth had sent invitations everywhere in his kingdom to noble families with daughters of marriageable age. Lisenth had begun formulating her plans as soon as the message had arrived. She would meet the prince, and he would be instantly charmed. And that was only the beginning. Lisenth had it all planned out. If she had even thought her shy sister was any sort of competition, she would have warned Dia to stay away from the prince. Both of them knew it wasn't necessary. No one would be looking at Dia when Lisenth was in the room.

What did Dia care about meeting the prince? No prince could ever be more charming than Sam.

CHAPTER 7

D IA FOLLOWED HER SISTER down the stairs and out the door
to the carriage, waiting to take them to the king's palace.
Outside, the sun still shone brightly in the evening sky. The
autumn air was cool and fresh. Around them, the whole city
bustled with excitement.

They joined an endless line of carriages all going the same
direction, toward the lofty towers of the palace. Lisenth fidgeted
impatiently as they made their way through the streets at a snail's
pace.

Dia was content to wait. Of course, the thought of seeing Sam
sent quivers of excitement through her, but she didn't like crowds
and felt shy in front of people. This would be her sister's moment
of glory, and Dia intended to remain firmly in the background.
All she wanted was a chance to spend time with Sam again. Her
thoughts instantly raced back to the evening they had spent
together on the balcony, how it felt to have him beside her.

At last, their carriage pulled up in front of the stairs, and
they got out. A long line of people moved slowly ahead of them,
and they took their places in it. At the top of the wide stone
steps, silver gates flanked by tall guards stood open, a herald

announcing everyone. When their turn arrived, he cried, "Lady Alladia and Lady Lisenth, daughters of Baron Ifereth of Bartal."

Lisenth curtseyed regally in the direction of the balcony where an old man with a golden crown on his head stood watching. Dia did the same. A girl beside the door gave each of them a small card. When Dia examined hers, she found a number printed on it in elegant script. 168.

Taking the card in her hand, Dia turned back toward the king. She had never seen King Hashoreth in person before. He was a tall man with snowy white hair and beard. On his arm, he wore a cuff with the royal crest. His posture was dignified, his expression serious. An aura of power surrounded him, and the whole crowd looked to him with respect. The guests in their fine clothes mingled and chatted in the enormous courtyard while the herald finished announcing everyone.

This event was meant to honor the prince, the king's grandson, now his only heir. Nearly twenty years ago, the king's younger son had murdered his older brother, heir to the throne, and when he was caught, the king banished him to the jungle. The scandalous news traveled like wildfire through all of Ischar.

Dia had been very young when it happened, but the horrifying story had never entirely gone away. Even now, versions of it traveled everywhere. Since that time, the king and his grandson were all that remained of the royal family.

A hush fell over the crowd as the king raised his hand in greeting. "I welcome all of you," he said in a commanding voice. "On this day, we celebrate my grandson's birthday. In a moment, he'll be coming out to say a few words to you. Before he does, I am pleased to offer an invitation to all the young ladies to meet him. You were each given a card. We will begin with the card with the number 1, and continue on from there."

The king held up his hand again, now displaying a small roll of parchment. "Our prince will be entertaining guests during the next seven days. He will extend his personal invitation to seven of you, whomever he chooses."

Gasps, giggles, and excited murmurs filled the crowd. The prince would choose from among them a few who he would get to know better.

Dia looked at her card again. 168. One hundred and sixty-seven girls would meet him before her. Perhaps he'd run out of time before they even met. His seven invitations would be all extended well before he got to her. That was fine. It wasn't the prince she was eager to spend time with. She scanned the crowd, spotting several guards in gray uniforms, but even from a distance, she knew none of them were him. Where was Sam?

Another hush fell over the crowd, and Dia saw her sister's attention riveted on the king. Lisenth held a card in her hand too, and Dia caught a peek at the number. 4.

The king smiled. "It is now my pleasure to introduce my grandson, Samanath Algorian, Crown Prince of Ischar." The crowd burst into cheers. A young man walked out onto the balcony. He was as tall as his grandfather and had the same commanding bearing. His hair was dark, and he wore a short dark beard. He wore a fine tunic trimmed in gold and a cuff with the royal seal around his arm.

Dia's eyes widened in shock. Her breath froze in her lungs. Even from this distance, she recognized him immediately. Prince Samanath Algorian was Sam—her Sam.

Carefully, she composed her features, hiding the shock on her face. Why hadn't he told her who he was? He could have told her from the beginning. By now, they'd spent lots of time together. He could have told her anytime, and he hadn't. Why not? A flash of anger surged through her. He knew she'd come from Bartal, that she hadn't been to Kulin before. She'd never seen him before.

Her mind went back to the day in the market, when he'd walked through the crowd with his face shadowed by his hood. He hadn't been hiding from a superior officer. He'd hidden his face because any number of people in the crowd would have recognized him.

Maybe he didn't want to see her again. She glanced down at the card in her hand. If he truly wanted to see her, couldn't he have arranged to give her the first card? Perhaps, to him, she had only been a plaything, something to pass his time while he had his pick of girls.

Lisenth would be furious if she realized. That night in the forest, it had been dark, Sam's face shadowed. She hadn't seen him clearly. She didn't know that it had been the crown prince who came to Dia's aid.

The party went on, and the guests enjoyed food and conversation. Prince Samanath began the lengthy process of meeting each young lady in the crowd. A long line formed, each girl with a little card in her hand. Dia followed the increasing numbers until she found herself at the very end of the line. Last. There was no one in the line behind her. Had he arranged it intentionally? Or had it been random chance?

When they'd spent time together on her balcony, she thought he wanted to see her again. Maybe she'd been wrong. Perhaps she'd misread his signals. Maybe it had only been a game to him.

As Dia waited in line, Lisenth appeared. Her walk was graceful and confident, and even in this crowd of people determined to look their best, she stood out. Scanning the crowd, her eyes fell on Dia, and she slipped through the press of people to stand beside her.

"I'm sure it was a good sign to be near the front." Lisenth displayed one of the royal invitation scrolls as if she wasn't surprised that she'd been among the chosen; she observed Dia's place in line with pity in her expression. "But don't worry. You weren't interested in trying for the prince in the first place. There must be many other young noblemen here for you to choose from." Her eyes appraised the crowd.

Suddenly, the cool courtyard felt hot. Dia hadn't cared about pursuing the prince before. Now she did.

The musicians began to play, and dancing commenced. Eldon and Thomas, the young men they had shared tea with the previous week approached Lisenth, and soon, she was in the center of a crowd, basking in their attention. The line inched forward. Dia waltzed a few times as young men asked the girls in line to dance, returning them to their places in time for their turn to meet the prince. Every now and again, one of the young ladies would come out gripping a scroll and looking elated.

Dia tried not to count them. Every time one came out, she continued to try. Did Sam intend one of the scrolls to go to her? It felt like years passed while the line slowly shortened ahead of her.

At last, her turn arrived. "Lady Alladia Ifereth," the chamberlain announced at the door. Finally, she saw him. Sam stood with two royal guards flanking him. His white and gold tunic was magnificent, setting off his dark hair and contrasting with his smooth brown skin. The young woman who had been in line before Dia was just exiting through a door on the other side of the room.

No matter what his explanation, Sam's eyes lit up as he saw her, and despite her anger, she felt a burst of excitement in her middle. She stepped forward gave the proper curtsey due to royalty.

He took her hand, ushering her back to her feet. "I was afraid you might leave before I could speak with you."

She smiled slightly. "I thought of it, Your Highness." She held up the card with the number 168. "Was this simply an accident?"

Sam met her eyes. "No," he admitted. "But I felt you should be last... because, somehow, after meeting you, I find myself unable to truly see any other woman." He glanced toward the empty doorway behind her and lowered his voice. "There is no one after you."

Joy and disbelief flooded through her, and her jaw fell open a little. Quickly she focused on schooling her expression. She stepped closer to him and spoke in a voice soft enough that only he could hear. "Sam, you very gallantly rescued me, and I have enjoyed every moment with you, but you don't have to feel obligated to..."

His eyebrows raised. "Obligated to what?" He stared at her. "I hoped that you enjoyed being with me as much as I did with you. I haven't been able to stop thinking about you since we met."

Her stomach rolled over as she held his gaze. His dark eyes held an expression that she'd never seen directed at her before. The room felt suddenly stifling, but she couldn't look away. "I did," she managed to say. "But I didn't know you were the prince. Surely a prince should be with someone powerful and beautiful."

Sam's gaze met hers. "Lady Alladia, I appreciated it more than I can say when you enjoyed my company without knowing who I was. In my position, many are attracted to my title rather than to me personally."

Dia drew in a slow breath. So that was why he hadn't told her. As she thought about it, she understood, and the knot of anger inside her dissolved.

His eyebrows drew together, his expression regretful. "You didn't deserve to be deceived, and I offer my most humble apology. Please forgive me?" His dark eyes fixed on hers, and she couldn't ignore the hope in them.

For a long moment they looked at each other. "Is there anything else you weren't truthful about?"

His eyes widened. "No, of course not."

She believed him as he said it. In the last few weeks, she'd come to know and trust him. "I forgive you. I only wanted to be with you. It didn't matter who you were. But I'm not a suitable companion for a prince."

"Why not?" he protested, his eyebrows raised. "You are brave, kind, and beautiful, Dia." He took her hand in his and kissed it.

His mouth was warm against her skin, and the sensation of his breath whispering over the back of her hand sent shivers all through her. She couldn't help but smile at him.

"You look absolutely stunning tonight." His eyes traced from her slippers all the way up to her eyes, not pausing, even for a moment, on the healing cuts on her arm. "The night we met, even rain and mud couldn't hide it."

No one had ever looked at her like this before. Dia recognized the look; she'd seen men direct it at her sister countless times. This was the first time she'd ever experienced the warmth of a man's attention herself. Tendrils of heat unfurled through her.

Sam turned to one of the guards and held out his hand. The man placed a scroll in it. Sam grinned at Dia. "The rest of the invitations are merely a formality. That sister of yours is competitive, from what you've told me. I didn't want her to be angry at you, so I gave her the first scroll. My grandfather insisted I extend seven of them, even though I tried to change his mind. If he had allowed it, I would have given them all to you."

He took the scroll and unrolled it. Moving to a small table, he took a quill and wrote. "In seven days, meet me at midmorning at the door of the palace stables."

"The stables, Your Highness?" The corners of Dia's mouth rose into a smile.

"Don't worry, Lady Alladia," he assured her. "I have a plan." He blew on the ink for a moment, rolled the scroll and gave it to her. "But I can't wait seven days to see you again. If you come back to the palace tomorrow at noon, I will meet you."

A quiver of excitement ran through Dia as she looked at the scroll. She'd never met with him openly, especially not now that she knew who he was. But her thoughts flew back to her sister and her carefully laid plans. Lisenth would be livid.

"What is it?" Sam asked, his eyebrows pulled together in concern.

She didn't want to tell him, but she wouldn't lie to him. "My sister will be angry. She knows I've been seeing someone, but she has no idea it's you. For weeks, she's been waiting to meet you. She wanted nothing more than to spend time with you. Until you gave me this, she assumed I was too plain for her to truly see me as competition. Now she will."

His eyebrows lifted in surprise. "How can she be angry at you? She must be blind not to see how extraordinary you are." He offered his hand. "Lady Alladia, will you dance with me?"

"Now? In front of everyone?" At the thought of the large crowd, her stomach clenched, and suddenly she couldn't breathe.

Sam bent to whisper in her ear. "I know you well enough to know you don't like to attract so much attention. Your sister won't be happy about it, but I'll be sure to ask her to dance later. If she has a measure of my attention, she won't have a reason to be angry at you. And if you dance with me, it would make me very happy. Please?"

His warm breath tickled her ear, and another delicious shiver ran through her. How could she refuse him? And why would she want to? Straightening her spine, she nodded, taking his arm as they went out into the courtyard together and joined the dancing. Maybe it was only her imagination, but Dia heard a tide of whispers surge through the crowd. Her insides quivered with nervousness.

Trying to ignore everyone else's eyes on her, she turned her attention to Sam. His gold-trimmed, formal tunic fit him excellently, showing off his athletic frame. Feeling as if this was all a dream, she put one hand on his shoulder and the other in his. The feeling of his hand on her waist reminded her of when he'd lifted her into the saddle so easily. He was strong and dependable. The thought that he might be a prince had never even crossed her mind. He'd never seemed arrogant. He'd simply been a young man.

For a few moments, the warmth of his arms around her almost made Dia forget the throng of people on all sides. When the music ended, crowds surrounded them. Everyone wanted to talk to the prince, and Dia slipped quietly away. She slid the invitation scroll into her bodice, hiding it.

A few more young men politely asked her to dance, and she graciously accepted. Lisenth had her own chance to dance with Sam. They spent two or three songs spinning gracefully through the crowds, while Lisenth wore a lovely smile.

They looked attractive together, but this was about more than appearances. Lisenth was determined to gain the power his position would grant her. Now that she knew Dia intended to interfere, Lisenth would make Dia pay for attracting Sam's attention.

⁕

Midnight was long gone when Dia and Lisenth slid into the carriage for the drive back to the earl's estate. Though exhaustion pulled at her limbs, a well of excitement flowed in Dia's middle. She'd seen Sam again, danced with him. Instead of completely fulfilling her desire to spend time with him, each time they were together only made it stronger. She kept her features smooth, not allowing her feelings to show on the outside, and pretended to rest, leaning her head against the seat. Her sister's voice interrupted her thoughts.

"Well?"

Dia opened her eyes and looked up at her sister. Lisenth's blue eyes were narrowed. Unable to avoid the conversation, Dia straightened up and met her sister's gaze. "Well, what?"

"*You* had the first dance with him!" Lisenth's expression filled with accusation.

Dia turned her gaze out the window to the dark city passing by. "He asked me to dance. I couldn't turn him down."

"Why would he ask *you*?" Lisenth's tone of disbelief and her question were equally insulting.

Suddenly, anger boiled up in Dia. "Just because I don't look like you, doesn't mean I don't have any value!"

Lisenth's eyes widened in disbelief, and she slid a little farther away on the carriage seat. Then she laughed coldly. "You *actually* think you have a chance with him! I never dreamed he would even notice you."

The anger still burned inside Dia. "I don't choose what he notices!"

Lisenth drew in a long calming breath. "Well, I have my invitation, and I'll be seeing him in two days. I'm sure he'll come around, if *you* leave him alone." Lisenth fixed her with a hard stare. "Don't see him again," she ordered.

Dia stared at her sister, speechless. Ordinarily she would never have interfered with Lisenth's ambitions. She'd always been inclined to clear the path between her sister and her desires. Until Sam. As unbelievable as it seemed, Sam liked her too, she wasn't willing to give up being with him. She liked *him*. Not his title, or his crown, or his palace. Just him.

Lisenth's demanding expression turned into one of disbelief. "You *are* planning to see him again! He gave you a scroll, didn't he? Show it to me!"

"No!" Dia protested. But her sister's quick fingers seized the scroll and pulled it from the front of Dia's dress. She reached for it, but Lisenth held it out of reach.

Unrolling it, she read it. "He sent you to the *stables*?" she snickered. "Maybe he's planning to hand you a shovel and ask you to clean up after the horses."

"Give it back!" Dia lunged forward to snatch the scroll. Her sisters grip didn't release, and the parchment tore into two pieces.

CHAPTER 8

WHEN DIA WOKE THE next morning between the soft sheets in her room at Lord Karvan's estate, a quiver of anticipation curled inside her along with a twist of worry. Only a few more hours remained until she would see Sam again. But now she knew she would be meeting Samanath Algorian, Crown Prince of Ischar. It was so much more pressure than keeping a secret meeting with one of the palace guards. Everything would have been so much easier if he really was only a soldier.

Dia wasn't about to reveal her plans for the day to Lisenth. Instead, she went to Countess Lavinia and asked permission to go walking and see more of the city. Her hostess agreed, as long as Roland would accompany her.

"Doesn't your sister want to join you?" Countess Lavinia asked, glancing toward Lisenth's room.

"Not this time," Dia replied. "Her appointment with the prince is tomorrow night, and she is busy preparing."

"But I heard you're meeting with him too, my dear," Lavinia said, smiling confidentially. "Is there anything you need?"

Dia returned her smile. "My appointment is not for several days. I have the final appointment of the seven." At least she wasn't worried about being last anymore.

Lady Lavinia smiled. "Very well then, you enjoy yourself today. You'll be safe with Roland. He can keep you out of trouble and carry your packages if you decide to purchase anything. Have a wonderful time." She smiled and kissed Dia's cheek.

Roland met her at the front doors of the estate. His livery looked crisp and tidy, and he smiled when he saw her.

"I'm afraid you've been dragged along on more adventures than you expected. Thank you for escorting me," Dia smiled back at him.

He bowed very properly. "Of course, my lady. I admit that things have been exciting. Might we happen to run into a certain young man while we are out?"

He hadn't heard yet. He still didn't know who Sam was.

"We might," she admitted, feeling her cheeks flush.

They left through the wide gates of the estate and strolled out into the city. Dia wasn't sure exactly how to tell him her real plans for the day. Instead, she walked in the general direction of the palace, sightseeing and window shopping as she went.

They made their way slowly through the city, and by the time the sun shone straight above them, they came to the gates of the palace.

Roland raised his eyebrows. "You're hoping to meet him here? Won't that attract attention, if he's on duty?"

"It might," she admitted. She climbed the steps with Roland at her heels and peeked through the gates into the courtyard.

"They won't let anyone in without an appointment," he pointed out.

"I know," Dia replied.

With a rattle, the gates opened, and a guard, a big man, heavily muscled and dressed in the gray uniform of the palace spoke. "I am Kerem, Captain of the Royal Guard. Please, enter, Lady Alladia."

Roland's eyebrows shot up in surprise, but he said nothing as he followed her inside. The gates closed behind them, and Kerem bowed to Dia. "If you'll please follow me, my lady."

Dia and Roland followed him across the marble stones of the courtyard where the party had been held, up to the ornate front doors of the palace. He led them inside. "Your attendant may wait here." Kerem gestured to an upholstered bench.

Dia turned to him. "Thank you, Roland. I will return in a short while."

"As you wish, my lady." Roland seated himself on the bench and Dia followed Kerem deeper into the palace.

Her soft slippers made no sound on the patterned carpets. They followed a long hall to its end and turned into a wide room comfortably furnished with soft chairs and couches. Double doors opened onto a garden.

Sam stood in the doorway. At the sight of her, a grin lit up his face. "You came!"

She hurried to join him, and he bent to kiss her cheek. "I missed you," she murmured, the words slipping out before she had a chance to consider whether they were appropriate.

He smiled down at her. "Me too," he replied. He bowed formally to her. "Lady Alladia, will you join me for a stroll in the gardens?" He offered his arm, and she took it gladly. "Does your sister know you came?"

Dia shook her head, looking down in embarrassment. "I didn't tell her. I only said I was going out to see the city."

"Perhaps that's for the best. And besides," he gestured at the lovely garden surrounding them, "this is the best part of the city to see. You were being absolutely truthful."

Dia's brows drew together. "Perhaps from one point of view, but she won't see it that way if she finds out."

Sam straightened to his full height, his features serious. "I will not allow her, or anyone else, to keep me from seeing you. Sooner or later, she will have to accept that—"

Dia looked up at him. "What?" Her voice sounded a little breathless. What had he been about to say?

Sam relaxed his expression and winked at her. "She'll have to accept that it's my choice who I spend my time with, and that you are every bit as valuable as she is. In fact, I would rate your value far above hers."

Dia looked down, her cheeks heating at his compliment. "She'd never believe you if you said that."

Sam took her hand. "I don't care. She may have gone to great effort to make you feel small, but that doesn't mean anyone else agrees with her. Well..." He pulled her close, and she felt him kiss the top of her head. "You are a little small."

She could barely breathe as his arms wrapped around her. With him so close, she felt his muscular frame against hers.

"Actually, you're exactly the right size," he murmured. Slowly releasing her, he offered his arm again. "Come and see the rest of the gardens. The view is breathtaking."

He led her toward a stone railing, and when they looked over, she drew in a breath in shock and clutched him, her stomach churning.

His arm tightened around her. "I know you don't like heights, but you shouldn't feel bad. This height is enough to make anyone dizzy. It's three thousand feet down to the bottom."

She peeked over the railing again. It wasn't just a little drop. The kingdom of Ischar lay atop a wide plateau bordered on three sides by stark, towering cliffs. The royal city of Kulin had been built at the edge and the king's palace extended right to the brink.

Clutching Sam's arm tightly, she took another look. Bits of the cliffs were visible on either side, but the cliff wall was so entirely vertical that it disappeared below the balcony. A few isolated towers of rock stood up from far below in a sea of green that spread in all directions. "Is that the jungle?" she asked.

His arm tightened around her. "Yes. With the lower altitude, the climate is much warmer down there. The forest is teeming with lush plants, trees, and animals."

Dia put a hand to her mouth. "Won't the wild animals eat anyone who goes down there?"

Sam smiled. "The jaguars try, but there are all sorts of other creatures. Yes, it's dangerous, but it's very beautiful."

She stared at him in disbelief. "You've... *seen* it? I thought only the worst criminals were sent down there. And none of them come back."

He smiled and placed his hand over hers on his arm. "It's a secret, of course, but a few of us have visited it for a short while. The royal guard watches the gate to the causeway constantly. They've allowed us through on occasion—with the king's permission—to spend a little time down there."

"You really went down there?" Her eyes were wide. From the rumors she'd heard, people didn't survive even a few days in the jungle. Sam must be tougher than she'd expected from a prince.

"I did," Sam nodded. "I felt it was important to know what it was like, since the penalty for the most serious crimes in Ischar is to be banished there."

She took another peek at the view. She couldn't help but recall that the king had banished his son. Her eyes went back to Sam.

"The rest of us have heard nothing but frightening rumors about the jungle. Do any of them... survive?"

"Some do. I'm not sure how many." Sam shook his head. "Some of the most dangerous of them have banded together, after a fashion. They can be vicious to each other, and they don't have an easy time cooperating."

The thought made her stomach roll, and Dia shivered. "Even if they deserve it, I hate to think about anyone being sent down there to die."

His arm tightened around her. "You have a kind and gentle heart. The judgement of banishment is only used in the most extreme cases. The judges bring all the information to the king. He is the one who has to make the final decision."

She took his hand in hers and looked up at him. "Does that mean that you will have to decide, someday? And your grandfather makes the decision now? I heard about his son. I'm so sorry, Sam."

His eyes filled with pain, and his jaw clenched.

She didn't want to ask him for more details, but if they were to understand each other completely, she had to know what had happened.

After a long moment, he drew in a deep breath. "I know there are many stories about what happened. Some of them are true. My uncle killed his brother and sister-in-law, and the king banished him."

Pain gathered in Dia's heart. They had all been Sam's family, and she could see how much it still affected him. "So, it's true? He killed your parents?"

Sam nodded.

Dia put her arms around him and held him. "I'm so sorry. The memory must be so painful."

He held onto her, taking in a deep breath. "It is. I don't like to talk about it. But I'm glad we did. Now you know one of the most painful experiences of my life."

"It's part of you," she said, pulling back to look up and meet his eyes. Hurt still shone in the brown depths.

He gazed back at her. "It's not all crowns and fancy parties. There are hard things about being king. When it's my turn to rule, I'll do the best I can."

"You'll do well," she assured him earnestly. How could he not? He was the kindest man she'd ever met.

"I fear you place too much confidence in me." He took her hand and brushed his lips across her knuckles.

The feel of his warm breath against her hand and his lips against her skin caused a delicious shiver to run all the way to her toes. He smiled again, and they resumed their exploration of the garden. Time flew as they strolled, and, when Dia looked at the sky, she was shocked to realize how low the sun had gotten.

Sam noticed it too. "I'm afraid I need to go." His voice was filled with regret. "Will you come back tomorrow?"

She smiled up at him. "You're meeting with another young lady tonight. You might want space to change your mind. Do you *really* want me to?"

He did not hesitate for even a moment before he answered. "Without a doubt."

"Then, yes," she managed to whisper, though she felt she couldn't breathe.

He pulled her close, putting his arms around her. She breathed in the scent that lingered on his cloak, forest leaves, leather and... him. "I'll be waiting until I see you again," she murmured.

———————•◆•———————

The walk back to the estate seemed much longer, and Dia realized she was ravenous. Somehow, the day had passed without her giving a single thought to food. Roland walked beside her. "Thank you for escorting me today," she said, trying to read his expression. "You must have been very bored, waiting for me."

One corner of his mouth rose. "Waiting in the palace is not the worst."

She smiled and raised her brows hopefully. "Then perhaps you would be willing to do the same tomorrow?"

Roland shook his head helplessly. "To meet Prince Samanath again? Are you sure you know what you're doing, Lady Alladia?"

During the day, someone must have told him who she was meeting with. She shook her head. "I'm not sure at all, Roland."

———————•◆•———————

The next evening, a gorgeously dressed Lisenth left the manor for her appointment with the prince. Dia had never seen anyone look so beautiful. Would Sam be dazzled by her looks? Hopefully not. Dia had spent enough time with him to know he wasn't the sort of person to be easily swayed by her beauty. And Dia didn't think Lisenth would truly appreciate Sam. Her ambition drew her to a throne and a crown. It didn't matter to her who wore it. Sam was a good person. He deserved to be with someone who liked him for himself—not his crown.

Dia's mind flew back to earlier in the day. She and Sam had spent hours, laughing and talking. They had taken a tray of food into the glass conservatory. Hidden among the exotic plants, they had shared a meal, talking about everything. She wanted to be the person he confided in. She listened as he told her about his life, his worries for the people of Ischar, and his hopes for the future. Already, she missed him.

Now, as Dia and Countess Lavinia sat together in the drawing room, working on needlework, the evening stretched long. Dia tried not to think about Lisenth and Sam together. A sudden commotion at the front doors announced Lisenth's return. A moment later, she glided into the drawing room and collapsed dramatically into a chair.

She smiled triumphantly. "It was wonderful." She sighed at the memory. "He might be a prince, but he must not be *too* pampered. I could have spent all evening just looking at those muscles." She sat up straighter in her chair. "They say noblemen have soft hands, but he isn't like that. Maybe he knows how to fight, because his hands—" She drew in a breath and let it out, then turned to meet Dia's eyes. "You probably didn't notice his hands."

Despite her best efforts to keep her expression impassive, Dia felt warmth rush to her cheeks. In fact, she *had* noticed his hands, calloused and strong but still gentle. She'd felt them at her waist as he lifted her onto the horse and again as they had danced. The memory of his arms around her threatened to make her blush even more.

Lisenth had already moved on. "It was a lovely meal, Countess. They spared no expense. As if I wouldn't already be impressed by sitting in the king's private dining room. When we came to Kulin to meet the prince, I never expected him to be so agreeable." She smiled and looked at Lavinia. "You know how it is, Countess. We are of noble birth, and we try to make the best marriage we can. It's not very often that a member of the royal family is looking for a bride. And you have to trust to luck. He might have been short, round, and insufferable."

Lavinia smiled knowingly. "Very true, my dear. There are disadvantages to marrying for position." She sighed quietly, looking away into the distance as if remembering the past. "There's little danger of him being short and round in the royal line of Ischar. They are an attractive family. King Hashoreth was very popular with the ladies in his younger days, I've been told."

Lisenth giggled. "That must have been quite some time ago."

Nodding, Lavinia smiled sadly. "Yes. I recall how much he adored his queen before she passed. His sons were tall and handsome, with his dark hair. The whole city admired them. I think every person in Kulin was there when Prince Kariman married. The king loved them both. It was such a tragedy..."

Lisenth leaned forward avidly. "Every person in Kulin has their own version of the story. Someone told me that Prince Adengo stabbed his brother right in front of everyone and Prince Samanath saw him do it."

"You shouldn't believe every rumor, my dear," Lavinia said, with an unaccustomed hint of sharpness in her tone.

"Of course not, Countess," Lisenth replied. "But having such a tragic story only makes the prince more romantic, don't you think?"

Dia felt her temper rising. She was quite sure Sam could have done without his painful past. He was a person after all, a real person who felt pain and sorrow, not just an object of gossip. Her hands tightened into fists.

"It won't be long before he asks me back to the palace," Lisenth said. "I'm sure he intends to. He just needs to finish with the seven appointments the king required that he set. He's only waiting until he's finished entertaining the others." Her eyes flew to Dia, and her lips tightened in disapproval.

Dia intended to go as he had invited her on the seventh day. But Lisenth had no idea that Dia planned to see Sam again tomorrow.

CHAPTER 9

AFTER SEVERAL SECRET TRIPS to the palace, Dia had brought Countess Lavinia into her confidence as they had a private moment, lingering over the remains of their meal in the breakfast room. The kind woman seemed to understand the situation. She'd known their family all of Dia's life, and maybe she observed more of the relationship between the sisters than Dia had realized.

"You need to tell Lisenth about this," Lavinia advised. "She is a proud girl, but I believe, underneath, she has a good heart. You know this can't be a secret forever, and she will be bitterly disappointed when the truth comes out. You heard her the other night. She expects another summons from the prince. When the invitation comes to you instead of her, she won't be pleased. It would be better if she hears it from you than anyone else."

"Do you really think so?" Dia asked. She bowed her head. "I know I have to tell her, but I've been putting it off as long as possible. I think she'll hate me when she finds out."

"Perhaps for a short while," Countess Lavinia admitted, patting one of her silver curls into place. "But not forever."

A wave of worry washed through Dia. "She's the one who... deserves to be royalty." Her eyes traced the pattern of the carpet.

Lavinia's voice sounded sharper. "Why would you say that, my dear?"

"Because—" Dia looked up to meet her eyes.

"Because she thinks so?" the older woman's eyebrows raised. "I've known you both all your lives. My dear Alladia, you have so much to offer. Never let your sister or anyone else tell you otherwise."

Tears of gratitude filled Dia's eyes, and she threw her arms around the countess. "Thank you."

Lavinia answered the hug. "It's true. If your dear mother were alive to see the beautiful young woman you've grown into, she would be so proud. Perhaps you might allow me to be proud of you in her stead."

"I would. Thank you!" Dia held her tightly, blinking back tears.

She needed to tell Lisenth the truth, and soon.

Dia felt better now that the countess was on her side. A carriage mysteriously appeared to whisk her off to her secret meetings with Sam, and Roland's schedule remained conveniently free to accompany her.

That day, when she met Sam at the palace gates, rain was falling. Instead of their usual stroll, they walked through the palace halls.

"Is Carrina still here? How is she doing?" Dia asked him.

"She is," Sam replied. "Would you like to see her?"

"Yes, please. I've been hoping she's all right."

Sam's brows lowered. "She has not improved as I wish she would, though our healers have been caring for her."

The infirmary was a long room at the end of a hall. Several beds lined both sides of the room. They found Carrina in one of them. On the night of their journey, in the dark and the rain, Dia hadn't gotten a good look at her. Now she saw a girl near her own age with blond hair. Her eyes were closed, one wrist splinted and her shoulder bandaged.

"Carrina?" Dia touched her uninjured hand.

At the voice and touch, the girl blinked, opening blue eyes to look up at her. "I remember you," she murmured, her voice weak. "You're Dia."

Dia nodded. "I wanted to make sure you were all right."

"Thank you," Carrina said. "You saved my life. You got me out of that coach and kept the wolves away."

Dia gripped her hand. Carrina gave her way too much credit. If not for Sam, they could easily both have been dead. She turned to meet his eyes. "Prince Samanath saved both of us."

Carrina blinked, her gaze unfocused. "Did they find the man who killed my father?"

Dia's eyes widened. "What man?" She had assumed that her father had been injured in the accident.

"I heard a sound like a windstorm. Something struck the carriage. Everything turned over. We were hurt. My arm was broken. When my father tried to help me, a man in a dark cloak dragged him out. He tried to get away, but the man held him. Then he put his hand on my father's head. After that, he didn't struggle anymore. Only a few moments later, he left my father lying there and came back for me." Her blue eyes were full of fear. "He put his hand on me. I don't remember anything after that until you came."

A windstorm? Or had it been a giant bird? Why would the Shadaroc attack these people? Maybe it had only been random chance, and it could just as easily have been Dia and her sister lying here.

"I'm very sorry about your father," Dia said. "We're trying to find the man who did this."

Carrina closed her eyes, and tears leaked from beneath her lashes.

"Just rest here. They will take care of you until you feel better." She looked to Sam for confirmation.

He nodded. "Of course, we will make sure she is cared for." Carrina's eyes remained closed, and Dia noticed how pale her skin was, chalky white. Her body lay motionless, as if she didn't have the energy to move.

Finally, Dia rose, leaving the girl to rest. With Sam at her side, she left the room.

In the hall outside, Sam paused. "They've given her the best of care, but she's grown weaker since the accident."

"Why would that happen? She was injured, but it didn't seem severe enough to cause this."

Sam shook his head. "No. And she's not the only one. Dozens of people in Kulin have become ill with the same strange condition."

Dia shivered.

"I fear the Shadaroc is behind it. The last time people got sick like this was at the same time as the sightings of the bird."

As they talked, he led her through the halls of the palace.

Dia had never seen a building so beautiful. Hand in hand, they wandered through a ballroom, a portrait gallery, and the glass conservatory containing tropical plants from the jungle.

"I love this room." Dia turned in all directions to take in the sight. She couldn't help but remember the time they had shared there.

Sam smiled at her delight. "You haven't seen all the plants yet." He pointed to an exotic purple flower. "Don't touch that one. It's poisonous."

Dia stepped back with a gasp. "How do you know which ones are safe?"

He laughed. "In the jungle, it's always best to assume everything is trying to kill you." He pointed out a shrub with fleshy leaves. "Maybe not quite everything. That one is very good for cuts and the sap prevents infection. It grows everywhere in the jungle."

They wandered the large room until they had seen all the plants and flowers. Sam led her to the door. "Are you ready to meet my grandfather? I've told him about you, and he wants to meet you."

Dia's eyes widened. "The king?"

Sam grinned. "Of course, he's the king. But he's my family, and I've told him you're important to me."

Dia felt her heart pounding. "He really wanted to meet me? Maybe another time would be better..."

Sam rolled his eyes and took her hand. "Not a chance. Come on." He led her down the hall to a door guarded by two armed men in gray uniforms. Sam knocked, and at the muffled reply from inside, he opened the door.

The old king looked up from his desk as they entered. A warm smile lit his wrinkled face as he saw them. Dia could tell from the way he looked at Sam that he loved his grandson.

Rising from his chair, he came to greet them. He took both of Dia's hands in his and smiled. "Welcome, my dear."

"May I present Lady Alladia, daughter of Baron Ifereth," Sam said.

"Lady Alladia." The king bent to kiss her cheek. "I knew your father, many years ago. It's been a long time since I visited Baltar province. He was a good man."

"Yes, Your Majesty. I'm afraid he passed away a year ago."

The king's expression fell a little. "I'm sorry to hear that."

"We miss him terribly. But it's been very kind of the Earl of Kana to host us during our stay here in Kulin."

The old man nodded. "Yes. We never stop missing our departed loved ones. I understand. Still, we are grateful to have you here. I heard about your bravery during your journey here." He smiled warmly at her.

Sam must have told him something of her misadventures. Dia returned his smile. "Thank you, Your Majesty, travel can be very difficult."

"So I hear."

He ushered them into a comfortable sitting room, where she settled onto a sofa beside Sam, the old man sitting across from them. Servants brought elegant trays of food and drink, and they talked and laughed. Dia quickly felt a portion of the same comfort with him that she felt with Sam. When the king finally rose, they stood up as well.

The old man shook his head. "I'm afraid I have another meeting, but I have enjoyed our time immensely. I hope I shall see you again soon, Lady Alladia."

"Thank you!" Dia appreciated his consideration. He'd been so much kinder than she had expected a king to be. She hugged him.

He bent to kiss her cheek. "Sam is an intelligent young man to spend time with you. He has my support to continue seeing you."

Dia felt the warmth of his words spread inside her. "Thank you, Your Majesty."

On the morning of the seventh day, Dia prepared for her official meeting with the prince. The torn remains of her invitation reminded her to be at the door of the palace stables at midmorning. Having no idea what to expect, or what to wear, she picked a blue gown. As she adjusted her veil, Lisenth entered the room.

She eyed Dia critically. "Is that what you're wearing?" She shook her head. "That color isn't your best. In fact..." She bent closer and looked intently at Dia. "What's wrong with your face? You don't look well at all."

Suspicion welled up inside Dia. "What do you mean?"

Lisenth wore a concerned expression. "You shouldn't allow him to see you like this. It would be best to reschedule."

"Lisenth," Dia kept her voice slow and calm. "The prince asked me to be there. I can't refuse."

"His invitation was a mistake," Lisenth announced. "My evening with him went so well that there's no need for anyone else to spend time with him."

"Did he *say* that?"

"Of course." Lisenth lifted her chin. "Today is the last of the appointments the king required him to make. After today, he will have fulfilled the requirement and be free to do as he chooses. He'll be asking me back to the palace by tomorrow. I'm sure there's no need for you to go today."

Dia squared her shoulders. "But he *did* ask me to come, and he's the prince."

"You shouldn't go," her sister repeated stubbornly, folding her arms across her chest.

Dia got to her feet and stood, meeting her sister's eyes. Irritation welled up inside her. "I'm sorry, Lisenth, but I am going."

Lisenth rolled her eyes. "Whatever you think best." Sarcasm dripped from the words. "I hope it turns out *well*."

Pushing back her annoyance, Dia went to the door and down the stairs. Lisenth didn't say anything else, or try to stop her. Outside the front doors, Dia slipped into the carriage and it rolled off toward the palace. She wasn't sure exactly where the royal stables were, but the guards would help her find them. Taking several deep breaths in and out, she tried to push the confrontation with Lisenth into the back of her mind. Her sister had already been angry. Not the best moment to tell Lisenth that Dia had been seeing Sam. Another time would be better.

Dia would be with Sam soon. All she needed to do was enjoy the short ride. She leaned back against the seat and closed her eyes for a few moments.

The sound of the wheels suddenly changed from the clatter of cobblestones to the softer sound of a country road. A glance out the window alerted Dia to the fact that they were going entirely the wrong direction.

"Roland?" She called to him, expecting him to be in his usual seat beside the driver. No one answered. "Roland? Where are you? Stop, please! You're going the wrong way."

Her only answer was the coach increasing speed as it rattled out of the city.

Every moment of travel took Dia farther from the palace. Already, the city was behind them and forests and fields lined the road. She had to find a way to stop this coach. Calling and banging on the roof yielded no response from the driver. Ignoring the obvious danger of jumping from a moving carriage, she tried the door. The latch didn't move. Someone was intentionally taking her away from Kulin. A shiver of panic moved through her. What did they plan to do with her when they reached their destination? Who wanted to get rid of her? Besides her sister, she could think of no one. Perhaps someone had discovered her meetings with Prince Samanath and wanted her removed from the city?

Could there be dangerous people among the nobility who would make sure no one ever heard from Dia again? By now, the whole city knew she'd received one of the prince's invitations. Since she was last on the list, they would all know that today was the appointed day. Maybe one of them had watched the estate for her to depart in a carriage. What had happened to Roland? She thought he'd been with her as they left.

Surely it wasn't Lisenth? Her sister wouldn't go so far as to harm her deliberately, would she?

When her churning thoughts yielded no immediate answers, Dia explored the carriage for options. Trying the door again, she found it completely immobile. The window openings were of sufficient size that her small frame could probably slide out, but it wouldn't be easy.

The carriage entered thick woods and, while Dia didn't look forward to being lost in them again, it was better than going quietly to some unknown fate. Now that they were alone on an empty road, the driver had slowed his pace somewhat.

Ignoring the indignity, Dia tucked her skirt between her legs. Kneeling on the seat, she stuck her feet out the window. Pushing against the upholstery, she slid her body out to the waist. Moving her hands to the window frame, she pushed herself out, dropping to the ground.

The carriage still moved at a good pace, and she struck the ground hard much harder than she expected, one ankle twisting beneath her. She rolled, coming to rest in the brush. The horses didn't stop, and she caught a glimpse of the driver. Even looking at the back of his head, she could tell he wasn't Roland. She wasn't waiting around to discover who he was.

Dia crawled quickly away into the woods until she was out of sight from the road. She brushed the dirt from herself and took stock of several places on her body that throbbed, bruised from her fall. The worst problem was her ankle. When she moved it experimentally, sharp pain stabbed up her leg. Walking would be a challenge.

Crawling over to a flat rock, Dia sat down, resting her back against a tree trunk. What now? Sam was back in the city expecting her to join him. When she didn't appear for their meeting, he would look for her. But how would he know where to search?

She wasn't even sure where she was. Somehow, she'd ended up in the woods, again, with no provisions, no warm cloak, and no means of defense. Most importantly, she had no transportation. Even her feet were not an option right now. Dia scanned the surrounding trees and undergrowth. If she couldn't find help before nightfall, she didn't intend to become easy prey for wolves again. The trees in this area were larger than those near the overlook. Some of them had wide, spreading branches. They were climbable, she realized gratefully, looking them up and down, even wearing a dress and avoiding an injured ankle. They looked high. Her stomach twisted at the thought of being so far off the ground, but she might be forced to climb to protect herself.

The day was warm and sunny now, but it would be cold when night fell. Already, there were a few small clouds on the horizon. Hopefully, any storms would wait until she found a way back to the city. Slowly, she made her way to the trunk of the tree that appeared to offer the most protection if wolves should come.

By nightfall, Dia's ankle had swollen badly. A long, slow day had gone by. She was hungry and thirsty, and no one had passed who might help her. The coach she'd been in had come back past her sometime in the afternoon. She had ducked low, out of sight until it was gone. Whoever the driver was, he wasn't on her side.

Sam would come to find her, but how would he know where she was?

Her empty stomach rumbled, but there wasn't much to be done about it. Darkness deepened around her, and patches of stars came out between the leaves. The distant sound of a wolf howl seemed inevitable. She looked up at the branches above her. Now, she had no choice but to go up.

A howl rang out, closer this time. Carefully protecting her ankle, she began to climb. Her first look at the ground below her caused a wave of dizziness. Sweat slicked her hands as she gripped the branches.

"Don't look down." She drew in a breath and forced herself to keep climbing.

Determination drove her to keep moving higher into the branches. Her stomach churned. Was she high enough to be safe from predators? She'd come so far, she had to be. Choosing a wide fork, she sat with her legs on the branch, her back against the trunk. As the warmth from her climb dissipated, a chill set in.

Pulling her knees up to her chest, Dia attempted to conserve all the warmth she could. The moon rose, gradually offering more light until she could see the tree trunks and a sky filled with broken clouds between the branches.

A huge dark shape flew over the forest and, for a moment, blocked out the light of the moon. Dia's stomach clenched at the sight of the Shadaroc. Until now, there had been no sign of it since the night she'd arrived. It circled and passed low over her hiding place. A rush of wind followed behind its wide wings as it passed. Was it landing nearby? Would it try to harm her? She couldn't help but think of Carrina, ill in her bed, and the cold blank features of her father, lying lifeless on the road.

Wolf howls rang out through the forest, and Dia huddled against the tree, grateful to be off the ground. The noise grew until a whole pack raised their voices, drawing steadily closer.

Where was Sam?

There was nothing she could do now but stay in the tree and hope she was out of reach. She clenched her teeth as she looked down. A howl sounded nearby, and a shape covered in silver fur came into view. It padded softly across the forest floor, pausing to sniff the ground. It followed the path she had taken earlier to the base of her tree.

It could probably follow her scent. Lifting its muzzle toward her hiding place, it snarled. Dia shivered, wrapping her arms around herself and holding her breath. Several more wolves slunk into the glade, joining the first. They all surrounded her tree. Abruptly, they lifted their noses to sniff the air. Something moved at the edge of the clearing, a shape, blacker than the gloom in the shadows of the trees. Her stomach twisted. She held herself completely still, barely breathing.

The shape moved forward, sharpening into the form of a man in a long, hooded cloak. He came forward until he stood in the moonlight. The wolves silently moved to surround him. Several of them raised their heads and looked into the gloom beneath the hood as if they were communicating with him.

As if he had received their message, he suddenly looked directly up at Dia. She remained frozen. Could he see her? He stared at her hiding place and didn't look away. His gaze didn't rove as if searching, he appeared to be looking right at her. What was she going to do?

Icy dread grew inside her. Carrina had said a man in a dark cloak had killed her father. Was this the same person?

The dark, hooded shape moved across the clearing and approached the bottom of Dia's tree. The wolves couldn't climb it, but a man certainly could, and she had no defense if he should decide to harm her. Her heart pounded, and she breathed in short shallow gasps, as he reached for the lowest limb.

CHAPTER 10

Dia's mind frantically reviewed options. Try to climb out of reach? She wasn't sure she could. Throw something down at him? What? She failed to come up with any workable plan, and her limbs froze in terror.

He climbed higher until he faced her. His features remained hidden in shadow except for the glitter of eyes. She wanted to move, to climb, to run, anything to get away from him. But she couldn't get her limbs to cooperate, and she remained motionless, still as stone, as he slowly reached out his hand to place it on her forehead.

Pressure built, beginning in the place where his palm touched her, but spreading outward over her entire body. It pushed against her like the vast power of an ocean wave. There was little room left in her mind, but her one coherent thought was that she could not allow the power to enter her. Gathering all the energy she could, she concentrated on forming a barrier that he could not penetrate.

Directly below the tree, the largest wolf raised its head and howled. Soon the others joined it. The man in the hood turned sharply toward them. With a hiss of frustration, he climbed swiftly down and moved away from the tree. The wolves surrounded him, retreating the way they had come.

Dia remained where she was, gasping for breath. Sweat beaded on her forehead. What had just happened? Her stomach still churned. She had narrowly escaped what she was sure would have been a terrible fate.

A moment later she saw a light. It followed the course of the road, moving slowly toward her. Another lantern came into view, then several more. Could it be help at last? Still shaking, her limbs stiff with cold, she climbed laboriously down from the tree and crawled toward the road. A few moments later, she heard his voice.

"Dia!"

"I'm here, Sam!" she replied. Her voice didn't come out as loud as she intended. She heard several more calls. They were getting closer.

"Dia, where are you?" His voice sounded frantic.

"Sam!"

The sound of his boots came through the fallen leaves and brush. A moment later, the light of a lantern shone causing her to blink.

He dropped to his knees beside her, wrapping his arms around her. "Dia! I was afraid I'd lost you. Thank the Soul Mother you're alive! Are you hurt?"

His fear revealed the depth of his concern for her, and she held him tightly.

"Are you all right?" He pulled back to examine her in the lantern light. Warm calloused hands brushed against her cheek. "You're freezing." Setting the light on the ground, he took off his cloak and wrapped her in it. "Are you hurt?"

"My ankle," she admitted, extending her leg. He hissed in sympathy, able to see the swelling, even in the dim light.

"What happened?" he demanded.

"I—" She sank into silence, trying to find words to describe everything that had happened.

"You can tell me about it as we ride," he said. "First, we need to take care of you. Are you hurt anywhere else?"

She shook her head. "If not for this," she pointed at the swollen ankle, "I would have started walking back toward the city."

"I know." He stood up and called back to the road, toward the other searchers. "She's here!" He bent down to pick her up in his arms. "I know some of what occurred, but we'll get you warm and safe, and then you can tell me everything. Dia… I was so worried. I knew something had happened to you, and I didn't know where you were."

"I'm all right, Sam. Thank you for coming for me. I knew you would." She put her arms around his neck and rested her head against his chest, grateful beyond words to have help and not to be alone with the strange creatures who wandered the forest at night. In a moment, they were back at the road, and several other searchers gathered around them.

"How badly is she hurt?" another guard asked.

She recognized Andar. He must have come to help search.

"Just her ankle," Sam replied.

"I'm grateful it's not worse," Andar replied. "There are wolves around. It's not a good night to be in the forest."

"We'll keep her safe now." Sam promised his friend while pulling Dia closer. "I'll make sure you aren't out in the woods alone at night ever again."

Relief flooded through her. "I didn't expect to be out here. It wasn't what I planned. I got into the coach at the earl's estate on my way to meet you. The driver had gone some distance before I realized that he intended to take me out of the city. Did you find out who that man was?" she asked. "The one driving the coach?"

"I did," Sam's voice sounded grim. "I'll tell you all the details soon, but now, we should be on our way. It won't be long until dawn."

The men and horses gathered. Sam slid her into his saddle and mounted behind her. "Is your ankle all right like this?"

In truth, it still throbbed furiously, but there wasn't much anyone could do. Hopefully, it would heal quickly.

"It's all right." While her injury remained painful, she didn't want to admit how much she enjoyed sitting in the saddle so close to Sam.

They joined the others heading back toward the city. Sam's arms tightened around her. "I was so worried. When you didn't come to meet me, I sent someone to Lord Karvan's estate. They told me you'd gotten in a carriage. Roland said that when he intended to escort you, someone grabbed him from behind and took his place. When I heard this, I went myself and had a discussion with your sister. Eventually, she confessed that she had hired a man to take the carriage out of the city to make sure you didn't keep your appointment with me. Perhaps she thought that if you didn't show up, I'd simply assume you didn't want to spend time with me. But I knew you would come unless some accident had happened. The man she hired was supposed to detain you for a little while and then bring you back to the city. At some point, he realized you weren't in the carriage. He seems to have fled. My only clue was the direction your sister instructed him to go. We've been searching since then."

So, Lisenth *had* caused the entire situation. "I'm so glad you found me," Dia said. "Maybe it was unwise to jump from the carriage, but I didn't know who that man was or where he was taking me. I didn't know if he intended to hurt me, or... worse, and I wasn't going to wait to find out."

Sam's voice sounded angry. "The whole thing is infuriating. I spoke very plainly to Lisenth. There is no way she could misunderstand. The earl and countess are aware of everything now as well. Under the circumstances, none of us felt that it was safe for you to remain under the same roof as your sister. I seriously considered locking her up."

Dia drew in a sharp breath. "You didn't..."

Sam drew her closer against him. "No, I didn't. But I wanted to. I can't figure out how the two of you are related. I've never met two more different people."

Dia couldn't help but laugh. "It's always been obvious that I don't look like her."

"Please tell me you won't ever *act* like her," he pleaded.

"Of course not." Her mind began to review her options. "Since I can't stay anymore with the earl, I need to make another arrangement. An inn or..."

"No need," Sam said. "That is, if you will accept my invitation to stay in one of the guest rooms of the palace. After this, I don't want to let you out of my sight."

Her eyes widened in shock. "T-the palace?" Could she really stay there? Would it cause a flurry of rumors? Maybe, but it would be wonderful to be so close to him.

"Dia, I did a lot of thinking while we searched for you." His voice was earnest.

A wonderful warmth grew inside her. "About?"

"You, of course." He drew her closer against him. "I realized how afraid I was of losing you, and how badly I want to be with you."

She didn't want to admit that she'd been thinking of him the whole time too. "And what did you decide?"

"First, that I need to be very clear with your sister about my future wedding plans. That she will never be included in them."

"I should have told her everything sooner," Dia admitted. "I intended to today, but she was already angry and I thought I would pick a better time. I didn't feel ready." After tonight, things had changed. "Now, I do."

"Good," Sam said. "We're going there first."

"In the middle of the night?"

"Yes."

Dia leaned closer against him. "Sam, before the wolves came, I saw the Shadaroc again."

She felt his body tense.

"Where was it?"

"It flew over the forest. I think it might have landed, but I couldn't see exactly where, and then, when the wolves came into the clearing, I saw the man. He was obviously with the wolves, like he was talking to them. They seemed to tell him where I was. Was he the Shadaroc in his human form?" The fear she'd felt earlier twisted through her as she remembered. He was still out there somewhere.

His arms tightened around her. "It must have been."

"He climbed the tree after me... I didn't know what to do."

"Could you see who it was? Did he harm you?" Sam held her close, worry plain in his voice.

She shook her head. "His face was covered. I couldn't see anything about him, except that the wolves were his friends. He didn't hurt me, but he frightened me!"

"The situation was far more dangerous than I realized. He might have killed you. I told my grandfather the night of the first sighting, and he's had men searching since then, but until now, no one has seen anything yet." His voice was grim. "We're in trouble. Everyone near Kulin is in danger. Please Dia, don't go out in the woods again."

She didn't want to tell him the rest of the details. After what she'd experienced, it was clear the man *had* tried to hurt her. The arrival of the search party had saved her.

They rode through the quiet night toward the city. No one else was out on the road. Ahead of them the lights of Kulin glittered. Sam directed his horse toward them. A short while later, its hooves clattered through the stone-paved streets, and they soon arrived at the earl's estate.

Sam pulled the horse to a stop. "We need to get you inside. I'm happy to carry you, unless you would prefer to walk?"

Dia hoped he would understand that she needed to be on her feet when she entered the house. Being carried would feel a little like admitting defeat.

"I will walk," she said firmly, "but I would be very grateful if you would assist me."

"Of course," Sam promised.

He lifted her down from the horse, setting her carefully on her good leg. Dismounting quickly, he put an arm around her waist, supporting her as she hobbled toward the door.

Even this late in the night, all the lights were on, and the doors were thrown open to admit them. The butler led them to the drawing room, where the earl and countess sat across from Lisenth. All three jumped to their feet at the sight of Prince Samanath and Dia.

Lisenth rushed forward to hug her. "I'm so sorry, Dia. It was all an accident! Please, say you'll forgive me."

Dia didn't know what to say. She fought the urge to slap Lisenth's face. What would that really solve? Lisenth released her, and Sam helped Dia over to a sofa where she sat down gratefully. He picked up a footstool and settled her injured ankle on it. Everyone stared at the dark purple bruising and swelling.

"Oh my!" The countess put a hand to her mouth. She turned to the butler. "Will you find someone to bring a basin of cold water for that?" He hurried out at her command.

Soon Dia held a cup of hot tea and a plate of bread and butter and slivers of cold meat. She took a few bites, but she couldn't really eat with everyone looking at her. She set her plate on the side table and took a deep breath. It was best to be direct.

"Lisenth?" Her sister came and knelt beside her.

"Yes?" Her concerned blue eyes met Dia's.

Dia returned her sister's gaze. "I understand you hired a man to take me out of the city in that carriage."

Lisenth's mouth dropped open a little at her directness. "He was only supposed to delay you a little so you couldn't meet the prince. He promised that no harm would befall you. This was all an accident!"

Hurt twisted Dia's expression. She fought to return her features to a mask of calm. "Did you give any thought to what it would feel like to be kidnapped, taken against my will to... who knows where? I didn't know if they intended to kill me or..."

Lisenth stood up, placing her hands on her hips. "Don't be ridiculous, Dia, he would never have hurt you." Her tone cut.

"Ridiculous?" Anger rose in her chest. She was very sure she'd never been so furious before. "Do *not* tell me I'm being ridiculous. You hired a man to kidnap me so I couldn't keep my appointment with the prince."

"You're exaggerating!" Lisenth protested.

Sam stood up, straightening to his full height. He glared down at her sister with his jaw clenched. "Lady Lisenth, exactly *what* is she exaggerating?"

Dia had never seen him look so angry before. His whole body was tense with it.

Lisenth could obviously sense it, and she took a step back staring up at him in dismay. "Your Highness, I'm sure you can understand that this was all a silly mistake. I can't imagine why your meeting with her would be important to you. There are many other girls with more to offer."

Sam took a step closer to her, and she backed up. His voice was cold. "Do you presume to decide whose company is important to me?"

"Of course not, Your Highness," Lisenth said hastily.

He glared at her. "Do you have any consideration for your sister's well-being?"

"Of course I do, she is dear to me."

"Dear?" Sam's eyebrows raised. "And yet, you don't care if she is injured, afraid, cold, hungry or attacked by dangerous animals?"

"But I never intended—none of that was *my* fault." Her face grew very pale.

"On the contrary. I believe it was *all* your fault." Sam said. "I've been considering all night whether you should be locked up."

Her jaw fell open again. "S-surely you wouldn't, Your Highness. This was only a misunderstanding. After the lovely time we had together the other night?"

He straightened his shoulders. "Lady Lisenth Ifereth, I promise you that, after observing your true character, I will *never* spend time with you again."

Lisenth's eyes narrowed, and she looked down at Dia. "But it can't possibly be because of *her*. There must be someone else. One of the other girls?"

"That is enough!" Sam exclaimed. "Let me make this *perfectly* clear."

His dark eyes looked hard, his tall form intimidating. He took a deep breath and with obvious effort, relaxed his hands from the fists they had been clenched into. Turning his back on Lisenth, he fixed his gaze on Dia.

The room grew dead silent around them. Sam bent to one knee and took Dia's hand. "Lady Alladia Ifereth, I love you with all my heart. Will you do me the great honor of becoming my wife and Princess of Ischar?"

CHAPTER 11

D IA'S HEART LEAPT AT Sam's words. In that moment, she might have left the ground behind and taken flight. Around them, the room erupted into exclamations.

"No!" Lisenth wailed.

Despite the chaos of the moment, Dia felt a wild heat building inside her. Everyone else around them faded until she saw no one but Sam. The anger disappeared from his expression, and his brown eyes were serious as they met hers, waiting for her answer.

She leaned closer to him. "Are you sure?" she murmured softly enough that only he could hear.

"Very sure." His eyes never left hers. "I love you, Dia. I want to be with you and no one else."

Her heart pounded in her chest, and the room felt suddenly hot. She smiled. "I love you too, Sam. Yes! I will marry you."

He kissed her hand, but she pulled him closer, threw her arms around his neck, and kissed his mouth. It was their first real kiss. Dia had never felt anything like it. As much as she'd enjoyed him kissing her hand, it was nothing compared to this. His mouth was warm and firm as it met hers eagerly.

He pulled back after a moment. If they had been alone, she wouldn't have let him stop so soon.

The time before the wedding was busy and exciting. To Dia, it seemed that King Hashoreth already had the event completely planned. He urged them to choose a date soon. The whole city bustled with excitement over the announcement of the royal engagement. They chose a date three weeks from Sam's proposal.

Dia now occupied a luxurious guest suite at the palace, and the royal physician had provided meticulous care to her ankle. The swelling went down every day; soon, she would be able to walk without a crutch.

Always uncomfortable as the center of attention, Dia had been forced to grow a little more used to it during the preparations for the wedding. As Sam's betrothed, she met many of the nobility. Most were supportive, at least on the surface. Maybe there were others, like Lisenth, who objected to Sam's choice, but no one spoke of it to her.

King Hashoreth was unfailingly kind. He never made her think she wasn't worthy of being with Sam. He even sent the royal tailor to measure and fit her for a wedding gown.

One night, a week before the wedding, Dia dozed off at her usual hour, but a vivid dream of her and Sam together had woken her up. Now she couldn't stop thinking about him, and she tossed and turned and couldn't go back to sleep. Despite the luxurious sheets and the beautiful room, she couldn't make herself relax again.

Sitting up, she slid her feet to the floor and wrapped herself in the robe she'd left across the back of a chair. The marble floor was cool and smooth against her bare feet. She lit a candle and took it with her as she tiptoed to the door and opened it. The guard in the hall looked at her in surprise.

"I'll be back in a moment," she explained. "I only need a breath of air."

He didn't try to stop her. The candle created a little pool of light as she moved down the dark hallway. Only a few of the lanterns were still lit at this hour. Aside from a few more guards at their posts, she saw no one.

She opened the door to the garden and slipped outside. The air was cool, fragrant with the scents of flowers and plants. It was silent, and she raised her eyes to the dome of bright stars above her. Still limping slightly, she made her way to one of the benches and sat down, drawing her feet up under her and wrapping her arms around her knees.

Drawing in a deep breath, she gazed into the sky. How quickly everything in her life had changed. But as she thought of her life back in Bartal, compared with being here in Kulin, spending time with Sam was the most important thing to her. When she was with him, life was brighter, more vibrant, more real than anything else up to that point. No doubts remained. She wanted to spend the rest of her life with him.

At a sudden sound, she turned to see someone standing there. She drew in a sharp breath and jumped to her feet, favoring her sore ankle.

The tall shadow spoke. "Dia! Don't worry, it's only me."

Recognizing Sam's voice, she sagged in relief. "You startled me." She took a slow breath in, trying to calm her racing heart.

He came forward and put his arm around her. "You didn't hurt your ankle, did you? I'm sorry I scared you. I didn't expect to find anyone out here. Why aren't you in bed?"

"I couldn't sleep," she admitted. "Will you sit with me for a while?"

He sat down on the bench, and she joined him, pressing close against the warmth of his body. His arm wrapped around her shoulders. "Were you worried about something?"

She shook her head. "Not worried, but this has all happened so fast. Before I met you, I wasn't sure I'd ever marry at all, and now... You..."

She could see his face in the faint starlight.

His eyes were concerned. "You're not having second thoughts, are you? Do you need more time?"

She ran her fingers through the short beard on his jaw, savoring the feel of the rough hairs. "No. No second thoughts. It's only that you seem too good to be true."

White teeth flashed in the dark as he smiled. "You think too highly of me. I promise you, I'm far from perfect."

Her own mouth turned up at the corners. "It's true, Your Highness, I esteem you very highly. But I don't think you're perfect." She paused, and they were silent for a moment. "There are difficult things buried in your heart. You conceal them from everyone. Will you tell them to me?"

"My secrets?"

She drew in a long breath. "That's not exactly what I mean, but I want to know everything about you. I think you're used to keeping everyone at a distance. But you asked me to marry you. Does that mean you trust me enough to let me in?"

His arms tightened around her and he kissed her forehead. "Dia, I don't know how you do it, but you see me more clearly than anyone else. Are you sure you want to know everything?

Sometimes I'm not strong. Sometimes I'm afraid. I'm the prince, and everyone expects me to be brave."

She already sensed that he wouldn't reveal himself easily. He was used to keeping his innermost feelings completely to himself. "I will help you through the hard things if I can," she murmured. "Will you tell me?"

"It doesn't seem right to burden you," he protested. "I love you."

Tears welled in her eyes. "But if we are to truly merge our lives together, we will share everything."

He dragged in a quick breath. "I'm not sure I can," he admitted.

She remained silent, waiting for him, giving him the opportunity to express himself.

Finally, he spoke. "I'm afraid of being abandoned. Except for Grandfather, everyone I ever loved has left me behind."

She kissed his cheek. "I'm so sorry, Sam. I won't leave you. I promise."

He buried his face in her hair and pulled her closer. "Dia, you accept me as I am, not as you think I should be. That means so much to me, more than you could imagine."

"Always," she murmured.

He took a deep breath. "I've never talked about this. In nearly twenty years, I've never spoken to anyone about it." He paused for a long moment. When he continued, his voice was tight with pain. "I was only a little boy, and one day, I ran into our room, expecting to run into my mother's waiting arms. Instead, I found her and my father lying dead on the floor."

She drew in her breath sharply. That was a part of the story she'd never heard before. "You are the one who found them?" Her voice cracked. "Oh, Sam!"

He drew in a deep, ragged breath and nodded. "I was only a child. Back then, I didn't understand murder or betrayal." His voice was choked. "All I could see was blood. So much blood. I was so young, and I'd never seen death before." His arms tightened around her.

"I'm so sorry." She held him close. What had that experience been like as a small child? She couldn't even imagine the horror and pain. She wished for a way to go back and save the little boy he'd been from what had happened.

His voice was thick with pain at the harsh memories. "They looked so much like they'd looked in life, yet horribly different. I didn't know what to do."

"No one should see that," Dia said. "Especially not a child. Did you have any other family?"

"Only my uncle," Sam said. "He was in the palace that day. But it was *his* dagger on the floor beside them, covered in blood. All the evidence showed that he killed them. Then he was gone, too. Grandfather banished him."

"You loved your uncle?" Dia felt him nod against her.

"I lost my entire family that day, except for Grandfather." He pulled back and looked at her.

The pain in his eyes was raw, even in the starlight, and her heart ached for him.

"I've never spoken of this." He looked away, lowering his gaze. "Not even to my grandfather. He would have been the only one who I might have talked with, but it was... something we couldn't discuss. I miss my parents, and I miss Uncle Adengo. I adored him as a child and followed him around every chance I got. Everyone loved him. He and my father were very close."

Dia gently brushed tears from his cheeks. "It must have hurt even more for him to have been involved in their deaths."

He nodded. "I can't help missing him. And that just seems wrong, after what he did. I shouldn't!"

"And you've kept this inside all these years?" How it must have weighed on him. He'd hidden it well. Other than the rumors she'd heard, she hadn't known the full story, and she'd sensed how much it still hurt him.

"Do you want to change your mind now that you know?" he asked. "This is the family you'd be joining, and few other people have such a cruel history. I understand if you want to walk away."

"No, Sam." She brushed his hair back from his face and ran her hand along his jaw. "I told you, I won't leave you."

He raised his eyebrows. "You're not the least bit worried that I might turn out to be as insane as others of my relatives?"

She laughed softly. "One bad apple doesn't ruin the entire family tree." Look at the way her own sister behaved. "I love you, Sam, no matter what."

He pulled her close again. "Dia, having you in my life is the best thing that's ever happened to me."

Was it really true? He touched her jaw gently, lifting her mouth to meet his. His lips were firm and warm and met hers eagerly. He wanted her. She'd never felt like this with anyone else—loved, valued, and cherished. Weaving her fingers into his hair, she pulled him closer.

The wedding day arrived sooner than Dia thought possible. Despite the nerves she felt at the prospect of appearing in front of everyone, she eagerly anticipated the moment. Her gown was white silk embroidered with silver and set with tiny gems that sparkled when she moved. A brilliant diamond set in silver rested on her forehead. A maid with a serious face had undertaken the task of arranging Dia's hair, gathering some of it atop her head in intricate braids and curls. The rest tumbled down in soft waves. A shimmering silver veil hung down her back.

It would have been the perfect moment to have a sister by her side, but, under the circumstances, that wasn't going to happen. She hadn't even spoken to Lisenth since she'd come to stay at the palace. Instead, Countess Lavinia arrived in time to oversee the last of the preparations.

She kissed Dia's cheek. "You are a vision, my dear," she exclaimed, wiping her eyes with a lace handkerchief. "Your dear parents would be so proud of you this day. I'm so sorry they aren't here to see it. You look radiant. You really do love Prince Samanath, don't you?"

Dia couldn't help but smile. "I really do." She hugged the sweet woman. "Thank you for being here with me today."

Sooner than she expected, it was time. The entire city seemed to have assembled in the great hall to watch Dia enter. She tried to focus her gaze straight ahead, not looking at the crowds of people on either side. Taking a deep breath, she squared her shoulders, lifted her chin and, limping only very slightly, walked up the center of the vast room.

Sam waited for her, dressed in a magnificent tunic of white and gold, ceremonial armor, and a cuff with the royal crest. The king stood beside him, white-haired and dignified. When he caught Dia's eye, he smiled.

King Hashoreth performed the ceremony. They both made their promises to the Soul Mother and to each other, to honor the bond between them, to love and cherish and remain faithful to each other.

When the ceremony was complete, the king gave Sam permission to kiss her. His arms surrounded her and his lips met hers with aching tenderness. The short stubble of his beard tickled her face. She never wanted him to stop, except, with a twist in her stomach, she remembered they were standing in front of a large crowd of people. They turned to wave and everyone cheered.

Sam and Dia shared a lovely dinner with all their guests and danced together while every looked on and applauded. Dia's ankle forced her to move slowly and carefully, but no one seemed to mind. Lisenth was present, seated at one of the furthest tables. Dia saw her several times, but she never managed to catch her sister's eye. As soon as the meal was finished, a crowd of people, especially young men, surrounded Lisenth, and Dia was glad. If someone else caught her sister's eye, that would be for the best.

Finally, silence fell, and the king raised a glass. "As you all know, I have waited a long time for this day," he said. A laugh rose from the guests, and Dia saw a barely noticeable flush color Sam's face. "The future of our nation is in the hands of my grandson. I have every confidence in him, and on this special day, I wish him and my lovely new granddaughter every happiness." He hugged them both and kissed Dia's cheek.

"Thank you," she smiled up at him as the crowd applauded.

Sam waved at them in response. "Thank you, Grandfather. And we thank all of you for wishing us well." He offered Dia his arm, and as everyone laughed and clapped, they walked down the long room toward the door.

Dia felt her cheeks heat as all the eyes followed them. They reached the door, and the guards opened it to allow them to slip out, and it shut behind them, leaving them alone in the hall. She took a long deep breath and put her hand over her heart, relieved to be out of the public eye.

Sam grinned at her. "You were magnificent."

She had to laugh, shaking her head. "I barely said a word. I believe we already discussed my feelings about speaking in front of people. That was to be your job. I'm only here to support you."

He slid his arms around her. "Is that what you plan to do?"

"Of course—" Her words were cut off as he kissed her. His mouth moved deliberately across hers and trailed kisses down her jaw to her neck. Her breath escaped in a gasp, and her knees felt suddenly weak.

She put her arms around him, her lips against his neck. "Sam."

He lifted her into his arms and started down the hall. "We're leaving before anyone else finds us here."

CHAPTER 12

F OR SEVERAL BLISSFUL DAYS, Dia thought of nothing other than Sam. The world existed outside a bubble where she spent time only with him, and they waited as long as they could before emerging.

One morning, ten days after the wedding, they woke together. "I have a meeting this morning," Sam whispered in her ear. His arms surrounded her, holding her close to the warmth of his body.

Of course, she knew that would be the case sooner or later. As the prince, he had important work to do. Except for recent days, much of his time was spent helping his grandfather. Sam would continue to take over more responsibility as time went on.

She reached up to brush her hand along his cheek. "Will you be gone long?" she asked.

His lips trailed kisses along her forearm as he pulled back to focus his dark eyes on her. "I'll make sure I'm not."

She smiled at him and placed the palm of her hand against his chest over his heart. She leaned close to say in his ear, "Do you know you're everything to me? I'll love you forever, Sam."

"Dia," he murmured, pulling her closer. "I don't know what I ever did to deserve you. I will love you forever, too." His arms tightened around her and she felt his lips against her ear. His kisses slid along her jaw. She turned to meet his mouth with hers.

That evening, Sam and Dia entered the royal dining room to find the king already seated. The old man got to his feet and came to greet them. He hugged Sam and kissed Dia's cheek.

"How wonderful to have you both join me."

Dia felt herself blush, recalling the many meals that had come to them on a tray for them to share alone in their rooms.

She sat down, and Sam slid her chair into place for her before taking a seat beside her. Servants quickly laid out two more place settings and brought in soup, placing a bowl in front of each of them. After the first bite, Sam raised his eyes to his grandfather, seated across from them.

"Is there anything I need to catch up on, since I have been..." he turned to wink at Dia, "...otherwise occupied."

Dia felt her face heat still further.

The old man laughed. "I can't imagine what you mean," he teased. "Take all the time you need."

The king wanted Sam to have an heir. It was vital to all of Ischar. The king stole a glance at Dia and smiled, but thankfully, he said nothing more about it.

His face grew more serious. "Marek and I have been searching for weeks, but we haven't found the sorcerer. Even more people in the city have become ill."

"You've taken all the usual precautions?" Sam asked.

The king nodded, taking another bite. "We searched for anything in common between those afflicted, any possible source of illness, water or food. Every effort has been made to separate the sick from everyone else, but despite our efforts, new cases appear every day."

Sam stared back at his grandfather for a long moment. "So, now you think it is... the same as all those years ago?"

The old man met his gaze for a long moment. "We've ruled out any other possibility."

Dia could see the pain in his eyes. They'd lost their family during that time, and now that Sam had told her more about it, she had a clearer idea of the pain the old man must be feeling.

"We need a way to fight the dark magic," Sam said.

The king looked down at his plate. "I've never said his name, not in all these years, but my... son had unusual abilities, and when he was banished, the illness disappeared."

Sam exchanged a glance with Dia. The king was talking about Sam's uncle, Adengo.

"And twice now, we've seen a Shadaroc near Kulin," Sam said, taking Dia's hand under the table.

The old man nodded, meeting Sam's eyes. "Until recently, the last sighting of the dark bird was at that time."

"Do you think it could be him? The Shadaroc is a form taken by dark sorcerers. If Ade..." Sam didn't finish the name. "If he practiced dark magic, maybe he is the Shadaroc."

The old man's expression tightened in pain. "I pray to the Soul Mother that the evil creature is not my son."

⁘

The next morning, Sam and Dia went to the dining room, expecting to share breakfast with the king. They found the room empty except for Marek. The old sorcerer sat alone, thoughtfully staring into a half-finished cup of tea.

"Where is the king?" Sam asked.

Marek shrugged. "I expected to meet him here."

Sam turned to the guard at the door. "Do you know where the king is?"

The man bowed. "I'm not certain, Your Highness. I have not seen him yet today."

"Thank you." Sam and Dia went to the door, and Marek got to his feet and followed them down the hall toward the king's rooms. They found the king's valet, Liam, just exiting the room.

"What's wrong?" Sam asked.

Liam, a thin, quiet man, getting on in years himself, had served the king for decades. "I'm not certain, Your Highness. The king is ill this morning. I was just on my way to find the physician."

"May we go in?" Sam asked.

"His majesty is in bed, but he would still want to see you." Liam held the door open for them.

They found him lying in a large bed, warmly covered, resting against several pillows. Sam hurried to his side and put his hand on his grandfather's shoulder. The old man looked exhausted, his lined face pale.

"What's wrong?" Sam asked.

The king shook his head slightly. "I... I don't know, Sam. I woke up feeling unwell."

"Are you in pain anywhere?" Marek asked, coming forward to stand beside Sam.

"No, only tired." The king's usually commanding voice sounded faint.

"What can I do to help?" Sam asked.

The king blinked and looked up at Sam. "Will you attend my appointments today? I'm afraid I won't be able to..."

"Of course," Sam promised immediately. "Don't worry about anything. Just rest."

The king nodded. His eyes went to Marek. "I'm grateful you're here, my old friend."

Marek nodded. "Always. But it grieves me to see you ill, my king."

"Thank you for all you've done to help me," the king said. "I'll try to rest and hope to recover soon."

Marek nodded, making his way toward the door.

The physician arrived, rushing to the king's bedside. He turned to Sam. "I will do my best to discover what's wrong. Give me some time to examine him, and I will send word."

"Of course." Sam nodded. Dia could tell he didn't want to leave, but they needed to give the physician space to work.

"We'll come and check on him again in a little while," she suggested, towing Sam toward the door. With a last look at his grandfather, he followed her out, closing the door behind himself.

Outside in the hall, Marek stood, his frail shoulders hunched. Sam placed a hand on his arm. "You're worried about him."

Marek nodded.

"We all are," Sam said.

The old man shook his head. "I fear this is my fault. He is King of Ischar. All our fates are tied to him and to you. He needs a stronger guardian. I've done everything I can, but if I were a younger man... Since I came here nineteen years ago, I've used my magic to protect him. Now, I fear it is not enough."

———◆———

The day passed in a rush of meetings. When evening fell, Dia stole a few quiet moments to watch the sunset from the garden. The sun had just disappeared, leaving the sky a brilliant canvas of orange and purple. Dia walked through the gardens, enjoying the beautifully tended plants and the crisp evening air. On one of the benches beside a small stone basin of water, she saw Marek. She might have passed, leaving him to his contemplation, but he looked up, smiling as he met her eyes.

"It's a beautiful evening, Princess. Would you care to join me for a few moments?" He gestured to the space on the bench beside him.

"I would be pleased to." Dia took the offered seat.

"Is the king any better this evening?" Marek asked.

Dia shook her head. "I'm afraid not."

He rubbed a hand across his face. "I can't believe I allowed this to happen."

Her eyes widened. "But it can't really be your fault, can it?"

"Since I came to Kulin to fight the Shadaroc, my power has protected him and Sam. If evil magic gains control of the king, it will control all of Ischar. All these years I've stayed close beside him to prevent that from ever happening."

"But with your protection in place, how could dark magic cause his illness?"

"I can't be completely sure. I've done everything I could to shield him, and I visited him this afternoon to attempt to restore his hallan. Something must have slipped through my shield. I fear I am too old to fight this battle. My power is not what it once was."

"Can you save him?" Dia asked.

"I will do everything I can," Marek promised.

Dia met his eyes. "The only real solution would be to stop the Shadaroc."

Marek nodded. "You're right, my dear. We must find him in his human form and force him to release the stolen hallan."

"Do you have the power to do that?" Dia asked, eyeing the man's frail body.

Marek smiled faintly. "Once I did. Now, I don't know. For the time being, I suggest we all work on identifying him. I cannot promise that my fading power would be anywhere close to enough to stop him, but I do promise to try."

Dia reached out and placed her hand over his for a moment. "You're very loyal to the king. I know he's grateful. We all are."

She took a deep breath, wondering how he would respond to the questions she really wanted to ask him. She glanced to the side and saw him watching her.

"It's all right," he said. "You may ask your questions."

"Have you always been able to use magic?"

The question didn't appear to bother him. He rubbed his chin as he recalled. "It was a very long time ago. I was a boy, maybe thirteen or fourteen, the first time I realized. Before that time, I had no idea."

"How did you discover it?"

One corner of his mouth lifted in half a smile. "To tell the truth, it was a random accident. I grew up on a farm, and one of the cows strayed. She was always a stubborn beast, and I went into the woods to find her. Dark came early, and I couldn't see where I was. When I came to a steep ravine, I didn't see the edge, and I stumbled and fell."

She drew in a breath. "Were you hurt?"

"I fell a long way. Truly, the fall should have killed me. Instead, something else happened. In that moment, I used the magic as a shield without even realizing it. Sometimes people with the gift go their entire lives without ever awakening it."

"And, besides falling off something, how do you awaken it?" Dia asked.

Marek smiled grimly. "It is in moments of extreme stress that we attempt to reach beyond ourselves, or deeper within ourselves. Fear or anger can bring the power forth. Even so, it takes years of training to be able to use it effectively. Sorcerers often use a stone or crystal to focus, amplify, or store hallan."

Dia couldn't help but remember the piece of crystal she'd found in the cave. Had it been magic that she heard coming from it?

"Now the dark sorcerer is taking energy from other people to gain more power?" she asked.

Marek nodded. "Yes. It takes a great deal of energy to do magic. Especially something like changing his shape."

"Have you ever changed yours?"

Marek smiled. "Those of us who commit not to harm others are more limited in what we can do. We use only our own hallan or what is freely shared to us by others. But yes. I have flown before."

Dia's eyes were wide. The thought of being so high up made her stomach turn over. "I'm better off on the ground. I don't like heights. What was it like?"

He smiled, closing his eyes for a moment as if the memory was pleasant. "It only lasted a few moments, but it was glorious. I won't ever forget the feeling."

Dia rose, smiling at him. "Thank you for answering my questions. I need to go and meet Sam."

The old man nodded and smiled. "I'm sure your prince had much to do today."

When Dia returned to their rooms, she found them empty, but it wasn't long before Sam returned. He sank onto a settee, looking exhausted. Dia sat beside him, taking his hand.

"I just checked on him again," Sam said, his fingers curling around hers.

"Is he any better?"

He shook his head.

"We'll find a way to help him," she said firmly. "I spoke to Marek about it. We won't stop until we find a way."

Sam smiled at her and brought her hand to his lips. "Thank you."

A servant summoned them first thing in the morning. The king was asking for Sam. They dressed hurriedly and went to his rooms. They found him still in his bed. If anything, he looked worse than before.

Sam took the chair beside the bed, and took his hand, his strong brown fingers contrasting with the old man's faded, liver-spotted skin.

The king looked up at him. "Sam?"

"I'm here, Grandfather. What can I do?"

"Sam, I need you to find..." His expression looked confused, and he blinked as if trying to bring his grandson's face into focus.

"What grandfather?"

"Help those who are sick," the old man said. "Marek will help too."

"I don't know how to cure them," Sam protested. "But we're still trying to find the sorcerer and stop him."

"You will," the old man said. "I think you will."

For a moment, he muttered, the words incoherent. Then his voice cleared. "Where is Adengo? And Kariman? I miss my sons. Where are they?" He looked at Sam, his expression vague.

Dia squeezed Sam's shoulder. His voice was quiet. "They're not here, Grandfather. I'm sorry."

"Mistake..."

"What?"

"Should never have sent him away..."

The old man's eyes closed, and he slipped into a restless slumber.

That night, Dia found Marek in the garden again, watching the sunset. "How are you tonight?" she asked, coming to sit beside him.

He smiled. "Well enough, Princess. You?"

"Well enough."

"We'll have rain before morning," he predicted, nodding at the clouds painted pink at the edges.

"How can you be so sure?"

He smiled. "Experience, my dear. After so long, I—" He fell suddenly silent, staring up at the sky. "Something isn't right. Can you feel it? He's coming."

Dia followed his gaze upward, seeing nothing but the empty sky. "Who? Do you mean the—" She didn't finish her question. A black shape appeared on the horizon. The Shadaroc.

"Finally, he shows himself," Marek said, his gaze focused on the distant bird.

"What can we do?" Her stomach clenched as the Shadaroc flew nearer, heading directly toward them.

"We do what we must," Marek said. "He's attacked the king. We must stop him." He stood up, moving away from her, out into the open courtyard.

Dia stared, fascinated, as he stretched out his arms and they became great silver wings. A moment later, his transformation was complete, and he launched himself into the air.

He rose above the palace, reaching the heights just in time to confront the Shadaroc.

For a breathless moment, the two powerful birds circled each other. A piercing screech, a challenge, echoed off the stone walls of the palace. The Shadaroc raised its deadly talons and dove toward the silver bird, who raised its own claws to block them. They crashed together. With a scream of pain, the black bird wrenched itself away, beating its wings to gain altitude and distance from its foe.

The silver bird pursued. In this form, its motion was nothing like the halting steps of a very old man; it was quick and graceful in the air, and it followed the Shadaroc. They wheeled and dove, striking at each other with hooked beaks and talons like swords.

The birds were built for speed, agility, and power. For some time, the silver bird maintained an obvious advantage, blocking every attack and striking its enemy hard. Then, the dark bird tucked its wings and plummeted like a stone toward its foe, no more than a blur of black feathers. With surprising agility for its size, the silver bird spun away from the attack, losing only a couple of feathers, which drifted slowly toward the ground.

The silver bird attacked, seizing the black one in a deadly embrace. They tumbled through the sky, falling faster and faster. At the last moment, they broke apart, regaining altitude with powerful strokes of their wings. Both determined to win, they crashed together again. The silver bird struck a powerful blow, causing the black bird to pull back. For a moment, they circled each other. With a shriek, the Shadaroc drove its talons into its foe, and in a tangle of feathers and wings, they crashed to the ground. The Shadaroc landed on top.

On the ground, several figures ran toward it. They looked so small next to the bird that it took a moment for Dia to realize they were men armed with spears, Sam among them. He thrust the weapon into the bird's body. It shrieked in fury, lashing out with wings and talons. Knocking the men aside, it vaulted into the air, a broken spear shaft still imbedded in its body. The wind of its wings blew down on them. In a moment, it was gone.

Dia ran across the courtyard to find Sam bending over Marek where he lay on the stones. The old man didn't move. Blood soaked through several places on his robe. More blood ran from beneath his body. Sam pressed his fingers to the old man's throat, searching for any sign of a heartbeat. After a moment, he shook his head.

The old man's eyes were open but unblinking, unseeing. Marek was gone.

The king's illness worsened over the next few days. Sam spent most of his time at his grandfather's side. Dia was often there with him. Worry lay heavily over the entire palace.

One morning, Dia woke early to find the bed empty and cold beside her. She looked around for Sam. Putting on a robe, she went to the door. Just as she opened it, Sam ran around the corner, his expression frozen in panic. The guard beside the door gripped his sword hilt, startled into instant alertness.

"Dia, come, hurry!" He took her hand and pulled her along.

With the guard at their heels, they went out into the garden, straight through the fountains and plantings to the railing at the edge of the cliffs.

It was easy to see why he was upset. A thin smear of blood ran across the white stone. When Dia looked back toward the building, she realized there were marks across the grass and a few small smears of blood, as if someone had dragged a body to the edge and...

"What happened?" she asked horrified. "Did someone..." the words didn't come. "Who?" Her hand flew to her mouth in shock. The base of the cliffs was three thousand feet below.

"Your Highness," the guard said. "I will alert Captain Kerem, and we will begin a search of the palace and grounds at once.

"Yes! Thank you!" Sam said. He turned back to Dia. "We have to check on Grandfather!"

Rushing back inside to the king's rooms, to their intense relief, they found the king still in his bed. They were delighted to realize he even looked a little better this morning.

"Are you all right?" Sam asked, hurrying to his side.

"Yes," he smiled slightly. "I'm beginning to hope I might beat this thing.

"Good!" Sam stared at him in surprise.

The king looked at Sam intently. "You look like you've seen a ghost, boy. What happened?"

Quickly, Sam explained what they had found.

The king's brow furrowed in concern. "Have Kerem and the rest of the guards conduct a thorough search. This is disturbing news. We need to know if someone is missing from the palace. Let's try to determine who it is before we decide what to do next."

"We've already sent word to Kerem. I'll let you know what they find," Sam promised. He stepped forward to hug his grandfather. "I'm so relieved that you're all right."

"As am I," the king replied.

Over the next few hours, the guards searched the entire palace several times over. They were unable to find any hint of a missing person. All appeared well. With nothing at all to go on, Sam was forced to cancel the search until they could obtain new information. The king had refused to send anyone down into the dangerous jungle until they knew more. Nothing could be done anyway. Not even a tiny chance remained of anyone surviving a fall from that height.

The next morning, Sam and Dia walked hand in hand to the royal dining room. The king stood when he saw them, apparently just finished with his meal.

"Good morning!" He hurried to hug them both affectionately. "I'm sorry I didn't wait for you, but there's much to do today. I felt so much better that I'm meeting with several of our councilors and a few of the nobility. There are many of our people in the city who are sick. We need to do more to help them."

Enthusiasm lit his wrinkled face.

Sam raised his brows in surprise. "What brought this on, Grandfather?"

"After having experienced this illness myself, I don't want anyone else to suffer." The old man smiled. "Now that I'm able, I feel it is time to take action."

"What can I do to help?" Sam asked.

The king smiled and clapped Sam on the shoulder. "Nothing today. We've had far too much excitement in the last several days. I'm sure a moment of quiet will be welcome. Spend time with your lovely bride. I'll fill you in later." He bent to kiss Dia's cheek and strode purposefully out of the room, several servants in his wake.

Soon, they were comfortably seated with breakfast in front of them, and they had the room to themselves. Sam shook his head. "That was strange. Of course, I'm happy he's feeling well and has so much energy, but..."

Dia understood what he was trying to say. "Something is different about him."

Sam's brows drew together. "Something..."

For a long moment, they were silent. Dia couldn't think of any way to describe what she meant. It was only a feeling.

CHAPTER 13

I N THE DREAM, SAM *saw the palace and the courtyard packed with people, all cheering and clapping. Dia walked through the crowd toward him, her face radiant. The glimmering white silk of her gown draped gracefully around her slender form; a white gem sparkled on her forehead.*

Love shone from her eyes.

Even in unconsciousness, he felt that he must be the most fortunate man alive to earn her love. And Dia gave it completely. The crowd gathered around them, wishing them well. Sam felt a hand on his shoulder and turned to see his father. His eyes widened, and he clasped him in a tight hug. How Sam had missed him, all these years. He looked exactly like Sam remembered, only Sam had grown up, and they were the same size now.

His father smiled at him. "I'm proud of you, Son. You've done well."

"I'm proud of you, too," a melodious feminine voice added.

His jaw slackening in disbelief, Sam turned to see his mother beside them. She looked lovely, her long dark hair just as he remembered. She wore a beautiful gown, as befitted the occasion, and a ruby sparkled on her forehead. She hugged him, and as he wrapped his arms around her, he realized how much smaller she felt in his arms than he remembered.

"Sam!" At the familiar call, he turned to see a smiling young man coming toward him through the crowd. "I missed you," Adengo said, pulling him close. "Look how you've grown! I missed you too, brother." He hugged Kariman fondly.

In disbelief, Sam smiled down at Dia. He never expected to see her with a gathering of his family. Now they were all here together, and his heart filled with joy. His grandfather made his way through the crowd to join them, laughing as he embraced each of them. "What a glorious moment!" He looked so happy. "Sam. This is your day. The future of Ischar is in your hands. I have every confidence in you, and on this special day, I wish you and my lovely new granddaughter every happiness."

Sam smiled at all of them. He felt loved and protected, surrounded by family. Dia smiled up at him as if she would adore him forever, her slender hand in his.

A huge shadow fell across the sky, and the wind of giant wings rushed across the people. Screams and shouts echoed through the courtyard. Sam looked around desperately, realizing that Dia was no longer beside him. He turned, frantically searching for her.

His father cried out.

"No!" Kariman's face was white with horror. He stared at a man in a dark hooded cloak with a knife in his hand. Blood ran from a crumpled form at his feet.

"No!" Sam echoed the cry, as he realized his mother lay there, her blood running onto the white stone beneath her. Kariman lunged for the man with the knife, and Sam felt frozen as he watched his father reach the dark figure and grab the hand with the knife. They grappled, and the man drove his blade in Kariman's heart. Blood flowing from the wound, he sank to the ground beside his wife.

Trying to drag his feet into motion, Sam looked around again, searching for Dia. She was still nowhere to be seen. The man in the black cloak turned toward the king.

"Stop!" Sam screamed, as the dark figure positioned himself behind the king and raised his knife. "Please!"

Sam ran toward them. They seemed farther away than they had been, and he ran, but he couldn't reach them in time. His grandfather turned at the sound of his voice, but the knife was already falling. The man in the cloak drove it into the old man's chest. With a final look at Sam, he sank to the ground.

Sam sank down beside him. "Grandfather!"

"Please help them, Sam," the old man's voice was faint. "You need to take care of the people now." He tried to say more, but he couldn't get the words out, and a trickle of blood ran from his mouth. His eyes looked up at Sam without seeing him.

Sam bent over him, weeping. He wasn't sure how long he stayed there. When he looked around, he saw no one nearby. Adengo was gone. The rest of the crowd had vanished. Sam knelt alone in the courtyard surrounded by the motionless bodies of his family.

He jumped to his feet. Where was Dia? Where was the man with the knife? Suddenly, he knew that he had to find her now, or it would be too late. He bolted across the courtyard and into the palace. Running through the halls, his breath coming in ragged gasps, he reached his rooms.

Throwing the door open, he looked around. The room was lit only by a single lantern on a table. He felt a moment of relief as he saw his wife in the bed. He moved slowly closer until he looked down on her. Horror felt like ice in his chest. She wasn't sleeping. Her beautiful eyes stared blankly up. Dark bruising surrounded the ivory skin of her slender throat.

He sank to his knees, clutching her. She was so utterly still. She was gone, like everyone else. Gone.

"No, Dia!" Sam couldn't bear it if she left him too. One by one, everyone he'd ever loved had left him behind.

"Sam!" Dia's voice sounded frightened.

He opened his eyes to see the familiar darkness of their room.

Dia was beside him, shaking him. "Sam! Please wake up."

He blinked. She was here. Alive. Dia wasn't dead. She was still beside him. Relief coursed through him, along with a sharp twist of nausea. He scrambled to his feet, running to the basin and vomiting. Every time he closed his eyes, he saw red blood against the stones, and Dia's eyes, empty and staring. He would rather die than see that.

Gentle hands rubbed his back. "It's all right," she murmured. "Here," she offered him a glass of water. He rinsed his mouth and then took a sip. She brushed his hair, damp with sweat, from his forehead, and then took his hand and led him back to bed, his body shaking. Drawing up the blanket, she covered him.

The dream had felt so real. He still wasn't sure that it hadn't been. When Dia slid into bed beside him, he wrapped his arms around her, pulling her close.

She snuggled against him, warm and living, and rested her hand on his chest. "Rest now," she murmured. "You'll be all right."

"It was a dream," he assured himself. He concentrated on his breathing, trying to slow his breath and calm the wild pounding of his heart.

"Only a dream," she repeated.

He drew in another ragged breath.

"Do you want to tell me?" Her voice was soft.

He couldn't tell her all of it. He dared not even voice the end of the dream, for fear that he would somehow cause it to happen in reality. There was no way he could tell her that part. He settled for a simple explanation. "I saw my parents," he murmured. "They were well and whole and with us on our wedding day. Grandfather too."

She listened quietly, her fingers making soothing circles on his skin. He took a deep breath, feeling a little calm returning, and he drew her closer to kiss her brow. "Dia, I'm sorry I frightened you." She felt soft and warm against him.

"It's all right," she whispered.

"I was so happy to have them there with us. But then…" he paused to drag in another breath. "A man with a knife killed them—my mother, father, and grandfather." Then, he had run back to his rooms to find *her* lying dead, and he'd known it would be his fate to be utterly alone.

Chapter 14

THE NEXT SEVERAL DAYS were busy ones. With his newfound energy, the king seemed to be everywhere at once. One morning, Dia and Sam managed to find him seated at an early breakfast.

"Good morning, Grandfather," Sam said.

The king smiled. "How are you, Sam? Dia?"

"We are well," Sam replied nodding toward a stack of papers in the old man's hands. "You look busy. What are you working on?"

The old man smiled. "In addition to helping the sick, I want to do more for the poor of our kingdom." His expression was determined. "We are blessed by a wonderful climate and a beautiful land. Our fields produce a bounty of goods, and we have more than enough to help those who are unfortunate."

"That's wonderful, Your Majesty," Dia agreed. "We would love to help you any way we can."

The king smiled and nodded.

"This new project is exciting," Sam said, "but I'm sure you miss Marek. He would have been a great help."

A fleeting spark of anger flashed in the king's eyes. It was gone so fast that Dia couldn't be sure she'd even seen it. Maybe she'd been mistaken. Why would a mention of his old friend make him angry?

"He was a good friend," the king said sadly. "I'm sure we will never stop missing him. He gave everything he had to Ischar, and we hold his memory in the deepest respect." He rose. Walking around the table, he kissed Dia's cheek and clapped a hand on Sam's shoulder. "I will let you know what I need soon."

Early the next morning, they were in the hall outside the king's rooms. They paused at the unmistakable sound of an angry voice. "I am King of Ischar, not some country noble! You'd better remember it. If this happens again, you'll be out on the street. I don't care how long you've been here."

The door opened, and Liam, the king's valet, hurried out, closing the door behind him. His eyes were tight, his jaw clenched.

"What happened?" Sam asked.

The valet shook his head. His own hair was nearly as white as the king's. He'd taken care of Hashoreth for most of his life. "The king is... unhappy this morning." He took in a deep breath. "I hope the mood will pass."

Sam gripped the man's shoulder. "I'm sorry, Liam. You've put up with all his moods for a long time. Is there anything I can do to help?"

Liam shrugged helplessly. "He's the king."

Most mornings, Dia spent a while in the infirmary, sitting with Carrina. The girl had no family left that Dia knew of, and she didn't want her to be alone while she was sick. The physicians checked on her frequently, doing everything they could to help. Despite their efforts, Carrina remained weak and pale.

Today she blinked, opening her eyes to look at Dia.

"How are you feeling this morning?"

"I'm all right," Carrina murmured. She smiled slightly. "I wish we had more time. You've been a good friend to me, and you saved my life."

Tears welling in her eyes, Dia smiled back, taking Carrina's cold hand. "When you're feeling better, I'll show you around the palace. Or we can go shopping in the city. You'll love it."

"That sounds nice," Carrina murmured, her eyelids falling shut. Her skin appeared deathly white, with dark circles under her eyes, and her skin felt cold.

Dia looked up to see the kindly physician beside her. He put his fingers beneath her chin to count her heartbeat. After a long moment, he met Dia's eyes.

"There must be some way to help her," she protested.

"I wish I knew how to fight this illness. I've done everything I can for her." He shook his head, his eyes downcast. He moved away through the rows of beds.

Dia remained, sitting beside Carrina as she slept. Suddenly the girl opened her eyes again, looking around terrified.

"What's wrong?"

"I thought he was here again. Maybe if he doesn't come back, I'll get better. He's here. He's here..." Her voice trailed off, and her eyes closed.

The king's project took shape quickly. He purchased a large building, not far from the palace, that had once been an estate of some kind. Soon, supplies were being gathered, staff hired, and the first of the ill and homeless began to receive aid. The king himself chose the people who were to work there.

He had plenty of resources at his disposal, and when the nobility and members of his court heard the details, everyone agreed it was caring of him to create such a nice place for the unfortunate. Within a few days, several dozen people were housed there, while representatives of the king looked after them and helped them to find training or work, whatever they needed to get back on their feet.

They had moved Carrina from the palace infirmary into the new place. It was very well staffed, and they could easily continue her care there.

When Sam and Dia toured the place, they couldn't help but be impressed. Carrina seemed comfortable in one of the rooms. There were many people working to help. Large numbers of the more well-off residents of the city had volunteered their time to run the place. In one of the central chambers, they observed a very familiar figure giving directions to several other workers. Her sister. Dia felt a twinge of unease in her stomach as they approached.

Lady Lisenth bowed to Sam, "Your Highness." She turned to Dia, and bowed again, only the smallest tinge of bitterness on her face. "Your Highness."

Dia nodded in response. "How are you, Lisenth?"

"I am well," her sister responded. If there was sarcasm in her words, it was deeply hidden. "It has been exciting to work so closely with the king to keep this place running."

"That's good," Sam answered. "We both wish you happiness. I apologize if I was harsh with you before. It's good to see you're doing so well and providing so much assistance to the king's new endeavor."

Lisenth managed a small smile. "I apologize if my behavior was... inappropriate. I hope you will join me in putting it behind us. There is much to be done here, and the king wouldn't be able to run this place without me."

⁃◆⁃

Two days later, Dia sat in the morning sunshine. Finally finding a quiet moment, she worked on knitting a pair of socks to be given away to someone in need. The work was relaxing after the busy pace of helping Sam and his grandfather. Sam was with the king now. One of the servants entered the garden and approached Dia, bowing. "Your Highness, there is a young woman at the palace gate asking to see you."

"To see me? Who is it?" Dia asked.

"Carrina."

"I'll come immediately," Dia said, laying her knitting aside and getting to her feet. Carrina must be feeling better if she'd gotten up and walked the short distance to the palace.

As Dia left the room, two guards stood outside the door.

One of them was Kerem. He smiled and bowed. "May I assist you, Princess?"

"I'm going to the gates, if you'd like to accompany me?" she asked him.

"Of course, Your Highness." He fell in behind her as she followed the messenger.

At the gate, a familiar girl with blond hair waited. She was on her feet, though she looked tired and deathly pale.

"She's a friend, you may let her in," Dia said, and Kerem opened the gate, holding it to allow her inside.

Carrina walked warily through and stood facing Dia. She appeared to be trembling. "Dia?" Her voice was quiet, barely above a whisper.

"How are you feeling?" Dia asked.

Carrina shook her head. "I'm trying to get better, truly I am. I'm just so tired. I wouldn't have come except that..." Carrina paused. "I had to. This is urgent. There is something wrong with the place the king set up to care for those in need. At first, I thought it would be a nice place. But many of the poor people who came for help have already fallen ill."

"Didn't they come there because they were ill already?"

"Perhaps some of them," Carrina admitted. "But they get worse when they come. No one coughs, they don't have a fever or any other sign of illness. Everyone there has food to eat, so they aren't starving. I have never seen anything like it. It just feels very wrong to me, and I'm so afraid. They go to sleep at night and wake up weaker every morning. I stayed awake one night, watching. And I saw..."

Her eyes grew large in terror, and she leaned closer to Dia.

"I saw a man, like the man who came the night of the accident and put his hand on my father's head. I watch him do the same thing to one of the sick people, an old man who was already very weak. By morning, he was dead, just like my father."

"And you saw this man put his hand on the old man?"

Carrina nodded. "Please help us? I didn't know who else to come to. I knew you would believe me. You were there that night. Please don't make me go back there!"

Dia hugged her. "No, of course I won't. You must come back to stay in the palace."

Carrina began to cry in relief and weariness.

"We'll make sure you are cared for here, and I will try to find out what's happening," Dia promised. "I will speak to the prince about it and let him know what you saw. Come with us, we'll help you back to the infirmary."

Kerem stepped forward to offer his assistance. Carrina leaned heavily on him while Dia supported her from the other side.

"Thank you," she murmured. "We must protect all the people in that place. They need help."

They hadn't gone more than a few steps before she slumped. Kerem caught her, lifting her into his arms.

"Thank you, Kerem," Dia said. "Will you please take her back to the infirmary? Please let them know that we must keep her here and watch her. I will speak to the prince about what she said."

"As you command, Princess." Kerem inclined his head toward her and then turned back toward the palace with Carrina.

With worry churning in her middle, Dia went back toward their rooms. She needed to tell Sam what she'd heard. She found him there, staring out the window. He didn't appear to notice her until she crossed the room to stand beside him. He turned and smiled as he saw her. "I didn't hear you come in."

"What are you thinking about so hard?" she asked, slipping her arm around his waist.

He sighed. "I was remembering when I was a boy, I would sneak away from my lessons and explore the palace, especially the places I wasn't supposed to go. I used to hide in the dungeon."

She laughed softly, picturing him as a mischievous child. He must have been adorable with those dark eyes.

"I've just been reviewing everything we know about what's happening. On the day my parents died, I saw my uncle down there, speaking to another member of the court." He rubbed his forehead. "It's been so long, and I tried so hard to forget that day. But they were talking about magic, and about a sickness spreading through the city. If my uncle used magic, maybe he knew something more about it than we do."

She looked up at him. "Sam, I think we're in serious trouble. Carrina just came to the gates asking me for help. They moved her to the new home for those in need. But she said she saw a man in the dark. He put his hand on a man's forehead, just as someone did to her father. By morning, the man was dead. She says many other people grow more and more ill inside. Something is very wrong."

He rubbed his chin, thinking. "It seemed a little strange to me that Grandfather suddenly became so involved in it. At first, I thought he was just being charitable, but what if there's something more?"

"What could we do about it? Is there a way we can see what's happening there?" Dia tapped one toe against the floor as she thought it over.

"Maybe I could sneak out of the gates and go there tonight," Sam suggested. "No one would know I was coming, and I'd be able to observe what's going on."

The idea frightened Dia. She'd never crept through the city in the dark before, but she didn't want Sam to go alone. "You can't go by yourself!" she protested. "I need to know what's going on, too. I'll go with you."

"What if it's dangerous?" he asked. "Will you please stay here where it's safe? I'll take Andar or Kerem, or one of the other guards with me."

She still didn't like the idea. "What else could this be but dark magic? We must be close to finding the sorcerer."

"I hope we are," Sam said.

"What about Adengo? He could use magic, couldn't he?"

Sam shrugged. "I don't know how much. He was learning it or had some natural ability. If he was willing to murder his brother, he certainly wouldn't care about harming other people to gain more power."

For a moment, his expression tightened in pain as he remembered what had happened. She reached out to touch his arm. He covered her hand with his and took in a deep breath.

"I saw him hide a key once," Sam said. "I think we should see if it's still there. Will you come with me?"

"Of course."

They slipped out of their rooms, moving through the palace toward the stairs. Sam appeared to be very familiar with a route that allowed them to reach the door without meeting anyone.

Dia couldn't help but smile. "You've come this way before."

He grinned. "So many times. But not for years. It's been some time since I tried to sneak away from my lessons." He picked up a lantern from a storage room as they passed and lit it.

They went down a long set of stairs. The walls were stone, bare of any decoration. The only light came from the lantern Sam carried. Dia didn't like the dark, and she walked close to him.

"I can't imagine why you came down here for fun."

She heard the smile in his voice. "Well, maybe looking for adventure would be a better description. Hiding down here made it very difficult for them to find me."

They saw no one else. At the bottom of the stairs, they entered a long hallway with doors opening on either side. The end opened into a larger chamber containing several cells with thick iron bars.

"There's no one down here...?" Dia looked into all the dark corners, dreading to see someone.

Sam shook his head. "We haven't locked anyone down here in a very long time. Those who commit crimes serious enough to warrant it are banished to the jungle." Holding the lantern high, he moved to the stone wall and walked along it. Near the far corner, he pulled out a loose stone and reached into the space to retrieve a ring holding two iron keys.

"What do they go to?" Dia asked as he held them up.

"I'm not entirely sure," Sam admitted. "But I have some ideas." He offered his hand, and she took it. "There are more rooms and passages through here."

They left the large room and entered a hallway that felt more like a tunnel. Dia began to wish for the sight of sky above her and for more air. She clutched Sam's hand.

"It's all right," he reassured her. "I've been down here a hundred times. I know the way."

There were several doors along the passage, and Sam tried both keys in each of them without success. They made their way farther along and saw several smaller doors. He handed her the lantern to hold while he tried the keys.

The lock on the last door at the end clicked open. When Dia brought the light to the doorway, it revealed a cramped storage space, empty except for a small chest. Sam picked it up and set it in the hallway. As she held the light for him, he tried the second key.

The lock opened.

Though she felt curious to look inside, the dark felt like it was closing in all around them. "Why don't we take it back upstairs?" she suggested.

He raised his eyes to her, and then nodded. "Very well." He tucked the keys into his pocket and picked up the chest.

She raised the lantern high and saw a flash of movement in one corner. Something scampered away from the light. Biting back a shriek, she jumped toward Sam. "Please tell me that wasn't a rat!"

He put his arm around her. "Come on." He guided her back down the hall. "I'm sure it wasn't."

He was obviously lying, but she chose to believe him as they hurried back past the cells and up the stairs. They made it back into their own rooms without meeting anyone, and Dia closed the door behind herself, leaning against it, breathing hard.

"Why do I feel we've just had our own adventure?" She looked at Sam.

He set down the chest and smiled at her. "You're very brave, my lady."

She returned his smile, still trying to catch her breath. "And you're lying through your teeth, my lord."

"Really?" He came nearer and slid his arms around her. "What did I lie about?"

"That was absolutely a rat." She shuddered in horror. "And I'm not br..." She didn't finish her sentence as he kissed the spot just below her ear. At the touch of his lips against her skin, she forgot what she'd been about to say.

In the quiet of their room, they opened the small chest and looked inside. It contained books and papers. Dia picked one up. "Do you recognize the handwriting?"

Sam nodded, his expression tight. "Adengo. I've seen his writing many times before."

For several moments, they sifted through the papers. A small leather-bound book lay beneath them. Sam opened it and thumbed through the pages. "It's a diary." He set it down as Dia took a larger volume from the bottom of the chest.

She opened it to see lists of strange incantations. Her fingertips tingled where they touched the leather cover. With a gasp, she closed it again. "It's a book of magic."

Sam looked sad. "They were arguing about magic that day in the dungeon."

"You were so small." Dia laid her hand on his arm. "What else do you remember?"

He rubbed his forehead. "It was so long ago, and I didn't understand everything they were talking about, but they mentioned a sickness. Adengo accused the other man of causing it."

"And who was he?"

"A man named Halderan, a member of the king's court. I remember everyone deferred to him because he was very educated. He was Adengo's tutor. He said something about Adengo being a talented student. Halderan sounded like he knew people were getting sick, and he didn't care."

"Just like the illness spreading now. Could Halderan have come back to Kulin?"

"It's possible." Sam picked up the journal, flipping through the pages. Nearly half the leaves were empty. Sam held the book open to the last entry. He read the words aloud. "I have no way to prove it, but I suspect that Halderan has magical abilities beyond anything we can imagine. His strength is more than any man naturally possesses. I found the spell to transfer hallan from other people among his things. I took the book and locked it away, but I fear he has already used it. The strange illness weakening our people is a sign of it."

Dia picked up the book again and looked through it. Her eyes widened at the words on the page. "It's a spell allowing him to appear to be a different person." She looked up at Sam in horror. How would they ever find the sorcerer if he could alter his appearance?

They both started as someone knocked at the door. Setting the books aside, Sam rose and went to open it. The king stood framed in the doorway.

"Grandfather?"

"Sam, how are you? I was just on my way back to my study and I wondered if you'd join me for a moment. There's something important I need to discuss with you." He looked past Sam's shoulder and his eyes met Dia's. He smiled. "Don't worry, my dear. I'll have him back to you very soon. You must have been busy. I've barely seen the two of you." His eyes flicked to the chest and the books and papers lying on the table. He clapped Sam on the shoulder. "Well, Sam?"

Sam's gaze turned back to Dia for just a moment before he focused on the king. "Of course, Grandfather." The door closed behind them.

Dia sat alone in the room, reading through Adengo's papers. It seemed clear from his notes that he was studying magic. He seemed to have had some kind of disagreement with his teacher. She searched for more information, but after reading everything through several times, she lowered the papers in frustration. Maybe if Sam looked through the collection, he'd be able to shed more light on them. Where was Sam?

She'd been reading for quite a while. The king had promised he wouldn't be gone long.

Dia left the room and went down the hall to the king's study. No guards were in sight, but someone stood outside the door. With a nervous quiver in her belly, Dia recognized King Hashoreth. His eyes were already on her, so she approached and bowed. "Your Majesty, are you finished with your meeting? Where is Sam?"

He took a few steps closer, gazing down at her. His eyes were hard and dark, nothing like the sweet old man who'd wished them well together. "Princess Alladia." His cold eyes held hers, and she couldn't help taking a step back. "Prince Samanath and I have worked well together for many years now. That must continue, just as before. Lately, I feel that he'd rather listen to *you* than to me. May I count on you to encourage him to fulfill his duty to Ischar and to me?"

"Yes, of course," she stammered.

He took another step toward her, malice slicing through his gaze.

"Good." He held her eyes for another endless moment.

Dia felt like she couldn't breathe until he turned away and disappeared down the hall. When he was gone, she hurried to his study. The door of the room was slightly ajar. She peeked in to see Sam in the chair, his body slumped forward over the desk.

CHAPTER 15

DIA RAN INTO THE room, rushing to his side. "Sam!" She shook his shoulder. He groaned but didn't wake. What had happened? She touched his cheek. His skin felt warm and damp with a light sheen of sweat. She shook him again. "Sam? Please wake up. What's wrong?"

He moved a little.

"Sam!"

Slowly, he raised his head and met her eyes. For a long moment, he stared at her, his expression completely blank. Beads of sweat stood out on his forehead and his pale skin. With one hand, he rubbed the back of his neck. When he took his hand away, she examined his skin but saw nothing out of the ordinary.

"Sam?" The worry in her belly expanded rapidly.

He blinked several times before his eyes focused on her. "Dia? What are you doing here? What happened?"

"Are you well?" She put her arms around him. First, King Hashoreth had behaved so strangely and now Sam? Something was very wrong.

He scrubbed a hand over his face. "Yes?" He took a deep breath and blinked again. "Yes," he said more firmly. "I'm fine."

"Can you walk?"

The question appeared to confuse him. He pushed himself up, swaying slightly on his feet. She pulled his arm around her shoulders, and together, they made their way back to their suite. Once inside, she helped him to a chair while she brought him a glass of cold water. He drank it gratefully.

"Are you sure you're all right?" She touched his forehead. His skin was damp with sweat, but he didn't feel feverish.

"I think so." He rubbed the back of his neck again. For a moment, he looked away, his gaze unfocused.

"What happened?" she asked again.

"I..." He rubbed his hand over his face. "Nothing. Nothing happened. I'm fine."

He obviously wasn't fine. What could she do to help? All evening, Dia watched Sam closely, but by the time a few hours had passed, he seemed to be his usual self. The effects of whatever had happened appeared to pass.

"Are you sure you still want to go out tonight?" she asked.

"I need to find out what's happening," he insisted. "I'm all right now. Truly."

Just after midnight, Sam drew on a long cloak and prepared to go. He kissed her. "Go to sleep," he murmured. "I'll be back before you have a chance to miss me."

She couldn't do it. A moment after he'd left, she threw on her own cloak and followed him. Staying far enough back that he wouldn't see her, she slipped through the silent hallways behind him. She was nearly to the gates, when strong arms seized her and a hand clamped over her mouth, silencing the shriek that would have escaped. She struggled instinctively.

"Why were you following me?" a voice hissed. A hand pulled back her hood. "Dia."

It was Sam. She drew in a deep breath, trying to calm herself. Tremors ran through her body.

"What are you doing?" he demanded. "You were supposed to stay in our room where it was safe."

He lowered his hand from her mouth and pulled her close into a gentle hug. "I'm sorry, I had no idea it was you behind me."

"I'm sorry," she finally managed to say.

"You're still shaking. I'm sorry I frightened you."

His familiar embrace quickly made her feel better.

He drew back and looked into her eyes. "Do you want to tell me why you're out here, sneaking through the dark, instead of in bed?"

"I was worried," she admitted. "I couldn't let you go alone. I thought Andar would go with you."

He shook his head. "He must have had some other duty. I couldn't find him. Well, come on then, we'll go together."

They crept to the palace gates.

"We look like we're attempting to commit some horrid crime," Dia pointed out as they approached the guards at the gate.

"It will be fine," Sam assured her. "They all know us." They saw Kerem among the other guards at the gates. Sam spoke urgently to him, explaining that they had a pressing errand and they would be back in a short while. The captain nodded in understanding.

The streets were silent and empty at this late hour. Dia gripped Sam's hand tightly and walked close by his side. It took only a few moments walking to reach the estate that the king had purchased for his project. Sam paused in a patch of heavy shadow, and Dia stayed close to him. From this vantage point, they had a good view of the doors. All was silent.

They watched for some time, until Dia was about to suggest that they needed to move if they were going to find out anything useful, when a solitary figure slid silently up to the side door. He threw back the hood of his cloak, and they caught a glimpse of white hair. Sam drew in a sharp breath.

When the dark figure disappeared inside, hand-in-hand, they crept after him. The heavy door was unlocked, and Sam opened it as silently as possible. A dark hallway revealed no one. As they followed the hall deeper into the building, several doors opened on both sides. A sliver of light escaped one of the doors. Not the warm orange glow of candle light, but an unearthly greenish glow. They crept nearer and peeked through the crack.

The still form of a young woman lay on the bed. A figure in a dark cloak knelt beside her and reached out a hand, placing the palm deliberately against her forehead. The green glow seemed to come from her inert body, coalescing at the point where the hand touched her head.

Dia watched, terrified, her jaw slack. Her mind flew back to her night in the forest, when a man in a dark cloak had rested his hand against her forehead in just the same way.

Something moved inside the room. Another girl appeared from the shadows and seized the man's hand in both of hers. "Stop!" she cried. "Leave her alone!"

The man in the dark cloak seized her at once, and she did not fight against his grip. Instead, she slumped in his arms. He placed her beside the other girl on the bed and put his palm in the same position on her forehead. She didn't move or try to struggle, but she whimpered in fear or maybe pain.

Sam pushed the door fully open. "Stop!" he ordered.

When the man turned to look at them, Dia recognized the time-worn features of the king. He jumped to his feet, striking Sam hard enough to knock him down. In a rush, he was past them, disappearing into the hall. Dia saw him go out through the doors before she ran to Sam. In the dark, she almost fell over him.

Someone must have heard the commotion, for a woman came down the hall with a candle in her hand. "What is going on here?" she demanded.

Sam picked himself up, rubbing his jaw. A red spot had already begun to swell. Dia went to the bed and shook the girl's shoulder. She girl stirred, blinking.

"There was a man in here," Dia told the woman with the candle. "We saw him attack this girl. Sam tried to stop him, but he ran out the door." She couldn't say she'd seen the king. Not now. They needed to find out what was happening. She turned back to the girl. "Are you all right?"

"I—I think so, Your Highness." The girl's voice was weak, and she sounded confused.

Sam was on his feet facing the caretaker with the light. "Please, do what you can for them," he nodded toward the two young women. "I will try to find out what's happening here."

"Very well," the woman said, setting the candle on a shelf and kneeling at the bedside.

Dia hurried with Sam to the outer door, but by the time they opened it, no one was in view. He stood for a moment, then leaned against the wall, taking in deep breaths.

"Dia? Did I just see what I thought I saw?"

She took his hand and gripped it. "I recognized him too. Your grandfather."

"But—" Sam rubbed his forehead. "That can't have been him. I know it *looked* like him, but how can it be him? I've been in a few fights before, but no one has ever hit me that hard. My grandfather is nearly eighty. He's in great shape for a man of his years, but you can't tell me he's strong enough to knock me down like that?"

Dia leaned closer to him. "Your grandfather wouldn't be creeping about in the dark trying to gather hallan from other people."

"You're right." Sam put his arm around her. "We have to find out what's going on."

The streets were empty and silent until they reached the palace. Despite the late hour, everyone inside seemed to be awake. There were extra guards at the gates. Kerem was no longer among them. Instead of allowing Sam and Dia quietly through, the guards seized them.

"What are you doing?" Sam demanded, fighting against them. "We only left a little while ago. You know who I am!"

"King's orders, Your Highness," the guards explained. Their faces looked grim. "We're taking you both to him now. If this is a mistake, you can explain it to him in a moment."

"Of course it's a mistake!" Sam growled.

Dia didn't try to fight the strong grip of a large soldier on either side of her. No one had ever seized her like this before. Terror pooled in her stomach. Their hands around her arms felt as hard as iron, and she couldn't pull away. Whatever they decided to do with her, she wouldn't be able to stop them. Ahead of her, six men held on to Sam. The guards marched them across the courtyard and into the palace. More people, guards, and members of the court gathered around them.

In the throne room, they saw the king, his golden crown splendid atop his white hair. He radiated power and strength. The guards brought them to face him. When the king raised his hand, a silence fell over the crowd.

The king stared at them, wearing an expression of deep sadness that didn't reach his eyes. "How could you do it?" He shook his head in apparent despair. "My own grandson. I hoped it wasn't true, but I know what I saw."

Sam's jaw fell slightly open in shock.

The king continued. "It broke my heart to discover that my own grandson, my heir, has been creeping through the city by night, murdering innocent people."

Sam struggled against the guards. "That's not true. I haven't murdered anyone," he exclaimed.

The king rested his fingertips against his brow and bowed his head. "Perhaps being heir to the throne was not enough power. You studied the very spell used to steal hallan from innocent people."

"No!" Sam protested. "I can't work magic."

The king nodded at one of the guards, and they recognized Kerem. "Bring it." Kerem came forward with something covered in cloth in his hands. "Please, tell everyone where you found it."

Kerem took a deep breath. "It was in the rooms belonging to Prince Samanath and Princess Alladia."

The king's expression was grim. He shook his head sadly. "So, it is true. I feared it might be. Please show all of them."

Kerem nodded and removed the cloth to reveal a spell book. It was the book they'd taken from Adengo's chest. The crowd gasped as the guard flipped through the pages displaying the spells.

The king spoke again. "And this treachery is only the beginning. Unless we stop him, Prince Samanath will destroy our entire kingdom. With a heavy heart," he placed his hand on his chest. "I condemn Samanath Algorian as a traitor to Ischar and sentence him to be banished."

"No!" Dia cried. Banished? It wasn't possible. The king loved Sam. And Sam hadn't done anything wrong. Her stomach tightened with icy dread.

"Grandfather?" Sam pleaded. "I didn't do any of those things. How could you—"

"Silence!" the king roared in a powerful voice. "For your foul crimes, you *and* your accomplice will be banished immediately."

"No! Please!" Sam begged, trying to break away from the guards, his eyes locked on the old man on the throne. "Do whatever you must to me, but not Dia! She never harmed anyone. You can't send her down there. It's too dangerous."

Instead of a kindly old man who smiled and sipped tea with them, an enraged king glared down, his eyes cold and cruel. Dia's heart pounded with terror. Sam struggled madly against the guards.

"Take them down the causeway," the king ordered.

CHAPTER 16

A S THE GUARDS ESCORTED them from the room, Dia's body grew numb with shock. What could she possibly say? The crowd faded into a blur of faces, and the iron hands holding her did not yield. The guards dragged them out of the palace and shoved them through the gates and onto the causeway. It was a narrow path without any barrier between the edge and the empty space behind it. The world spun for a moment when Dia looked down, even though in the dark she couldn't see the dreadful drop. Tears burned in her eyes.

They began the journey along the causeway. Several guards escorted a struggling Sam down the path ahead of her. Abruptly, he stopped fighting them. His protests became suddenly silent and his head hung down. Now the guards were supporting him. What had happened?

"Sam?" she cried. He didn't answer.

The guards took them down, the causeway winding endlessly back and forth across the cliff face at a steep incline. The journey seemed to take forever. Dia's thighs burned with the effort of walking down the hill. As they descended, the air grew noticeably warmer. Eventually, they reached the bottom and a second gate.

The guards removed the cuff inscribed with the royal crest from Sam's arm and pulled the signet ring from his finger. They pulled the gold from Dia's arm as well, and the jewels from her forehead.

She looked up at the guards. Their faces were all familiar. "Please! Don't do this," she pleaded. "We didn't hurt anyone."

The nearest one took a deep breath and looked down at her. When he met her gaze, there was pity in his expression. "I'm sorry, Princess, but this is the king's order."

"But you can't obey King Hashoreth anymore! Something is wrong with him!" Her voice sounded desperate.

The guard shook his head. "I'm sorry."

They unbarred the powerful gates, took Sam and Dia through, and left them standing alone. The gates shut again with a thud. The sound of marching feet faded as the guards retreated back up the causeway, leaving them truly alone. Sam sank to his knees, gripping the back of his neck.

"Sam?" She knelt beside him. "What's wrong?" Beads of sweat stood out on his forehead.

"What happened?" he muttered, looking around in confusion.

"The king banished us, and they took us out of the city. Now we're at the bottom of the causeway."

Sam blinked and looked around again, taking in the gates, shut fast behind them, and the dark jungle only a few paces away. Strange calls and cries echoed in the dark. Sam put his hands on either side of his head, groaning in pain. "I don't know what's wrong, but my head is splitting. You need to *run*, Dia, now! Get as far away from the gate as possible and get off the ground."

"I'm *not* leaving you!" She tried unsuccessfully to pull him to his feet, and he groaned again. The sound of voices came from off in the brush, and her heart pounded in her chest. "Please, Sam."

Dragging with all her strength on his arm, she managed to get him on his feet and lead him toward the shelter of the trees. They plunged into the thick growth, hiding among the foliage, not a moment too soon. The sudden clamor of cries and voices rang out in the clearing, and Dia shrank deeper into the undergrowth, dragging Sam with her. He sank to the ground, and she focused on silencing her rapid breathing, hoping to keep them hidden.

Several dark figures appeared, entering the clearing from different directions. If Sam and Dia had still been standing by the gate, they would have been surrounded.

"Where are they?" a harsh man's voice growled. "Search."

The men dispersed, combing through the surrounding jungle. One passed to one side of where Dia hid, slashing at the undergrowth with a blade that came inches from her face. She held in her scream as their footsteps crashed through the undergrowth in search of them.

Suddenly, rough hands seized her from behind, dragging her out of her hiding place. Now she screamed and struggled wildly, only stopping when a blow crashed against her head. Where was Sam? He would help her. She opened her mouth to cry out for him but then clamped it shut again. They hadn't found him yet, and he was sick, not ready to fight. If she called for him, it would only alert these men that she wasn't alone. They would find him and hurt him.

Thick undergrowth scratched at her as the man dragged her back into the open space. "Here!" he said, holding her. In a moment, several others gathered around.

"What did you find?" someone asked. Another struck a spark and lit a torch. In the sudden flare of light, Dia saw a circle of ragged, dirty men. Their hair was unkempt, their beards untrimmed. Their eyes widened in surprise as they stared at her, and some of them had their mouths open in shock.

"They sent a woman down here?" one of them snickered.

The man with the torch brought the light nearer and gazed down at her. "It's true," he said in disbelief. "They never sent a woman down before." Their eyes roamed over her body in a way that made her want to scream. The man with the torch took another step closer.

His eyes surveyed her face, and he smiled slowly. "So beautiful." He raised his fingers to brush her cheek. "What did you do? You must have made the king *very* angry. I'd like to know what it was." His fingers brushed her shoulder, feeling the fine silk of her gown. "Such a pretty dress. You obviously had money up there." His eyes looked her up and down, slowly, lingering too long on her chest. "My name is Ravi. Who are you?"

Dia stared back at him, not answering.

Ravi grinned. "That's all right. You don't have to talk to me. We'll have plenty of time to get to know each other. I can find out everything I need to know for myself. I'm afraid we'll have to search you. You might be hiding something valuable or maybe carrying a dangerous weapon."

Dia struggled against the hands gripping her. "Don't touch me." She tried not to let her fear show in her voice, but her limbs shook with terror. These men could probably see it easily.

The man laughed again, handing the torch to one of his companions. He put his hand on her shoulder. She shoved it away. He seized her, putting his arms around her and pulling her close. She struggled against him, loathing the feel of his hands on her skin.

"Let me go!" She intended her voice to sound commanding. Instead, it sounded desperate.

The sounds of a fight broke out all around them, blows and cries.

Ravi turned to see what was going on, still gripping Dia. Several of the men already lay on the ground while the others battled a dark shape. He threw down another attacker and stepped forward into the light.

Sam.

His jaw was set, and his dark eyes burned with fury. "Let her go!"

The men didn't obey. They stood frozen, staring at him.

Sam moved suddenly. The man holding the torch dropped it to defend himself, but Sam's fist struck him down. Several of the men had already fled, leaving only the man who held Dia. He released her as Sam attacked him, grabbing the machete in his hands and wrestling the weapon from his grip. As Sam raised the blade, the man followed his friends, fleeing into the jungle.

Sam stood with his blade ready, turning in all directions, looking for enemies. When nothing moved, he turned to her and offered his hand. Dia almost collapsed in relief as his fingers closed around hers reassuringly.

"We have to get away from here," he said. "They'll soon be back."

He released her hand and knelt beside the unconscious ruffians, gathering weapons, a few articles of clothing, anything useful. They didn't have much. Sam rolled everything into a bundle. He threw it over his shoulder, and they hurried away into the dark jungle.

Tightly woven vegetation closed in around them. Branches scratched Dia's arms and caught at her long skirts. It didn't matter. She pushed on, willing herself to take each painful step away from the men who had attacked. After a time, when all was quiet around them except the night sounds of the jungle, birds, insects and strange cries she couldn't begin to identify, they stopped to catch their breath.

"Are you hurt?" Sam asked.

Dia tried to answer, but it came out as a muffled sob. Sam dropped the bundle, pulled her into his arms, and held her. His embrace felt better than anything else in the world. She'd been so frightened back there. If he hadn't come...

"It's all right," he murmured. "We're going to be all right."

She put her arms around him and held on. His sympathy made her cry even harder. "How? How are we going to be all right?"

He laughed grimly. "I guess you have a point."

"We've lost everything, Sam. Our lives are gone. We have no way back. And your grandfather, or something that looks like him, is back there, hurting people, and no one is left to realize there is something terribly wrong with him."

His arm tightened around her, and his hand stroked her hair. "I know we're in trouble now," he admitted. "But we'll find a way. There must be some way to stop him."

"I was really worried about you back there. I think you passed out. You said your head hurt, and you weren't yourself. Do you remember?" Dia drew back and looked up at his familiar features, indistinct in the dim light.

His brows drew together. "No."

"Something is very wrong, Sam. When I found you in your grandfather's study, you didn't look well. What if it gets worse?" She reached up to touch his cheek. "Do you remember what happened in there?"

He shook his head. "No, I... I don't know if there's anything I can do about that, but I will do my best to keep you safe down here. We need to get farther away from the end of the causeway and then find someplace to rest."

Rest? Was he serious? "What about the jaguars and snakes... and..."

"Just stay close to me." Sam picked up his bundle, took her hand, and led her deeper into the jungle.

CHAPTER 17

IN THE DARK OF the jungle night, they wound their way between giant trees, trailing vines, and undergrowth. They walked as quietly as they could. As the noise of their own passage grew less, Dia became aware of the living sounds of the forest. A thousand kinds of creatures made the jungle night a symphony of beauty—and terror.

By the time they'd traveled for a few hours, the night grew old, and exhaustion dragged at Dia. The day had been long and stressful in the extreme, and her whole body cried out for relief. Finally, they climbed into the branches of an enormous tree to rest. As she knew from experience, it wasn't easy to climb in a dress, but she succeeded in the end, her heart pounding from the height. The ground felt a long way away. This wasn't the first time she'd taken refuge in a tree, but at least she wasn't alone this time. She tried to avoid looking down as they settled themselves in the forks of the giant branches.

What were they going to do? Their people had banished them. Their lives were gone. Fear and worry twisted through her, but exhaustion took over, and Dia fell asleep.

When she woke, it was blessedly light again. Sam still slept, although he twitched and muttered in his sleep. Still, he was alive—they were both alive. She took a deep breath. They had survived their first night in the jungle.

Gently, she nudged his shoulder. "Sam?" He started at her touch, but didn't open his eyes. "Are you all right?" She shook him again.

He blinked and put a hand to his head as if it hurt. He groaned and rubbed his other hand over his face. For a long moment, he stared at her. There was something wrong with his eyes. They looked furious and cold, and his expression different from any she'd ever seen on his face before.

"Sam?" Her stomach tightened.

He shook his head again, closing his eyes and rubbing his forehead again. After several long moments, he opened his eyes. This time, they were warm and familiar. "Dia? Where are we?" He looked around at the tree.

"Does your head hurt?" she asked.

He nodded. "Yes, but the pain is fading now. I'll be all right in a moment." He took in a deep breath, sitting up and looking around. "I remember now. We fought a band of outcasts, and we slept in this tree."

She smiled in relief, leaning back against the tree trunk. He seemed himself again. "That's right. You were wonderful. I thought they were going to..." Her voice trailed off before she finished her sentence. She didn't even want to think about what those men would have done to her.

"I won't let anyone hurt you," he assured her.

His promise warmed her heart. She couldn't imagine a more caring husband. With no hesitation, he'd taken on a whole gang of criminals for her. She couldn't even find words to express how grateful she was to have him beside her, but what were they going to do here in the jungle?

"If we don't find a way home, how are we going to help the people back in Kulin?" Dia couldn't help but remember Carrina and all the sick people.

Sam nodded, taking another deep breath. "Whatever we saw, that thing wasn't my grandfather. I'm sure of it. Adengo's notes described the Shadaroc changing its appearance." Sam's expression was grim, his jaw tight. "I think it killed him."

"Oh, Sam!" She pulled him close. Tears ran down her face. "I'm so sorry."

"He was the last living person who loved me." Sam's voice sounded choked, and he wrapped his arms around her. "Except for you. Please don't leave me. Dia, you're all I have left."

She held him tightly. "You're everything to me." Whatever the challenges of their situation, they would endure them together. "I love you. I'll never leave you."

He held her for a while before pulling back. "We need a plan to go back and fight the Shadaroc, but we aren't ready to take that on yet. If we die down here, there's nothing we can do for our people."

"Do you think Adengo might still be alive?" Dia looked around at the trackless growth around them.

"I don't know," Sam said. "What would I say to him if we found him? Hello, Uncle, you were banished for murdering my parents. How have you been?"

Dia shivered at the thought.

"Our first plan should be to move farther away from the end of the causeway and those men who attacked us," Sam decided.

It wasn't much of a plan, but it was a start. They climbed down to the forest floor and assessed their situation. Sam had collected a machete, two knives, and a water skin. He laid out a few pieces of ragged, dirty clothing. "I'm sorry. I don't have anything better to offer." He looked at her silk dress, already significantly the worse for wear. "Your gown is lovely, my dear, but a little conspicuous down here."

"And difficult to walk in," Dia added, eyeing the scavenged clothes. Now was not the time to be picky. In the past, she'd been privileged to wear beautiful dresses, but her previous adventures in the woods had quickly taught her exactly how impractical they were in the wilderness. As much as she wanted to look beautiful for Sam, survival was far more important. She sorted through her options and picked out the least offensive. Sam handed her a belt with one of the stolen knives in a sheath attached to it.

She raised her chin to meet his eyes. "I don't know how to use it."

"It's only for... emergencies," he explained. "I'll show you a few things later when we have a moment."

She nodded, swallowing hard. The idea that Sam would teach her how to use a weapon had never crossed her mind before. For now, he was right. They needed to get moving.

"Help me?" She turned away from him, and he began to undo the long row of buttons up her back. Her breath hitched at the familiar touch of his fingers against her skin, and she turned to kiss him.

For a moment, all her fears faded as she focused on the way his mouth moved against hers. He deepened the kiss for a moment before he broke it and pulled back.

"I don't want to stop." One side of his mouth turned up in a smile. "But I need to get you somewhere safe."

She didn't want him to stop, either, but he was right. She nodded and turned so he could finish the buttons.

Dia removed the gown and dressed in the stolen clothing, using the belt to hold up trousers much too large. Her shoes weren't well suited to the woods, but they would have to do. She rolled up the bottoms of the pants so they wouldn't drag on the ground. The sleeveless tunic hung almost to her knees. She must look ridiculous.

Sam switched his fine tunic for a ragged one. In the old clothing, he no longer looked like a prince. He looked like a tall young man who could have been anyone. They collected their discarded clothing and other belongings and added them to the bundle. Sam slung it over his shoulder, and they started off through the jungle.

Between the giant trees, their smaller descendants battled for space, and ferns and vines crowded between everything else. Occasional game trails wound through, and they followed them as often as they could. The day brightened as they walked, the morning mist burning off as the day grew hot. Insects buzzed, and the sounds of animals and birds surrounded them.

Clouds gathered as they walked. A clap of thunder provided the only warning before rain poured down, quickly turning the ground to mud and making it difficult to walk. They took shelter beneath a tree with leaves so wide they barely allowed any of the droplets through. Dia sat beside Sam, her arms wrapped around her knees. Rain soaked her to the skin, and mud coated her feet. She stared out into the jungle.

After a while, the rain stopped, leaving the leaves decorated with glistening drops. Getting to their feet, they went on. They walked for hours, and Dia's empty stomach growled. Sam must have been hungry, too. He stopped, turning aside to a tree laden with pale green fruit. "I know these from when I was here before, and we have one in the conservatory." He picked a fruit and offered it to her before taking one himself and biting into it. "There are so many kinds of plants down here. I know a few more that can be eaten, and a few that are good for healing, and a few that are poison."

She smiled. "You told me to be careful of all the plants unless I know what they are."

He returned her smile. "That's right."

Other than the potted plants back at the palace, Dia had never seen any of the vegetation that grew here. She took a tentative bite of the fruit. It was slightly sweet, but also starchy, with a large pit in its middle. She nibbled the rest around the pit and then reached for another, following Sam's lead in eating several, grateful not to be so hungry anymore.

After they finished, they walked around and found trees that had dropped nuts, perfect to gather and fill their pockets for later. Sam had taken a waterskin from their attackers that they filled along their way at a spring of fresh, cold water coming from the bottom of the cliff.

"This is good water," Sam said, refilling their supply. "The springs coming down from above are good to drink. Just don't gather water from out there. Often, it's not very clean." He gestured toward the sea of trees.

They drank again and moved on. A troop of chattering monkeys passed overhead, moving through the treetops. Once, a large snake slithered past them. Dia repressed a shriek as she jumped away from it, clinging to Sam. "I hate snakes," she confessed.

He held her. "You're shaking. I guess you like them even less than you like rats."

She couldn't help but smile. "I'm sorry I'm not braver." Her head rested against his chest, and his strong arms comforted her.

"You don't give yourself enough credit. You're very brave."

As the sun sank behind the plateau, they halted to watch it. Soon, darkness would fall. They needed to find a safe place to rest. Abruptly, Sam dropped her hand he'd been holding and stepped away. She looked up to see his expression completely changed. He looked angry, his eyes hard and cold. Fear washed over Dia, and she involuntarily stepped back.

"What's wrong, Sam?"

He didn't answer. Though he looked right at her, he didn't appear to recognize her. He gazed at her as if he were a completely different person, someone who hated her. Dia took another step away. His eyes turned to something out in the jungle that she couldn't see. He took several steps as if he were going to leave. In the middle of a step, he froze, sinking to his knees, with one hand on the back of his neck. He groaned.

Dia rushed to him, kneeling beside him. His eyes were closed, his skin pale and clammy. "Please tell me what's wrong!" she pleaded.

He blinked at her, pain in his eyes. "Head hurts," he mumbled.

"What can I do?" There had to be some way to help him.

He shook his head, closing his eyes again. After a few moments, he opened his eyes and appeared to see her now. "Dia?" he appeared confused. "What happened?"

"You... were angry. You looked as if you were going to walk away into the jungle." She touched his forehead. Some color had returned to his face now.

"What?" he asked. "I don't remember being angry."

"You're all right now." Relief flooded through her. "Come and have a drink of water and something to eat." They sat together at the base of a tree and used rocks to crack open the nuts they had gathered.

As night fell, they climbed into the tree branches. Taking refuge in high places was inevitable in the jungle. Without the aid of complete exhaustion and minimal rest the night before, Dia might never have slept. Despite her discomfort, her eyes closed.

Hours later, she lifted her head. Jungle sounds had awakened her. A large body made a slight sound as it brushed through the small branches. Her insides tightened in terror, and she sat up on the branch.

"Sam!" she hissed, shaking him. "Wake up, something is coming."

He didn't respond. She shook him again. Finally, he stirred, one hand rubbing his head. He opened his eyes and looked up at her.

"There's something out there, coming closer!" She pointed out into the dark, where a pair of eyes shone in the dark.

"Why did you do it?" he demanded.

"Do what?" Shock raced through her. He'd never spoken to her like that, his tone hard and angry. She couldn't imagine what he was talking about.

"Why are you working against me? Every time I turn around, I find you trying to stop me." His voice was sharp, and he stared into her eyes, his anger focused on her.

Her heart pounded wildly. "No! I've never tried to stop you! Please turn around. Something is out there in the trees." She pointed into the branches behind him.

On the branch, he sat up slowly, his eyes never leaving her. "Did you think I wouldn't find out it was you? That you would get away with it?"

Fear jolted through her. How could she get him to return to himself? She responded as well as she could. "No, Sam, whatever it was, I'm sorry!"

He lunged forward, seizing the front of her shirt and dragging her to face him. "You think that saying sorry will make this go away?"

"Please stop, Sam! It's Dia—you don't know what you're saying!"

The fury on his face terrified her. She'd never seen him with such hatred and violence in his expression, particularly never directed at her. He'd never even been angry at her. It was one of the things she loved most about him, the way he was so careful with her feelings.

She tried to pull away from him, but his grip held her firmly.

"I'll make you pay for working against me!" he yelled.

"Sam! Please! I'll do whatever you want."

Over his shoulder, the eyes crept closer. "Sam! Behind you—please wake up!"

CHAPTER 18

DESPITE DIA'S DESPERATE WARNING, Sam didn't even glance at the dark jungle behind him. "Don't try to distract me!"

The eyes edged closer. A shaft of moonlight illuminated the long, feline body of a jaguar.

"Sam, please wake up!" Her voice was tight with desperation and her breath came in gasps.

"I. Am. Awake." He held her by both arms and shook her roughly.

With a snarl, the cat sprang. As its claws struck him, Sam's body jerked, and he released Dia. She lunged forward, grabbing the hilt of the machete fastened across his back and pulling it free. He yelled as the cat dragged him along the branch. Reaching over him, Dia swung the blade straight at the eyes. She felt the weapon strike fur, and the cat hissed angrily, releasing Sam and backing up slightly.

Dia held out the blade in her shaking hand.

The jaguar advanced. Dia's heart pounded wildly as she lifted the blade. The big cat was no more than a vague shape, blacker than the night except for a glimmer of moonlight here and there on its sleek coat.

It slashed at her with sharp claws, and she thrust her blade at it. Sam lay flat on the tree limb between them. If she backed away, it would take him. Snarling, it attacked again. Claws raked her arm, leaving lines of hot pain behind, but she refused to back down. She struck a harder blow, and the animal yelped in pain and retreated. She watched it for a long breathless moment, until, with a final snarl, it turned and slunk away.

The night grew quiet again, except for the usual sounds of the jungle. Dia sat down on the limb, shaking all over. She almost dropped the machete. If she did, what would she do if something else came along? She needed to keep the weapon close. Choosing a safe place between the limbs where it couldn't fall, she set it down.

Sam lay across the branch. He still muttered, restlessly trying to move. Already, he was off balance, and if he moved much more, he would fall. Resolutely not looking at the black depths below, Dia edged closer and tugged at him. He was so heavy, and he wasn't helping at all. Inch by inch, she dragged him to safety.

Muttering angrily, he yelled and struck out. His knuckles met her cheekbone, knocking her back against the tree trunk. For a moment, she couldn't see. She slumped against the rough bark, holding her throbbing cheek.

Her eyes welled with tears. Sam had hit her. The pain of an attack from the person she trusted most was worse than the pain in her face.

Dia retreated as far as she could along her branch. Wearily, she watched the bits of moon between the trees move slowly across the sky, while Sam lay where he was. She waited in the dark, searching the jungle for any sign of danger, and watching Sam. Gradually, her racing heart slowed, and the adrenaline faded, leaving her drained and shivering. Slow hours passed before the light of dawn filtered down through the leaves. In the new light, she looked at Sam. He lay utterly still now, exactly where he'd been. All across his back, blood soaked the torn fabric of his tunic. It looked bad. She wanted to go to him and tend his injuries, except... what if he hit her again?

She remained where she was, watching him warily, as he slowly opened his eyes and blinked. Finally, he moved his head a little and looked up at her.

"Dia?" he murmured. "Are you all right? What happened?"

It was Sam. Really him. She began to cry in sheer relief.

"What's wrong? What's the matter?" He tried to get up and lay back with a groan.

She wiped her eyes. "Stay still, you're hurt."

"I don't remember what happened." He looked up at her. "But you're hurt too." He pointed toward the blood on her forearm. "Was it like before?" His expression was anguished. "I said and did things without realizing where I was or what was happening?"

Dia stared back at him, not wanting to tell him what had happened.

"You have to tell me." He met her eyes directly.

When she still didn't speak, a look of horror grew on his face. His eyes locked on her cheek.

She could feel it swelling.

"I can see it in your eyes," Sam said. "It's my fault you're hurt. Did I... hit you?"

She gave a tiny nod.

Sam closed his eyes, looking pained. "Dearest, can you ever forgive me? I'm so sorry. I deserve to be beaten for doing it."

More tears fell down her cheeks. "I wouldn't have come near you until you felt better, but you were slipping off the branch. I had to keep you from falling. It wasn't your fault. You didn't know what you were doing."

He shook his head. "That's no excuse!"

She sniffed and wiped her eyes. "Let me see your back. I would have done something for it last night, but I needed light, and I was afraid... afraid to touch you."

Pain filled his eyes at her words. It didn't seem fair to blame him for something he hadn't done intentionally and didn't remember doing. They needed to learn the reason for his behavior. They needed a solution. He wouldn't choose to act like that on his own. The sadness on his face twisted her heart.

"I'm sure it will be fine. It's no more than I deserve."

She wiped her eyes again. "You don't deserve it! Whatever that thing is that looks like the king... he *did* something to you. It's not your fault."

Very slowly, Sam sat up, his jaw clenched, his expression tight with pain. They climbed down, Sam moving slowly and stiffly. When they reached the ground, they walked a short distance until they found another small spring. Sam sat down on a rock, and she helped him pull off his tattered shirt. Her stomach rolled as she got a clear view of the long gashes. One set of claw marks began at his shoulder and raked down his back. The other began just above his waist, curving inward, ending just before it reached his spine.

She couldn't stop the tears that filled her eyes as she cleaned the cuts. He didn't say much, but his jaw clenched, and his hands balled into fists. When she finished, he pointed out a shrub with thick fleshy leaves.

"Pick some of those. Squeeze the juice onto the cuts. It will help prevent infection. Injuries are dangerous down here."

Dia picked several large handfuls. The leaves had a strong scent that reminded her of the lemons from the little tree growing among the other tropical plants back at the palace. She set them on the rock beside Sam.

"They have a strong smell," she broke one and held it out to him.

He wrinkled his nose as he sniffed. "That's the one."

She washed the cuts on her arm first and dripped some of the juice onto one of them. It burned like fire, and Dia held back a yell, thankful that the fierce pain faded after a moment, and she could breathe again. What about the rest of the cuts? It had to be done. She used her knife to slice the underskirt of her court dress into strips for bandages.

"Can you help me?" She held several of the leaves out to Sam.

He took them, and she gritted her teeth and held out her arm. He crushed the leaves and dripped the liquid into the cuts. More fiery pain exploded through her arm. She didn't breathe and for a moment she couldn't think. Then it passed, and Sam wrapped the bandage and tied the ends together.

"Does it sting?"

She gulped in several deep breaths. "So much!"

He sighed. "Why didn't you tell me before I did that?"

"And what good would that have done?" She raised one eyebrow. "I'm done. Now it's your turn."

The whole process took a long time. She had to go back to the shrub to refill her supply twice. She could see the muscles in his jaw clench as she applied the liquid. It broke her heart to hurt him, but she had to do it.

They walked a long way that day. By sunset, Dia was so exhausted that she could barely put one foot in front of the other. They stopped and ate fruit and cracked nuts on the rocks as evening settled over the jungle. When they'd finished eating, they climbed into the branches—their new nightly routine. Dia watched Sam, alert for any sign of a change in mood. He'd seemed entirely himself all day, smiling at her and holding back branches so she could pass, but what would happen during the night?

For now, they settled into the forks of a giant tree. It was a blessing to rest, but Dia was afraid that if she fell asleep, she'd wake up to find that *other* Sam. Despite her fears, exhaustion took her, and she dozed.

She startled awake with a gasp when she heard the angry snarl of a big cat. Where was the machete? As she felt around herself blindly, she saw the dark outline of Sam raise the weapon. He struck hard at the animal and it yipped in pain. He jerked back to escape its slashing claws and struck it again with the blade. It snarled and slunk away, disappearing between the branches. He turned back to her, the weapon still in his hand.

Was Sam himself? Her eyes locked on the blade and her heart pounded wildly in her chest.

He only lowered it with a smile she could barely see in the dim light.

"I'm sorry to wake you like that." He settled back down beside her. "It's gone now. Hopefully, we can get some rest."

"Thank you," she murmured, leaning her head against his shoulder. How much time did they have before his awareness slipped away again?

The night passed with no further excitement, but it was difficult to sleep after everything that had happened. Eventually, the sun rose, shining into the mist that lay over the forest. Birds and monkeys called in the branches. Sam and Dia climbed down from the tree. After a few moments search, they found water and fruit. Dia washed her face, and the cold liquid refreshed her. It was a new day. Sam was beside her. Maybe the worst of his strange condition was behind them.

With the morning sun quickly growing hot above them, they set off through the trees. They'd been traveling for a while when Sam suddenly stopped. He stood frozen in the middle of the game trail they'd been following.

"I'm going the wrong way," he announced suddenly. "I have to go back." He turned around, passing her without a glance, and headed back the way they had come.

Dia ran after him and put a hand on his arm. "Please stop."

He threw her hand off, and turned to face her, fury in his eyes. "There's a reason you don't want me going back there, isn't there? You're trying to stop my plans."

He had lost control again. What would he do next? She took a step back.

He followed her, his eyes never leaving hers. "You should never have gotten involved if you didn't plan to finish this."

Maybe it was better to go along. "I will finish it," she said firmly. "We will go back and take care of it."

He nodded, his jaw tight. "You'd better. This was your responsibility, and you have to pay for what you did." He took another menacing step toward her. She moved away, but he followed, seizing her arm. "This was your plan all along, wasn't it? You planned to sell me out."

"No!" she protested. "That's not how it was at all, please listen."

"I've heard enough lies!" He raised his fist and tried to hit her, but this time, she saw it coming and twisted violently to avoid the blow and escape his grip.

Once free, she bolted away.

"Get back here!" he snarled.

Dia ran. What else could she do? Sam followed. He was faster. Her heart pounded and her breath came in gasps. A glance over her shoulder confirmed he still pursued. He would catch up. If only he'd come to himself before something awful happened.

Her flight came to a sudden stop as she rounded a large tree and collided with a man. Though she'd never seen him in the daylight before, his face was familiar. He was one of the men who had surrounded them at the bottom of the causeway. Ravi.

CHAPTER 19

A	s Dia attempted to scramble away, Ravi caught and held her. "You!" He recognized her, and he wasn't alone. A group of men followed him.

By the time he realized that she'd been running thoughtlessly through the jungle for a reason, Sam was there. She ducked to one side as he hit the man holding her. Ravi stumbled back, losing his grip and allowing her to slip free. The other men tried to grab Sam, but that only made him angrier. He whipped out the machete and attacked them. A few of them drew weapons to block his blows. Attacking with insane strength, he took two of them down quickly. The rest fled.

From behind a tree, Dia watched him as he turned in all directions, looking for someone else to attack. She kept herself out of his sight. At last, he stood still, breathing hard. His eyes glittered with malice that she had never seen in him before.

Dia remained still and hidden until Sam rubbed his forehead and staggered away in the direction they had originally been going. Slipping silently through the trees, Dia followed him, taking care to stay out of sight. She saw no further sign of the outcasts. Sam went on for a long time, occasionally slashing at bushes with his machete.

How long would it last? There must be some way to wake him up, to bring him back to himself. He came out of the trees into an open area. A wide, slow-flowing river crossed their path. Already Sam stood on the rocky shore. The far side was a dense wall of jungle with giant trees spreading roots down into the water. Dia didn't want to go out into the open where she would be visible to anyone passing by, but she couldn't let Sam out of her sight. She loved him. He was the last, most important piece of her life remaining, and there had to be a way to cure him.

Sam stepped into the river, not even appearing to realize what he was doing. He moved deeper until the water reached his waist. Dia saw a ripple on the surface near him. Something was there, hiding, invisible beneath the surface. Her focus flew back to Sam. He was holding his head now, the machete still in one hand. He cried out in agony, his entire body stiffening.

Ignoring any potential danger, Dia ran out onto the open bank. "Dia!" Sam cried.

Suddenly his body lurched, and he fell into the water, disappearing beneath the surface. Horrified, Dia saw the coils of a huge snake break the surface. The enormous reptile had Sam.

She drew her knife and plunged into the water, striking at the thick, reptilian coils with her blade. The water swirled and bubbled. The top half of Sam reappeared, wrapped in a snake as thick as a tree trunk. He reached an arm out to her and she seized his hand, pulling with all her might. She chopped at the snake again and blood turned the water red, but it didn't release him. Dia refused to let go of Sam's hand, even as the snake dragged them both under.

Dia splashed and fought, feeling the smooth powerful coils of the snake moving through the water. Clawing her way back to the surface, she gulped in a breath. She still clutched Sam's hand, but his grip felt looser now. No part of him was visible except his arm. Desperately, she hacked at the snake with her knife.

"Let him go!" she demanded, striking it over and over again.

The snake rolled again, dragging her from her feet and beneath the water. She stabbed at it a few more times, and kicked, trying to find her way back out into the air. At last, she got her feet beneath her and stood, breaking the surface, coughing and gasping. Another hand grasped Sam's arm alongside hers, and she saw a young man beside her. He took his own chop at the coils with his machete and yanked on Sam's arm. The snake's grip loosened, and Sam's head and shoulders came into view.

After one last blow from the machete, the snake retreated, slipping soundlessly away into the murky water. The man dragged Sam back onto the bank, lifting him and pounding on his back. Water ran from Sam's mouth, and when the man set him down, he lay on the ground motionless. Were they too late?

She refused to even think it. Dropping to the ground beside Sam, she shook him. "Breathe!" she demanded. He didn't respond. "Sam!" She bent over him, placing her lips against his and breathing air into his lungs. She tried several times while he remained motionless. "No, you can't die. You can't."

She placed her hands against his chest. If only she could give him some of her own life energy. She would gladly spend it to help him. Her energy surrounded her and she willed it to flow from herself through her hands into him. The palms of her hands felt warm where they contacted his body.

"Live," she ordered. "Breathe!"

For an agonizing moment nothing happened. Then Sam coughed and gagged.

Dia clutched him, sobbing in relief. She clung to him as he cleared his lungs. He was breathing. He was alive. She searched his face. "Is it you again?" His eyes, his expression, everything was familiar. He stared up at her in confusion.

She turned to see the young man who had helped them. "Thank you!"

He nodded in acknowledgement. "I'm not sure a girl who attacks a snake that size with that little knife needs my help." He nodded to the weapon which now lay in the shallow water. He didn't appear to realize how terrified Dia had been. Only her fear for Sam had driven her to attack.

"I had to." She waded in to retrieve the knife and replaced it in the sheath at her belt.

The man still watched her in surprise. He wore ragged trousers, worn boots, and was shirtless, his sun browned skin indicating that was common for him. A small bag hung across his back, and a knife and machete hung from his belt. He was nearly as tall as Sam, with chestnut brown hair reaching his shoulders and a short beard. Was he one of the criminals banished to the jungle? If he was, he hadn't harmed either of them when he had the opportunity. He looked young, a few years younger than Dia, but he obviously knew how to handle himself in the jungle. How had he come to be here? Could he have been banished as a child? Why?

"I'm very grateful that you did, but why would you help us?" she asked.

The young man nodded toward the river. "I saw the snake."

"The only people we've met down here have tried to attack us." She needed to explain that it felt dangerous to trust him, in spite of the aid he'd given them. Dia studied his face. There was something familiar about his features.

"I understand." He met her eyes frankly. "Were you just sent down?" He glanced toward the cliff wall, barely visible through the trees.

She nodded.

"You should know, there aren't many women down here, and you'll need to watch yourself. Don't go anywhere alone. Most of the men won't care if they harm you." His face flushed slightly beneath the tan.

She shuddered at the memory of the outcasts they had encountered. "We've already met some of them."

He rubbed his forehead. "They gather at the bottom of the causeway if they see the lights as they bring someone down. Most people wait right by the gate and don't last an hour."

Dia shivered. She and Sam had been luckier than she realized. Kneeling beside Sam, she helped him sit up. "How do you feel?"

"Much better than I would as a snake's dinner." He smiled slightly. "Thank you both for saving my life." He looked at the man. Getting to his feet, he held out his hand. "I'm Sam. Dia is my wife."

"Kael," the young man replied. After hesitating a moment, he took the offered hand and shook it. He looked at Sam. "Well, what did you do? Everyone has some sort of story of why they ended up down here. They were framed, or it was all a mistake. Something."

"We're not criminals," Sam said firmly, meeting Kael's eyes. "But we are in trouble. And so is everyone we left behind up on the plateau. A dark sorcerer has disguised himself as the king. He sent us down here."

"He even banished her?" Kael glanced toward Dia. "Even knowing what would probably happen to her down here?"

Sam nodded. "I begged him not to, but he didn't listen."

"Is he a shape shifter?"

"A Shadaroc," Sam said.

Kael stared at them with raised eyebrows. "If that's true, we have a big problem on our hands, even down here. Are you certain? Did you see the giant bird?"

Sam nodded.

Dia met Kael's gaze without looking away. "It had wolves following it. And it was too big to be anything else."

"We have seen it here too," Kael said. "A few weeks ago, it flew down into the jungle. When I went to the place where I saw it land, I found three men dead, not a mark on their bodies, no blood. They were just dead." He took a long deep breath. "I hoped it wouldn't come back. This is serious news. I must tell my father. He's the leader of the village, and he doesn't allow just anyone inside. From time-to-time, others of the outcasts come to us claiming to have a change of heart and asking for our friendship."

"And?" Sam asked.

"Some of them prove themselves to us and become accepted. Others only seek to betray us."

"Would you be willing to give us the opportunity to prove ourselves?" Sam asked.

Kael surveyed them again. He glanced at Dia.

"It would mean so much to us," Dia said. "You've already aided us, but we still need help. Sam isn't well."

Kael stared at Sam, scanning him for any sign of illness.

Dia looked up at Sam, not wanting to say it in front of him, but what else could she do? If Kael agreed to help them, she had to warn him. Sam was very dangerous at times. "Sometimes he's all right, but other times not. It's been growing worse. He says and does things he would never normally do. He doesn't know where he is or what's happening around him."

Pain filled Sam's eyes. He turned to Kael. "I only meant to protect her, but sometimes I can't." He bowed his head, shame in his expression. "And it's worse than that. I hit her."

Kael's eyes flashed to the bruise on Dia's face. A quick spark of anger crossed his expression.

Sam looked at Dia now, his eyes pleading. "I didn't mean to. I love her, and I would never intentionally hurt her. I don't remember doing it."

Tears welled in Dia's eyes, and she reached up to touch his face. "It's not your fault. There must be a way to help."

"My father is a skilled healer," Kael said. "Maybe he knows of a cure. I will take you to him."

"Thank you! We would be very grateful," Dia exclaimed. Maybe there was hope that Sam would recover in time.

They followed Kael off into the jungle. He moved swiftly and quietly, his brown skin blending into his surroundings. Dia tried to move like he did, slipping easily between the branches and vines.

For hours, they walked until the sun slid down into the west. Dia wondered if they would find a safe place to spend the night before darkness fell. She watched Sam closely, alert for any sign of another bad spell. For now, he walked beside her, holding her hand, and helping her over fallen logs and rocks.

But she had learned that it couldn't last.

The change was sudden.

It was worse this time. Sam stood right beside her when he changed. One minute, he looked as he always had, her husband, her soulmate, his loving smile shining toward her. Then, his eyes hardened and his expression became one of hatred. His fingers tightened around hers in a savage grip.

"I knew it!" he snarled, jerking her toward him. "I know what you've done." He seized the knife at her belt and raised it.

Dia screamed.

Kael grabbed Sam's wrist with both hands. They struggled and fought. Eventually, Kael managed to force the knife out of Sam's hand, and it fell to the ground.

"Get the knife," Kael instructed. She darted forward to pick it up.

Sam yelled and fought. They rolled on the ground. In this state, it seemed likely that Sam would overpower Kael and hurt him. If he got free, he would come after her or wander alone in the jungle. It was already getting dark. He might not even survive the night in his condition.

So, Dia crept up behind them as they fought and hit Sam on the head with a rock. She struck him hard enough that his body went slack and crumpled to the forest floor, but he still breathed. Bursting into tears, she sank to the ground beside him.

CHAPTER 20

KAEL DISENTANGLED HIMSELF FROM Sam's inert body, grabbed his bag, and pulled out a length of rope. He tied Sam's hands behind him. When it was done, he sank back to the ground, breathing hard.

"Was he like this before?"

She nodded, wiping her eyes.

"How are you still alive?" He stared at her with wide eyes.

"He never tried to stab me before. This was the first time..." She was overcome by the memory of the terror she'd felt and the terrible purpose in Sam's eyes. He would have done it. She would have been dead, and he wouldn't even know what he'd done. She realized she was shaking all over. Staring down at the rock still in her hand, she dropped it with a gasp. "How badly did I hurt him?" Sam's body lay limp on the jungle floor. She knelt beside him and touched his face. His skin still felt warm, but she could see blood in his hair. "I'm so sorry, Sam."

She turned to Kael. "I had to hit him. Otherwise, he might have hurt us and then wandered the jungle until another jaguar found him."

Kael's eyebrows shot up. "You're apologizing to *him*? He pulled a knife on you. Don't you think he's the one who should be apologizing to you?"

Tears spilled from her eyes. "I know. But he was never like this before. I know he loves me. Will he be all right?"

"I'm sure his head will hurt," Kael said, "but I think he'll be all right. Did he hurt you?"

Her hand throbbed where he had gripped it too hard, but she would be fine. She shook her head.

"Good. If we hurry, we can reach one of our outposts. We'll be safe there for the night, and it's not far away." Kael rigged a crude stretcher from tree branches and rolled Sam onto it. He looked at Dia, assessing her strength. "Can you lift one end? Maybe his feet will be lighter."

She nodded and took up her end. By the time Kael lifted his side, Sam felt dreadfully heavy. Still, she had to do this. They needed to get Sam somewhere safe. He groaned from the stretcher, and she almost stopped to go to him, but they couldn't delay now. They had to reach safety before it got any darker.

Branches and tangled undergrowth blocked their path, and Dia tripped constantly as Kael's longer stride pulled her forward. Sam had begun to move on the stretcher, twitching and jerking, pulling at the ropes binding him.

Exhaustion swept over Dia in waves. She couldn't remember the last time she'd really slept, and Sam was so heavy. Her arms and shoulders burned, and her back ached. But she continued on, her one thought that she must get Sam to safety.

Blackness had descended on the jungle when Kael finally stopped in front of her. She almost lost her balance at the sudden halt. She couldn't see anything. The shadowy form of another person appeared beside her. Dia jumped and almost shrieked in fright, but the newcomer only had a brief whispered conversation with Kael.

"This is Altan," Kael explained. "He's one of our men. He'll help us get to the outpost."

Dia wanted to collapse in relief. When Altan took over carrying Dia's end of the stretcher, she was beyond grateful. She rubbed her aching arms and shoulders as they walked.

Moving more quickly now, they soon came to a tall rocky outcropping looming out of the dark jungle. She saw a faint glimmer of light. As they got closer, she realized it was torchlight coming out of a cavern in the black cliff face. It lit an irregular passageway. Without the light, she might never have dared enter the cave, but Kael and Altan didn't hesitate as they went in, and she followed them. They passed a gate made of thick stalks of bamboo lashed into a lattice. A man guarded the entrance and closed the barrier securely after they passed.

Kael nodded toward the crude gate. "It keeps the jaguars out."

The passageway twisted and turned until they came out into a spacious cavern. There were a few other men there, some sitting, some lying on rough pallets. Kael and Altan set Sam down.

"What are we going to do with him?" Kael asked. The other men came and gathered around, looking down at Sam. Dia went and knelt beside him.

Sam opened his eyes and struggled against the ropes. His eyes burned with fury. "Let me go!" he snarled.

Dia backed away to a safe distance.

He thrashed around and then began to get up. Kael pushed him back.

"No!" Sam yelled.

Kael held his legs down. "Quick, tie his ankles." The others rushed to obey.

"I'll pay you back for this," Sam raved. "I'll kill you. You're all in on it, but I know who started it." He looked straight at Dia. Terror pooled in her belly.

"Do you know what's wrong with him?" Kael asked.

"No," she cried. "He was in a room with the sorcerer. When I found him, he was unconscious. I finally woke him up, but he looked sick. Since then, sometimes he's all right, and sometimes he's like this."

Kael came to stand beside Dia and put a comforting hand on her shoulder. "Hopefully, my father will know how to help him."

She looked up at him. It was kind of him to help since they had been strangers before today. He had stepped in, just as Sam had that rainy night outside Kulin when they had met.

Kael's expression was kind, and something in his face reminded her of Sam. That was why she'd thought his face looked familiar.

"Do you think your father will be willing to try?" There had to be a way to return Sam to his right mind. She wanted the man she'd fallen in love with back. The man who was unfailingly kind to her.

"He will do what he can," Kael said, staring toward Sam, who continued raving. The others had gone back to their places, leaving him alone in the middle of the cavern. He turned to look at Dia. "How did you make it this far through the jungle with him?" His eyes went to the bandage around her forearm.

Dia's memory flew back to the experience with the jaguar that had clawed Sam and earlier today with the snake.

"You must have had a terrible time." Kael's voice held concern.

Dia's eyes suddenly filled with tears. She had been terrified, over and over again. She'd been attacked, afraid, hungry, dirty, and she'd lost the help of the man she loved. "I did," she admitted. "I sincerely appreciate your help today, Kael."

His expression showed embarrassment at her thanks. "Get some rest. I'll keep an eye on him for now." He showed her a woven mat. "There's not much down here to make blankets out of, but it's never very cold, so we don't worry too much."

"It will be wonderful to just sleep," she said sincerely.

This was a huge improvement over sleeping in trees, and the gate at the mouth of the cavern would keep predators out. Kael had promised to watch over Sam. Dia lay down on the mat and sank immediately into exhausted slumber.

Hours later, she woke to hear Sam's voice.

"Dia?"

She blinked, opening her eyes to see a dim light coming into the cave from a small high opening. She sat up, ignoring the protests of abused muscles and hurried to his side. "I'm here, Sam. It's all right."

"I can't move."

"We had to tie you. You were trying to attack us."

"I'm sorry. I'm so sorry. Please tell me I didn't hurt you?" Regret was plain in his voice and expression.

She wouldn't tell him he'd tried to. "I'm all right."

He looked around the dim cavern. "Where are we? Is Kael still with us?"

"Yes. We're taking you to a healer, and we hope he can help you." She placed a comforting hand on his arm.

"I don't deserve your concern after what I've done." He closed his eyes and shook his head.

"It's not your fault. You're sick. I hope you'll be better soon. For now, we'll do what we can to help. You must be hungry and thirsty."

The other men in the cave were stirring by then, and Kael came over. Sam looked up at him. "Thank you for what you did yesterday."

Kael nodded and turned to Dia. "How long?"

She stared back in confusion. "What?"

He gazed at Sam appraisingly. "How long do we have until he goes crazy again?"

Dia shook her head. "There's no way to tell exactly. Several hours?"

Kael looked at Sam's bound hands and feet. "But we can let him stretch a little, at least?"

A quiver of fear twisted her middle. They needed to take care of Sam, but each attack made her more wary. After a moment, she nodded.

Kael untied the ropes, and Sam sat up, rubbing his wrists. He had fresh blood oozing from his back. Dia's bandages had not survived the encounter with the snake. Sam got to his feet, and Kael offered him water and food, which he accepted gratefully.

When he'd eaten, Kael led Sam outside for a moment of privacy. They returned, Sam still rubbing stiff muscles. He pulled off his shirt and allowed Dia to clean the cuts. Kael handed her a handful of leaves from the shrub rumored to prevent infection. She reapplied the sap to Sam's injuries.

When they had finished, Sam sighed. "That's so much better. Thank you."

Kael nodded. "We need to get to my father. Can you walk?"

Sam nodded. "Yes, but you should tie my hands again. I don't know how long I will last."

Kael tied Sam's hands, and they left the cave. Altan came with them. He was a quiet man, with dark hair just beginning to gray. He rarely spoke, just offered his assistance when they needed it. They walked for half the morning before the shift in Sam happened again. Dia watched helplessly as he yelled and tried to attack them, even with his hands tied. It took both Kael and Altan to tackle and secure him.

They found no way to get Sam to cooperate. Their only option was to keep him securely bound, and carry him along, struggling and raving. Progress was difficult like that. Even with the two men doing most of the lifting, sweating with the effort, Dia rapidly grew exhausted. When they paused to rest, Dia went a safe distance from Sam and sat down. She loved her husband, but she wasn't sure how much more she could endure.

"Are you all right?" Kael came to sit beside her.

She laughed bitterly. "This whole thing is so ridiculous. We got married five weeks ago. And it was wonderful. Now here we are wandering the jungle with Sam tied up. I never imagined…"

"Why did the king banish you?" Kael asked.

"We saw something terrible," Dia admitted. "We followed the king and found him using dark magic to drain the life from a girl. He knew we'd seen him, and by the time we got back to the palace he claimed Sam was a traitor and a murder, and that we were the ones practicing dark magic, and he sent us down the causeway."

"And you think this dark sorcerer has taken the place of the king?"

Dia nodded. "We believe that's what happened, and we fear for the rest of the kingdom left in his power."

Kael looked from her to Sam as if just connecting something. "Sam. Sam? Dia, who is Sam?"

She looked over at Sam, where he lay tied hand and foot, still struggling. "Samanath Algorian, Prince of Ischar."

Kael's eyes widened. "He's the prince? The beloved grandchild of King Hashoreth, the only heir to the throne? And the king banished him. Just like that?" He let out a low whistle. He rubbed his forehead. "It can't have been the real king who banished you. He's dead. My father found him in the jungle three weeks ago."

Dia's eyes widened. "It's been less than a week since we were sent here."

"That proves your story. From what I've heard, the king loved his grandson more than anything. Those two were the only members of the family left in Ischar. I can't imagine the prince committing a crime severe enough for the king to send him down here." He met Dia's eyes. "And you? The prince's new bride. Why would he *ever* send you?" He eyed her critically. "Are you more dangerous than you look? Are you trained to fight? You took on that snake."

Dia's eyebrows shot up. "Not at all! That was desperation born of an emergency. I think he sent me here because he knows I love Sam. He feels that I'm standing in the way of his plans."

Kael's eyes met hers. They were brown like Sam's. "That's not a crime worthy of banishment."

Trying to ignore the sound of Sam raving, she wiped at the tears welling in her eyes. Back in Kulin, her sister had thought Dia had gained a story-book ending, and now look at her. Would Lisenth have fared any better if it had been her who married the prince? Dia took a deep breath and raised her eyes back to Kael. "What about you? How long have you been here?"

"My father was banished before I was born."

That was surprising. "You've lived in the jungle your whole life?"

He grinned. "It's not so bad. It does keep you on your toes, but..."

"Have you ever been up to the plateau?"

He shook his head. "My father's told me about it, but I've never seen it for myself. I don't miss it. I grew up in the jungle. I love the trees and the vibrant life here. And the animals."

"Even the snakes?" Dia shuddered.

He laughed. "I'm not afraid of snakes, or the stinging ants, or even the spiders who lie in wait to hunt birds."

Dia scrunched her eyes tightly shut, not wanting to even imagine spiders big enough to eat birds. She took a deep breath. "Tiny birds. They are very, very small birds."

"What?" His brow wrinkled in confusion.

She looked up at him. "The birds the spiders hunt, they're very small, right?"

He laughed. "I'm afraid not. The spiders are big. But don't worry, they are rare, and seldom bother people. Usually, they only come out at night."

She pulled her knees up to her chest and wrapped her arms around them. The thought of hunting spiders creeping through the midnight jungle was terrifying.

"You're really scared." He stared at her as if just realizing it. "Don't worry. I'll make sure nothing happens to you."

As Dia looked at him, intending to thank him, Sam yelled. "Let me go! I'll kill you for this. I'll break every bone in your body."

She bowed her head, not wanting Kael to see her crying again. He must have been able to tell, because he put a comforting hand on her shoulder.

"Don't worry," he murmured. "We'll find a way to fix this. We'll keep trying until we find a way."

A chill washed over Dia despite the warm air. What if there was no way to fix it?

CHAPTER 21

FOR TWO MORE DAYS, they made their slow and painful way toward the village. Sam had only a few periods of lucidity. During these, he stretched, ate, washed, apologized to all of them, especially Dia, and then allowed himself to be bound again. Sometimes he walked with them for a while before he began to threaten and rave and struggle.

Evening was falling over the jungle when they followed a small river up into a little round valley. Between the trees, Dia saw a spectacular waterfall. They followed a narrow path that climbed up the rocks to one side of the falling water. The way led into a narrow fissure in the rock.

Dia followed the others inside. The rock walls were smooth on either side. They came to a gate made of thick logs. Kael pounded his fist against the door.

"Who's that with you, Kael?" someone inside asked.

"I have a man who is ill, and his wife. He needs my father. Please let us in," Kael said.

The heavy door swung open, and they carried Sam inside and set him down. A man shut the gate behind them. He stared at Sam in confusion, and when his eyes fell on Dia, his mouth fell open a little in surprise.

He was young, perhaps the same age as Kael, with wavy dark hair that hung untrimmed around his shoulders. Also, like Kael, he was shirtless and unshaven, but he grinned at her. Kael smacked him. "Turgen, this is Princess Alladia Algorian, *wife* of the Crown Prince of Ischar."

Turgen's grin dimmed a little at the word wife, but he bowed gallantly and kissed her hand. "Your servant, my lady."

"We need my father's help. Where is he?" Kael asked.

"I would be happy to stay with her Highness while you find him," Turgen offered, smiling warmly.

Kael smacked him again. "Just go get him, please."

Turgen winked at Dia and disappeared.

Dia stared around in wonder. Inside the gate was an open space with cliffs surrounding it on all sides. High above, tendrils of jungle growth clung to the edges of the rocks. Beyond them, a wide circle of evening sky was visible.

In the clearing lay a little village of huts constructed of bamboo and dried leaves. Several people went about their work, gathering up fruit that had been drying on racks, smoking fish or game meat, weaving baskets. Children played between the huts.

A moment later, Turgen returned, a man walking beside him. He was tall and appeared to be of middle age, reminding Dia of a younger Hashoreth, or even an older Sam. His dark hair was mixed with gray, but there was a definite resemblance.

He hurried to them and asked Kael, "Is it true? The prince and princess?" He looked at Dia, and then down at Sam. "Is this Hashoreth's grandson?"

"Yes," Dia offered her hand, "and I am Alladia Algorian."

The man smiled, taking her hand and kissing it, the gesture as formal and proper as any used in the royal court back in Kulin. He turned his gaze back to Sam. "This is Samanath?"

She nodded.

"He's grown considerably since I saw him last."

Dia looked up at him in surprise. "You know him?"

He raised his eyes to meet hers. "I am Adengo."

Shock stole her breath, and for a moment, her knees felt weak and trembling. This was the man accused of murdering Sam's parents. He'd been here in the jungle all this time, creating any sort of life he could in the wilderness. She placed a hand over her heart and finally managed to draw in a sharp breath.

Adengo's brown eyes met hers frankly. "Then you know who I am?"

She nodded, speechless.

He straightened his shoulders. "Princess Alladia Algorian, I did *not* murder my brother and his wife." His voice was firm, and his eyes, so similar to Sam's, bored into hers.

Perhaps she was naïve, but she felt the truth of his words, especially now, when she and Sam had been falsely accused and banished. She stared back at him, trying to form the words she needed. "What happened?"

"A dark sorcerer was hiding in our midst. He urged me to join him. When I refused, he killed my brother and his wife and made it appear that I had done it. At the time, I desperately hoped my father would believe me when I told him I was innocent, but he didn't." Adengo looked into the distance, remembering. "I would never have done such a thing. I loved my older brother, and I loved Sam. He was only six." Adengo looked down at the stretcher again. "He used to follow me everywhere."

Hopefully, she wasn't making a mistake, but Dia trusted him. She met Adengo's eyes. "I believe you're telling the truth."

Adengo bowed his head. "Thank you."

"Sam missed you all these years. Your father did too."

Adengo's expression tightened in pain. "I wish I had the opportunity to speak to him again before he died." He looked toward the cliff. "I... found him."

Dia's eyes welled with tears. "We already feared the worst, but we couldn't be sure until Kael told us. Back in Kulin, a man who looks exactly like Hashoreth is ruling our people."

"You were right," Adengo said. "Whoever he is, he is surely *not* the king. I buried my father." He glanced quickly up toward the towering cliff hidden behind the trees. "Lady Alladia, it's been nearly twenty years since I've seen any of my family. You are welcome here. I see you've already met my son, Kael."

"Yes. He's done so much for us. We might never have reached you without his aid." She lowered her gaze to Sam. "My husband is very ill. Can you help him?"

Adengo knelt beside Sam and touched his forehead. Sam's eyes flew open. "Let me go!" he snarled. "I'll kill you for keeping me bound. Release me!"

Adengo turned to Dia. "This is serious. How long has he been like this?"

"It started just as we came down here, a little over a week ago. Can you cure him?"

"I will do everything I can for him," Adengo said. "But I cannot promise that a solution is within my power. I must learn more, and I'll need more time."

"What do we do with him in the meantime?" Kael asked, looking down at Sam.

Adengo glanced toward the edge of the village. "For now, I suggest Turgen's jaguar cage."

They took Sam to the other side of the compound. Against the cliff wall was a large square cage made of bamboo lashed together. Turgen appeared as if he'd been watching for them.

"We need to borrow it," Kael nodded toward the enclosure.

Turgen grinned. "I guess my plan can wait." They opened the door. It took three men to wrestle Sam inside and cut his bonds. Kael barely made it to the opening ahead of Sam. They dropped the bar into place to hold the door and then stepped back, breathing hard. Sam tried to grab them through the bars.

"Make sure someone watches him every moment," Adengo said.

Kael sighed, looking at his cousin inside the cage. "I'll take the first turn."

"When I finish my shift at the gate, I'll find some others to relieve you, and then I'll take a turn," Turgen offered.

"Thank you," Adengo said, nodding to them both. "Please don't leave the gate unguarded."

Turgen looked guilty for a moment. "No, of course not." With a last glance at Dia, he disappeared.

"Thank you all for your help." Dia looked around at each of them.

They nodded.

"Will you come with me?" Adengo offered. "I will share what comfort I can with you. And we must decide what to do."

"Yes, thank you." Dia followed him to a hut made of bamboo and thatched with a thick layer of palm fronds.

At the door stood a slender woman with dark hair and beautiful brown skin. She offered Dia a kind smile.

Adengo smiled at her. "Kani, we have guests. This is Princess Alladia Algorian. My niece, since she married Prince Samanath."

Kani's eyes widened in surprise, but she offered a kind smile. "Welcome, Alladia."

Adengo turned back to Dia. "This is Kani, my wife."

He held the door of the hut open for her. "Please come in. As you can see, we live very simply here." The inside was furnished with chairs and a table made of bamboo and low cots in the corners.

"Please sit." Adengo gestured to a chair.

Dia settled into the crude chair and found it far more comfortable than anything she had sat in since she'd left the palace. She rested against the chair back with a sigh. She was so tired. Her mind spun, trying to untangle the events of the past. Was she wrong to believe Adengo?

She hoped not. For now, she needed to trust him. He might be her only hope of saving Sam. Adengo offered her fruit and small round cakes. He sat down, and Kani sat beside him.

"Thank you." Dia helped herself and took a bite out of the cake.

He gestured toward the plate. "We make them from a tuber that grows in the jungle. Please, you must be hungry, though many people fare much worse than you their first time in the jungle."

A pang of guilt twisted her insides. "I would have done so much worse alone. Sam protected me as long as he could. Can you help him?"

"I hope so," Adengo replied. "I will need some time to prepare. Even if I succeed, the cure is likely to be unpleasant for him. Please, tell me everything you know about the Shadaroc and what happened up there."

Dia recounted the story of her first sightings of the enormous bird and told him of Carrina and what she'd seen the night they were banished. "We found the king—well, someone who looked like the king—using magic to extract power from the people there."

Adengo nodded soberly. "Hallan. It is life energy, or soul energy. Any kind of sorcery gathers this power from people and uses it. I have limited skill as a sorcerer myself, but I only gather hallan in small amounts from people willing to give it. A dark sorcerer will take from others against their will. He can drain them until they have nothing left, and they die."

Dia looked at Adengo and nodded. "That's what he's doing, isn't he? That's why he searched for people who were poor or alone. He thought he could use their hallan, and no one would miss them."

"Yes," Adengo said. "And when you tried to expose him, he had to get rid of you. I assume he expected you to die down here."

Dia remembered the day when she had found Sam in his grandfather's study, his face blank, sweat standing out on his forehead. "He did something to Sam. They were alone together. That's when Sam started getting sick."

"Could you see anything? Any sort of wound or injury?"

"He kept rubbing his neck, here, as if it hurt." Dia put a hand to the back of her neck. "I couldn't see anything, but maybe I should check again in the daylight."

Adengo nodded. "I agree. Perhaps the sorcerer used something to poison his mind. His behavior indicates that. If this man is impersonating the king, then having Sam's mind under his control would be very useful to him. Essential, in fact."

Dia fought back tears. "He warned me that I must influence Sam to do his duty and to cooperate. He said that Sam would rather listen to me than to him. The whole thing wasn't like Hashoreth. I think he wanted to control both of us. That's why he..." Her eyes went to the door of the hut, in the direction of the cage. "Can you find a cure for Sam? He's a good man, and he wants to serve his people. He showed nothing but caring to me, before..."

Adengo put a comforting hand on her arm. "I hope you believe me when I say I'll do everything I can. Now, get some rest, and when the sun comes up, we'll get started. It's better if you're not alone for the time being. We must leave Sam where he is for now, but you are welcome to stay here with us." He gestured to one of the cots.

"Thank you," Dia replied. "Your hospitality is most welcome."

He grinned. "I'm afraid the comforts I'm able to offer are sadly limited, but I find that several days in the jungle make even the most pampered of the nobility grateful to receive them."

Dia smiled. "Very true, but I'd like to hope I would have been grateful anyway."

"Get some sleep. We'll be back in a short while." He patted her shoulder, and they left her.

Dia stood for a long time in the doorway, looking out at the shadows of the jungle and the shapes of the huts. A man walked by, and even in the dim light, she recognized Kael. She called his name softly, and he stopped and came to her.

He looked down in concern. "Are you all right, Lady Dia? We had a long day."

"I'm tired," she admitted. "But we'd never have gotten here without your help. I thought your face seemed familiar from the moment we met, but now I realize it was a family resemblance."

He smiled. "Sam's my cousin, and he doesn't know it."

Dia came closer and laid her hand on his arm. "There was no way for you to know who we were, and you helped us when you didn't have to. You saved both our lives. You have my sincere gratitude, and I trust you."

He put his hand over hers. "Thank you. I want to help."

She looked up into his face. "Kael, will you tell me more about your father? Adengo says he didn't kill Sam's parents. Everyone up there, King Hashoreth, even Sam, they all believe he is guilty."

Kael sighed heavily. "It all happened before I was born. But people grow up quickly in the jungle, and I'm not a child anymore. I believe I see my father clearly. He's taken care of me and all the others in this village. I've never seen him harm anyone or take advantage. And I've never known him to lie, not in all these years. Though he feels pain and sorrow for what happened, he doesn't seem to have the darkness of guilt inside him. So, judging by the man I know him to be, he would never have killed his brother."

"Thank you, Kael." Dia wanted to believe him, and she hoped he and Adengo were both telling the truth.

"Get some rest, my lady," Kael urged, and then disappeared around the corner of the hut.

Dia lay down on the low cot, finding it more comfortable than she'd expected. She stretched out, trying to relax the knots of tension throughout her body. The sounds of the jungle night surrounded her, and she tried to remind herself that there were stone walls and a gate between her and any predator who might wander by. She was safe to rest.

Just before she dozed off, Sam called her name. "Dia?"

Some small part of her wanted to ignore him, but the rest of her vaulted out of bed and rushed to the cage. "I'm here, Sam. How are you?"

He made a low sound that wasn't quite a laugh. "I'm in a cage. And that's probably for the best. Where are we?"

She couldn't see his features clearly in the dark, but she moved closer to him. "This is Kael's village. His father is going to do what he can to help you. He's preparing tonight, and he'll start in the morning."

"What will he do?"

Dia shook her head. "I don't know, but he's going to try to discover what's wrong."

Sam sounded miserable. "I'm so sorry, Dia. I only wanted to protect you, never to hurt you. Never."

She leaned against the bars, tears welling in her eyes. "I know, Sam."

"I love you, Dia," he murmured, coming up to the other side of the barrier. "Please forgive me."

"I will. I do."

They were silent for a long moment, and she missed having him close. She murmured a prayer to the Soul Mother, that She would return Sam to her. His love was the best thing that had ever come into her life.

"Sam..." she whispered.

A strangled gasp escaped her lips as iron hands closed around her throat.

CHAPTER 22

D IA'S MOUTH OPENED IN a silent scream. She had no breath to make a sound. With all her strength, she kicked and struggled, trying to free herself from the hands strangling her.

In the dim light, she got a look at Sam's face. He wore an icy sneer as his hands closed even tighter around her throat. She kicked at the bars of the cage and tried to twist away from him. Bright lights swam before her eyes. Now, her arms and legs felt too heavy to move.

Someone slammed into her from the side. Other hands tore at the ones around her throat. For an endless moment, they struggled until the iron grip broke, and she collapsed to the ground, dragging in a life-giving breath.

Shouting men surrounded her. Sam was yelling and laughing. Her stomach churned at the sound, and she nearly vomited. Someone pulled her a safe distance away from the cage. She couldn't muster the energy to open her eyes.

Someone picked her carefully up from the ground, lifting her into their arms.

"What happened?" Adengo's voice demanded.

"He tried to strangle her!" Kael replied furiously. His voice was just above her. It must be him carrying her. "I was keeping watch. He called for her, and she came. He told her he loved her, and a moment later he had both hands around her throat."

"Put her here," Adengo instructed. Dia felt Kael put her down on a cot. A soothing hand brushed her forehead.

She opened her eyes to see Kael and Adengo in the light of a lantern.

"Just lie still and rest," Adengo said.

Something cool was placed against her throat, and it eased the throbbing pain a little.

"Are you hurt anywhere else?" Adengo asked gently.

She shook her head.

"You're safe now. I will watch over you."

The pain in her throat made it impossible to think of anything else, but the cool compress helped. Adengo kept applying it until, gradually, the pain eased enough that she fell asleep.

———◆———

Dia woke to find the sun streaming in the door of the hut. The moment she tried to move, the pain reminded her that she'd been crushed and bruised. Was she safe? She looked around quickly.

Kani sat in a chair beside her. She laid a gentle hand on Dia's shoulder. "We will do what we can to help," she assured Dia. "You're safe now."

Moving slowly, Dia sat up. Kani offered her water in a cup made from some kind of round shell. Dia took a sip, but swallowing sent pain shooting from her throat. She put a hand over it.

"It will take time to heal," Kani said. "Outside, they are trying to help Sam."

Dia didn't attempt to answer, but she got to her feet. When she peeked out the door, she saw several men approaching the cage. Adengo appeared to be directing the others. They held ropes. She stood in the shadow of the hut, watching.

Dia held her breath as Kael opened the door of the cage. With a yell, Sam charged out, attempting to attack him. The others were ready, grabbing him from both sides. Sam yelled and cursed and threatened them.

She wanted to cover her ears so she couldn't hear him. His familiar voice, which had always been so kind before, was now vicious and cold. She hoped she never heard him speak like this again. For several moments, all she saw was a group of scuffling bodies. As Sam fought wildly, Kael and the others pulled his arms behind him and tied them. Sam tried to tear himself free, but there were too many of them, and they eventually wrestled him to the ground, holding him immobile.

Adengo knelt near Sam, a large basket of supplies beside him. In the bright daylight, he carefully examined the back of Sam's neck. Dia left the hut, feeling a little unsteady but able to walk. She went to them. Adengo raised his head to see her coming. He beckoned to her. Pushing aside the ends of Sam's hair, he pointed to a tiny black spot on his skin. Was that the place? She'd never examined his neck with care before. Was it simply a birthmark? Had it been there before?

"I think that's it," Adengo said. "Is this the place that hurt him?"

She nodded, not sure what would happen if she tried to speak.

Adengo met her eyes for a long moment. "I think the Shadaroc inserted something into his flesh to influence his mind. I will try to help him regain control."

She nodded. It was just what she had suspected. The sorcerer had deliberately taken Sam's sanity and forced him into violence.

How could they leave the piece of darkness lodged in Sam's mind? "Can you remove it?" Dia's voice was a faint, raspy whisper.

Adengo shook his head. "Of course you want me to take it out, but I can't now. If I do, it will damage his mind permanently. There are only two ways to remove it. The first is for the sorcerer who put it there to remove it voluntarily and release Sam."

That wasn't likely to happen. "Second?"

"If you kill the sorcerer, you'll be able to remove the splinter safely." Adengo met her eyes.

He must know how impossible that seemed now, but maybe they could find some way.

Adengo put a hand on her arm, his eyes full of concern. "I will do what I can for Sam now. You should go."

She shook her head. After all they'd been through, she couldn't just leave. She had to know if they succeeded in helping Sam. Maybe he would be himself again soon.

Adengo took a deep breath, accepting her choice. Looking around at the group of men, he gave directions. "You two hold his head still. You three hold his legs and body, the others make sure he can't get his hands free."

Sam struggled as they gripped him, and he yelled. "I'll kill all of you if you touch me! Let me go!"

Adengo ignored him and bent low to examine the skin surrounding the black spot. He took a small keen knife and placed it against the skin. Meeting Dia's eyes, he said, "Get ready."

She nodded back.

He made a cut down the back of Sam's neck. At the feel of the blade, Sam yelled in rage and pain and struggled futilely against the hands and ropes that held him. Blood welled from the cut, running down his skin. Dia's stomach clenched. It was painful to see him hurt. No matter what happened, she was sure she'd always feel the same. This was *Sam*.

Adengo mixed several powders into a bowl and poured the mixture into the wound. Sam screamed and tried even harder to escape, but his uncle just added a series of liquids next. After a moment, Sam quit struggling and collapsed into stillness.

"Good." Adengo nodded. He took out a wide bracelet made of silver and set with a cloudy red stone. He turned to Dia. "This will help transfer a little hallan to him. I hope it will be enough to combat the evil."

Adengo placed the bracelet around his wrist. He nodded to Kael and the others. "Please turn him over."

They turned Sam so he lay on his back. His eyes were closed. Adengo placed his hand with the bracelet on Sam's forehead. The strange stone glowed.

"Can you hear me, Sam?" Adengo's voice was steady and calm.

"Yes," Sam answered. In that moment, he sounded like himself.

"There is another influence in your mind. Are you aware of it?" Adengo maintained his touch on Sam's forehead.

"Yes," Sam repeated. Now his words came out from between clenched teeth. "But I don't want to do what he says."

"It's time for you to regain control." Adengo's tone was firm.

Suddenly, Sam's eyes flew open, and he laughed. "You won't get rid of me! I'll have my revenge. None of you will escape." He struggled wildly against the ropes and the hands holding him. He tried to wrench himself away from Adengo's touch.

"Sam. You are in control. Come back."

Sam yelled in pain, and grew still, panting. "I'm here." He groaned. "Help me, please!"

Adengo kept his hand steady against Sam. "You have all the strength you need. You are in control."

"I'm in control. I'm in control," Sam chanted.

"I cannot remove his influence now," Adengo admitted. "You must lock him away. Form a wall in your mind, and imprison him behind it."

"He's too strong." Sam struggled.

"No," Adengo said. "You have the power to overcome him. You can do this."

Sam drew his brows together, appearing to concentrate. His body jerked and his voice changed. "You will not bind me!" he yelled.

Adengo maintained his calm pressure. "Come back, Sam."

"I can't," Sam panted, desperation plain on his face. "I can't do it. Please, help me."

Dia couldn't stand to watch him struggle on his own any longer. She went to his side and bent over him. His eyes scanned her face, and he laughed coldly. "Still here? I thought I killed you last night. You won't get away."

Dia's stomach clenched, and tears welled in her eyes.

Sam jerked and struggled. "No. No," he protested. "I won't let you hurt her. Dia?"

She wasn't sure if she could speak. She swallowed past the pain her throat. "Sam," she whispered.

His brown eyes met hers and she saw the real Sam in them. "Dia!"

He yelled in pain again and then appeared to lose consciousness. Adengo removed his hand and looked at her. "I've done all I can for now. It will be up to him if he is able to regain control. In the meantime, we will lock him up again until we know whether he succeeded."

They removed the ropes binding Sam and carried him back into the cage. He lay very still as they secured the door.

"We will keep at least one man guarding him at all times," Adengo ordered. "I will take a turn as well." Kael and the others nodded. He turned back to Dia. "Get some rest. There's nothing else we can do but wait."

Dia put a hand on his shoulder. "Thank you," she managed to whisper.

He covered her hand with his and gave a reassuring smile. He gathered his supplies and carried them back toward his hut. She couldn't picture Adengo murdering his brother or anyone else. There was no deceit in his eyes, and they lacked the calculating gleam of someone who desired power and was willing to kill for it.

Dia turned her gaze back toward the cage and Sam's unmoving form inside. Shame flooded through her when she realized how relieved she was that they had confined him again. She couldn't help being afraid of him now.

A gentle arm came around her shoulders. Kani stood beside her. "Come with me. You need rest."

***

Dia wasn't sure how long she dozed. She wanted to know what was happening with Sam, but she was also terrified. What if she went back to see him and he attacked her again? What if he appeared to regain his reason, and they let him go, only to have him slip out of control and kill her?

The last attack had been a close call, she couldn't deny it. A few more moments and she wouldn't have survived.

She sat up and looked out the door of the hut. It was dark now. She didn't know how much of the night had passed. Someone had left her a plate of food and a waterskin. She ate and drank gratefully, though, each time she swallowed, pain burned through her throat.

It must be late. She didn't see anyone moving around. In the faint starlight, she tiptoed closer to where they had left Sam. Hidden in the shadow of one of the huts, she heard voices from the cage. She recognized Adengo's voice.

"Sam?" Adengo asked.

A groan was the only response.

"Do you know where you are?"

"The jungle." Sam's voice sounded hoarse.

"That's right." Adengo's tone was soothing. "Do you remember who you are?"

"I'm Samanath Algorian, Crown Prince of Ischar, or I was... before they banished me."

"Do you remember who I am?" Adengo asked.

Sam drew in a breath in shock. "Adengo!"

"Sam, I didn't murder your parents. Someone else killed them and placed the blame on me. I pray that you can believe me. I swear on my life that I would never harm either of them."

Sam's voice was tight. "I believe you. Now I know who killed them. It can't have been you. I remember that day we were together in the dungeon. No one else saw us there except Halderan. You had your dagger with you. Halderan left, and you walked with me back up toward my rooms. You left me only a moment before I found my parents dead. There is no way you could have killed them. There wasn't enough time. Halderan was in my mind and I couldn't get him out. While we were connected, I saw into his mind too. I saw enough to be sure he killed them, not you."

"No! Not me," Adengo exclaimed. "I loved Kariman. And you... I would never have taken your parents from you. I'm so glad to see you again, Sam."

"Please forgive me for believing it was you, all this time. I'm sorry."

"You were a child," Adengo said. "There's nothing to forgive."

"I missed you, and so did Grandfather," Sam said.

"I missed you too."

"Where is Dia?"

Dia wanted to go to him, but she didn't know how she could hide her fear if Sam saw her now. She stayed still, hidden in the shadows.

"Do you remember what happened?" Adengo asked Sam, his tone careful.

Sam remained silent for a long moment. The sound of his breathing quickened until he gasped for breath. "No! Did I really do those things?" His voice was tight with pain. "I remember hitting Dia when she tried to help me. It seems like a bad dream. Did those things really happen?"

"I'm afraid they did," Adengo said. "The sorcerer poisoned you. You weren't well."

"He's still in my head. I can barely hear him now, but he made me do it. I remember my hands around her throat!" Desperation filled Sam's voice. "She felt so small and soft, and I knew when I tightened my grip, I would kill her. No!" Sam yelled. "Where is Dia? Did I kill her?" She heard him struggling wildly.

"No. She's here. She's all right," Adengo assured him.

"How can you say that?" Sam cried. "I promised I would spend my life honoring and protecting her. I nearly strangled her."

Dia rested her back against the wall of the hut, and sank to the ground, pulling her knees up to her chest. Sobs shook her body, as she heard the sound of Sam's agony and grief. She should go to him.

But she couldn't. She wanted to, but she couldn't make herself face him. Not at this moment. She couldn't make herself move from that spot. Eventually, dawn filtered down through the trees.

She heard footsteps approaching her, and she hastily wiped the tears from her face and looked up to see Kael.

He offered his hand. "Come on."

She took the hand and allowed him to pull her to her feet.

His tone was comforting. "You don't need to be here."

Fresh tears fell at his words. She needed to be near Sam, even if he didn't know she was there and even if she couldn't be with him now. There were no words to explain all this to Kael. Maybe he understood, because he put his arms around her and held her as she cried.

He led her back to the hut, and she sank onto her cot and curled into a ball. Kael went out, returning with water and food. Setting them where she could reach them, he left with an awkward pat on her shoulder.

———

Adengo found Dia in exactly the same place hours later. "I'm sorry, my dear." He put a kindly hand on her arm. "I know you love Sam, and he loves you too. If not, this situation wouldn't be so painful. Are you ready to see him?"

Dia shook her head. She wasn't ready.

"How long will you put it off?" he asked gently. "I released Sam this afternoon. He appears to be in complete control of himself. I have assigned four guards to watch him every moment for a few more days, just to be sure..."

Dia wiped a hand across her eyes. "Does he want to see me?" she asked in her scratchy whisper.

"Of course," he assured her. "More than anything. But he is waiting for you to decide to see him."

Her heart twisted. This was her Sam, and how could she refuse? Gathering the threads of her courage, she sat up, wiping her eyes. "All right," she whispered.

"Wait here for a moment," Adengo said. "I'll be right back."

He soon returned, extending his hand to help her up. Once upright, she took a long, fortifying breath. "I'm not sure I can do this," she whispered.

"You're not alone," Adengo said, offering his arm. The gesture was graceful and courtly. He wore ragged clothes, but she saw past them to the prince he had once been. She took his arm, and they went out. Sam stood waiting in the space between the huts. Two of the men from the village stood on either side of him, ready to seize him if he showed any sign of violence. Sam's posture was tense, his body rigid.

A band of icy terror twisted inside her at the sight of Sam. Dia couldn't help but remember the chilling sneer on his face as his big hands gripped her neck. She felt the power and strength in his arms which should have been used to protect her but instead had been used to attack. No. This was Sam. She loved him, and he was in control of his actions now, wasn't he?

He stood completely still, as if afraid to move, even slightly. From his eyes, he was himself again, but the stark pain in them was new. Slowly, with Adengo at her side, she approached him. The muscles in his jaw tightened as she drew near. His eyes were locked on her neck. The bruises he had left would stand out against her pale skin.

When she raised her chin to meet his gaze, she saw the pain in them even more clearly. Tears welled in his eyes. Moving slowly, he bent to one knee. "Forgive me. Please, Dia," he pleaded. "I remember everything now. I never meant to hurt you. But I know I did."

Her heart ached for him. She forced the words past the pain in her throat. "It wasn't your fault, Sam, none of it. Of course I forgive you."

He reached for her hand.

At the sudden movement, Dia jumped back with a gasp.

The agony showed plainly on his face as he slowly lowered his hand.

CHAPTER 23

I T TOOK TWO WEEKS before the worst of the pain in Dia's throat eased. She had seen Sam often, but he had kept his distance, not trying to touch her or even come near her. After ten days, Adengo had removed the guard on him, and he'd showed no sign of violence or insanity.

Dia had many opportunities to speak with Adengo. The better she knew him, the more certain she became that he was telling the truth about his brother's death. If he were truly violent and cruel, he'd be out in the jungle with the other outcasts, not here, cultivating a peaceful community.

One morning, she saw Adengo and Kani at work cleaning the tubers which made an important part of their diet. They smiled as she joined them and began to help.

"Good morning," Kani said.

"Good morning." Dia picked up a tuber and began peeling off its outer husk.

"I'm glad you're here," Adengo said. "I can see that you're very good for Sam, despite the challenges you've faced together. You are an extraordinary person to have come so far."

Her cheeks warmed at his praise. "That's kind of you to say."

He met her gaze. "I believe you are extraordinary for another reason, Dia."

Her eyebrows raised. "What do you mean?"

"Not every person can work magic. Very few have the ability born in them to sense the flow of hallan, but I believe *you* are such a person."

Dia felt her jaw slacken in shock. She laughed, thinking he must be joking, but he met her gaze steadily, no trace of humor in his expression. The laugh faded. "You're serious?"

He nodded. "I would never make a joke about something like that. I believe you possess the natural ability, and you could study sorcery if you chose."

Why would he think she possessed any magical skills? She was ordinary. She'd never considered this before, not even in her dreams. "I would never take hallan from someone else!"

He smiled slightly. "I understand completely. I feel the same way myself. But the use of hallan freely given to you is much different from taking it from someone against their will."

A shiver ran through her at that thought.

"Sorcery requires a strong will," Adengo said. "Maybe no one has ever observed that will in you before, but I have."

She almost laughed again. "In me? You think that I have a strong will? Maybe you haven't noticed all the times I've been frightened or not been able to solve a problem on my own?"

He put down the root he'd been working on and wiped his hands on a piece of cloth. Meeting her eyes again, he smiled and raised one hand, palm toward her. "Try to touch the power," he instructed. "Place your hand against mine."

Dia met his eyes for a long moment. He genuinely seemed to believe she could do... something. More than likely, nothing would happen, but she set down her work, raised her hand, and placed her palm against his.

"Now clear your mind, open yourself to feel the flow of hallan." His voice was deep and calm.

Drawing in a long breath, she closed her eyes and attempted to obey. It was difficult to clear her mind; thoughts of Sam, worries and distractions all flitted through it. Gradually she obtained a sense of calm, and for a moment, she sensed the energy flowing through each of them, and the point where it met and mingled at their joined hands.

As quickly as it had come, the elusive sense disappeared. She looked up at Adengo.

He smiled. "Very good for a first attempt."

She shook her head. "You're making it sound like it went better than it really did. I have no real skill at this."

Adengo lowered his hand, and she did the same. "People study for years to achieve any level of control over hallan. For many, emotion helps to connect them with the power. Many beginners achieve results when they are angry or possessed by another strong feeling. It is much more difficult to touch the power when you are calm. Think about what I said. You don't need to decide anything now. We can try again another time."

She nodded. "I will."

◦◦◦

That evening, the entire village had gathered around a fire in the open space between the huts. During her days here, Dia had met nearly everyone who lived there. The people were a mix of men who had been outcasts at one time, and the native people of the jungle. There were more men than women, but still a good number of families.

All of them were loyal to Adengo. They treated him with deep respect and listened when he spoke. Tonight, he'd asked all of them to gather. They passed around baskets of fruit, plates of meat roasted over the flames, and piles of the little cakes they ate so often.

Standing tall, his leadership unquestioned by anyone in this group, Adengo faced the assembled people. "We have a serious problem," he said. "The Shadaroc has taken the king's place. He now has control of everyone in Kulin, and his darkness will quickly spread to all of Ischar." Adengo looked up past the cavern walls, toward the looming blackness of the cliff. "Ischar might seem far away down here, but if we don't act, the people will remain in captivity. Many of them will lose their lives."

There was muttering at this statement. Many of these men had been banished. They didn't appear to feel much loyalty to the kingdom that had cast them out.

Sam stood up beside Adengo. "I know none of you owe Ischar anything," he added. "But if we can defeat the dark sorcerer, I would welcome any of you who want to come home."

There were murmurs at this, and the villagers looked at each other. They cared about each other, and relied on their friends, but survival was difficult in the jungle.

"This isn't the first time the Shadaroc has come to Ischar," Adengo went on. "I tried to expose him nineteen years ago. I failed." He turned to Sam. "When your parents were killed, I was banished, and the dark sorcerer escaped."

Dia's eyes were on Sam as he focused on his uncle, listening intently.

Adengo went on. "I tried to explain to King Hashoreth—my father. I wanted him to understand what had happened. I never wanted to harm my brother or his wife, but the Shadaroc made it appear that I had. I desperately wanted him to believe me, but he didn't. He banished me." He turned to look at Kani, sitting beside him. "I made a new life here."

Adengo took something out of his pocket. It shone silver in the firelight. Dia gasped as she recognized the king's medallion. Hashoreth had worn it every day. Her eyes darted to Sam. He stared at it, lines of sorrow etched on his face.

"You... you found him, didn't you?" Sam's voice sounded choked, and Dia felt a powerful urge to go and try to comfort him. She almost did. A shiver of fear stopped her. It felt dangerous to be so close to him. With an effort, she remained in her seat.

Adengo leaned toward Sam and handed him the locket. "I'm sorry, Sam. At his passing, you are the rightful king of Ischar."

"No." Sam wiped his eyes with his hand. "Until we defeat the Shadaroc, I'm no one."

A long silence settled over the group. Dia stared into the fire, except when she sneaked glances at Sam. She knew how much his grandfather had meant to him. The two of them had been so close. Until this reunion with his uncle and cousin, his grandfather had been his only family. He'd been left with no one. Except her.

And she had kept her distance from Sam. Dia hadn't meant to abandon him, just as he hadn't meant to attack her. But it had happened, and she couldn't ignore the effects of it. She couldn't help being afraid of him. Still, she wanted him back. She missed him, missed being close to him.

"I only know of one way to truly destroy the Shadaroc," Adengo said. "We must get close enough to him to drain his power. I have created a conduit, similar to the one he uses to steal hallan from others." Dia had seen it before, the bracelet he had used to help Sam.

"And how would we do that without him destroying us?" Sam asked. "Another sorcerer already tried to fight him, and the Shadaroc beat him. Do you remember Marek?"

Adengo nodded. "He was a good man, and an experienced sorcerer. He came to Kulin to search for the Shadaroc, before I left there. It's not good news if Halderan beat him."

Sam shook his head. "He's not going to let us walk up to him and attack him."

"No," Adengo said. "I have some of the same skills Halderan possesses, though my power is not as great as his, since I refuse to enhance it by draining hallan from others. My strength should be enough to capture his attention, at least for a short time. I will need help to defeat him."

"I will go. Ischar is my kingdom," Sam said, getting to his feet. "I can't ask anyone else to accept the responsibility."

Dia felt a quiver in her belly. Her fear remained strong, but anger welled up inside her. She had fled from this sorcerer long enough. She stood up. "I will go," she said firmly. "Ischar is my kingdom too."

Sam's head whipped around to face her. "It's too dangerous. He's powerful, and he will try to kill us."

Despite his protest, she stood still, stubbornly staring back at him. "The Shadaroc tried to take everything from me, and I will not stay here waiting. I must do what I can. He deserves to pay for the people he's killed and hurt."

Sam met her gaze and nodded slowly.

Adengo looked around the circle. "Is there anyone else who would undertake this dangerous quest?"

Altan stood up. "It's been many years since I've seen Ischar. I'll go."

Adengo nodded at him.

"So will I."

Adengo turned toward Kael, now on his feet. Adengo's jaw tightened, and Kani's features froze. Neither of them wanted their son to volunteer for this risky journey, but how could

Adengo refuse Kael now? His shoulders slumped as he nodded. "Very well. We will go together."

"How will we get inside the palace?" Kael asked. "From what my father says, it has strong walls and gates, and they guard it well. We need to get close enough to reach the sorcerer."

Adengo looked at Sam. "If you can get us through the city gates, I can get us into the palace."

Sam raised his eyebrows. "What, is there a hidden passageway?"

"Of course." Adengo grinned.

Sam's eyes widened. "And no one else knows about it? You never told me?"

Adengo shook his head. "We were boys when we found it. Only Kariman and I knew. Even my father never realized it was there. And I wasn't about to tell *you* at the age of six. I can only imagine the trouble you'd have gotten into!"

A guilty expression crossed Sam's face. "Probably true," he admitted. He rubbed his jaw. "The guards at the city gates shouldn't be too difficult, unless they recognize us. I'll keep them from seeing my face. But if we arrive in a group looking like we just walked out of the jungle, they'll never let us through. We'll need to disguise ourselves and sneak through one or two at a time. When we reach the top of the cliffs, we will move that direction."

Adengo nodded in agreement. "Very well."

Dia looked around at the others who had committed to go. Any one of them might be killed in this attempt, or they all might. The fear rose up inside her again at the thought, but she wasn't going to stay behind here while Sam went back to Ischar to face their enemy.

In the center of the group, the fire had burned down to coals. In twos and threes, everyone dispersed to find their beds.

Dia stood in the doorway of the hut, looking at the small patch of clear sky between the leafy branches. Soon, the village was silent. Everyone else had gone to bed. She listened to the night sounds of the jungle, grateful for the protection of the village.

The distant howl of a wolf sounded from somewhere out in the forest. She stared into the dark toward the gate, and shivered. She hadn't known there were wolves down here.

"Dia?"

The whisper startled her, and she drew in her breath, turning to see a tall shadow in the dark. Sam. She quelled an instinctive burst of panic. He was Sam again. Her Sam. He wouldn't hurt her. Slowly and carefully, she took a step toward him.

"Did you hear the wolf?" she asked.

"Yes." He took a step toward her now. "Would you allow me to take your hand?"

Dia's heart pinched. How sad that he had to ask. How sad that she thought it over before she extended her hand.

The moonlight touched his fingers as he, very slowly, reached out to her. With extreme care, he took her hand in his and brought it to his lips. The warmth of his breath caressed her skin. The feel of his mouth against her hand made her shiver and her heart pound. How she wanted everything to be like it had been before.

More wolves howled, and she looked fearfully toward the jungle.

"They can't get through the gate," he assured her.

From far above, the shadow of giant wings fell over them, blocking out the stars. The Shadaroc circled and dove to fly low over the village. It passed close enough for them to feel the wind of its wings. Dia stared upward, paralyzed by fright. Sam's hand tightened around hers.

In a moment, it was gone.

"Does it know we're here?" Dia asked. "It has a connection with you. Can it tell where you are?"

Sam scanned the sky. "I don't know. I hope not."

Dia scanned the sky as well. "What about this village? This depression in the rocks could easily be seen from the air. But it doesn't know where we are, does it?" Without the element of surprise, their difficult mission could easily become impossible. "I'm afraid," she confessed. If only she could ask him to hold her like he used to. The feeling of his arms around her was so comforting. At least, it had been.

"You don't have to go." His voice was gentle. "You'd be safe here until it's all over."

He was wrong, and she felt the conviction of it deep inside herself. She *did* have to go. It was the only chance of truly saving Sam, and it was the only way she could move forward. The Shadaroc had already attempted to kill her several times, and he meant to destroy many of her people. In order to have any chance of stopping him, she must confront him again. It was inevitable.

CHAPTER 24

D IA HAD NEVER BEEN so filthy in her entire life. She wanted nothing more than the longest bath of her existence and to scrub herself clean all over. When she consulted with Kani, she advised her that the pool below the waterfall was the best place to bathe.

"You can't go alone, dear," Kani said. "The jungle is too dangerous. Here are some clean clothes. They're not very nice, but you'll have to make do." She gave Dia a plain tunic and a pair of cropped trousers. Nothing fancy, but they were clean and would fit much better than what she had been wearing.

"We make our own soap." Kani presented Dia with a lumpy piece and a ragged piece of cloth to use as a towel.

"Thank you so much," Dia said fervently.

Sam, Kael, and Turgen were leaning against the rock wall beside the gate. Dia took her armful of supplies and marched up to them. "I need to go to the waterfall," she admitted, feeling her cheeks heat slightly. All their eyes suddenly fastened on her and she felt horribly uncomfortable. Everyone here must realize why she wanted to go there.

"I would be very happy to escort you, my lady." Turgen offered his most charming smile.

Sam's eyes widened, and he put a heavy hand on the young man's shoulder. "No. I believe that honor will be mine."

Kael stared at Sam with narrowed eyes. "And are you sure it's safe for you to go anywhere alone with her?"

Sam wanted to object, but instead, pain clouded his eyes. "I hope it is."

"Why don't you ask her if she feels safe?" Kael took a step forward to face Sam. "What if your *condition* comes back?"

Dia felt a wave of terror at that thought. When she met Sam's eyes, she saw a flash of the same fear. He feared that idea even more than she did. With all her heart, she hoped it never happened. The only way to banish the fear of it, for either of them, was to defeat the Shadaroc and cure the poison in Sam.

The two men were still arguing as she went to the gate, opened it, and walked into the passageway. With no further discussion, they both followed her. She followed a trail that led down to the pool below the falls. A few moments later, they came to the clearing where the waterfall plunged into a wide pool.

"It's beautiful," Dia murmured.

They followed the path to a flat ledge at the edge of the water. She set down her things on the rock.

Kael cleared his throat. "We'll just wait on the other side of those rocks."

In a moment, they both vanished, and she looked around and found herself alone. The water was clear, and she could see to the sandy bottom. With another glance around, just to check, she undressed and slipped into the water. It was quite cold, but it felt refreshing after the warmth of the air. She used the soap and scrubbed. Just as she finished rinsing her hair, she realized she was not alone in the pool. A long sinuous reptilian body moved through the water, and one of its coils brushed against her arm.

She couldn't prevent the horrified shriek that burst from her lungs as she jumped back onto the rocks. Sam was there in an instant, wrapping his arms around her. "What is it?"

"Snake!" She pointed to the edge of the pool where its long body departed into the brush.

Kael held his machete ready, but looking down at the snake, he grinned. "Green Boa," he said, bumping the departing coils with the toe of his boot. "Harmless."

A hint of a flush showed on his tanned face as he glanced at them, before disappearing back around the rocks.

Dia took a deep breath. She had been terrified of snakes even before the incident in the river. And the one in the pool had been large.

"Are you hurt?" Sam murmured into her hair.

She became suddenly conscious of his arms against the bare skin of her back, one hand against her waist. "I'm all right. It just scared me." It felt so good to rely on him when she was frightened. She had missed being able to look to him when she needed someone.

"I'm happy to help."

His arms pulled her closer, and with her ear against his chest, she felt his heart beat faster. She was suddenly conscious of her undressed state and heat rushed to her cheeks. How much had Kael seen? More than enough. She slipped out of Sam's embrace and bent to grab the ragged towel, dried herself hastily, and pulled on her clothes.

Gathering up her things, she found Sam still waiting. "Thank you." She smiled at him, her cheeks still flaming after the entire ridiculous scene.

They planned to leave the village in a few more days. Each of them had made what preparations they could. The sky had cleared after an afternoon shower, and Dia had just finished helping Kani scoop the centers out of a basket of coconuts and spread them to dry in the sun. As she ate a piece of the crisp white fruit, the flavor sent her mind back to that day in the market with Sam, when they'd eaten chocolate and coconut. It seemed years ago now. So much had happened.

"Dia?"

Turning toward the voice, she saw Adengo in the doorway of the hut.

"We'll be leaving soon. Any training I can give you will help keep you safe. The Shadaroc must guess that you have power. Perhaps he could sense it, and that is the reason you are the one who saw him."

She'd never considered before that perhaps the Shadaroc had been searching for her specifically. Had he craved her power?

Adengo nodded. "The first thing you must learn is how to prevent someone else from taking your hallan. It requires power to create a shield."

"A shield?" So, there was a way to protect herself from her enemy. That was good news.

Adengo took out the cuff with the red stone spand held it up. "Come inside and sit down. We will try it."

Dia took a deep breath and nodded, following him into the hut and taking a seat.

"Hold out your hand," Adengo instructed.

She extended her arm, and he slipped the cuff onto her wrist.

"Now," he met her gaze, "put your hand against my forehead and feel my hallan."

Her hand trembled slightly as she reached out and placed her palm against his head. A shock flew from her hand, up her arm, and ran through her whole body. All at once, she was aware of her own hallan, the energy infusing every cell in her body. Through the link, she felt him, the power and vitality of his life, flowing through his body.

"Good," he murmured. "Now, try to take a little."

Shoving down her uncertainty, Dia obeyed. She needed to learn all she could from Adengo. She closed her eyes, focusing on the link, on the power. Reaching out, she drew a small amount from him. The extra power flowed into her, warm and glowing. It felt euphoric. No danger would ever have power over her. She could do whatever she chose and no one would stop her.

Without even making a conscious decision, she reached for more. There was more, and she could have it. She must have it.

A barrier blocked her way. When she reached the wall, she pushed against it. The rest of the delicious energy lay behind it. All she needed to do was break down the wall. She concentrated, shoving against it, hammering at it. The boundary held firm.

"Dia?"

A voice called her name. Who would interrupt her in her pursuit of power? She would take what she wanted. She pushed harder against the wall.

"Dia."

In a flash, her reason returned. She had taken hallan from another person. It had only been in training, but she had tried to take more. She'd wanted it.

Dia gasped, horrified, and wrenched her hand away from Adengo. What had she been doing? How could she have done it? Tears welled in her eyes. "I—I—? Did I hurt you?"

Adengo looked back at her, his expression calm. "I'm not hurt." His voice was firm.

"But I—I could have hurt you if I had taken more? I could have kept taking it until there was no more."

"Yes. It is difficult to resist the power once you feel it. It requires great discipline."

She shook her head. "I didn't know it would feel like that." She drew in a shaky breath.

He took the cuff and replaced it on his own wrist. "You felt the shield? I would not allow you to draw any more power."

Dia nodded.

"I want you to make your own shield. Concentrate on creating a barrier in your mind. Do not allow any of your own hallan to leave you."

Still shaken by what she'd felt, she drew in another breath, attempting to prepare.

Adengo put his hand on her forehead.

She felt intense pressure, centralized on the point where his hand rested but spreading outward through her whole body. The sensation was instantly familiar. When the Shadaroc had found her in the forest, he'd climbed into the tree where she hid, put his hand on her head, and she'd felt exactly the same thing.

At the moment, she'd been determined not to let him in. She did the same now. She pushed back with all her strength, concentrating on holding the line. At last, the pressure eased, and Adengo removed his hand.

"You did well."

"He did that to me, that night in the forest," she said.

"So, this wasn't your first time. Even so, your skill is impressive. Most people have little resistance. If you were anyone else, he would probably have killed you that night." His brown eyes held hers. "You are a remarkable person, Dia. Keep practicing your defense. You will need to use it again."

Two days passed. Dia saw Sam only from a distance as he helped the other villagers with their chores or took a turn on guard. She spent time with Adengo, allowing him to teach her. In the evenings or other quiet moments, they sat together practicing Dia's growing magical skills. Adengo was a good teacher, patient and calm. As they finished one of their sessions, several of the villagers gathered. Kani among them.

"It's time to wash our clothes," she said, smiling. Dia joined them.

As the group of villagers walked down the trail toward the pool, Dia didn't want to admit that she'd never done her own laundry. The jungle certainly emphasized how pampered she'd been before. Still, there was an earthy simplicity to this life that she liked. Would it really be so bad to stay here? She'd met Sam without knowing he was a prince. Down here, he wasn't.

As they knelt beside the water, she sneaked a glance at him where he stood guarding the villagers as they washed their clothes. He stood still, only his eyes moving, watching the surrounding jungle for any sign of danger. Even dressed in ragged clothes, she still admired his handsome features, his broad shoulders. Her eyes traced his muscular arms, his strong hands.

The horrible memory of those hands around her throat flashed across her mind, and she did her best to shove it away. It hadn't been Sam who wanted to kill her. She drew in a breath and looked away from him.

Kani worked beside her, patiently offering a few tips as they worked. "Adengo told me about you and Sam," she said. "I'm sorry for what happened to you both."

"Thank you."

"I haven't known either of you long, but I can tell he cares about you," Kani said. "He watches you. His focus is constantly on you."

"I love him," Dia said.

Kani nodded. "Then don't let fear cause you to push him away. You're right to be afraid, but it isn't really Sam that you fear, is it? It's the other darker mind inside him. That mind belongs to someone else. Perhaps you can help him resist it."

The memory of the cold sneer on Sam's face as he tried to kill her flooded back into Dia's mind, and she shoved it down. Kani's words made her want to hope things could get better. "Maybe you're right," Dia said. "I know what happened was never his choice. I don't blame him, but I can't help feeling afraid."

Kani patted her hand. "I understand. Move slowly, and give yourself time to heal."

In preparation for the journey back to Ischar, Adengo brought her a rough knapsack, and together they packed dried fruit and meat and a few other useful items.

"We'll be in danger," Adengo reminded Dia. "Perhaps you more than any of us. I know Halderan. He craves power, and he has been looking for a strong ally for many years. That's what he wanted from me. When I refused to give it, he destroyed my life and killed my brother and sister-in-law. He will want the same from you."

"But I don't have enough power to help him. He must realize I have no idea what I'm doing."

"He would rather teach you himself," Adengo said. "He will want control over what you can do, control over you. Be ready."

Dia swallowed hard.

Adengo patted her shoulder. "Just remember, you're stronger than you think you are."

She hadn't spent any time near Sam. They hadn't spoken since the night they had seen the Shadaroc. What would he think of the skills Adengo was teaching her? Would the magic create even more distance between them? He had already lost so much to magic. But she couldn't stop learning now that she'd started. They would need the magic when they met Halderan.

Dia took advantage of every free moment to practice. Every lesson Adengo taught her helped her discover something new, and each time they worked at it, she grew more comfortable feeling hallan.

They left the village at sunrise to begin their journey. Pockets of mist still lay over the forest, and the birds and monkeys called to each other in the canopy. Kael led them, knowing every tree and trail. Adengo followed him. Dia walked in the middle, followed by Sam, while Altan brought up the rear.

"The causeway is too well guarded," Kael explained as they moved into the forest. "We can't get up that way. We'll go east instead of west. The way is longer, but there is another way up onto the plateau, less direct, but I don't think the king and his guards know about it."

They walked for five days without encountering any other people. Most afternoons, the skies opened, and it rained hard. They sheltered under trees or rocky outcroppings during the worst of the deluge. When the storm passed, the sun shone, sparkling on the clear droplets spread over the forest. As soon as the rain ended, the birds and monkeys resumed their activities, and the travelers went on.

Kael led them to caves or protected nooks in the forest where they could sleep. If none of those could be found, they spent the nights in the branches of the huge trees. They all took turns on guard. Dia insisted she take her turn like the others, but she hated to feel alone in the jungle night as the others slept. The dark nights, alive with the sounds of insects and animals, brought back the memory of being attacked by a jaguar when Sam was ill. Shivering at the thought, she rubbed the nearly healed claw marks on her arm and watched the dark forest carefully.

Only a few times did a predator come near them, and Kael quickly frightened it away. Travel was so much easier with a guide who knew the jungle. Dia couldn't help but watch Sam. Even under her continual scrutiny, he showed no signs of his previous condition. She would not bring up how much easier travel became when he wasn't fighting against them.

Dia often caught Sam's eyes on her, but he didn't try to touch her, and while he was courteous when he spoke to her, he didn't bring up their situation. It was continually on her mind, and she guessed he felt the same. She didn't avoid him, but she didn't try to get closer to him. She still fought the fear that flooded through her when she remembered what had happened. There had been no warning in that moment. Even though he was himself again, she feared he would change. How could she overcome the reaction she had to her fear? She needed more time.

Dia walked at the best pace she could, but she couldn't go as far or as fast as the men. They never complained about her speed, and she was grateful. However long it took, they would reach their destination. What would they find when they got back to Kulin? It would be dangerous. For now, she concentrated on enjoying the journey, every tree and flower, every breath and heartbeat. Any of them might die in the coming confrontation.

After a long day of travel, exhaustion weighed down Dia's limbs. The sun sank into the distant jungle. "There's a place we can stay," Kael said from the head of their group. "Just a little farther."

Inwardly, she groaned, barely managing to keep the sound from escaping her lips. A little farther could mean many things. No distance ever seemed to tire Kael. He led them on, and she trudged after him, her eyes on her feet. A hand touched hers, and she looked back to see Sam just behind her.

"We're almost there."

He was close enough to touch her. Despite the faint sliver of fear, she loved having him beside her. She couldn't help but smile at his optimism. "Thank you." She squeezed his hand.

They walked together, and she loved having him beside her. Attempting to push her unease into the background, she concentrated on how good in felt when he held her hand. She watched him, but his eyes remained warm and kind, and he seemed himself. She smiled up at him and intertwined her fingers with his.

Thank the Soul Mother he was all right. During those terrible days, she'd thought the man she loved was gone forever.

Darkness had fallen by the time they reached a cliff face with giant tree roots guarding a small open space at its foot. They gathered in the sheltered nook and ate a meal of fruit, nuts, and dried meat. Sam sat beside her. He bent closer to whisper in her ear. "My brave Dia, no matter what happens to us, I'll love you for the rest of my life."

"I love you too," she murmured.

She was so tired, and he felt so good beside her. She rested her head against his shoulder. He put his arm around her and pulled her closer. The others had all settled down for sleep, except for Kael, who stood guard a short distance away.

"I understand if you can't forgive me for what I did." Sam's whisper was so low only she could hear it.

She turned to answer softly in his ear. "I *do* forgive you, and I never blamed you. None of it was your fault. But I still need a little time to work through this. I'm trying not to be afraid."

"You're afraid I might suddenly change and hurt you?"

His warm breath on her ear, and the solid strength of his body against hers were reassuring, but she had to be honest. "Yes."

His arm tightened around her. "I would rather die than hurt you."

Dia woke sometime in the black darkness at the distant howl of a wolf. A soft gasp escaped her lips before she was alert enough to silence it.

"It's all right," Sam whispered beside her. "Altan is still keeping watch. The wolves are still a long way off. It'll be my turn on guard in an hour or two."

"Why aren't you sleeping?" she murmured.

He bent close to reply. "I was. I started thinking of you and I woke up."

The warmth in his tone sent butterflies through her middle. Having him so near had brought back memories for her too—not just the frightening ones but good times they had spent before they were banished.

"I can't stay away from you, or even stop thinking about you," he whispered. "You're my wife. I want you back."

His fingers brushed softly along her jaw, finding her chin and raising her lips to meet his. The kiss began gently, with infinite care and tenderness, his lips soft against hers. It felt so right that she didn't stop to think. Instead, she pulled him closer. When he deepened the kiss, she responded.

Her heart was pounding before he pulled back. She would have pulled him close again, except that another wolf howled, closer this time.

Altan's voice came out of the dark. "If they get any closer, we need to climb."

The others were awake now.

A huge dark shape soared over the treetops. Two, then three times, it passed over them, but they made no light and no sound. They all watched the sky until the stars faded and a misty dawn lit the jungle, and they traveled on.

CHAPTER 25

TWO NIGHTS LATER, SAM woke suddenly in the deep dark of the jungle night. He listened intently, sure some sound had woken him. His eyes roamed the lush vegetation all around him, but he saw no sign of danger. The night was quiet except for the usual sounds of jungle life. Dia lay at his side, curled up in slumber, her breathing soft and peaceful. She needed her rest. They'd walked a long way that day. He closed his eyes.

Sam.

His eyes shot open again. Someone had called his name. Dia hadn't stirred beside him, and he saw the sleeping forms of his friends around them, all except Altan, who stood nearby on guard. Sam could just make out his shape, a little distance away, looking out into the dark jungle, paying no attention to Sam. Who?

Something stretched and stirred inside his head. *Did you think you could keep me locked away?*

Sam's stomach clenched at the sound of the voice he hated. He bent all his concentration on shoring up the wall holding that other consciousness captive.

He thought he heard the distant sound of cold laughter. *Sam, you're not strong enough to keep me in here. Sooner or later, I will get out. And I'm going to kill her.*

Sam glanced down at Dia, sleeping so trustingly beside him. The starlight glowed on the smooth pale skin of her arms and her throat. Her breathing was quiet and even. She looked slender, fragile, and vulnerable.

The sudden memory of his hands around her throat overcame him, his mind and will bound, while his enemy attempted to destroy the person he loved most.

With all his might, Sam thrust the voice back behind the wall. Breathing in gasps, his jaw clenched, he looked down at Dia. No matter what else happened, he couldn't allow his enemy to hurt her again. By some miracle, she'd forgiven him. Now, she was just beginning to trust him again. He'd meant what he told her, that he'd rather die than give in to the voice again.

He remained still, staring out at the jungle, concentrating on the wall in his mind. He imagined making it thicker, higher, impenetrable. That other mind *could not* escape to harm Dia. He wouldn't allow it. There was no way he could sleep again. The rest of the night passed slowly.

Before dawn, Altan woke them. "Men coming."

It was unlikely the newcomers would be friendly. Everyone stirred and prepared to flee or fight if they were found. Waiting in silence on the branch of an enormous tree, they watched a company of outcasts pass beneath them. Dia took Sam's hand and gripped it tightly.

It meant everything to him that she turned to him when she was frightened. He intended to be the one she could always rely on.

When the forest was quiet again, they traveled on. Sam focused on the sounds of life in the wilderness surrounding him. Dia walked beside him, and their friends were with them, but in the quiet of his mind, he heard the distant sound of the sorcerer imprisoned in his mind, trying to escape.

They halted for the night on a sheltered ledge at the bottom of the great cliff. It was Sam's turn on guard. He took his place standing against the wall of rock while the others settled for sleep. He'd been staring out into the jungle when he felt fingers brush against his hand.

Dia stood beside him. She looked up at him, giving him the sweet smile that never failed to melt his heart. Her caring was obvious in the expression, but Sam didn't deserve her love. Maybe he never had. But he wanted it, like he wanted air to breathe. He fought to control the urge to put his arms around her and never let go.

"May I kiss you?" he murmured. "Please?"

In answer, she moved closer to him, sliding her arms around his neck. He pulled her closer, drawing her against him, her mouth to his. Her lips were soft and sweet, and he wanted the moment to last forever. He wanted her to stay there in his arms.

Far too soon, she broke the kiss and slipped away. "Good night, Sam. I love you."

"I love you, too." The chill of her absence surrounded him. He wanted to follow her, to pull her back against him.

Turning to look at him over her shoulder, she smiled and returned to the others, settling down to sleep.

His eyes traced her slender form as she curled up and closed her eyes. There was no doubt she was the best part of his life. He would do everything he could to make sure no one ever hurt her again.

A cold laugh sounded in the back of his mind. *You are weak! I won't be imprisoned forever, and when I get free, she will be mine.*

No! Sam focused on the word. No. No. He couldn't let the sorcerer escape and harm Dia.

See if you can stop me, Prince Samanath. I am stronger than you.

No. I'm strong. I'm in control, Sam chanted to himself. I will stay in control.

He stood for a long time concentrating on the idea of control, and the barrier in his mind. Midnight passed, and Kael took over his post as guard. Sam lay on the ground near Dia, closed his eyes, and drifted into sleep with the sounds of the jungle surrounding him.

In his dream, Sam walked through the palace gardens. Lush flowers and plants surrounded him, and the sun shone down brightly, the clear sky spread wide above him in the way it never did in the jungle.

Well-dressed people stood in little groups, laughing and chatting and eating delicacies from small plates. No one looked at Sam, no one seemed to notice him, until he saw Dia slipping through the crowd toward him. The aquamarine silk of her gown shimmered, and the smooth strands of her hair mingled with a translucent silver veil. She was so beautiful. She smiled at him, her eyes bright with love. They were together. Contentment filled him, until the moment was broken by a cry.

Sam turned to see King Hashoreth standing atop the stone railing. He was only a handsbreadth from falling, nothing behind him but space and the jungle thousands of feet below. Sam ran toward him, focused on nothing but helping him down out of danger.

His grandfather's eyes focused on him. "Protect them for me, Sam." As he finished the words, a figure in a dark cloak appeared, shoving the king off balance. Arms flailing, he fell.

Sam ran, his heart pounding, but he was too far away, and his grandfather plummeted from sight. "No!" Sam screamed. He reached the edge and seized the man, ripping the dark cloak away. "You killed my grandfather!"

Hashoreth's face looked back at him when the cloak was gone. "Don't worry, Sam. I'm not dead. I'm right here. There's nothing left to worry about."

Sam tried to confront him. "You killed him!"

Hashoreth shook his head. "That can't be true, Sam. I'm right here. Now, you and I can work together to rule Ischar."

"But you're not him! You're not my grandfather. You killed him and took his place."

A cold smile grew on the old man's face. "You can't stop me."

The expression chilled Sam to the bone. But then, fury flared up in Sam, burning away the cold. "I won't let you do this!" He had to stop the imposter. The time had come to fight back. He leapt forward, seizing the man by the throat. Someone must stop him. Sam had to destroy him.

Despite Sam's grip on his neck, the man's eyes met his. Sam couldn't allow his determination to waiver.

All at once, the imposter disappeared, and it was Dia he held by the throat. He released her instantly, but she crumpled to the ground. Agony coursed through Sam, and he knelt beside her. Her beautiful eyes stared blankly back at him, and she didn't move at all. Dark bruising surrounded the ivory skin of her slender throat. Frantically, he laid his ear against her chest, hearing no sound of a heartbeat, no movement of breath.

"No!" he gasped. His hands had done this. Sinking to the ground beside her, he clutched her still body, holding on to her desperately. He couldn't let her go.

Sam's eyes jolted open to see the dark jungle and cliffs. He couldn't breathe. Every muscle was clenched, and his gut churned with nausea.

"Sam!"

Slowly Dia's voice penetrated his confusion. She wasn't dead. The sorcerer hadn't forced him to kill her. She was here. It had been a dream. He dragged in a breath.

"It's all right," she said, placing a cool hand on his forehead. "You're all right, Sam. Breathe."

He drew in another ragged breath. He realized he was clutching her arm, much too tightly. "I'm sorry," he gasped, removing his fingers. "It was only a dream."

"That's right." She brushed her fingers along his jaw.

Her soft voice and the gentle feel of her hand on his face soothed him. He took in long, deep breaths, trying to calm his mind, relax his body, and focus on where he was now. Dia was here, she wasn't hurt. He turned to see Adengo on his other side.

"I'm sorry, Sam," his uncle said. "I wish there was more I could do to help." He dug in his pack, pulling out a packet of medicinal herbs. He gave Sam a section of a long slender root. "Chew this, it will help a little."

Sam was alarmed when his hand shook as he took it. He chewed the woody root and tried to slow his breathing. Dia moistened a piece of cloth from the water bottle and applied it to his forehead.

"You'll be all right. We'll get through this together." She held his head in her lap and whispered to him until unconsciousness slowly took him.

CHAPTER 26

As the afternoon sun began to descend, Dia stopped as Kael held up a hand in warning. He bent low over the forest floor ahead of them. "Someone passed this way since the last rain. Several men."

"Outcasts?" Adengo asked.

Kael nodded. "None of our people are in this area. The rest of you, find someplace to hide, and I'll go take a look."

They waited in a shallow cave, a single room with a smooth, sandy floor, for Kael to return. After a while, when there was no sign of Kael returning, Adengo got to his feet. "Stay here," he instructed Sam. "Altan and I will find him." They disappeared out of the opening.

Dia and Sam were alone. It was the first time since they'd met Kael that they'd been alone together. No one else stood guard in case something went wrong. Dia felt a quiver in her stomach as Sam sat down beside her. She sneaked a glance, only to find him already looking at her.

"Are you afraid of me now?" he murmured.

Some part of her was, but maybe that would never go away. Even if that were true, she still loved him, and she chose to trust him. She met his eyes and answered firmly. "No."

He drew her close and kissed her. His mouth was warm and firm, and the brush of his hands against her skin made her heart beat faster.

"I know I don't deserve your love. I don't deserve you," he murmured, pulling his lips from hers and trailing kisses down her neck. "But I can't help wanting you."

Her breath hitched at the feel of his mouth against her throat, and she could barely get the words out. "I promised I would never go." She had made that promise before the worst of their trials had happened. Though she'd had moments when she wondered if she could keep it, she wanted to. "I won't leave you."

He pulled back and raised his eyes to meet hers. "Even after what I did?"

She blinked back tears. It hadn't been Sam that had done it. "Even then."

Tears welled in his eyes, but he smiled and drew her close against him. "You're the best part of my life."

When Dia heard Adengo's voice at the mouth of the cave, she slid away from Sam and got to her feet. He followed her.

"Kael's back," Adengo said. "We need to go."

As they slung their bags over their shoulders and left the cave, Adengo filled them in. "Kael found a group of the outcasts, and we are changing our path to avoid them. If we move quickly, we should be able to avoid a confrontation. He will meet us a little farther along."

They hurried through the thick undergrowth, trying to be quiet. Adengo stopped abruptly in front of Dia, and she looked past him to see Kael. The young man couldn't move. Four men held his arms, and another pressed a knife against his throat.

The one holding the knife grinned as he saw them. It was Ravi. Dia remembered him from their earlier encounters, a dark-haired man with a thick beard. "Adengo, old friend, I thought you should be here to watch me kill your son."

"What do you want from me?" Adengo's eyes were on the knife against Kael's skin.

"You live a nice life in that village," the man said. "I'd like you to turn over your position to me. I can lead them just as well as you."

"Let him go, and we can talk," Adengo said.

"Oh, it's not that easy." Ravi's grin was cold.

For a long moment, they all remained still. What were they going to do? Sam stepped from behind the others to stand protectively in front of her. As he moved, the man with the knife suddenly spotted him. His eyes locked on Sam and his jaw dropped a little open.

"It's him." His feet shifted uncomfortably, and his eyes darted around as if looking for an escape path.

"Who?" another outlaw asked.

"The crazy man. We're not fighting him. He killed two men last time."

He made a sudden leap for the cover of the underbrush. The others released Kael, vanishing into the forest. A moment later, they were alone.

"Thanks," Kael nodded at Sam. "Let's get out of here."

They ran.

Kael led them through the jungle, and they ran until Dia thought her lungs would burst. Finally, they stopped, gathering between the giant roots of a tree. When they paused for a moment, Adengo embraced his son. "I'm so glad you're safe."

Kael slapped his father's back. "Thanks to Sam." He turned to grin at Sam. "Your last meeting with them must have made quite an impression."

It had. It was a moment Dia would never forget.

"There are more outcasts gathered," Kael said. "More of them than we usually see together. It will be dark soon, and we need to put some distance between us."

As night fell, Dia heard something behind them. "What's back there?" she asked Sam. It sounded like someone was following them.

They increased their pace, but the pursuit grew nearer until they all heard it closing in. Several people were following them. They pushed forward, only to come out into a wide clearing brightly lit with torchlight. A large group of outcasts stood in the open space.

As they turned to run back the way they had come, the men who had been pursuing seized them. Their friends rushed to help. At least eight men tackled Sam. Someone grabbed Dia from behind. She struggled but couldn't break his grip. The others fought too, but they were outnumbered. The sounds of fighting quieted as their attackers wrestled them to the ground. For a moment, it was quiet.

The howl of a wolf broke the silence. Then another. Dia looked up. In this open space, no trees hid them from the sky, and the bright light of torches would be visible for miles above the dark jungle. In the moonlight, she saw it coming from a long way off; it was only a black speck in the distance at first, but growing larger all the time.

Wolves ran into the clearing, snarling. Several men still held Dia and her friends, but others turned to defend themselves. With their attention occupied, they didn't see the black shadow until it was directly above them. Dia looked toward the sky. Giant talons swooped down toward them. She ducked low. With a blast of wind, it passed, gripping two of the men who'd been holding Sam in its talons. The bird lifted them into the sky, and they screamed as it dropped them into the jungle.

The Shadaroc wheeled and dove at them again. Panic and confusion took over the clearing. Men ran in all directions. The outcast holding Dia released her and fled. She scrambled to her feet and darted toward the cover of the trees, two of the wolves charging after her. She bolted to the edge of the jungle, leaping for a branch to pull herself up but not fast enough. Sharp teeth closed on her leg and hot pain flared from the bite. With all her strength, she kicked it directly in the snout, and it released her and fell back. The second wolf snapped, just missing her, as she pulled herself up into the tree and out of reach.

Dia climbed higher until the leaves and branches hid her from view. She could still see down into the clearing, and men fled in all directions as the Shadaroc dove low several more times before it flew off and disappeared.

Before long, the wolves followed it away into the jungle.

With the danger passed, the outlaws gathered themselves together. They collected their injured friends, and Dia heard them deciding where to begin the search for their prisoners. "They went this way," one called, leading a group off into the trees.

Dia wanted to run and keep running, but if she moved now, someone would spot her. Where were Sam and the others?

For hours, the outlaws searched, but Dia didn't hear them find anyone. What was she going to do? By now, dawn was only a few hours away. They would certainly spot her as soon as it got light. She needed to climb down before then, but how could she find her companions?

Dia crept back down the tree. She needed to keep moving in the direction they'd been going before their mishap. As much as she dreaded being alone in the jungle, it was by far preferable to spending time with the outcasts.

In silence, she slid to the ground and tiptoed away. She'd gone only a little distance from the tree, finding her path in the moonlight, before a dark figure loomed in front of her. He seized her as she turned to run, pulling her hard against him.

"This is my lucky day," he hissed.

She recognized Ravi's voice.

He sounded smug. "Now I have you, and your crazy boyfriend is nowhere in sight."

"He's right behind me," Dia lied. "Out there in the trees, can't you see him?"

Whether the man believed her or not, he began to turn uneasily, looking out into the forest for any sign of movement. Taking advantage of his distraction, Dia drove her elbow hard into his gut and twisted out of his grip. She ran, branches whipping at her, underbrush clutching at her legs.

Hard fingers clamped around her arm, dragging her to a stop. She twisted, attempting to wrench her arm away from him.

"That wasn't very nice, my lady." He pulled her closer.

She brought her knee up sharply, aiming for his crotch.

He turned his leg, deflecting the blow. "I don't know why you hate me so much," he said. "None of us is going to escape the jungle. It's a hard life down here. You need an ally. If you stay with me, I can keep you safe."

"Leave me alone," Dia demanded.

"You'll change your mind in time." He pushed her against the wide trunk of a tree and moved closer, pining her body against it. "You'll see how much I can help you." His hips pressed against her. One hand kept a bruising grip on her arm, but the other began to wander over her body.

Dia threw all her strength into fighting him. She *had* to get away. He kissed her neck, and she struggled harder. "Stop!" Such intimacy was reserved only for Sam. This could not be tolerated. She twisted and fought, but he was bigger than her, and much stronger.

"It's better to stop fighting," he murmured.

"No!" Her fear moved into the background as anger welled up inside her. This man had no right to force himself on her. He must be stopped.

Finding an energy buried deep inside her, she seized it and hurled it toward Ravi. The burst of power wrenched him away from her sending him staggering a few steps away. "What—?"

Dia bolted away into the trees, shoving through the tangled jungle growth. After a few moments, she paused, listening, her heart pounding. No sound of pursuit came from behind her. Adengo had never taught her to use her power as a weapon, but tonight, she needed to protect herself.

From the darkness ahead of her, a voice spoke. "Dia!"

It was Sam. He stepped from the shadow beside a tree into a patch of faint moonlight. Relief flooded through her, and she ran to him. He took her hand, and they hurried away.

They had been moving for some time before the sun rose past the distant horizon, allowing morning light to filter down through the jungle foliage. They heard no sound as they walked except the native birds and animals. Beside her, Sam's eyes went to the blood on her leg. "You *are* hurt. Why didn't you tell me?"

The injury ached, especially after walking on it for so long, but she shook her head. "It's not too bad. There wasn't time to do anything about it before."

"We should do something now," Sam insisted. "Let's find water."

They paused beside a small pool fed by a stream of falling water. Dia pulled her shoe off and allowed Sam to wash the wounds. Her leg was heavily bruised beneath the bloody punctures left behind by the wolf's teeth. He left her side and returned a few moments later with a handful of healing leaves. Gently, Sam cleaned her injury and applied the disinfecting sap. She gritted her teeth against the familiar sting.

"I started searching as soon as we escaped the outcasts," he said as he worked. "I'm sorry I didn't find you sooner."

She let out a breath in relief and smiled. "I'm so glad you did. When we got separated, I was afraid I'd be alone, just waiting for them to find me. I'm so grateful we found each other."

He returned her smile. "If I hadn't found you, I would still be looking."

His dark eyes focused on her, and the truth of his words warmed her.

After Sam cleaned and wrapped the injury, they left the pool. With the morning mist lying heavy on the jungle, they searched for hours, looking for any sign of their friends. The day brightened, burning off the tendrils of fog. They saw no one else. Their path led them along the edge of the towering cliff wall.

"There." Sam pointed to a small flat shelf a little way up the rock face. "Let's rest for a while. We should be able to see a little more from up there. Maybe it will help us find them. There's a wide ledge leading up."

Dia didn't even want to look at the cliff, but his idea made sense. If they kept moving around, they might only grow farther from their friends. They picked fruit and filled their bags, and then moved to the base of the cliff.

Dia's chest tightened as she looked at the climb. She shook her head. "I can't."

Sam smiled. "You can. Just stay on the inside, near the wall, and don't look down."

She didn't want to climb up. Sam stepped closer and tilted her chin up to look at his face. He gave her his most charming smile. "You can do this."

"No—"

His lips found hers, covering her protest. His mouth was warm and firm, and she couldn't help but remember how it had been before. She never wanted him to stop. The fear inside her dissolved into warmth.

He drew back and met her gaze. "Now. What were you worried about?"

"It's high."

He leaned closer, nearly bringing their mouths together, but stopping just short. "It's not that high. Is there really anything to worry about?"

There was. Dia was sure of it, but at the moment, she couldn't recall what it might be. Together, they moved cautiously up the ledge onto the small, flat area. Dia sat down close against the cliff wall, as far from the edge as she could get.

He smiled at her. "We can rest here and enjoy the view."

"I'll rest," she said. "*You* enjoy the view."

He scanned the jungle for several moments before sitting beside her. "You climbed up here with no trouble. You're very brave."

She shook her head. "My heart is still racing."

Taking her hand, he smiled. "I hoped it was my presence making your heart race."

Laughing, she gripped his hand. He lifted their joined hands to his mouth and kissed her wrist.

"We need something to eat." He released her hand and opened his pack. With their backs resting against the cliff, they ate a meal of fruit and dried meat. When they were done, they sat together, looking out over the jungle. Sam put his arm around her, and she moved closer, resting her head against his chest.

How she'd missed being close to him. It felt so right and familiar to be together.

He brushed his fingers lightly along her arm, slowly, from her shoulder down to her wrist. He drew her hand to his mouth and kissed the palm of her hand. Her eyes closed at the sensation of his lips against her skin. He moved to her wrist, the prickle of his beard rough against her skin.

A gasp escaped her lips.

She wasn't sure she felt ready to be so close to him, but she didn't want him to stop. He raised his head, and she kissed him, allowing her loneliness and longing for him to flow into the way she clung to him. He lay back, pulling her on top of him, wrapping his arms around her.

He groaned. "I've missed you—so much." His kisses blazed against her lips, and she responded, pulling him even closer.

Abruptly, Sam gasped and pulled away.

Dia sat up, startled. "What is it?"

His jaw clenched. "I—I need a moment." He looked away from her, scanning the jungle as if he hoped to see something.

She put her hand on his arm. "What's wrong, Sam?"

He drew in a heavy breath. "It's *him*. His voice is louder than it was." He met her gaze, his pupils dilated and his expression a little dazed. "I want you, Dia, enough that I almost lost control. I want you so much that I almost forgot to hold up the wall in my head."

No. He couldn't lose control. Dia slid rapidly away from him. She wanted him too, but they could *not* allow the sorcerer to take control of him again. Had it been her fault? She should never have kissed him. "I'm sorry."

He rubbed his head. "No. It's not you. You didn't do anything wrong." He looked out over the jungle again.

Dia's eyes followed his. They needed to find Adengo. He could help Sam.

The afternoon lengthened as they sat together, now with a few feet between them. They didn't speak or touch each other. Sam sat with his forearms resting on his knees, his head down. She wanted to comfort him, but what could she do?

The sun set behind the cliffs, and the air cooled. "Let's climb down and try to find somewhere safe to spend the night," she suggested.

He nodded.

They moved slowly down the ledge to the bottom. Dia let out a sigh of relief at being back on the ground again. They moved off into the jungle, looking for somewhere sheltered. The light was fading fast, and there was no hope of finding their friends in the dark.

Behind her, Sam paused, holding his head with both hands. "No. No." He didn't meet her eyes. "Go back."

Her heart began to pound.

"I can't let him out," Sam said. "I won't." He stood still, his body motionless, his jaw set.

"You can do it," she encouraged him.

He nodded. "I can do it. I can do it."

She needed some way to help him. What could she do? When the gurgle of water sounded ahead of them. Dia took out her empty waterskin. "Stay here for a moment. I'll get some water. Have a drink of water, then we'll keep walking. It's going to be all right."

"All right," he repeated, nodding.

Dia hurried toward the sound of water and filled the container from a clear pool. What would she do if Sam lost control?

Gathering her determination, she went back the way she had come.

Coming around a tree, she saw Sam. He hadn't moved, standing still, gripping his head as if he could hold his skull together. His chest heaved. "Can't hold him," he muttered. "Stop. Go back. I can't—" He raised his head and saw her. Darkness was already growing in his eyes, and he said one more word. "Run."

Dia bolted.

Her feet slipped and skidded on the uneven ground as she dodged protruding roots that reached out to trip her. Heavy crashing steps pursued her. She ran until her side ached, and she gasped for breath in the heavy, humid air. The light grew dimmer, and trying to keep her steps quiet, she hid in a patch of brush.

Holding her breath, she listened. He was still back there. Footsteps grew closer. Her lungs burned, but she didn't dare move or breathe. He passed her, moving away into the trees. She remained where she was, hidden as the darkness deepened around her.

The sounds of the jungle at night swelled up around her. Sounds she had once feared now soothed her. It was his sudden footsteps, approaching again, that caused Dia to run.

"Come back, Dia!" His voice sounded terribly familiar, and yet not like himself at all. "Running won't help. I *will* find you."

Hours passed with her running and then hiding in the dark, fleeing when he got too close. Exhaustion dragged at her, but she couldn't stop, couldn't let him catch her. She stumbled through the branches and vines, over the uneven ground.

How long would the darkness last? If he still hunted her at dawn, he would find her easily in the daylight. Even now, the black sky was lightening to gray. Could she use magic to stop him? The idea of using her hallan against Sam was repulsive, but she was running out of choices.

She crouched at the base of a large tree, melding herself into the heavy shadow there, remaining as still as possible. All was quiet for a time. Too quiet. She realized the normal night sounds had gone silent around her. The roar of a jaguar sounded, out in the dark.

It roared a second time, much closer.

Now the big cat moved silently. Only a quick gleam of eyes in the dark alerted her to the creature stalking her. If she didn't move, it would pounce on her. If she moved, Sam would find her. Would it be better to face the jaguar? She had no good options left. Her heart pounded in her chest, and her knees trembled as she slipped from her hiding place.

A hard hand seized her wrist.

"Well." Sam's voice, his tone as cold as ice. The voice came from his mouth, but it didn't sound like Sam. It wasn't him.

Whipping around, she saw his tall form in profile in the fading darkness. She struggled, attempting to pull her hand away from his powerful grip.

"You should never have tried to run."

She glanced over her shoulder to see a sleek feline body at the edge of the clearing, gathering itself to spring. With all her strength, she twisted her body, wrenching her arm out of his hand. The jaguar sprang toward them, and Dia threw herself down, rolling to one side.

With a snarl, the beast pounced on Sam. Hissing in pain as its claws struck him, he kicked it away from himself. He just had time to draw his knife and yell a wild challenge before the cat attacked again. For a moment, she saw only two black shapes struggling. The animal snarled and then yipped in pain. It retreated, and Sam followed, striking it one more time with his knife.

With a yelp, the cat slunk away into the underbrush.

It grew lighter every moment, and Dia knew there would be no more hiding from him. Sam's eyes locked on her, the knife still in his hand, and the monster inside him looked out from the shell of her husband. Dia had no other choice. She scrambled to her feet and ran.

CHAPTER 27

IN PANIC SHE SPRINTED, jumping over fallen logs and stones, moving as fast as she could, but knowing he could catch up with her any time—the pain in her leg from the wolf bite slowed her as much as the exhaustion of the last several hours. Underbrush scratched at her; tangled roots attempted to trip her, slowing her progress even more.

She charged around a giant tree, certain that she would not make it another step more and ran headlong into a man. In the gray light of dawn, she realized it was Adengo. He caught her.

"It's Sam!" she gasped.

Sam was only a moment behind. Before he could reach them, Kael stepped from behind a tree, seized his knife hand, and struck his head. Sam crumpled. Kael took off his pack, rapidly pulling out rope. A moment later, he had tied Sam securely.

Adengo held Dia. Her body shook violently. "It will be all right now," he murmured. She burst into tears.

Kael approached them. "Please take Dia a little way up the trail and find a place she can rest. I will take care of Sam."

Adengo released her, and Kael took his place. Trying to regain control, Dia watched him go to Sam and kneel beside him. She couldn't look, and she buried her face in Kael's shoulder. How had she let her guard down? She had wanted so badly to believe that Sam would remain himself. How foolish she'd been to believe it.

"Come with me," Kael said gently, ushering her away from them.

She didn't try to object as he led her through the trees to a rock face with a shallow depression in it. Dia sank down on the sandy floor, curling herself into a ball.

Kael's hand rested on her shoulder. "We won't let him hurt you. It will be all right."

How could she believe him? How could it possibly be all right?

When Dia opened her eyes, the sun had moved. Her head ached from crying, and her throat felt tight. Her body was stiff and sore from her long flight.

Kael sat beside her, looking out into the trees. "They're coming."

A wave of fear swept over her, and she sat up, sliding to the back of the stony nook. She watched them come, Adengo in the lead, walking softly between the trees. He met her eyes and nodded. "He is himself again."

How could Adengo be sure? Sam had tried so hard to remain in control, and he'd failed.

Sam stepped into view from behind his uncle. He gazed at her, his eyes full of shame and pain, but their brown depths were entirely Sam.

She took in a deep breath. He was all right. For now.

—◦◦◦—

They rested where they were for another day. Kael disappeared silently into the jungle to look for Altan. Adengo sat beside Sam to clean and treat the claw marks left behind by the jaguar. They weren't nearly as bad as the first time they'd tangled with one of the big cats but still looked painful. Sam sat still, not saying a word, while his uncle worked on him.

"You haven't been in the jungle long," Adengo said, raising one eyebrow. "I've never seen anyone so eager to fight with jaguars. You should learn to stay away from them."

Sam's jaw tightened, but he didn't reply.

Very slowly, Dia began to relax a little. She wasn't seriously hurt other than scratches and bruises. She rested and ate, then rested again, trying to overcome the exhaustion. Sam avoided her, not even looking at her.

Every time she turned away, she felt his gaze on her.

Dia stayed close to Adengo. The temporary closeness she'd shared with Sam had vanished. More than anything, she wanted it back. But how?

An hour before sunset, Kael returned, a slightly battered Altan at his side. He had a cut across his forehead, and he held one arm close to his chest. Dried blood stood out against his skin. They gave him water and food, and Adengo tended his wounds. When darkness fell, they set their guard and rested.

—◦◦◦—

Dia opened her eyes to see morning light spreading through the trees. She didn't feel ready to continue their journey, but they couldn't stop now. They had to go on. Halderan was up there in Kulin, waiting for them. A wave of anger rose inside her. The sorcerer had tried to kill her several times. Worse than that, he'd tried to force Sam to do it. The sorcerer had been in Sam's head. He fully understood how much pain it would cause Sam, and he didn't care. He'd hurt too many people already.

How could she fight him? He was old and powerful, drawing from a well of knowledge that she could only imagine. Still, he had destroyed her life, and she must do something to oppose him. If she acted now, maybe there was still time to save the people of Kulin. Maybe she could still save Sam.

In her heart, Dia knew that, even if she failed, she had to try. They had to stop Halderan.

She got up and walked over to Sam where he sat slumped on the ground, his head on his folded arms. She gripped his shoulder. He turned to look up at her, his eyebrows raised. "I won't let him do this to us," she said, her gaze holding Sam's. "Are you ready to go?" Slowly the ghost of a smile crossed his face, and he got to his feet.

They traveled on, and for a few more days, they made steady progress on their journey. As the sun sank, they arrived at the mouth of a cave. This one was nothing like the small sandy caverns they had sheltered in before. A chill breeze wafted from it, and Dia shivered despite the warm night.

"How deep is it?" she asked, nodding toward the back of the cavern.

Kael grinned. "It's huge. No one knows for sure. But if we want to get back to the top of the plateau, we have to go in."

"Have you been inside before?" She stared wide-eyed at the black tunnel before them.

"Many times," Kael said. "It will take a day or two to get through, but we can do it."

"In there? An entire day... or two?" her voice cracked. A whole day in the dark and the cold?

"It's the only other way I know to get to the top," Kael said. "Unless you want to go back to the causeway gate and knock. I haven't been all the way onto the plateau this way, but I've been through the cave."

The idea of going back to the causeway made Dia shiver. She'd already had more than enough contact with the outcasts. Apprehension filled her as she stared into the cave. It wasn't going to be pleasant, but it was better than the other option. They made what preparations they could, filling their bags with fruit and nuts. Kael assured them they'd be able to find water inside. They carefully prepared dozens of wooden torches, tying them into bundles.

"Get some rest," Adengo advised them. "Sleep now. I will watch."

As dawn brightened the forest outside, they turned their backs on the sunlight and warmth, lit the first torch, and began their dark journey. Kael held the flame aloft and led them. The gradually shrinking point of white light that marked the entrance soon passed out of sight. Inside the cave, the air felt damp. Some of the walls shimmered with moisture. The warm orange glow of flame provided the only light. Beyond the edges of its flickering glow, the cavern was utterly dark. It was cold inside, a strange contrast to the heat of the jungle.

Dia followed Sam through the dimly lit passageways. His footsteps fell steadily, and she firmly resisted the temptation to stop him, so she could look into his eyes. After their scare a few days ago, she wasn't sure how firm his control was. She made sure Adengo wasn't far behind her in case something went wrong.

Poor Sam. He didn't deserve to have another person force him to act in ways he never would on his own. She sensed the pain recent events had caused him. Now, he walked silently, not touching her, not speaking, his footsteps making a steady rhythm against the stone.

They took a course that wound back and forth, climbing steadily. After a few hours of travel, they came to a vertical rock face that required them to climb. She hated heights under any circumstances, but she had succeeded in climbing onto the ledge with Sam just a few days ago. She would try her best. Still, Dia did not feel confident in her skills. What if she reached a point where she couldn't reach any hand or foot holds, and there was nowhere else to go? Or what if she lost her grip and fell to her death, possibly taking Sam, just behind, with her?

Maybe he heard the pace of her breath increase with her fear. Sam broke his long silence and murmured, "It will be just like climbing the other day. You can do this."

She took in a deep breath and repeated it to herself. *You can do this.* Sam supported her. Even now, he did everything he could to help her.

"Here," Kael's voice came down from the top of the rock shelf. A length of rope fell down beside her. "I've anchored the other end. Tie it around yourself."

Dia obeyed. The rope made her feel a little more secure.

"It will stop you if you slip," Kael said. "But it won't feel good. Try not to fall."

She shook her head. That was the best advice he had—try not to fall?

Finding a secure hold for each of her hands, she gripped the rock. Taking in a deep breath, she moved one foot off the cavern floor. A moment later, she lifted her other foot. A tendril of panic wound through her as she realized that her hands and feet where they gripped the rock and a slender line were all that connected her to the rock face. She focused her gaze on the rope leading up the cliff face.

Drawing in a deep breath, she reached higher. Despite being terrified, she had to go on. Higher and higher she climbed. The muscles in her forearms burned, but the flickering light of the torch above her grew closer. She focused on it, determined not to look down.

At last, she reached the brink, and Kael helped her up onto the ledge.

"Nice job." He grinned at her, loosening the knot and removing the rope.

She returned his smile, breathing hard, her hands still shaking, but relieved and proud of her accomplishment. Behind her, Sam pulled himself over the edge, and they all sat resting for a while.

In the constant blackness inside the caverns, time disappeared. Dia had no way of knowing how long they'd been inside. For what seemed like days, they climbed on and on, taking occasional breaks for food and drinking from pools along the way. She grew more exhausted. The temptation to beg the others for a break grew stronger, but she stubbornly refused to be the only one who needed a rest.

By the time Kael finally halted them, she felt ready to collapse. They stopped in a cavern, dryer than some, but filled with strange rock formations. "Try to sleep a little," he advised them. "I'll watch and keep an eye on the torch."

The uneven rock floor was uncomfortable, but desperate for rest, Dia sank down gratefully anyway. The stone was hard and chill beneath her.

"Do you want something to eat?" Sam offered her a piece of jerky.

"Thanks." She took it and started to chew.

He settled beside her. She wrestled down a sharp twinge of fear at having him so close. Part of her wanted to move farther from him to create a safe space between them, but she hadn't seen any sign of him changing since she'd run from him a few days ago. Silently, she drew in a slow breath. For some time, they ate together in silence.

Sam turned his eyes to meet hers in the orange light. "No matter what else happens when we get back to Kulin, I have to stop Halderan. Whatever it takes. He killed my parents, my grandfather, and he wants to kill you. I won't allow him to do it."

She put her hand over his and gripped it. "I'm so sorry about your family, Sam."

He put his other hand over hers. "They're gone now, at rest. You are my family now, and I will do everything I can to protect you. May the Soul Mother grant that we have the strength to defeat him."

The cavern grew silent as they all settled to sleep. Dia clenched her jaw in a vain attempt to keep her teeth from chattering. The others appeared to be resting, but the cold surrounded her, depriving her of sleep. Shivers wracked her body.

Sam moved closer. "Dia? I can keep you warm, if you let me."

By then, she was so cold that she forgot to be afraid. She slid closer to him, and he wrapped his arms around her.

"Your hands are like ice." He pulled her closer, and she rested her head against his chest. He felt familiar and so warm. It felt right to touch him and have his arms around her. She wished for a thick warm cloak like the one Sam had loaned to her that rainy night back in Ischar. It seemed a thousand years ago now. Would their lives ever be free from running? Unsure of what lay ahead, she snuggled closer to Sam and allowed exhaustion to claim her.

After a few brief hours, they went on, too cold to remain still any longer. It took a long time before the exertion of climbing warmed Dia enough to stop shivering. The muscles of her arms were sore and tired, but they had to go on.

Another exhausting trek brought them to the end of the caverns. In the dark, Dia barely saw the opening, but she smelled a breath of warmer, dryer air infused with the fragrance of growing things, and outside, the sky sparkled with stars. They made their way out into a little rocky hollow surrounded by brush and trees. The night was still around them. She took a deep breath and looked up at the sky, never more grateful to be able to see the stars.

Outside, the air lacked the prevailing chill of the caverns. Dia was so exhausted that she sank to the ground and let the others explore the area as she curled up, hidden beneath the branches of a thicket of trees and slept.

Sometime in the night, chill set in again, not as cold as the cavern, but enough to have her seeking warmth from Sam. Beside her, his warm, strong arm pulled her to him, resting his head near hers. What would she do without him? But what if he lost control again and listened to that other voice in his mind? The conflicting thoughts battled for dominance in her head. There had to be a way to cure him completely. How else could she ever completely trust him? But she needed him. His people needed him.

When they all awoke, they sat in a circle, sharing a meal. Adengo took out his silver bracelet. The red stone glowed faintly.

"It is the power of hallan. Soul energy," he explained, holding it up. "My abilities are small next to the Shadaroc. But he takes power from many people, and he doesn't care if he kills them to gather the fuel to work his magic. I take only a little at a time from people who are willing to give it. The energy I have is contained here. I will use it in our fight against the dark sorcerer."

Marek had tried the same thing, and he'd lost his life in the attempt. Dia's gaze went to Adengo. His eyes appeared calm and his expression determined. If he feared he was going to his death, he hid it well. In his hand, the stone glowed brightly for a moment.

"Can you change your shape, as he does?" Sam asked.

Adengo nodded. "For a short time at least. I will have to choose how to use what power I have. I will give my own life force as well, as much as is required to defeat him. Will each of you give of your own energy to increase my magic?"

He looked around the circle, meeting each of their eyes. Kael rose and offered his hand to his father. Adengo touched the stone to his palm. Its light brightened at the touch. Kael blinked, swaying on his feet before he sank to his knees. He remained where he was for a moment, just breathing, before he got back to his feet. He stumbled a little on his way back to his seat. The others stared at him.

"Are you all right?" Sam asked.

Kael took in a deep breath and then released it. He nodded. "It's already passing."

Dia stood up and held her hand out to Adengo. Sam followed her. "No, Dia, wait."

She ignored him. This was her fight as much as anyone else's, and she would do her part.

Dia nodded to Adengo, and he touched the stone to her hand. For a moment all the energy in her body vanished at once. Her knees trembled. For a moment, she wondered if she would collapse, but she willed herself to remain standing.

"Dia?" Sam's voice was full of concern. He turned to his uncle. "What did you do to her?"

Adengo met his eyes steadily. "She'll be all right in a moment. She's stronger than you realize."

Sam turned back to her.

She took a deep breath, feeling stronger by the moment. "I'm all right, Sam."

He stepped forward and offered his own hand to Adengo. At the touch of the stone, his body crumpled, sinking to the ground. Dia bent over him. He stared up at her, his eyes wide. "Did—did it feel like that to you?"

She nodded. "Breathe. It will pass in a moment." Perhaps her brief experience with hallan made it easier for her.

Altan came forward and took his turn. After the strange exchange, they sat resting for a while as the sun grew higher.

Only a short while later, Dia felt like herself again. Now she knew what it felt like when someone drained her hallan. The experience of losing power and energy was opposite to the rush of feeling when she gained it. If she ever borrowed the power from someone else, she would remember what they were truly offering her.

Sam took a little longer to recover, but after resting and eating, his energy returned to normal, and they resumed their journey. As they left their camp behind, Dia saw that it had been hidden in a notch in the cliffs. Their way now ran much nearer the cliff edge. She looked out over the jungle and felt her stomach flip at how high they were. They had climbed well over a thousand feet and were now about half way up the towering wall. Kael led them along a narrow ledge that climbed steadily upward.

"We'll reach the top of the plateau by tomorrow night," Kael said, shading his eyes with his hand, as he gazed up the rock face toward their goal.

They moved steadily up the trail as the sun sank, leaving their path in heavy shadow. They walked in silence, their feet barely making a sound against the stones. The quiet evening suddenly rang with the howls of wolves. Horrified, Dia saw sleek gray bodies running up the narrow path toward them. Sam stepped protectively in front of her, pulling out his machete.

In a moment, the wolves were on them. Dia's breath was rapid and shallow, as Sam struck at the nearest with his blade and kicked the animal. It yelped and backed up. Altan grunted as sharp teeth closed on his arm. Kael came to his aid, striking the animal and forcing it to release its hold.

For several moments everything was a tangle of fur and teeth and fighting men. Three wolves jumped on Kael, driving him to slip from the cliff edge to cling to the rocks. Altan grabbed him, dragging him back to the safety of the ledge. Adengo struck down another wolf with his machete.

Dia screamed as two of the beasts leapt at Sam. As he drove one back, the other snapped at his leg. With only her small knife in her hand, Dia lunged forward to strike it. Snarling, the animal turned from Sam and bit at her. Its teeth grazed her side as Sam whirled to knock it away from her.

The remaining members of the pack turned and fled back the way they had come. A few had gone over the edge, and four of the animals lay on the stones dead or dying. Quiet descended over the rocky ledge. Dia stood with her companions, trying to catch her breath. They looked around for further danger.

"What are they doing here?" Kael asked, wiping sweat from his brow.

At that question, cold fear expanded in her belly. Dia searched the clear evening sky. "It's here."

CHAPTER 28

THEY DIDN'T SEE THE Shadaroc coming. From above, the enormous bird dove past them, sending a violent blast of wind across the ledge where they stood. Dia crouched against the rocks to keep her balance. The sudden wind drove stinging dust and sand against her skin, and she narrowed her eyes against it.

"We have to get out of here!" Sam yelled. "Hide." He straightened up, offering Dia his hand.

"That way!" Kael pointed back down the hill.

It was their only option. The climbing path ahead was bare rock with no cover at all. They turned and fled back the way they had come toward a sheltered fold in the cliff. This time, they saw the bird approaching. At first, it appeared small in the distance, as if it was only the size of an ordinary hawk. It moved fast, growing quickly nearer. When it swooped close, its giant wings blocked out the fading sunset, seeming to cover the entire sky.

The bird flew directly at them, giant talons reaching for them. Dia dodged out of its way, diving toward the ground, and Sam followed, covering her body with his own. He stiffened and grunted in pain. The bird must have struck him.

How badly was he hurt? "Sam!"

The bird passed by, winging away to turn and attack again.

They got up and kept going. Taking her hand, Sam pulled her forward. A thick stripe of blood spread across his back, appearing black in the dim light. He was hurt. He'd taken the impact of the huge talons, placing himself between them and Dia. She needed to see how bad it was. She had to help him.

The bird struck with its beak the next time, knocking Kael and Altan hard against the rock wall. One of its wings struck Adengo and Sam, driving them to the ground. The Shadaroc hovered there, flapping its enormous wings and blasting them with wind. It came closer, reaching out.

Giant talons closed around Dia. She screamed, trying to twist away, but the claws surrounded her, pinning her in place. It lifted her from the ground. The bird beat its great wings, gaining altitude in a series of sickening lurches. Dia's stomach churned, and she almost vomited at the sight of the towering cliffs and the jungle, visible only as a dark carpet of trees impossibly far below her.

The wind tore at her hair. She felt the unearthly speed of their flight. Any moment now, the bird would drop her, and she would fall to her death. She closed her eyes, trying to breathe. The talons gripped her too tightly. If it tightened its grip any more, she would be crushed, but if it loosened...

Dia wasn't ready to die. Closing her eyes tightly, memories of Sam flashed through her mind. She saw the time they had spent together at the palace before the king banished them, happy memories of Sam smiling at her, the warmth in his eyes when he said her name, the way she couldn't help but respond when he touched her skin. She loved him, and he loved her. If these were her last moments, she would remember that above everything else.

She had no warning before the bird opened its claws, releasing her into the air. Her shriek of terror cut off abruptly when she struck a ledge of rock. The fall hadn't been deadly. She still lived. The pain along one side of her body where she'd landed proved that.

Dia lay on the stone gasping for breath. For several moments, she did nothing other than breathe. Hot pain burned through her left hip and shoulder, but she was alive. Finally catching her breath, she blinked, taking in her surroundings.

She wasn't alone on the ledge. A man in a long black cloak stood over her.

Instinctively, she dragged her aching body farther away from him. He stood still, observing her efforts with no attempt either to stop her or to help. Her slow movements brought Dia to the cliff wall, and she pushed herself into a sitting position, resting against it. She gripped her injured leg and stared back at him.

The man in the dark cloak stood still, staring at her dispassionately. She didn't doubt for a moment that they were deadly enemies. A sense of creeping dread came over her. A powerful aura of malevolence surrounded him so strong that she felt it to her bones. She needed a weapon, some way to defend herself. Her knife. She reached for the sheath at her belt and found the blade still there. Her fingers closed around the hilt. As the man took a step toward her, she drew the blade and pointed it at him. "Don't come any closer!"

He paused where he was, looking between her and the little knife. He pulled the hood from his head, and she recognized the white hair and features of King Hashoreth. It wasn't him. Even with the same face, she could tell the difference easily this time. She'd never seen the real king wear the cold sneer he wore now.

"You're not Hashoreth," she said firmly, gripping the knife and keeping it pointed at him.

"No. I am not." He stared at her.

"You're Halderan."

He nodded. "That's right. Princess Alladia, why are you trying to return to Ischar? What could you hope to gain by it? You must realize only death awaits you there. Everyone in Kulin is under my command. Ischar is *my* kingdom now."

"No!" Her voice sounded small and thin against the unyielding rock.

When he took another step toward her, she raised her knife again.

Glancing at the small blade, he shook his head in disgust and waved his hand. The weapon tore from her grip, skittering across the rock until it teetered for a moment on the edge and then fell. When he stepped even closer, she tried to slide away from him, but her back was already against the cliff face.

Halderan gestured to each side, to the edges of the small rocky shelf they stood on. "There's nowhere else for you to go."

She glanced upward to see the cliff rising sheer above them and behind him to the vast expanse of empty air.

Moving slowly, he edged closer until his gaze bored into hers. Though his eyes remained the same brown as Hashoreth's, now they glittered with malice in the dim light. He knelt beside her and placed his hand on her forehead. Pressure built beneath his palm where it touched her skin, stronger than before. It felt as if something were outside hammering against her, attempting to get in. Adengo had been right when he trained her to form a barrier. She needed to protect herself.

Halderan had done this to her several weeks ago when she'd been alone in the forest. She hadn't doubted, then or now, that he intended to harm her. This time, the attack was more powerful. It required every scrap of her will to resist.

Why her? What reason could he have to pursue *her* in particular? She wasn't special. Until Sam had come along, no one had ever given her a second glance. No one had ever singled her out for anything. She was shy, quiet, and plain when compared with her tall, stunning sister. But the sorcerer remained determined to destroy her.

Anger welled up inside her. The Shadaroc moved through Ischar taking whatever he wanted, harming whoever he chose without a thought for anyone else. He needed to be stopped. Dia looked up into those cold dark eyes.

"Take your hand off me!" She kicked him with her good leg.

He grunted as her foot collided with his knee, and he clamped his other hand over her ankle, pinning it to the rocks. "You will die if you don't learn to cooperate," he hissed.

For a long moment, he left his hand against her forehead, and she felt the mounting pressure against her mind. The attack grew even more forceful, but she would not, *could* not, yield to him.

Finally, he removed his hand and backed away.

She remained where she was, trying to catch her breath.

He shook his head. "Why are you still fighting against me? I could crush you at any time. At first, I thought that would be the best course, since you have already interfered with my plans several times. But you have great potential, and because of that, before I destroy you, I'll offer you the chance to change your mind." He got back to his feet, still gazing down at her. "You will learn to work with me, or I will kill you. The decision is yours." Halderan glanced toward the edge with its deadly drop. "Try not to fall." He laughed coldly. "There is no safe way off this ledge other than flying. Haven't you stopped to think that if you only stopped fighting against me, I could teach *you* to fly?"

Standing on the edge, he raised his arms. They widened and lengthened until they became great wings. His body, head, and legs transformed into those of a bird. Leaping from the precipice, he soared into the air, leaving her alone.

For a while, Dia waited, savoring his absence. She had no idea how much time she had before he returned. Despite his warning, maybe she could find another way off this ledge. She needed a way back to Sam and the others. They must have seen the Shadaroc carry her away. What could they possibly do about it? Did they know where she was? Maybe they had seen where he left her. Maybe they could reach her... somehow.

Dia pushed herself to her feet. Sharp pain flared from her left hip when she attempted to walk. She limped heavily, but her leg supported her weight, and she hoped that meant nothing was broken. A wave of dizziness washed over her as she stood. For one thing, from that vantage, she could see off the edge, and that wasn't good.

It took only a moment to explore the narrow ledge. It consisted of a flat space only a few feet wide and two or three times that in length. When she looked up, the cliff towered above her, and she couldn't see the top. It was possible she could climb a little way, but, a short distance above her, the cliff jutted out. She had no chance of climbing that. Looking down, she spotted a few other ledges but no way to reach them from here and no more chance of escape from them than where she was. Sometime during her flight here, she'd lost her knapsack. Now, she had nothing with her. Even if she didn't fall, she'd starve on this barren ledge.

Squinting far across the cliff face in the gathering night, she looked for the slender path she'd been walking with Sam and the others. A jutting fold in the rocks hid the place from view. She couldn't see where they were, which meant they most likely couldn't see her. They would have no way of knowing where the bird had taken her or if it had simply released her to fall to her death in the jungle like it had the outcasts.

She slumped against the rocks, pulling her knees up to her chest.

The last glimmer of sunset quickly faded. Dia sat, her back against the stone, watching the stars come out. She needed a solution. As the night passed, the Shadaroc didn't return. Dawn found her shivering and chilled, still watching the sky, slumping against the stones in exhaustion.

The cold of night passed as the sun rose higher. She grew warm and then hot as the cliff face captured the sun. She had no water, no food, and no way to escape. Afternoon brought the blessed relief of shade, and she slid into the shadow as soon as it was wide enough to cover even part of her.

As darkness fell again, the temperature dropped, and she sat with her back against the stone, her knees pulled up against her chest. The rush of wind heralded the approach of the enormous bird. It dropped a bundle onto the rocks and landed on the ledge. As she watched, its shape blurred until a man stood there. Halderan stared at her appraisingly. "You must be thirsty," his voice dripped with mock sympathy. He nodded toward the bundle. "There's water and food in there."

Dia stared back at him. He hadn't come to offer relief, unless she gave in.

"You can have all of it, if you're ready to cooperate." His cold eyes met hers.

She would rather die than help him. "I will not." She held tightly to a fragment of hope that she would find something other than those two options. Maybe Sam and her friends would find her.

Halderan approached her. She wanted to kick him again, to fight, anything. But what could she really do here on this ledge? She didn't move as he knelt beside her and placed his hand on her forehead. She felt the pressure again, like some powerful force trying to break into her skull. Despite feeling physically worn out, her determination hadn't faded.

With all her will, Dia resisted him, refusing to allow the assault inside.

After a long moment, he hissed in frustration and got back to his feet. "I can wait as long as it takes, my dear." He met her gaze. "You can't escape, and you can't overpower me. You can fight as long as you want."

He walked to the stock of supplies and placed his boot against it. With his eyes on hers, he pushed the bundle over the edge, and it fell out of sight.

Dia fought the tears that welled in her eyes. She wouldn't give up, not yet. Sam was still out there, trying to find a way to help her. She was sure of it. When she made no answer, the sorcerer allowed his body to shift and flow into his avian form, and he flew away.

Alone again, Dia let the tears come. Raising her hand to wipe them away was too much effort. She rested her head against her knees and cried.

—◆—

Dia lay parched in the burning sun, waiting for the life-prolonging shade. Her sense of time had faded. Her mouth was dry, her tongue swollen, and her lips cracked. She was too tired to even roll over, though the sun burned against her skin. How long would it take for her to die? She no longer knew how long it had been. Her eyes closed, and she drifted. When she woke, the shade of the cliff had covered her, and the rock felt cool beneath her. Did that mean she would have to live through another night? She didn't know if the chill or heat was worse.

The rush of giant wings and the increase wind answered her question. The night was always worse. That was when he came.

Too weak to move, she could barely register that, instead of turning from bird to man, strong talons closed around her body, lifting her into the air. The cliffs rushed by in a blur. Kulin spread out beneath her, with forests and fields surrounding it. The bright sun sank toward the west.

The immensity of the sky surrounded her while the whole world spread beneath her. The height of it made her head swim and her belly churn.

The Shadaroc flew toward the city, descending toward the forest not far from the walls. Nausea rushed over Dia as the carpet of trees rushed up to meet them. Her empty stomach heaved, but there was nothing left to come up.

The bird dropped her in a small clearing. She struck the grass and rolled. Her mind urged her to run, to flee, as soon as his talons released her, but her body ignored her. She lay where she had fallen, gasping from the shock of impact and still retching.

A hard hand seized her, dragging her upright. Hashoreth's familiar features twisted into a sneer. "You don't look very well, Princess." His eyes traveled over her. "For someone so small and weak, you've been more trouble than I would have thought possible. Why do you fight so hard? You must be miserable. Don't you realize I can make you feel better? All you need to do is help me. Is that so bad?"

Halderan's temporarily kind expression didn't fool her. He didn't really care whether she was miserable. Increasing his own power was his only goal. What more could he want from her? "You already have the city, the whole kingdom. Why should my decision even matter to you?"

He stared at her coldly, without answering, and then moved in the direction of the city, dragging her with him.

Why should it matter?

She turned the question over and over in her weary mind. Why? He'd already won. Everyone acknowledged him king. All of Ischar was his. Yes, she and Sam had made their way back from the jungle to try to stop him, but what chance did they even have?

As the realization settled over her, she drew in a sharp breath. No matter how unlikely, they must have some chance of succeeding; otherwise, why should Halderan care? The very idea felt preposterous at the moment, but he must have some reason he desired her hallan so much. After all he'd done to her, he hadn't killed her.

What would he do next?

As the sun set, he walked out of the forest, dragging her with him to meet a company of men in the crisp gray uniforms of the royal guard. Dia recognized all of them. Kerem stood right in the front. His tall form straight, muscular arms at his sides. His expression, which had always been kind in the past, now appeared strangely blank. He stared at her without a hint of warmth or recognition.

The darkness in his gaze reminded her instantly of Sam, back in the jungle, when he'd been under the sorcerer's control. An icy silver of terror wound its way through her. How many minds had Halderan taken?

He dropped her at the feet of the company of guards. "I have no doubt that Prince Samanath will come looking for you. In a way, I'm grateful to you for leading him back here. It will be easier to rule this land with him at my side."

"He won't obey you," Dia protested.

The sorcerer laughed. "He has no choice. There is no way he can escape the splinter in his head. He might have tried to lock me away for a time, but he can't get me out of his mind. Sam is a stubborn man. Most people don't last an hour trying to fight me, and he's battled on for weeks. It's only a matter of time before his mind breaks under the strain. There's no escape for him. He is already mine."

Halderan bent to one knee, and leaned close to Dia. "You should reconsider. If you prove yourself useful enough to me, I might make a bargain that would give you back your prince. That is what you want isn't it? More than anything?"

Her stomach clenched. How did he know so much about what she wanted?

He straightened up, laughing coldly. "I thought so. I've seen *his* mind. It's overrun with a pathetic devotion to you. I've never heard anyone's mind scream so loudly as his did when I forced him to hurt you."

The sorcerer turned quickly to address the guards. "Take her to the dungeon."

CHAPTER 29

KEREM'S BIG HANDS CLOSED around Dia's upper arms. The white-haired figure of the king disappeared in the direction of the city, leaving her with the silent company of guards. Without a word, they closed in around her and marched her toward the walls.

She had to keep fighting. Sam still fought, and she had to do the same. She couldn't give up while he still tried to stop Halderan. But Dia was in no condition to walk. Her injured leg slowed her movements, and lack of food and water made her weak and dizzy. They'd only been walking for a few minutes before everything faded.

She felt the ground against her back and realized she must have fallen. Men's voices came near as the guards bent over her. "Bring that water," one of them said.

Dia felt a trickle of water on her forehead. How long had it been since she'd had any?

"Water," she gasped.

They lifted her head and placed the waterskin so she could drink. The cool liquid felt blissful in her parched mouth, and she gulped down as much as she could.

"Get her up," Kerem's emotionless voice said. "We don't have time for this."

"Give me a moment," another guard protested. "Look at her drinking, she hasn't had water in a long time."

Dia recognized Andar's voice. What could he do to help under these circumstances?

He held the water so she could drink. "No wonder she fainted," Andar said. "Wherever the king has been keeping her, he hasn't treated her well."

"His orders were to take her to the dungeon," Kerem growled in a tone entirely opposite his usual manner.

An iron hand seized her and dragged her painfully up. She cried out.

"You're hurting her," Andar protested. "The king didn't order us to harm her. There's no need. I'll carry her."

She felt arms lift her, and the bruising grip relaxed. They were moving again.

"Thank you," she whispered, blinking up at Andar.

He didn't speak, but he nodded.

Dia drifted in and out. Heavy booted footsteps echoed as they passed through the back gate and beneath the wide city wall. They were soon inside the palace and moving down the dark stairs to the dungeon. Dia smelled the familiar scent of damp, chill air.

She opened her eyes to see a glimmer of light. A couple of lanterns sent a small glow into the darkness. When they reached the bottom of the stairs, the sinister rattle of chains grew closer.

"You can't be serious," Andar protested.

"King's orders," Kerem hissed. "Do you have some objection?"

Andar didn't reply.

A big hand grabbed her arm, yanking it away from her body. A heavy iron manacle closed around her wrist. Kerem took her other arm, extending it and locking another band around it. They were connected with a short length of thick chain.

"Bring her."

They crossed a large chamber. Dia remembered the room from her explorations with Sam. On that day, the cells along one side of the room had been empty. Now, horrified, she saw the forms of several people inside.

Some slumped dejectedly against the walls, others lay on the floor as if they didn't have the strength to move. She recognized a few of the nobility, but many of them wore the clothing of tradesmen from the city. The prisoners were a mix of men and women, some old, even a few children. They couldn't possibly all be criminals.

One of the figures in the cell was very familiar. Even in the dim light, Dia recognized bright, golden hair. Her voice barely worked. "Lisenth?"

Her sister turned to look at her through the iron bars, blinking as if she couldn't believe her eyes. "Dia?" Her eyes welled with tears. "I thought I'd never see you again!" The tears were running down her cheeks now. She reached out through the bars toward her sister. "I'm so sorry, Dia. I treated you horribly, and I thought I'd never get a chance to tell you."

Dia own eyes filled with tears, and she extended her hand toward her sister's. The heavy chain stopped her. A moment later, she was dragged from the room. There was no more time to talk.

"Dia!" Lisenth's voice faded behind them as they moved down the hall and into a small stone room.

Andar set her down gently. "I'm sorry, Princess," he murmured, straightening up again. He was gone in a moment, and the door slammed shut. Only a tiny silver of light came in from the crack beneath the door.

The room was empty. The cold stone walls closed in around her, and she began to shiver in the chill air. Why were all those people locked up down here? What had her sister done? Where was Sam? Was he coming here to try to help her? If he did, he'd find the Shadaroc waiting for him.

With no light to indicate the time of day, Dia quickly lost track. As quiet hours passed, she heard a lock in the door. Quietly, the key turned, and a dark form came close and thrust something into her hands.

"Take it. I'm sorry I can't do more."

It was Andar. He was gone in a moment, and the door closed behind him. Dia realized she held a chunk of bread and a slice of meat in her hands. Desperately hungry, she ate them quickly. In the faint glimmer of light, she saw that he'd set down a bucket as well. Water? She found it was nearly full, and she drank gratefully. At least all the people here weren't completely under the Shadaroc's control. But what could the others do?

Dia stirred at the sound of the heavy door opening.

"Princess, can you get up?" She recognized Andar's voice. "Come with me. I think I can get you past the guards. We have to get you out of the palace. I overheard the king. He's planning to..." His voice trailed into silence.

If he didn't even dare say it aloud, it couldn't be good. A sharp twist of fear penetrated her exhaustion. Dia climbed laboriously to her feet. Andar quickly stepped forward to help her, wrapping her in a long cloak and pulling the hood up over her head.

"Follow me, quickly."

Taking her arm to help her along, they left the cell. The passageway was dark around them, only a glimmer of light coming in from one end. "We'll get you up the stairs and out the back gate," he said.

Dia hurried as quickly as she could. The manacles were heavy on her wrists, and she attempted to keep the chain from clanking. The dim passageways seemed silent, and even as they passed the cells full of people, no one said anything. Andar led her back to the stairs, and they climbed up quietly. Dia's heart pounded in her chest, but they reached the top without being challenged. Two guards stood beside the open door, and she paused when she saw them.

"Keep moving," Andar said. "They won't stop us."

Dia obeyed. They reached the last step and came out into the hallway. The guards remained frozen in position, standing at attention as if they couldn't see the two people creeping past them out of the dungeon. Maybe they would escape after all.

At a sudden sound behind her, she turned to see a towering figure. His large fist struck quickly, passing Dia to strike the back of Andar's head. He swayed and stumbled at the unexpected blow but regained his balance and stepped protectively in front of Dia.

Kerem faced Andar with no trace of emotion on his face. "Treason!" he growled.

"No!" Dia cried, stepping out from behind Andar. "That's not true. He didn't do anything wrong. I made him do it."

She grabbed Kerem's arm as he swung his fist toward Andar. He was too strong for her attempt to do much. He shook her off, and the two men grappled. Andar landed a hard hit to Kerem's jaw, but the bigger man kept coming.

Andar grunted as a blow like a sledge hammer pushed past his attempt to block and struck his body. Kerem followed it with a vicious hook. When his fist struck Andar's jaw, his head snapped to the side, and he swayed on his feet, then collapsed slowly to the floor.

Grabbing Dia's arm, Kerem pulled her toward the stairs. Both the guards were watching her now, their faces frozen in shock, but they didn't try to stop him. Without a word, he dragged her back down the stairs to the dungeon.

Once he looked at her, she met his eyes. "Please, Kerem! You were my friend. Please don't do this."

He gave no sign that he even heard her. He took her to a larger room lit by torches and seized the chain between her manacles, stretching her arms over her head. He placed it over an iron hook embedded in the stone, shoving her face-first against the wall. Her feet barely reached the ground, leaving her on tiptoe.

She turned to look at him behind her. "Kerem, please. It's the sorcerer in your mind making you do this. Please don't."

He didn't answer. His only response was to raise a whip. When the blow fell, a line of searing pain erupted across Dia's back. A strangled cry escaped her lips. "Please don't!" she begged. "I didn't do anything wrong!"

Another lash struck her. Her jaw clenched against the pain. Her resolve to endure quietly broke down after the first few strokes, and she cried out. The room spun around her. After a few more lashes, she realized she was hanging by her arms, no longer standing.

When he finally took the chain from the hook, she collapsed to the ground, and darkness took her.

⁛

Dia woke in her cell. She lay on her belly on the cold, hard stone. Her back was on fire. Long lines of searing pain crisscrossed her skin. There was no help, no relief. Her sense of time worsened. Day and night were gone. There was only lying on the floor, her teeth clenched against the burning pain, occasionally crawling to the precious bucket of water to drink.

The door opened. When she saw Kerem, she shrank back against the wall, overcome by the urge to flee. There was nowhere to go. He took her back to the same room and hung the chain over the hook, just as he had the first time. Raising her arms pulled against the already damaged skin of her back, and she moaned.

"Dia! What did they do to you?"

Dia's eyes flew open at the sound of the familiar voice. She wasn't alone with Kerem in this terrible room. She turned to see Lisenth chained just as she was. What was her sister doing here now? Her golden hair hung in knots and tangles, and her gown was torn and dirty. Lisenth's blue eyes met hers, wide with terror.

"What are they going to do?" Her voice was tight with fear. Her eyes traced the cuts on Dia's back.

Kerem stood behind her, his wide shoulders and bulky frame making her slender form appear small by comparison. Lisenth shrank away from him, her breath ragged in panic, her body shaking in fear.

"Kerem, no!" Dia begged. He had always been a kind person before. He would never have done any of this without the sorcerer controlling him. "Please! Don't do this. She's my sister. Please!"

He ignored her. When the lash fell, Lisenth screamed as it struck her. A line of blood appeared across her back. This couldn't be happening. Long ago, Dia had promised to look out for her younger sister. This could not be allowed. Kerem must be stopped. Someone had to stop him. Lisenth hung her head, tears making tracks down her dirty face, and her shoulders shaking with sobs. Despite all the pranks and the times Lisenth had been cruel, Dia still loved her.

There was no one else who could stop this. It had to be Dia.

Another lash fell. When the bloody welt showed along her sister's back, Dia knew exactly how it felt.

Lisenth screamed and cried. "Please, someone help me! Please!"

Hot rage welled up inside Dia. The anger came in waves, and she embraced it. She needed more. Searching inside herself, she connecting with the weak, hesitant glow of her own hallan. It seemed small, but its power was bright and clean. There was more hallan within Lisenth and within Kerem.

As he raised his arm for another blow, Dia seized the hallan within herself and struck out. When the power hit him, his whole body jerked, his eyes fixing directly on her.

"What did you do?" he snarled, staggering toward her.

His big hands seized her wrists. Where they touched, Dia felt his hallan connecting with her own. The extra energy flowing through his body felt like life-giving oxygen to a drowning person. Greedily, she drew it inside herself. Power.

CHAPTER 30

A S THE BRIGHT ENERGY burned through Dia, the manacles binding her wrists cracked and felt away. The magic strengthened her, easing the pain of her injuries, soothing damaged joints and tissue, beginning to knit torn flesh together. The pain eased, allowing her to stand. Her entire body pulsed with the influx of energy. Her head spun. She drew in a long breath, savoring the feeling. This was bigger than the taste she'd experienced in the jungle with Adengo.

Before her, Kerem trembled. He dropped his hands away from her and took a step back, sinking to his knees. The energy she savored was *his* hallan. Dia had no right to take it from him.

Kerem gripped his head in his hands. The gesture reminded her painfully of Sam. This man needed help. Could she provide the same kind of aid that Adengo had given Sam? After that, Sam had been able to regain control of his mind.

Dia stepped forward and placed her hand on Kerem's forehead. This time, instead of draining him, she gave back. While she touched him, she sensed the agonizing sliver of darkness at the base of his skull. While the sorcerer lived, she couldn't remove it.

Instead, she reached out with her power to surround it. She sent tendrils of clean hallan through the rest of his mind.

"Kerem? Can you hear me?"

For a long moment, he didn't reply. He finally spoke, his voice faint. "Yes, Princess."

"Can you hear the other voice in your mind?"

He nodded slightly. "Please take him out! I don't want to do what he says."

Adengo had explained this back at the village. If she removed the splinter now, it would destroy Kerem's mind.

She met his eyes. "I can't take him away now. You must find a way to lock him up." Sam had done the same thing. "Build a wall in your mind and imprison him behind it." He nodded and closed his eyes.

For a long moment, Kerem remained silent, his jaw clenched, and his expression tight with strain. "Help me? Please?"

Dia drew in a deep breath and focused on sending more hallan into him.

After several moments, Kerem sighed and looked up at her. "I can barely hear him now."

She met his gaze. "You must hold the wall. Do not let him out."

He nodded, and got back to his feet, looking at her in confusion, as if he only just realized where he was. "Princess Alladia? What are you doing here?" He put his hands to either side of his head. "Wait... I remember?" His gaze traveled up and down her ragged clothes and battered body. He looked past her to see Lisenth still chained against the wall. "Did I do this?"

His body began to shake, and tears welled in his eyes. "No! I'm sorry." The words came out from between clenched jaws. "I didn't mean to. I didn't want to."

Dia put a comforting hand on his arm. "It wasn't your choice."

His hand flew to the back of his neck. "He put something inside me. After that, I had to do what he said. I couldn't stop, no matter how much I wanted to. He made me do... terrible things."

She put her hand on his shoulder. "I'm sorry, Kerem. No one deserves to have their actions controlled by someone else. I have to stop him."

He took the keys from his belt and unlocked the manacles that bound Lisenth.

She ran to Dia and hugged her. "You saved me. Even after I was so cruel to you, and I didn't deserve it. I'm so sorry for everything I've done. You always looked out for me. Please forgive me!"

Her sister was alive. Somehow, the conflict that had hung between them felt smaller now. She met Lisenth's gaze. Her sister's blue eyes welled with genuine remorse, something Dia had never seen there before. She put her arms around her younger sister and held her.

"I'm sorry I was jealous," Lisenth said, hugging her tight. "I was so angry when you became a princess instead of me. It was never what you wanted in the first place. But I realize now that you really love Sam."

"That's right," Dia said. "I love *Sam*. Not his crown, if he ever gets it back. Just him." Where was Sam at this moment? She needed to find him.

"I knew you hadn't done what they accused you of. You wouldn't hurt anyone. I thought you were dead down there." Lisenth's eyes welled with tears. "I thought I'd never see you again, no matter how badly I needed to apologize."

"Thank you," Dia said. "There will be time for us to talk more, but the sorcerer is up there, and I have to stop him."

Lisenth's eyes widened in shock. "No! You can't go, Dia. He'll kill you. He's already killed so many..."

A sharp sliver of fear twisted inside Dia. "I know he will try. But if I don't face him, he'll keep killing other people. Stay down here where it's safe. Don't let him find you."

Lisenth gave Dia one more tight hug before she fled down the corridor.

Kerem remained beside Dia. His brows drew together in anger. "I agree with her, Princess. You should stay here too. I will find the sorcerer. He and I have unfinished business."

"You need magic to fight him," she protested.

Kerem shook his head. "I don't care. I will never allow him to control me again."

Dia took in a deep breath. "You'll be in terrible danger if you attack him. I don't see any hope of winning."

Kerem met her eyes. "The same is just as true for you."

"Perhaps. But I have magic within me, and I will use it to fight him." They had come too far, and she couldn't stop now. Perhaps he felt the same.

She squared her shoulders and nodded at him. "We'll go then."

He nodded. She followed him, and they started up the stairs. Part of the way up, he froze in the middle of a step. The king's cold voice floated down from above. "Have you completed my orders, Captain?"

Kerem answered in the same flat tone he adopted when the sorcerer controlled his mind. "Yes, Your Majesty."

"Has she broken yet?"

Dia's stomach clenched. The king was talking about *her*.

Kerem took several more steps upward, and Dia followed him. He was determined to face the king. She wanted to stop him, to beg him to go back and hide somewhere safe. Fear swept through her, but she had to face the king too. Kerem paused in the doorway, and she shrank into the shadows behind him.

Moving suddenly, Kerem lunged toward the king, driving his sword into his body. The king screamed in rage and pain as the weapon bit into his flesh. It was a solid blow, but not a deadly one.

"Kill the traitor."

Four other guards moved with unnatural precision to attack Kerem.

"You are not my king!" Kerem yelled. "King Hashoreth would never order me to harm the innocent. You ordered me to whip a defenseless girl. I would never have done such a thing until you forced me." He aimed another stroke at the king, and one of the other soldiers blocked it.

Kerem's blade struck one of them down quickly. The other three displayed no hint of emotion at the loss of their comrade and continued to advance.

From the shadows of the doorway, Dia watched the fight. She had no weapon. All she had was magic. Gathering the power of her hallan, she spread it into a shield surrounding Kerem. The barrier blocked several strokes that might have struck him while he continued to fight.

The sorcerer's eyes suddenly fixed on Dia where she stood in the doorway. A cold smile lifted one corner of his mouth. A sudden burst of power struck Dia. She stumbled a few steps back, nearly falling down the stairs, but managed to regain her balance on the second step.

The three guards had surrounded Kerem. He struck down another of them and lunged toward the sorcerer again. As his back was turned, the remaining two soldiers struck him, one blade slicing the back of his shoulder, the other piercing his back below his ribs. Kerem grunted in pain, but finished his attack. His weapon struck the sorcerer.

Dia held her breath. The blow should have struck him down. Instead, it glanced off. Climbing back through the doorway, Dia extended her power, trying to restore the shield. For a moment, it held, and the weapons deflected harmlessly off it.

The imposter king waved his hand, and another blast of power struck her, pinning Dia against the wall. Kerem gasped as two blades struck him. Frantically, Dia tried to replace the protection around him, but one of the soldiers attacked again, driving his blade deep into Kerem's body.

Dia struggled against the power that held her. Unable to free herself, she could only watch as Kerem sank to his knees.

"I'm sorry, Princess," he gasped. Blood poured from several wounds. He slid slowly to the floor, a trickle of blood running from the corner of his mouth. Dia's heart froze.

There was nowhere to run. With Kerem no longer fighting them, the other guards seized her, the power holding her against the wall dissipating as they gripped her hard. They dragged her farther into the hall, where she stood blinking in the daylight coming in the windows. The sorcerer faced her. He wore King Hashoreth's golden crown and the armband with the royal seal.

"Princess Alladia, I knew you would embrace your power, given the right *motivation*."

The rage she had felt earlier still burned. What he called motivation was nothing more than torment.

He smiled approvingly at the fury in her expression. "Now you know how it feels to take hallan from someone else. Do you want to feel it again? I can help you."

"I won't be like you!" she protested.

His brows rose. "Is that your final decision? This is your last chance to join me."

"Never!" She yelled, struggling to tear herself free of the guards.

"As you wish," he said calmly. "Since you have repeatedly refused to see reason, we are finished here. You will be executed. Now."

Her stomach twisted in panic.

The guards on either side of her pulled her after Halderan as he walked to the garden door. He paused in the doorway, raising his hand in greeting. From outside came the cheers and shouts of a large crowd.

Dia struggled against the guards, but they didn't release her. Struggling to find calm and control, she attempted to gather her hallan.

The imposter turned back toward her, a contemptuous sneer on his face. A casual wave of his hand smothered the power she had fought so hard to gather.

Outside the door, a sea of faces greeted her. The entire area was packed with people staring at her. Her stomach quivered under the gaze of so many. Some of them shouted when they saw her. The crowd parted to create a path for the guards. They crossed the space to the wall and stopped. The fake king stood just a few steps higher than the rest of the crowd, a majestic figure with the sun gleaming on his crown and his snow-white hair.

Dia felt all eyes on her, conscious of her filthy shoes, ragged clothing, and the bloody stripes marking her back.

"My people." At the king's powerful voice, a hush fell over everyone. "Just a few short weeks ago, we pronounced a sentence of banishment on Princess Alladia Algorian. Despite this, she has returned to Kulin attempting to murder me and seize control of Ischar." He gestured to the fresh blood on his side. "I will not allow it. Banishing her was not enough. She must be executed."

Dia's stomach clenched. Her time had run out. She didn't know where Sam and the others were, and there was no way they could help her now. The guards dragged her to stand beside this man who had taken everything from her. Despite the cold fear flooding through her, the anger was still inside, and she couldn't keep silent any longer.

"This man is not Hashoreth!" she yelled. "He is the Shadaroc, a dark sorcerer. He will steal the life from Kulin. Don't let h—"

His hand struck her face, cutting off her words, snapping her head back and knocking her to the ground.

"Silence!" he roared. "You are finished!" He dragged her to her feet and then onto the top of the balustrade. Only inches away now, the gaping void of space opened wide beneath her.

Still stunned from the blow, she tried to stop herself. Her fingers scrabbled against the stone, trying to find a grip. From the corner of her eye, she saw movement. Out there in the crowd, a man shoved past people in a desperate attempt to reach her. Sam. He was here. Somehow, he'd found her.

He was too late.

The sorcerer hurled Dia from the top of the wall out into the empty air.

The wild rush of air carried away her scream as she fell. The wind shrieked past her as she plummeted. Every muscle clenched, and her heart froze in her chest. Death rushed up to meet her. But she couldn't leave the Shadaroc behind to destroy everyone.

Fight.

There must be a way to fight him.

Another wave of fury rose up in her. She couldn't die like this and let him win. These were her people. She could not fall.

Dia stretched her arms against the blast of wind, spreading them as wide as she could. Somehow, they were wider than they had ever been. Impossibly, they were wide enough that she could catch the wind and ride it. As she concentrated on her body, it became lighter. Her skin, feathers. Her arms, wings.

When she spread wide, strong wings against the wind, her fall became a gentle glide. The air currents lifted and buoyed her up. She was safe in the sky. Her sharp eyes saw every detail, all the way down to the jungle. The paralyzing fear of being so high up vanished entirely. Flight was glorious. The air became her home.

CHAPTER 31

WITH HIS HEART HAMMERING in his chest, Sam raced toward the wall where Dia stood, ragged and injured, but alive and upright. He heard the crowd shouting as she was sentenced to death.

Then his brave, beautiful Dia straightened her slender shoulders. "This man is not Hashoreth!" she yelled. "He is the dark sorcerer. The Shadaroc. He will steal the life from Kulin. Don't let h—"

Halderan struck a vicious blow, driving her to the ground.

Sam's yell of outrage was lost in the shouts of the crowd. He had to reach her. This was the nightmare sensation of trying to run toward a goal forever just out of reach.

"Silence!" Halderan roared. "Your time is up!" He dragged her to the top of the wall, and before Sam could reach them, hurled her off the edge of the precipice.

Every muscle clenched, and hot pain tore through Sam's chest. He sank to his knees. A strained silence fell over the crowd. Sam was aware of nothing beyond the agony coursing through him. Dia was gone. The sorcerer had destroyed her without a second thought, giving no care for the rare person she had been.

Dark rage burned through Sam. He raised his gaze to the man wearing the shape of his grandfather. Drawing his weapon, he got to his feet.

Before Sam could reach him, the old man stepped up onto the top of the wall and spread his arms wide. His form shimmered and shifted until a great black bird replaced him. It leapt into the air. Why would he change his shape now, in front of everyone?

Like a streak of light, a brilliant white bird dove from the sky, claws extended to strike the black one. Its talons dug into his back and the Shadaroc shrieked, twisting away from its grip. Beating their great wings, they climbed and dove, twisting in the air to attack each other with sharp, hooked beaks and deadly talons.

The snowy white bird must be Adengo. He battled the Shadaroc with all his strength. Barely daring to breathe, Sam stared upward as the battle in the sky unfolded.

The white bird was strong and graceful, but smaller than the Shadaroc. The crowd watched the skies in stunned silence as the battle raged above them. It went on for a long time. Sam saw blood in several places, standing out sharply against the white feathers. He clenched his hands into fists. The black bird was winning.

From the side, another giant bird of prey challenged the Shadaroc, this one with silvery plumage. The two birds combined their efforts to overcome the Shadaroc.

Directly above the courtyard, they crashed together. The Shadaroc dug long talons viciously into the white bird, and the beautiful creature tumbled down to the stones of the courtyard. The black bird prepared to dive, ready to deal the killing blow.

Before it reached its fallen foe, the silver bird drove into it from one side, protecting its injured companion. If one of them was Adengo, the other could only be—

His body numb with shock, Sam ran toward the fallen bird.

When he reached the place where it had landed, instead of a bird, he found Dia lying crumpled on the stones, blood running from gaping wounds on her chest and shoulders. "Dia!"

When the king had thrown her from the wall, she hadn't fallen. She'd flown.

"Dia!"

Now she didn't respond to his voice. She couldn't be dead. Not after all that had happened. He applied pressure to the worst of the wounds, trying to stop the bleeding. She was alive. Her heart still pumped. She still breathed.

After several moments, she blinked and opened her eyes. "Sam?" Her voice was barely a whisper.

Relief coursed through him at the sound of her voice. "Just lie still. Don't try to move. You're hurt."

Pain clouded her gaze. "I—I tried to stop him, Sam. He's too strong. I fought him." Her eyes drifted closed again. He hadn't realized she had magic within her.

Focused on her, he was barely aware of the battle raging above him, until both birds plummeted to the stones, the Shadaroc on top. And when they changed back into men, he rose tall and strong, while Adengo lay bleeding and injured on the stones.

A moment later, with great effort, Adengo dragged himself to his feet.

Still wearing the form of the king, Halderan stared at him in disbelief. "I thought you were dead after all this time. Look at you, my old pupil."

Adengo faced him, ignoring the blood running from his injuries. "I came back to stop you."

Halderan laughed. "That's very touching, but I proved myself stronger in the skies. You can't stop me."

"Maybe not," Adengo said. "But I still have to try."

Halderan released a current of raw power from his hand to strike his enemy. Adengo blocked it. They traded a few blows back and forth, but Adengo's power weakened visibly with each one. Finally, his defenses shattered, allowing a blow to strike his chest. He sank to the ground.

"No!" Sam cried, getting to his feet to face the sorcerer. He stood frozen, facing the man that had killed his family. He needed something, a weapon that had the power to defeat the sorcerer. What did he have left? Only a knife.

Halderan knelt beside Adengo where he had fallen, reaching out to place his hand on his adversary's forehead. The glow of power grew between them. At the touch, Adengo struggled, trying to bring his power to bear against Halderan. He managed a few flashes of energy before he lay still.

For a long, terrible moment, Halderan continued to draw hallan from Adengo. Then he got slowly to his feet, straightening to his full height. He stared around the courtyard at all of them. "Is there anyone else here who dares to oppose me?"

Sam stepped forward. He had no magic, no chance. He knew it, and his stomach churned with dread. As soon as he was dead, the sorcerer would kill Dia. Sam had to act.

"I oppose you! You murdered my parents and my grandfather. You took King Hashoreth's place and tried to kill my wife, and you have killed countless innocent people. Adengo spent all those years in the jungle, and now—" his eyes darted to the crumpled figure on the ground. "I won't let you go on!"

"Very well, Prince Samanath." Halderan opened his arms in invitation. Drawing his knife, Sam advanced toward him.

"You can't fight me, Sam," Halderan said. "And I don't think you really want to."

A surge of power struck Sam. For a moment, all he saw was light. The power swirled through his head until it reached the wall he had so carefully built in his mind. Like a giant wave, the power struck the barrier, washing it away as if it had never been. There wasn't even time to scream as the flood rushed through Sam's mind, sweeping away every shred of resistance.

The voice in his mind was his own voice now.

"Do you still want to fight me, Sam? This was all simply a... misunderstanding, wasn't it?"

In a hidden corner of his mind, the original Sam screamed. On the outside, Sam felt his body stop moving. He stood straight and calm. He felt the expression on his face relax. He put his knife back in its sheath at his belt. His voice sounded calm, even serene.

"Yes. It was only a misunderstanding. You're right. You're the only family I have left, and I don't want to fight you. I'm sorry, Grandfather. We need to work together, now, to take care of Ischar."

Halderan glanced at the still form of his enemy. "And Adengo?"

Sam's gaze went to the man on the ground. It all seemed so simple now. "He killed my parents. You were right to banish him."

"That's right," Halderan said, his features relaxing into a smile. "This has only a been a mistake. As we go forward, we can both work to care for our people."

Sam nodded, smiling in return. "Yes, Grandfather. That's a good idea."

His mind calm now, Sam walked forward to stand with the king. Side by side, they faced the crowd of people. "Ischar is safe this day," the king proclaimed. "The traitors have been punished, and I have my grandson back at my side, loyal to me and to Ischar."

No! The remaining sliver of Sam screamed inside his mind. No. Don't do this.

That part of himself wanted to run to Dia, to care for her injuries and make sure she was safe. He wanted to help his uncle. He needed to stop Halderan.

At his grandfather's side, Sam walked across the courtyard to stand looking down at Dia, where she lay on the stones. She had fought with every bit of strength she had, and she had lost. Her skin was white, and blood stood out harshly. Her eyes were closed, her breathing shallow and fast.

"It's unfortunate, but I've come to realize that she will never help us," Halderan said. "It's time to let her go. I realize this might be difficult for you, Sam, but it's time. You must do this for the good of our kingdom. You'll feel better when it's all over. You will find another wife who will be better for you."

"Better," Sam heard his own voice agreeing.

Sam stared down at her familiar face, her features tight with pain. Even so, she was beautiful. She loved him.

Yes! He screamed at himself. She loves you. And you promised to take care of her, never to hurt her. You cannot allow him to force you to hurt her again.

Halderan's eyes fixed on her, and he stepped closer to her, towering over her as she lay on the ground at his feet. He had won. "It's over, Princess."

Dia looked up at him and blinked, her eyes still dazed.

"Are you ready to let her go?" he asked, turning to Sam.

"If you believe it's for the best," he heard his own voice reply.

Halderan nodded.

Sam drew his knife. Horrified, he watched his own hand raise his blade.

Dia looked up at him. "Sam?" her eyes widened as they locked on the knife in his hand. "Fight him, Sam. Don't let him do this to us. Please, Sam!" She turned her gaze back to him. And she looked all the way through him to the tiny corner of his mind still his own. "I'll love you forever."

His hand trembled.

This is Dia! He screamed at himself. You cannot harm her. I won't allow it. You are not me! This is my mind, my hands, and I will not hurt her!

His hand shook harder. Sam couldn't move. He couldn't put the knife down, nor could he use it to attack her.

Her beautiful eyes still gazed up at him. "Please, Sam! I love you. You don't want to do this." Very slowly, painfully, she gathered her remaining strength to drag herself up from the ground and stand before him. She looked up into his eyes. "Please? Don't hurt me."

He felt sweat on his face. Every muscle in his body clenched as his mind fought the sorcerer's influence.

"Kill her," Halderan ordered. "Kill her, now!"

Sam stood still. As the small corner of his own mind refused to be silenced, blinding pain shot through his head, and he screamed.

"What are you doing?" Halderan roared. "Do it!"

The pressure in his mind increased. Sam stood, panting. "Get out of my head!" he begged. "Please! I'll do whatever you want if you take the pain away. Anything except hurt Dia." He screamed again. The pain was unbearable, but he couldn't harm his wife.

The pressure became too great. Sam could no longer remain still, but he couldn't hurt Dia. Instead, Sam raised the knife and drove it toward Halderan. He struck a glancing blow before the sorcerer's power smashed into him. He felt a blinding flash of pain and then nothing.

CHAPTER 32

As Sam crumpled to the ground at the sorcerer's feet, Dia realized that Halderan's energy flowed around and through a single point on his wrist. She couldn't see anything; the sleeve of his coat covered it. But Dia felt it. With both hands, she reached out to seize his wrist. Her hands closed around metal, a cuff like the one Adengo used to transfer hallan. The power flowed through it.

She ripped the bracelet from his arm and placed it on her own.

A look of abject horror crossed his face as she reached up to put her hand against his forehead. "No more!" she shouted. "You will never take anyone's life again."

Desperately, he clawed at her arm, trying to grip the bracelet, but she left one palm against his head and held the other well out of his reach.

The power swirled and pulsed within him. It belonged to hundreds of souls, maybe thousands. With the aid of the cuff, she felt it. It was like a river, made up of uncounted different currents, each with its own color and texture.

Dia claimed them all. The current of power flowed into her, filling her.

Halderan gasped, his eyes wide and his skin deathly pale now that his power had been taken. He sank to his knees, still weakly reaching out for the bracelet. Dia knocked his hand away.

Now, Dia sensed exactly what Halderan had done to Sam. A slender, potent shard of Halderan's darkness hid inside Sam. It lay against the base of his skull, poisoning his mind, stealing his will.

She whirled back to face Halderan where he knelt on the stones. "Remove it!" she demanded. "Let Sam go!"

"It will never come out," he sneered. "You cannot have him back. Samanath is *mine*."

She knew what she had to do.

Dia met Halderan's gaze. "You are a murderer. You have taken countless lives for your own gain. No more!" She straightened her spine and squared her shoulders. "Though I have yet to be crowned, I am the rightful Queen of Ischar, and I sentence you to die for your crimes."

His eyes widened in disbelief. His dark eyes filled with fear as he shrank from her.

Dia gathered all her will and focused it on him. She touched his forehead, channeling the energy through the bracelet. Halderan could not be allowed to harm anyone else. The remaining power of his own hallan flowed through his body, and she drew every scrap of it into the bracelet. Fingers, toes, organs, muscles, mind, she drained every part of him.

He screamed in rage and pain, trying to twist away from her grip, reaching again for the bracelet. She shoved his arm away, and her hand followed him inexorably, scouring every scrap of hallan from him. He sank down onto the stones, his skin turning a horrible shade of gray. His breath sounded strangled. Soon, he couldn't scream anymore. He couldn't breathe. Halderan collapsed, unmoving.

For a long, heady moment, the energy of hundreds of people pulsed through Dia, granting her the power to do anything she chose. It was her choice whether to protect or destroy. She could wear any shape she desired. Anytime she decided, she could change herself back into a bird and soar into the sky. The crowd stared at her, fear on their faces. It was like nothing she'd ever felt before. The power taken from one soul back in the dungeon had only been a taste. This was bigger than she could ever have imagined.

Beneath the rush of wild emotion, her own reason spoke. She never wanted to control anyone by fear. Beneath the euphoria of the power, she recalled herself, and looked down at Sam, lying so still at her feet. She sent a thin sliver of power to him. Delicately, it probed the back of his neck. He twitched as if it hurt him, but Halderan was dead, and the poisoned sliver had to come out.

Dia wrapped the power around it, shielding the rest of Sam's mind from the infection. It wasn't going to be pleasant, but she had to do it. With a sudden jerk, she wrenched the poisoned splinter out. He screamed, his body jerking convulsively. Then he lay still.

She directed a bright stream of power into him to strengthen and heal him. His health began to return. Dia directed the power in the same way through her own battered body, soothing, healing and strengthening. It eased the pain of the wounds left by the Shadaroc's talons, soothed the sting from her back and her injured leg. She would need time to recover completely and for her wounds to heal entirely, but the pain eased, and a measure of her strength returned.

She sent power flowing into Adengo, where he lay on the ground. His wounds began to heal themselves. Though his body remained battered, he would survive.

Dia's eyes returned to the crumpled remains of the sorcerer. Halderan was dead. It was finished.

Dia took in a long, deep breath, savoring the feeling of power within her. It belonged to hundreds of people, perhaps more. She must send the power back to the souls it belonged to. With their hallan restored, they would be healed.

She released the stolen energy.

It darted away in a thousand tiny points of light, racing back toward the weakened souls who desperately needed it, some returning to the drained people below in the dungeon. Hundreds of glowing sparks of energy flew out into the city, seeking the lives they had been drawn from. With a sense of profound rightness, Dia felt them slide back into place, the stolen hallan returning to the souls it had come from.

She dropped to the ground beside Sam, turning his head to examine his neck. A thin shard of absolute blackness protruded from his skin. She gripped it between her fingers and pulled.

For a moment, she tugged fruitlessly, the splinter still lodged firmly. Then, it moved. She pulled harder, and at last, it came free, a rush of blood following it. She dropped it to the stone, the toxic sting of it burning her fingers. She put her hand against his neck, searching for any more feeling of evil. The wound still bled, but his blood was clean now. She rested her ear against his chest. Though he hadn't moved, his heart still beat, and she let out a sigh of relief.

Her eyes darted back to Halderan. He remained where he had fallen on the stones, unmoving. His skin was shriveled, eyes sunken into his skull, flesh withered. His disguise had faded away, and his long, thin face no longer resembled King Hashoreth. Slowly, the people began to gather around them, staring down at Halderan.

"Is he dead?" a nobleman asked.

With the cuff still surrounding Dia's wrist, she felt the flow of energy through all the people. While she wore it on her wrist, she was sure Halderan had nothing left. "Yes."

Suddenly, the silence broke as they cheered. They surrounded Dia, shouting, "Long live the queen!"

"Wait!" she yelled, getting to her feet. The shocked crowd fell silent as she fixed her gaze on them. "Sam and I have given everything to defeat this sorcerer. Before we do anything else, I need you all to listen to me."

They looked at each other in silence and nodded, their eyes on her. They would listen. Everyone would know the truth today.

Dia pointed toward the gruesome, shriveled thing lying on the stones. "Look at his face. That is *not* King Hashoreth. The Sorcerer Halderan came to Kulin over twenty years ago. Back then, he took the shape of the Shadaroc when he chose, but also disguised himself as an ordinary man while he attempted to place himself in a position of power. He made our people sick by stealing hallan from them." The crowd nodded. Anyone old enough to remember that time recalled the sickness and fear.

Dia went on. "Halderan killed Crown Prince Kariman and his wife. He framed Prince Adengo for their murders, causing him to be banished. Prince Adengo has been in the jungle all these years, separated from his family and friends. Today, he returned to help us fight Halderan, at great cost to himself. With all our hearts, we welcome him back to Kulin and back into the royal family." There were murmurs of assent and many glances toward Adengo where he lay on the ground, several people attending him.

"When King Hashoreth lost the magical protection of his faithful friend, Marek, Halderan killed the king and stole his shape," Dia said. "Why else would an old man who loved his grandson more than anything else turn on him? The real king died at the foot of the cliffs, and he rests in the jungle. Halderan banished Crown Prince Samanath and myself. All his accusations were false. Sam never harmed any of our people, nor did I. I swear it to you."

Dead silence fell as she said it. The crowd was still, frozen by the shock of her words. She held their eyes, looking for any sign of dissent. "After what you have all seen today. Is there *anyone* who doesn't believe me? The splinter in Sam's mind gave Halderan control over his actions. It is gone now. Prince Samanath is himself again. Are you ready to accept him as your king?"

They looked at each other. Some of them shifted uncomfortably, but they voiced their agreement.

"Very well," her voice was as hard as granite. "Samanath Algorian is King of Ischar. Today, you have named me queen. With that authority, I remove his sentence of banishment, as well as Prince Adengo and myself. We must stand together now and never allow evil to creep into our city. Will you give us your loyalty?"

The people shouted and cheered.

Chapter 33

As the noise and confusion in the courtyard died down a little, Dia turned to a pair of royal guards. "Where are the other guards who fell under the sorcerer's control?"

One of them came forward and knelt. "My queen, besides Captain Kerem, there were four others. Two dead, now."

She nodded. "Bring me the remaining two. They must receive the same help that I gave Prince Samanath. Go at once." The two guards gathered several others and hurried away.

Dia found another of the guards and beckoned him forward. "There are many people locked in the dungeons by the sorcerer, my sister among them. Release them. See that they receive food, drink, and a healer's care."

"Yes, my queen." He headed for the stairs to the dungeon.

She turned back to the crowd of couriers and nobility. "Now, the rest of you, gather everyone from the palace and those who are nearby in the city. We will speak to them in the courtyard shortly."

They bowed and scurried off to obey her orders. The guards began ushering the crowd away, toward the outer courtyard near the gates where they expected Dia to address them. Soon, she stood alone except for the remaining members of the royal guard.

When she looked down at Sam, he was awake. His brown eyes were fixed on her with a mixture of shock and fear.

He looked at her, gazing at the bright tendrils of hallan swirling around her, almost as if he weren't sure she was the same person. She met his gaze for a long moment. Would he still feel the same about her after everything that had happened? Could he?

Dia removed the bracelet from her wrist and tucked it into her pocket. "It's still me, Sam."

She drew in a deep breath. Would he reject her? Had the power within her created too great a distance between them? For a tense moment, she waited.

Slowly, the corners of Sam's mouth lifted in a smile. "I always knew you were meant to be a queen."

She dropped down beside him, burst into tears, and threw her arms around him. For a long moment, they held each other.

Slowly, Sam pushed himself to his feet and offered his hand to help her up. He put his arms around her once more. "When he flew away with you, I thought I'd never see you again. I knew he would hurt you. And I couldn't stop him. I swore I would always protect you, and I couldn't—" He bowed his head, and she reached up to brush tears from his cheeks.

"It's over now, Sam. We're safe."

He pushed aside the torn fabric of her tunic to look at her. "How could he do this?" he murmured brokenly.

"He... forced me to use magic to defend myself. What he really wanted was for me to join him. Instead, he helped me find the power to stop him."

Sam met her eyes for a long moment. "He was a fool to underestimate you."

The guards placed Adengo on a stretcher and lifted him. Kael and Altan were already beside him. Sam and Dia followed them to the infirmary, where the healers waited. Immediately, they began working on the wounds left by the Shadaroc's talons. Adengo's skin looked terribly pale beneath his suntan.

Sam and Dia came to stand beside him. Adengo opened his eyes and looked up at Dia. "You did it. I knew you would find your power."

She put her hand on his shoulder. "It wasn't only me. By myself, I would have failed. We couldn't have stopped him without you."

He smiled slightly as his eyes drifted closed again.

Dia took the sorcerer's bracelet from her pocket and put it on. With it in place, she felt the hallan flowing through herself and the men around her.

Sending a stream of power toward Adengo, she directed it toward each of the wounds in turn, binding the torn flesh together, finishing the work of healing she had begun earlier in the courtyard. The lines of pain on Adengo's face smoothed.

The wounds weren't completely healed, but now they looked smaller, cleaner, and weeks old. Some color returned to his face.

"Thank you," he murmured, looking up at her. "After you fought so bravely, I pray you have already done the same for yourself."

She nodded. It had been essential. She wouldn't have been able to keep fighting if she hadn't taken strength and healing from the hallan. Placing her hand on his shoulder, she said. "Rest. You're safe now." Dia removed the cuff from her wrist and returned it to her pocket.

She looked up at Kael and Altan, who had been watching over Adengo. "He'll be all right. They will take care of him. You've both done so much to help us. We will be honored to give you any reward you want."

Altan smiled. "How about a hot bath, a good meal, and a soft bed?" He looked at Kael, who shrugged. Altan laughed. "He's never had a hot bath in his entire life. He doesn't know what he's missing."

Dia smiled. "They will take care of you." She nodded toward the servants waiting near the door. "Get some rest. There will be plenty of time to decide what you want to do."

"We must return to our family," Kael said. He nodded toward his father. "He misses my mother and sisters."

"They are welcome to come back here with you," Sam said. "I promised that any of you who fought Halderan would be welcome to return home." His gaze went to Altan.

He bowed to Sam. "Your Majesty, I am very grateful for your pardon. But after having lived all these years in the jungle, I have seen the effects of banishing serious offenders there. Many of them are cruel men, and they do not treat anyone well, especially not the people who lived in the jungle before. It isn't fair for Ischar to send the worst of their criminals there."

"You're right." Sam nodded. "After seeing what it's like, I realize we should never have done that. I will give my aid to correct the situation. Thank you for your help, today and throughout our journey. We will speak more of it later."

Altan nodded.

Sam looked at Kael. "You have our sincere gratitude. And you and all your family are welcome here anytime you choose to come. You belong to the royal family, no matter where you go."

Kael grinned and stepped forward to embrace Sam and Dia.

A moment later, with Sam at her side, Dia climbed to the balcony overlooking the courtyard. Every bit of space was packed with people. It was time to address them. This was the first time Dia had spoken in front of such a large crowd. After the events of the day, she almost forgot to be nervous about it.

Dia could have tried to prepare before she spoke to them, to change her appearance back to what they expected her to look like. She chose not to. Dia faced her people wearing the ragged, stained clothes she'd worn on the journey from the jungle. This was a day for honesty, and it was important for all of them to see the truth of what had happened.

Sam stood beside her, and they both spoke to their people. The news of Halderan's death and the miraculous recovery of many of the sick in Kulin would spread far and wide. The remains of the sorcerer were already on their way far from the city to be burned. The palace staff immediately set to work cleaning the stains from the white stone and repairing the damage left behind by the battle.

At last, their address was over. Everyone had gone except for the guards. Dia couldn't help but feel a little apprehensive as she eyed their polished weapons. They were meant to protect the royal family. It would be some time before she could fully trust them again.

The short, round man who served as head of the household explained to Sam and Dia that it would take the palace staff only a few moments to make sure their room was prepared. "Though with your grandfather gone, you should really be moving to the king's quarters," he pointed out.

"No," Sam said quickly. "Not yet. Please let all the staff know not to disturb his room, or any of his things. Not until I give the order."

"As you command, Prince Samanath." The head of the household bowed. "The healers will continue to tend to Prince Adengo. They will keep you informed of his condition. He eyed the blood on Dia's clothes. "Surely the healers should be tending you as well, Princess?"

"No, thank you," Dia said firmly. She wanted time in private to process everything that had happened, not someone else fussing over her.

His brows raised. "At least let me send a few of the healer's salves and bandages to your room. And hot water?"

"Very well," Dia nodded. "I would be grateful. If I require more help, my husband will assist me."

Soon, Sam and Dia stood outside the door of their suite, silent guards posted on either side of the entrance. They both stood frozen for a moment. Sam cleared his throat and opened the door, ushering Dia inside. He closed the door behind them and locked it securely.

Dia stood for a moment, frozen, looking around in disbelief. The moment felt completely surreal.

"Is it wrong that it feels so strange to be here?"

The room looked exactly as it had before. They both looked around. Sam methodically checked every nook and corner, searching for any sign of danger. Dia walked into the dressing room with Sam behind her. Their clothes still hung neatly. Nothing had been disturbed.

Sam's fingers brushed softly against her shoulder. "It breaks my heart to see what they did to you. I should have found a way to stop them."

Dia shook her head. He shouldn't be blaming himself for Halderan's actions. "How would you have stopped him? You did everything you could. He injured you too." She laid her hand on his arm and walked to stand behind him. She felt his hallan and the long wound across his back from the bird's claws.

She remembered the moment vividly. Her own fear, the savage wind of the bird's passing. She recalled the weight of his body covering her, putting himself in harm's way to keep her safe.

"You were protecting me."

He turned to face her, resting his hands on her shoulders. "And *you* were protecting all of us. From now on, when I see the scars left behind, I will remember how brave you are. You saved Ischar."

Dia didn't feel brave. She had only done what she must.

She turned Sam around again, brushing her fingers along his back, tracing the path of the cut, leaving behind glistening sparks of hallan.

He sighed gratefully as the power eased the pain of his injuries. "Thank you."

"Do you think we're safe here?" she asked. "We always trusted the guards before... until your grandfather ordered them to seize us."

He turned to face her, nodding in understanding. "It will take some time for us to trust their loyalty." His dark eyes met hers. "And me? How can you trust me? I'm not sure why you're here in this room with me at all, after everything I did."

The pain in his eyes made her heart ache. She looked up at him and reached up to brush his cheek with her fingertips. "Halderan was very powerful. I watched him use every bit of that power attempting to force you to kill me."

"Dia, I almost—" He sank to his knees and looked up at her. "How can you ever trust me again? He took my will. He took control of my hands." He looked down at them holding his palms up and spreading his fingers.

Dia put her fingers beneath his chin and lifted until his eyes met hers. "He's gone. Dead. And he will never come back. He can't touch you with his evil again."

"How can you be sure?" His gaze was pleading.

She took Halderan's bracelet out of her pocket and put it on. Immediately, she felt the flow of hallan from herself and Sam. She drew him to his feet and put her arms around him. The power of their hallan glowed brighter. Bright strands flowed around them and intermingled.

"No darkness remains in you," she said. "If there were any left, I could see it. I see everything inside you, every corner of your soul. He's gone, Sam. There's only you."

The power swirled around them sparkling on the surface of their skin. It glowed in Sam's eyes. Dia released the power, took off the bracelet, and set it on the table beside them.

For a moment, all was quiet. The light faded, leaving them in darkness.

"I never felt anything like that before," Sam murmured. "I could feel... *you*. I've loved you all this time, and I had no idea you had... *that* inside you."

Her lips lifted in half a smile. "Me neither. And I am more than content to let that part of me sleep, for now. I hope it will never be needed again."

How could either of them know what the future would bring? The only thing she was sure of was that they would face it together. Standing side by side at the tall windows, they looked out over the city.

"Tomorrow will be a fresh start." Sam put his arm around her, drawing her closer to his side. "Because of you, the sun will rise with new hope for our people."

ACKNOWLEDGEMENTS

Thank you for reading this book! Thank you family, friends and fans for supporting me during the creation process. I cherish the opportunity to bring to life stories born in my imagination and share them. I hope you enjoy reading them and that we have many future adventures together.

About the Author

aj@ajparkwriting.com
www.ajparkwriting.com
Stay In Touch – Join my email list and download a FREE Story
https://BookHip.com/XKTAJDB

AJ Park is the author of several fantasy adventure books and has won multiple writing awards. She grew up reading everything she could get her hands on, and continues to cultivate her life-long love of stories.

When she's not working on the next book, she loves climbing mountains, being outdoors, and spending time with her family. She loves meeting new friends, being part of the local community, and works for a digital marketing firm that helps businesses grow.

THE RING KEEPER

PROLOGUE

Callonen

HIS WORSENING ILLNESS MADE travel difficult. Emperor Callonen wished for the strength to ride his horse as he always had instead of sitting in a carriage. At least his guards offered him the small kindness of not mentioning the change. No one dared speak of his deteriorating physical condition. They all hoped he would get better. He needed a solution. If he didn't fine one, Callonen's death would leave every person in his empire vulnerable.

The carriage rolled toward the edge of the Warding, surrounded by a protective army. Sarine couldn't afford to allow any harm to come to their emperor. Without him, and the enchanted defense of the Warding he wielded, the demons would destroy their people.

"Emperor, I think we should have ignored his message," General Gray said from his seat opposite, his expression sober behind his dark beard. "What could he possibly have to say that will aid us? It's too dangerous for you to be so near the border."

Callonen's stomach clenched. The message from his traitorous brother had been unexpected in the extreme. Years ago, the last time they had spoken face to face, Haldreth had driven a dagger into Callonen's heart. Only a miracle had saved him that day.

No, not a miracle. A young woman had saved him. She had loved him and sacrificed everything to save his life. The memory of Allia awoke a sharp familiar pain in his chest. He recalled the sound of her voice, the way her golden hair had caught the sun, the touch of her hands. She had seen his true self more clearly than anyone else. In all these years without her, he had not felt whole. For a moment, he concentrated on breathing, focusing on controlling his emotions enough to speak again. "No. He will not aid us."

"Then why should we hear what he has to say?" Gray protested. "He plans to destroy us. This whole meeting is probably a trap."

"We won't leave the Warding," Callonen assured him. "For now, we still have the power to keep the demons out of our land. Maybe can learn something useful from what he says."

The edge of the Warding, invisible to the human eye, was defined by lines of armed men on both sides. Outside, the heavily armed troops of Ara in blue uniforms congregated. Inside the protection of the Warding, Callonen's men stood guard in orderly rows.

As the carriage stopped, Callonen drew in a deep breath. A strong urge to escape flooded through him. He would order them all to turn around instead of going through with this. How could he face his brother again after what Haldreth had done? He'd been a peaceful man all his life, but now Callonen felt the urge to attack, to make his brother pay for the pain he'd caused. Haldreth deserved to die for the crimes he'd committed.

General Gray moved to the door and got out, turning back, subtly providing support. As Callonen stood upright, exhaustion dragged at his limbs, pain twisted through his muscles and joints. No matter how his body felt, he had to face his brother. For a moment, he feared he couldn't walk without aid. Gray remained close beside him, ready if that should be the case.

Callonen moved forward, one step and then another. His loyal soldiers in dark green uniforms lined his path on either side. They were good men, every one of them. He would do what he had to do to protect them and the rest of his people.

With halting steps, Callonen walked toward the front, attempting to conceal his weakness as much as he could. A familiar figure approached the border from the other side. Haldreth's appearance hadn't changed much. Dark hair and beard, their father's brown eyes. He looked older, but he remained a mirror image of Callonen, his identical twin.

Callonen was the one who had changed. The illness had attacked his body, aging him prematurely. The changes were obvious now, as he faced his brother across the empty space between the soldiers, and he saw the triumph on Haldreth's face.

"Callonen!" Haldreth called jovially. "It's good to see you, brother!"

Ignoring his pain and weakness, all of Callonen's muscles clenched, tightening with a visceral need to attack. His jaw clenched back the words that threatened to come out in a flood of despair and pain. *You took Allia from me. I loved her with all my heart, and she was everything to me! I intended to cherish her for the rest of my life.* Despite knowing that Haldreth would hear the desperation in his voice, he couldn't prevent the question that escaped his lips. "Where is she?"

A long, awkward moment of silence fell. The soldiers on both sides stood perfectly still while Callonen faced his brother.

At first, Haldreth's face betrayed no emotion other than vague confusion. "Who?"

Callonen glared at him, attempting to control the trembling in his hands.

Haldreth's eyes widened in realization. "Oh, you're talking about that servant girl who worked at the palace. The two of you were… friends."

Hot rage flooded through Callonen and he struggled to keep his body still, his expression calm. Haldreth meant to goad him, to force him to lose his remaining shreds of control.

Haldreth laughed coldly. "Let the past go, brother. It was a long time ago. Seventeen years is a long time to hold a grudge. I can't believe you're still asking about her." He tapped his chin as he thought. "What was her name? Hannah? Leah…?"

"Allia." Callonen hadn't spoken her name aloud in years. The pain was too great.

Haldreth smiled, slapping his thigh. "That's right," he rubbed his chin. "I remember now. Allia." He shook his head. "Not the smartest girl. For some reason, she never would cooperate with me, no matter how I tried. She's long gone."

Callonen hadn't thought his heart could hurt more, but the pain in his chest increased at his brother's words. Haldreth had taken Allia, determined to control her for her power. He would have used *any* means to force her to his will.

"I didn't ask you here to talk about her," Haldreth said. "I wanted to know how you were. You don't look well, brother."

"No," Callonen ground out. His brother knew that already.

Haldreth shook his head in mock sympathy. "That's terrible. How long has this been going on? Probably about four months now?"

Fear, like a silver of ice, penetrated Callonen as everything came together at the words. Four months. "It's a spell," he gasped. He looked up at his brother. "You did the same thing to father, didn't you? I should have realized."

Haldreth raised his eyebrows. "Me? How could I affect our dear departed father's health? I haven't been in Sarine for years."

"Before you left, I saw your spell book with an enchantment to cause someone to die of old age within a year. Father wasn't even sixty, and he could have had many good years. How could you—" Callonen felt his knees weaken, and he swayed on his feet. Gray stepped closer, taking his arm to support him.

Haldreth's cold eyes bored into Callonen's. "If you believe that's true, then you know exactly how much time you have left. Just a few short months. We are family. I thought we should speak once more before it was all over. Perhaps you already knew that Allia gave birth to a child."

Yes. Callonen had received that news.

"You haven't found her, have you?" Haldreth asked, his voice deceptively casual.

Callonen's voice shook with rage. "I would never tell you where she is!"

Haldreth smiled. "So, you don't know either. No matter. I sent my demons to hunt her. It's only a matter of time before they find her."

Unable to leave the Warding himself, Callonen had sent many of his best people to search for the child over the years. They still searched. There seemed little hope they would find the girl before Haldreth's dark servants did.

"Dear brother," Haldreth said, shaking his head, "why are you still trying to fight me? Sarine *will* be mine. You have nothing left. Give up now. You don't have long anyway, and there's no cure for your illness."

Giving up seemed logical. If so many other lives hadn't depended on him, Callonen would have done it long ago. But Haldreth had lied about one thing. There *was* a cure for his condition, Allia's enchanted ring. There would be hope if they could find the ring.

Hope.

Haldreth nodded to his soldiers. Yelling, they drew their weapons and surged forward to attack.

THE RING KEEPER

CHAPTER 1

Ana

Travelers rarely used the rutted dirt track running past the only inn in Bright Springs. But all morning, carts and wagons rolled along. Ana saw them through the windows as she cleaned the tables and swept the floors. The harvest had just begun. It was too soon for anyone to be taking their crops to market, and it made no sense for so many to be traveling.

By midday, a noisy crowd of villagers and travelers packed the inn. No one wanted a room for the night, but they all wanted a meal. In the kitchen, Tari prepared food as fast as she could. Ana ran back and forth with orders, coins and heavy trays laden with food. Fergen would be pleased. This might be the most profitable day the innkeeper had ever had.

Fergen entered the common room, his gray hair and stocky frame familiar among the crowd of strangers. He led another group to the last empty table. "Why are so many people on the road today?"

Ana hurried over to take their order.

"I'm not staying in Gildan," a big bearded man in the worn clothes of a farmer was telling the innkeeper. "Harvest or no harvest. My grandfather lived in the old kingdom more than sixty-five years ago. He was there when it fell. If the same thing is happening here, we want no part of it."

"The same thing?" Fergen asked. "What are you talking about?"

"The village of Gildan was attacked," the man growled. "And the day after, anyone who had gotten even a scratch was burning with fever. They were poisoned. I'm not the only one who remembers what happened in the dark times. It was the Shekkar."

The room froze. One of the villagers dropped a mug, and it broke on the floor. A terrified silence replaced the voices.

"Are you telling me the Shekkar attacked Gildan?" Fergen finally asked into the ringing silence.

"They came in the middle of the night. We didn't see them, but I know it was them!" The man faced Fergen.

"How do you know? The Shekkar haven't been seen for nearly forty years. Not since the old emperor destroyed them with his enchanted sword. Who could have brought them back?"

The bearded man shook his head. "I don't know who, but someone did. In the north, there have been rumors of them for years, but they've never come anywhere near here, until now. I'm not waiting around for them to come after my family." He waved a big hand at his wife and children, clustered around the table. He nodded toward the road, where wagons were still rolling along. "I'm not the only one who thinks so. We've worked all year for this harvest, and it makes me sick to leave before we can bring it in. But I'd rather abandon it than be dead."

His words echoed around the room. The unnatural stillness dissipated slowly as the crowd resumed eating and talking. Their voices were hushed now. Ana gathered the pieces of the broken pottery into her apron, collected a few coins, and left the farmer and his family with a pitcher and mugs while she went to the kitchen for their food.

It took hours for Ana and Fergen to finish serving the midday meal. The inn's kitchen was empty of food save for a few scraps and an enormous stack of dirty dishes. Ana found Tari surveying the pile, a look of dismay on her kind face.

"What a day," the cook exclaimed. "We'd better clean these quick. There will be more customers here tonight. Can you work on them while I start some meat roasting?"

Ana tied back her hair and was busy at the washbasin when Fergen came in, running a hand through his gray hair. "Did you ever see such a crowd?"

"Not in Bright Springs," Tari answered. "Did you find out where they're going?"

Fergen glanced at Ana and gave the cook a warning look.

Ana turned from washing dishes to face him. "You don't have to hide it from me. I heard what they said." She was sixteen, no longer a child who would wail and cry in fright. "What are the Shekkar?"

At the word, Tari dropped the dish she was drying onto the floor, where it landed with a loud clatter.

Fergen took a deep breath, his lips tight, and his face unsmiling. "They're demons."

⚬

When the dishes were finally finished and Fergen gave her permission to take a break, Ana left the kitchen and walked up the hill into the quiet woods. She craved the silence of the trees after the noise and bustle of the inn.

A little way up the hill, she came to her favorite oak tree. Over the years, she'd climbed it so many times that she had worn the bark on its limbs smooth from finding the same handholds over and over again. The late afternoon sun filtered down through the leaves and made a pattern of light and shade on her skin as she sat in the wide fork between the branches, hidden from sight. This had been her secret place as a child, and it was still a haven of peace and solitude for her.

Beyond the edge of the woods, she saw houses and bits of the fields where farmers brought in their harvest. Nothing could be heard but the tranquil murmur of oak leaves in the breeze.

She wanted to stay until the sun set, but Fergen expected her back in time to help with the dinner rush. It had been the same every night for the nine years she'd lived at the inn, though today had been far busier than usual. Fergen, the kind old innkeeper, had taken her in, a child alone in the world, after her grandmother died.

In the stillness, Ana heard the distinct sound of footsteps beneath the tree. Was it one of the boys from the village? She looked down through the branches.

Two strangers walked between the trees, pausing every few steps to bend low and look at the ground. Ana knew everyone in Bright Springs, and she'd never seen these men before. Were they part of the crowd of travelers today? If that was true, what were they doing in the woods?

Silently, she watched them. They wore packs on their backs, confirming her guess that they were traveling. The one with dark hair knelt on the ground, looking at something. The other had light hair that hung in unruly waves. "Are you sure?"

The kneeling man looked up from the ground. He frowned behind a short dark beard, and his brows were pulled together in worry. "The tracks are clear. No human made these. You can see the marks of their claws in the soil. They're here."

He stood, and Ana's eyes widened as she stared at the long blade at his side. She realized the other man wore a similar weapon strapped across his back, the hilt sticking out above his pack. No one in Bright Springs wore a sword. She'd never seen weapons that big before.

"When?" The man with light hair rubbed the back of his neck.

"They look fresh. I'd say, last night."

"It's this town, then. It has to be. They passed through Gildan on their way here. Everyone in this place is in danger. If they were here last night, they'll be back as soon as it gets dark. She must be here, and we have to find the girl before they do." He turned and took a step away.

The dark-haired man shook his head. "Not the town. Here. The tracks are everywhere around this tree." He pointed to several places surrounding the oak. He paused, looking down toward the inn, the way Ana had come. Bending down, he examined the ground. "These tracks don't match the others. Someone walked here."

Peering down between the branches, Ana watched him. He examined her tracks along the path she'd taken from the inn into the woods. No one had ever bothered to follow her before. She wasn't important enough, unless it had something to do with her secret. Ana possessed a strange ring. It was silver, set with a sparkling green gem. Peculiar symbols marked the inside of the band. On her deathbed, her grandmother had warned Ana never to tell anyone about it. All these years, she'd worn the ring on a leather cord around her neck, hidden beneath her clothes. It was a constant reminder of the secret, but until now, she hadn't given much thought to her grandmother's warning. She pressed her hand against the stone, feeling a strange tingle in her skin like the ring had a life of its own.

The men followed her tracks a little way down the hill. Ana breathed a sigh of relief as they went away. Then they turned and came back to the base of her oak. "See the tracks there. They come right to the tree."

Ana pressed herself against the bark, out of sight. These men were following her, and from their conversation, they weren't the only ones. Her stomach tightened. All the talk in the inn that day ran through her mind. Now strange tracks had led these men to this very spot. No one but Ana ever came here.

One of the men climbed the tree. Ana heard his boots against the bark and the soft sound of his breath as he pulled himself up. Soon, he appeared between the branches, and they stared at each other. Her eyes darted to his shoulder, wondering if he still carried his sword, but he'd taken it off with his pack before he climbed the tree. He wore a dagger at his belt, but his hands were nowhere near the hilt.

Up close, he looked barely older than the village boys who worked in the fields. His expression seemed friendly. He had a straight nose and a strong jaw covered by a short beard.

"Who are you? And why are you following me?" she demanded.

She didn't know these men. Maybe they were dangerous.

Seating himself on a branch, the young man raised his empty hands palm out in a nonthreatening gesture. "I'm sorry I startled you. Please, don't be afraid." His voice sounded kind. "I'm trying to find someone. She's in danger, and we came to help."

Ana stared back at him. That wasn't what she'd been expecting him to say. What was he talking about? It almost sounded as if he knew about the secret. Grandmother had been very clear that Ana should tell no one because it was dangerous. Something terrible had pursued Ana years ago when she was a baby. Could it be the same thing that had left tracks all around her tree?

"Do you wear a ring? Silver, set with a green stone?"

Ana's eyes widened. How could he know about it? Was he a friend or an enemy?

She stared back into his eyes and held up her hands. "No. This village is too poor for anyone to wear jewelry."

He returned her gaze. "I know it's a secret. But if you or someone you know has the ring, you're in great danger." He looked at her with serious gray eyes. "My name is Zarek." Pointing to his friend on the ground, he continued, "That's Dane down there. May I ask your name?"

She'd been warned never to share her real name, so she gave him the shorter version she'd used all her life. "Ana."

Zarek met her eyes, his expression earnest. "I promise we would never hurt you, Ana. We came to help. There are dangerous things in this world, and we've sworn an oath to find the girl with the ring, protect her and take her to safety. Do you believe me? We only want to help."

She stared into his eyes and nodded toward the ground. "Tell me what made those tracks."

He cleared his throat and rubbed the back of his neck before he finally spoke. "Shekkar. Demons."

Ana drew in a sharp breath, her eyes wide. Even before the rumors she'd heard today, the village boys used to tell stories about Shekkar just to frighten her. Everyone knew demons would rip you apart if they caught you. They had destroyed an entire kingdom, their poison killing thousands. Now, it wasn't just an old story. "And you think they're following me?"

He stared at her for a moment before he nodded.

Cold dread twisted her stomach. If the Shekkar were hunting her, they would kill her. She had no way to run fast enough or far enough to escape them. Tears welled in her eyes, and she blinked them back. Ana was too old to cry like a baby. She didn't want Zarek to notice.

"They're coming soon. We need to go!"

He was right. His words startled her into motion, and she followed him as he climbed down.

"Hurry," Dane called up from the ground. "It will be dark soon. We have to get everyone indoors. The whole town is in danger!"

"We have to tell Fergen." Ana pointed down the hill toward the inn.

"Is that where you live?" Dane asked.

"Yes."

Dane looked at Zarek. "The Shekkar will follow her trail there. But the rest of the people should barricade themselves in their houses. I'll meet you at the inn. Get her inside. Tell them to bar the doors."

Zarek removed his sword from its place on his pack and belted it around his waist.

Ana led him to the back door, and she ran into the kitchen. "Tari, where's Fergen?" she asked the gray-haired cook.

"What's going on? Who is that?" Tari eyed Zarek in confusion.

Fergen appeared in the kitchen door. "Hurry, Ana! Almost every table is already full." His eyes tightened in suspicion as he looked at Zarek. "Who are you?"

"My name is Zarek. I serve the Emperor of Sarine. I came to warn you that the inn is going to be attacked."

The blood drained from Fergen's face, and he took a step backward. "When? Who? Not the—"

"Shekkar. Demons of dark magic," Zarek said. "My friend has gone to warn the rest of the village. The demons will be here soon. We need to bar the doors and windows. Get everyone out of here. Tell them to stay hidden indoors. Go now!"

Fergen ran back to the common room, and he only had to utter one strangled word, "Shekkar." His customers scattered at his warning.

Ana helped Fergen pull the heavy shutters closed, and he dropped the latches into place. They barred the front door.

"The demons are coming. You should go too," Zarek said, putting his hand on Fergen's shoulder, gesturing toward the kitchen door.

Fergen glanced down at Ana. "What about Ana? If she's not safe here—"

Zarek met Ana's eyes, then looked back at the innkeeper. "They're following her."

Ana's stomach clenched.

Fergen stood beside her and put his arm protectively around her shoulders. "If she's in danger, I'm not leaving her."

Ana turned to hug him tightly. He had always treated her with kindness, even though she was only an orphan.

"There's no way you can fight them." Zarek shook his head. "They'll only kill you if you stay. Take the cook and run. Get somewhere secure. Find a place to hide!"

Fergen didn't want to go, but Ana couldn't let him get hurt because of her. She threw her arms around him. "You've done so much for me. You always took good care of me. Please don't let them kill you! I couldn't bear it."

He held her close. "Every day I've had you in my life, I've been grateful. I love you Ana, please be safe!" He kissed the top of her head and released her. "I'm sorry. I'm so sorry." He took Tari by the arm, and they disappeared into the gathering darkness.

Ana helped Zarek check the doors and windows again. Then he pushed chairs and tables against the front door.

Outside, night covered the village. Dane ran in through the back door. He slammed it behind him and slid the heavy bar across it. "I told them to get indoors and stay there." He was breathing hard. "They didn't all listen." As if to punctuate his words, a scream rang out from somewhere in the darkness.

Ana stood trembling. Fergen was gone, along with everyone else she knew. No one was left except these two strangers.

Outside, something clawed at the door, and Ana didn't dare to breathe. It scratched at the walls, hunting for a way inside. A hard blow struck the door. It held. From the other side came a shriek of frustration. Ana cringed away from the sound.

Zarek gripped the hilt of his dagger and took a deep breath. His jaw clenched. Dane came into the dining room, drew his sword, and stood watching the door, tense and ready, the weapon in his hand. From outside in the dark, they heard terrified voices and running feet. Someone was out there. They called out, and Ana wanted to help them. A man screamed first, then a woman.

Zarek drew his sword and held the weapon ready, his eyes on the door.

Outside, it grew silent. Whoever had been out there, they made no other sound. Ana took a deep breath, then another. The quiet didn't last. More blows came at the front door, and more shrieking. The door creaked and groaned and shook on its hinges. Would it keep them out? Or would the thing outside find more of her friends and neighbors and kill them? Would it find Fergen and Tari?

She couldn't stand that. "They're looking for me! If I go out there, will they take me and leave the others alone?"

"You can't do that, Ana," Zarek said firmly. "They can't get the ring. If they do, many more people will die."

"People are dying now! Can't you just take the ring and go?"

He shook his head. "It's too late for that. They're already following you."

"They're breaking in. You're going to have to take Ana and run," Dane said. "Get ready to slip out the back door."

Zarek took Ana's hand and headed for the kitchen.

The attack against the door redoubled. Ana heard blows from all around the building now. From the front of the inn, they heard the sounds of breaking wood and shattering glass. Abruptly, the assault on the back door ceased.

Zarek met her eyes. The muscles of his jaw clenched. "Get ready to run."

"It's time." Dane's voice sounded hard as he looked at Zarek. "You're faster than I am. Take her and go. I'll hold them off and then follow you."

Ana's breath came fast and shallow, and her heart pounded in her throat. Zarek raised his sword.

"Go. Now!" Dane ordered, standing in the kitchen doorway, his blade in his hand. Several black shapes burst through the front door, shrieking. Dane held his sword ready.

Zarek pulled Ana through the back door. She screamed as a black shape towered above them, blocking their path. Shoving her back, he attacked the black thing.

The demon screeched and tried to claw at them, but Zarek's sword deflected the blow. Ana heard its razor-sharp claws scrape against the metal. While his sword held the creature back, he drew his dagger. The blade glowed faintly green in the darkness. He struck at the demon, driving the blade home until it fell, unmoving.

"Run!" Zarek ordered, tucking the dagger back into its sheath.

They dashed away from the village, following the edge of a stream, stumbling over the uneven ground in the moonlight. Ana ran as fast as she could, but it didn't feel fast enough. Zarek pulled her along, urging her to greater speed.

The night was quiet around them, except for their rapid breathing and the sound of their feet pounding against the ground. Ana looked back over her shoulder and saw Dane behind them, running hard. Beyond him, black shapes followed. But Zarek was heading the wrong way.

"Don't go—" she gasped, pointing ahead of them. "There's—cliff—"

Zarek didn't listen. For a few moments, they widened the gap between them and their pursuers. But the demons would soon cut off their escape. The small stream beside the town drained into a larger river that had carved a deep cleft in the land, and Zarek was coming to the brink of the cliff. He stopped and looked over the edge. Ana glimpsed a black chasm with a silver ribbon of water at the bottom.

Dane caught up with them. "That way!" He pointed along the edge of the canyon. They followed the cliff downstream.

The Shekkar cut across the distance, heading straight for them, gaining fast. Ana could hear the demons clearly now, and their horrible voices sounded triumphant. They were about to claim their prize. She stopped on the brink of the cliff, frozen, the yawning space open below her. Zarek had placed himself between Ana and the Shekkar, his sword in one hand and his dagger in the other. But there were too many enemies to fight, and they charged toward him, black claws outstretched.

The foremost of the creatures struck at him. He blocked the blow with his sword, but poisonous claws seized the weapon, twisting it out of his grip. A flash of moonlight lit the sword blade as it spun away, landing behind the demon.

Zarek sheathed his knife and darted straight toward Ana. As his shoulder slammed into her, his arm seized her waist, and his momentum propelled them out into the black abyss. Ana screamed as they fell.

THE RING KEEPER

CHAPTER 2

Ana

COLD AIR RUSHED BY Ana as she fell, the black rock of the canyon flashing past. They struck the water, and from that height, it felt like a solid wall. Her face and arms exploded in pain. Their momentum sent them deep under the surface. The impact tore her away from Zarek and knocked the breath from her lungs.

She flailed, frantically trying to find her way back to the surface of the dark water. There was nothing to hold on to, and the current tossed her in all directions. Something seized her leg, pulling her. Confused and disoriented, she felt like she was being dragged deeper into the water.

Ana felt them break the surface, and dimly, she realized Zarek had brought her back from the depths. He towed her toward the bank, hauled her out of the water onto the gravel shore and struck her back. A little water ran from her mouth. Additional blows brought up more, and she coughed violently. She sucked air into her lungs and felt the stones of the bank beneath her as she lay, coughing and gasping.

Dane slogged through the shallows toward them. "Is she hurt?" He knelt down beside them.

"We hit hard. She has water in her lungs." Zarek ran his hand through his hair. "I didn't mean to hurt her. I wouldn't have jumped—I didn't know what else to do!"

"You did what you had to do." Dane bent over Ana. "Carry her and watch her. We'll check on her again when it gets light. Come on, we need to go."

Ana's lungs burned, and she still wasn't sure which way was up. Zarek slid one arm under her shoulders and the other beneath her knees and picked her up. He must be very strong because he easily got to his feet holding her. No one had held her like this since she was a small child. She wanted to tell him to put her down, except she couldn't gather the breath to speak and she wasn't sure she could walk.

The dark canyon walls towered above them, the moonlight gleaming on smooth rock. Ana hid her face in the front of Zarek's shirt. Her ribs throbbed where his shoulder had struck her, her skin felt raw where she'd hit the water, and her soaking wet clothes felt chill in the night air. Unsuccessfully, she tried to hold back the tears that escaped from the corners of her eyes. Now she was crying like a baby and being carried like one.

They kept going. Ana had several more bouts of violent coughing, but when they passed, she breathed more easily.

Zarek set her down to walk, but exhaustion slowed her steps. She struggled along until, eventually, the rose pink of dawn lit the east. Dane stopped in a sheltered place beside some rocks and took off his pack and sword. Ana collapsed to the ground. Zarek dropped his own gear and sat near her. It felt good to be still, and she rested her back against the stone.

"How badly are you hurt?" Zarek asked. Putting one finger under her chin, he gently turned her face to the morning light to examine where she'd struck the water. His brows lowered, and his mouth turned down in a frown. "I'm sorry." He released her chin and shook his head.

But Ana knew he'd done the best he could. If he hadn't jumped with her, the demons would have caught them. "I..." She swallowed and tried again. "You didn't let them catch us." She spoke with difficulty, and her throat felt raw from coughing up river water.

Zarek stared back at her, his eyes widening in surprise at her answer.

"Where are we?" She scanned their surroundings. This was already farther from home than she'd ever been before.

"We're at the bottom of the canyon below the village. This river flows down into Lake Bethor."

Everyone she had known, the only home she remembered, had been left behind last night. She looked at Zarek. Another fit of coughing passed before she could speak again. "Did they kill everyone in the village?"

He rubbed the back of his neck. "I don't think so. Most of them are safe."

"What about Fergen and Tari? What if the demons killed them?"

"They didn't," Dane said from where he sat on a rock nearby.

"How can you be sure?"

He took a deep breath and met her eyes. "Because the demons are following us."

Ana felt a sharp twist of fear in her belly, and she shivered. This was it. They were all going to die. As soon as night fell, the Shekkar would hunt them. And this time there would be no shelter, no cliff to help them escape.

A muscle in Zarek's jaw tightened.

Ana's chest constricted until she couldn't breathe. Her voice sounded strangled. "They're going to kill us. We're going to die."

Dane came over to her and bent to one knee, gripping her shoulders. His brown eyes appeared stern. "We are not going to die. We are going to run, but we can escape them."

Ana looked back at him. "How is that possible? I've heard the stories. If they don't tear us apart, they're going to poison us, and there's no cure."

"There is one cure," Zarek said. "The ring. You do have it, don't you? It's the reason they're following you."

Ana hadn't trusted them with her secret before, but what choice did she have now? They had both saved her life last night, at great risk to themselves. If they wanted to harm her, why would they do that?

She clutched the ring where it hung under her shirt. Pulling it out, she drew the cord over her head and made a fist around the ring. "This is why they're following me? Then let's get rid of it!" She stood up, faced the churning white water of the river, and drew her arm back to throw.

They launched into motion so quickly, she barely saw them moving before they both gripped her wrist.

"Don't!" Dane pleaded. "You can't. If we lose that ring, the empire of Sarine will fall and no place in the world will be safe from the demons. Many more people will die. Besides, it's too late. The Shekkar are already hunting us."

That was too much pressure. Ana didn't want the lives of thousands of people to be in her hands. She scrunched her eyes closed, but that didn't stop the tears from running down her cheeks. Closing her hand tightly around the ring, she sank to the ground, and they released her arm.

How could she possibly escape the Shekkar? Ana shook her head. "It's only a matter of time before they kill me."

"We won't let that happen," Dane promised.

Beside him, Zarek nodded in agreement. He rose and took a deep breath, as if to shake off the worry, and grabbed his sodden pack. From inside, he retrieved his flint and started gathering sticks. Still clutching the ring, Ana got up and stretched her stiff, sore muscles. She hung the cord back around her neck and began gathering wood. Dane helped too, and in a little while, they had a good fire going. Ana sat with her knees pulled up to her chest, as close to the flames as she could.

They spread wet clothes and blankets from their packs to dry on the bushes. Zarek peeled off his wet jacket and shirt and hung them up. He lay back on the sandy riverbank with his eyes closed.

Ana blinked and looked back at Dane. "You promised you would protect me. What if they kill you?"

Dane rubbed his face and met her gaze. "If something happens to one of us, you could use the ring."

"What do you mean... use it?" Ana stared at them in confusion.

"You don't know what it does?" Zarek sat up, his eyebrows raised in surprise.

Ana shook her head. It was a ring. Was it supposed to... do something?

"That ring can heal any injury," Zarek said.

Ana stared back at him in shock. "What? How?" Then her eyes widened. "Do you mean that back there, I could have saved the lives of those who were injured?"

Dane shook his head. "No. The demons would have caught us too. We would have to escape them before you'd have a chance to use it. And you can only heal one person at a time. The ring uses your strength and will to heal, but the process is painful. It would be several days before you could do it again."

"But if one of you were injured, then I could heal you?"

"Yes."

"What if I can't do it?"

"We're hoping that you can," Dane said. "We serve the Emperor of Sarine, and he wields a magical power called the Warding that keeps the demons out of Sarine. All we have to do is get over the border before they catch us. The emperor is ill, and we're hoping you can heal him. If he dies, the Warding will disappear, and the demons will destroy Sarine."

"And you think I can heal him? Why don't we give the ring to someone else?"

Zarek got up from where he'd been resting and sat beside Ana. "Once you put it on your finger, it will not come off again. The ring belongs to you."

He was right. Ana didn't want to give it away. The ring was the only possession her mother had left her. Maybe she wouldn't have actually been able to throw it in the river, even to save her own life. Pulling the cord from beneath her collar, she stared at the ring. Strange symbols were engraved on the inside of the band, and the green gem sparkled in the sunlight. What would it be like to heal someone? Painful, they had warned her. But she wasn't willing to give up this final link to her family.

She removed the leather cord and slid it onto her finger. It fit exactly.

Zarek was worried about her. They were all in danger, and he felt sorry for the shock and pain she had been through in the last several hours. He wanted to keep her safe.

Ana's eyes widened, and she gasped. Zarek was still there, standing beside her. He hadn't moved or spoken, but now that she wore the ring, she could sense what he was feeling.

He was determined to protect her and get her safely to Sarine. And Zarek would never harm her. She felt his loyalty, as if she knew what was in his heart. She stared at him in wonder. "You really do want to help me."

Zarek grinned. "I told you I did."

She took a step nearer to Dane and found she could sense him, too. His feelings shared the same desire to protect her, and the same loyalty to Sarine.

Last night, Ana hadn't had much choice but to trust them, and she wondered if it had been foolish. If she believed this new sense, then she had been right to count on these men.

"Maybe we can make it." With this new knowledge, she felt more hopeful. "If they catch up, can we fight them? I don't know how." She looked at Dane's sword. "But you both do."

Dane sighed. "I wish I could. Ordinary weapons don't hurt them. That dagger is the only thing we possess that can." He pointed to Zarek's weapon.

Zarek sat up and patted the hilt. "The dagger is enchanted with the power to kill demons, just like Emperor Caldoreth's sword, Blackbane. I didn't know for sure it would work until last night, but I killed one of them."

"That's more than anyone else has done since the sword was stolen," Dane said. He felt hope and relief when he said it, and Ana relaxed a little.

"The wizard Zarekathus helped Caldoreth found the empire of Sarine. His son Callonen is emperor now," Zarek said.

"Za—re—kath—us?" Ana stumbled over the name.

"Just remember, Zarek-athus," Dane said, grinning. He nodded at Zarek. "His mother named him after the wizard. I think she hoped he would grow up to be a brilliant scholar."

Zarek smacked his friend.

Dane only laughed. "You're better with a blade than a pen and ink." He glanced at Ana. "Zarek might be young, but he's the most skilled soldier in Sarine."

Ana gazed at Zarek with wide eyes. He shifted uncomfortably under her attention.

Turning back to Dane, she asked, "You mean he can beat you?"

Dane grinned. "He can beat anyone. Here." He tossed her a damp shirt. "Put this on and hang up your clothes. I'll stay with you, and Zarek can find us something to eat."

Ana took the shirt and went behind the rocks to change. It felt strange to put on clothing that didn't belong to her. Dane's spare shirt was much too large, which was a blessing after she peeled off her soaked pants. The hem came nearly to her knees, and she had to roll the sleeves up to expose her hands. She felt embarrassed to walk around partially dressed in front of two men who had been strangers only a few hours ago. But it was much better than wearing wet clothes.

Dane had pulled off his shirt and jacket while she was gone and now hung them up.

She touched the fabric of her borrowed shirt. He could have had at least one dry piece of clothing if he hadn't shared with her. "Thank you," she said. She hung up her tunic, pants and jacket and huddled close to the flames.

He turned at the sound of her voice and smiled. "You're welcome."

It didn't take Zarek long to come back with a rabbit. He sat down by the fire and began skinning and cleaning it. His hands moved skillfully. When he finished, he placed the rabbit on a spit over the fire to roast and went to scrub his hands at the edge of the river.

"How far is it to the Warding?" Ana asked, looking up at him as he returned to the fire.

He rubbed his wet hands against his pants. "It will take several weeks to get there," he admitted.

"Don't worry. We'll make it," Dane promised.

"Why do the demons want the ring?" she asked.

"They serve the king of Ara. He wants to destroy Sarine. And right now, Emperor Callonen is very sick," Dane said. "But we know he's still alive because the demons are chasing us. If he dies, they won't bother with us. They will simply go to Sarine and destroy it. We were searching for the ring to save his life."

Ana felt her stomach twist. "And if I can't heal him... it would be like... back there? The demons would kill everyone? How do you know it will work? Have you seen it heal before?"

"When I was little, back in Sarine, a young woman named Allia saved my life with the ring," Zarek said.

The blood drained from her face at the sound of the familiar name. Before she died, Grandmother had told Ana her mother's name was Allia.

"You know that name?" Zarek asked, observing her reaction. "Then you are Cirana? After all this time, we finally found you?"

She nodded. "Allia was my mother. But Grandmother told me never to tell, that if people knew, it would be dangerous. I guess she was right."

Zarek nodded.

"But, Allia—you know her? Where is she?"

"I knew her," he corrected quickly. "I'm very sorry, but she died many years ago."

Ana's momentary hope crumbled. All her life, she'd wondered about her mother. Had Allia loved her? Why hadn't they stayed together? It made sense that she was dead. If Allia had been alive and had loved her, she wouldn't have left Ana alone.

Ana nodded sadly. "I understand. But will you tell me about her? My grandmother said she named me Cirana. I've never told anyone my real name before. Everyone always just called me Ana. You said you knew her. What did she look like? Tell me everything you remember about her."

"I remember her." Dane shook his head sorrowfully. "It was the first year I joined the Emperor's Guard. Half the soldiers in the palace were secretly in love with her. She had the most beautiful smile, and she was always kind to everyone."

"It was almost seventeen years ago," Zarek said. He turned the meat roasting over the fire. "I was only six when she left the city. My parents were so grateful to her for saving my life. I remember she had long golden hair, lighter than yours. Her eyes were different. I don't remember exactly, maybe green? My father and his friend Harrow went to look for Allia. Harrow was badly hurt on the way back, but he made it to the Warding and said he'd hidden Allia's child and the ring. He must have meant you. We guessed she'd passed the ring on to you before she died."

"So we can ask Harrow about it!"

Zarek shook his head. "The Shekkar had attacked him. He didn't survive their poison."

"Your father and his friend rescued me." Ana looked at him. Her mind tried to avoid the terrible truth. "But your father... He came back, didn't he?"

Staring back at her, Zarek shook his head.

The truth settled over Ana. It was her fault he had lost his father. Tears stung her eyes. "You must hate me." She felt her hands clenching into fists. "I'm the reason he's dead. You loved your father, and he's dead because of me."

Zarek took her hand. At his kind touch, she allowed her fingers to relax into his. It felt good, and she appreciated the comfort he offered as it flowed through her. "That's not true, Ana. Stop and breathe. With the ring, you can tell what I'm feeling. You know I don't feel that way. I don't hate you. My father thought that protecting you and your mother was worth risking his life for. I will do the same. I promise I won't let anything hurt you."

———— ✦ ————

For six nights, they followed the canyon downward. The white river roared beside Ana, reminding her not to slip. Zarek frequently offered his hand to help her down from the boulders. The cliffs on either side of the river had gradually lowered, but they had spent the long nights climbing through the rocks. Ana pushed hard to keep up with them.

Tonight, the stars turned slowly in the clear sky above them. When Ana turned to look at Zarek, and she saw him staring behind them. Was something back there?

"Dane! Demons!" Zarek yelled above the sound of the water. Dane looked back. "Behind us?"

Zarek pointed back the way they had come.

Continue the story in the full version: https://www.amazon.com/Ring-Keeper-AJ-Park-ebook/dp/B0CZPMDZ3V